Shakspere Wood

New Curiosum Urbis

a guide to ancient and modern Rome

Shakspere Wood

New Curiosum Urbis
a guide to ancient and modern Rome

ISBN/EAN: 9783337382353

Printed in Europe, USA, Canada, Australia, Japan

Cover: Foto ©Andreas Hilbeck / pixelio.de

More available books at **www.hansebooks.com**

THE NEW

CVRIOSVM VRBIS:

A GUIDE TO

ANCIENT AND MODERN

ROME.

BY

SHAKSPERE WOOD.

LONDON:
THOMAS COOK & SON, Ludgate Circus, E.C.
SIMPKIN, MARSHALL, & Co.

ROME: THOMAS COOK & SON, 1B, Piazza di Spagna.
NEW YORK: COOK, SON, & JENKINS, 261, Broadway.

1875.

TABLE OF CONTENTS.

INTRODUCTION.

In the following pages the author endeavours to guide the stranger among the remains of the series of cities succeeding generations of Romans have built, one upon the other; through the streets of that which belongs to the period closed on the 20th of September, 1870; and over the sites where the new city of Rome, the capital of Italy, is rapidly springing into being. The information given has been obtained exclusively from original authorities; through an intimate acquaintance with the cities of Rome, both ancient and modern; and by accurate notes taken on the spot, as regards the contents of picture and sculpture galleries, and other collections, the position of the component parts of which are constantly being changed. It is the intention of both the author and publishers to keep this Guide up to the present date—not the date of 1874, when these words were written—but the latest which the hand of time has inscribed on the pages of history. But while noting day by day what changes may occur in things and places here described, or what additions may be necessary through new discoveries made—it may be well to look back upon those, interesting to the traveller, which have taken place within a few years, and particularly during the last four, since Rome once more assumed a position of political importance in the world.

Recent changes.

Up to the time when Pius IX. had occupied the papal throne for a period beyond the general average of the reigns of Popes, Rome was as distant from London or Paris, calculating by time, as New York or St. Petersburg are now. She was to all intents and purposes a city of the past—no railway crossed her territory, no telegraphic wire carried intelligence to other countries of what was occurring within her walls. Without commerce, without communication, she was virtually cut off from the rest of mankind, and sunk to be the mere Sacristy of the Roman Catholic Church, and an interesting place of sojourn for students of art and antiquity, and for those few wealthy persons who had time and leisure at their command.

Passports.

The passport system was retained in Rome in the most rigorous sense, long after it had been abolished in other countries, except as a matter of momentary political necessity. Five years ago no Roman could obtain his passport in less than three days, and then only on the production of a certificate from the curate of his parish that he had satisfied all the requirements of the Roman Catholic religion. It is scarcely longer since when Her Majesty's Consul, receiving on a Saturday afternoon, after the Papal Police Office was closed, intelligence of a near relation lying dangerously ill at Marseilles, was unable to get his papers regulated by the authorities in time to leave Rome before the following Monday evening. Although the use of passports is now abolished in Italy, it is no disadvantage to have one. It may, at Post-offices and other places, serve to establish a person's identity in the absence of better credentials.

With no gas in the streets, with a censorship of the press which prohibited the advance of litera-ture within the Papal dominions, or its introduction from abroad, she remained in darkness both ma-terial and moral, long after the light of civilisation had spread rapidly elsewhere. While superstition reigned within, it can scarcely be a matter for wonder that ignorance and prejudice regarding her should exist without, and particularly with reference to the climate.

There can be no doubt that seventy years ago, The Climate. when each of the 365 or more churches was a separate cemetery, Rome was far from a healthy city. One of the first things Napoleon the First found himself obliged to do when he occupied Rome, at the beginning of this century, was to establish an extra mural place of burial. The ad-vantage of this reform was even recognised by the Popes, and intermural interment was gradually prohibited, first within one church and then within another, among the more fever-stricken districts, until it was finally abolished altogether — ex-cept occasionally in the case of some wealthy English convert, to whose remains it was desired to pay especial honour. Now there is no respect for persons in this regard. There were also many Causes of other causes of unhealthiness. Such a thing as a unhealthi-ness. water closet was absolutely unknown ten years ago; and to say nothing of the houses occupied by the Romans, those let to foreigners of wealth and position were unprovided with anything but a common open privy—often situated in the kitchen —disseminating miasma throughout the house. The bye-streets were often impassable for filth, and to within the last few years it was impossible for women to pass along some of the streets connecting the Corso with the Babuino, so continually were they used by men for that convenience the houses did not afford. In the courtyards of nine-tenths of the houses there were open wells sunk to a considerable depth, the sides of which were green with damp. These also created miasma and unhealthiness during the hotter months; and in the grounds of the many private villas within the walls, built by wealthy persons, but occupied by their impoverished descendants, were stagnant pools of water— where once there had been gushing fountains— covered with rotting verdure and spreading malaria all around. Up to a very recent period it was the custom to flood the immense Piazza Navona—then a vegetable market—with water every Sunday during the month of August. It was made a kind of popular festa; those who kept, or could afford to hire carriages, used to drive backwards and forwards through the water, stirring up the refuse of decayed vegetables below, while the poorer sat around in crowds enjoying the fun. When the sluices were opened, some of the accumulated refuse of the week was carried off. The remainder, soaked with water, lay and rotted in the sweltering

August sun. And yet people wondered why August should be so unhealthy a month, or so many people be struck down with fever.

The abolishment, however, of intermural interment did much to lessen that unhealthy influence supposed to exist in the pure air of the country, and other causes were in gradual process of removal by the Papal government; for, although it was adverse from any reforms which would turn the tide of civilisation through Rome, its interest was concerned in what might prevent a sufficient influx of wealthy persons, and thus some time anterior to Rome becoming the capital of Italy, sufficient of the evils had been removed to make Rome by no means the least healthy city of Italy. But the bad name remained, and the question is continually asked, why there should still be so strong an impression that the climate of Rome has particularly unhealthy qualities. The cause is not far to seek. The opposition made by Rome against the advance of modern civilisation necessarily spread throughout the other states into which Italy was divided, and over which Rome maintained a powerful influence. Up to ten years ago few persons came to Italy, except to take up their residence for some weeks at least, in one or other of the principal cities, and chiefly at Florence, Rome, or Naples. Rome, on account of its many objects and points of interest, was the most attractive for a lengthy stay; and consequently Florence and Naples waged a continual war by spreading alarming reports to prevent persons

Antagonism of other cities.

going on to Rome, or remaining there. And among those most active were, and in fact still are, medical practitioners interested in keeping, in the city where they had established themselves, those who had sought the climate of Italy. "You must not think of going to Rome before November, if you have the slightest regard for your health," to those on route southwards; "You must not dream of remaining in Rome after Easter," urged Naples, in hopes of attracting persons there for the summer, who might have lingered in Rome, and spent the hotter months at L'Ariccia, Albano, or Tivoli. At both places alarming reports of epidemics violently raging in Rome, at times even, when she had never been healthier, were constantly spread; and articles were constantly appearing in English medical journals of authority, written by those interested not only in Florence and Naples, but in Pau, Mentone, Nice, Sorrento, and many other places, in which it was sought to prove that the climate of Rome was at all times unhealthy, and at some even deadly. The favourite argument was a comparison between the number of births and deaths, and that with regard to a city with so immense a population of celibates, monks, nuns, priests, soldiers, &c., that, were it the healthiest spot in Europe, the number of deaths must, as a matter of course, be in excess of the births. In 1873 the total number of births was 7201, and the deaths 8479; but of this 8479 no fewer than 5496 ! ! were unmarried persons. Then it is urged that the death rate is high in propor-

tion to the population—no doubt it is; but so is the
rate throughout Italy ; attributable to the inferior
condition of medical science, and to other causes,
altogether apart from climate ; and when the death
rate of Rome is compared with that of other Italian
cities it exhibits a very different picture from that
which popular ignorance, prejudice, and individual
interests would present.   The following table is Average mor-
tality.
taken from a volume of statistics recently published by the Italian goverument :—

City.	Population.	Deaths.	Average per 1000 inhabitants.
Turin ..	212,644	5791	27·2
Palermo ..	219,395	6259	28·5
Messina ..	111,854	3234	29·0
Leghorn ..	97,097	3046	30·1
Rome ..	248,307	8479	34·0
Bologna ..	115,957	3951	34·0
Florence ..	167,069	6122	36·6
Milan ..	199,009	7361	36·9
Genoa ..	130,296	4972	38·1
Venice ..	128,901	4919	38·1
Naples ..	448,335	17,205	38·3
Trieste ..	123,098	5083	41·2

These figures need no comment.   Excepting Rome one of
the healthi-
Palermo and Messina, which are in Sicily, they est cities.
show that of the ten principal cities of the Peninsula, only two—Turin and Leghorn—are healthier
than Rome ; one—Bologna—is on a par with her,
while six—Florence, Milan, Genoa, Venice, Naples,
and Trieste—are from $2\frac{1}{2}$ per 1000 to 7 per 1000
less healthy than she is.

The same exaggeration which has been applied
to the unhealthiness of Rome applies also to re-

maining in Rome during the summer, and to the supposed danger of entering it before October, or of remaining beyond May. Of course, between those months English people are liable to suffer inconvenience from the heat, but it seldom reaches, even on the hottest day, the summer temperature of Boston in the United States. Precautions must necessarily be taken against peculiarities in the climate during those months, as it is requisite to guard against the bleak east winds and other variations of the climate of London; but the dangers are very slight, and the precautions very easy and simple. The Roman fever is nothing more than what is known in the United States as chills and fever; and, unless complicated with other diseases, is seldom or ever fatal. The symptoms are easily recognised, and give plenty of warning for the use of preventives. It is preceded by a general feeling of lassitude and discomfort for some days, accompanied by a sensation of aching in the joints, and a disposition to yawn. When English people feel thus out of sorts they generally attempt to walk it off, and augment rather than diminish the evil. The best thing is to consult a medical man at once, and he will prescribe an ordinary aperient, such as people can generally prescribe for themselves, to be followed by a few grains of quinine, to be taken an hour before eating three times a day for a couple of days. This is a sovereign preventive, and cuts off the complaint before it has time to develope. The quantity of quinine to be taken is no more than amounts to an ordinary tonic, and quinine, like port wine or whiskey, is only detrimental to the system when taken in large quantities. It is not uncommon for persons newly arrived in Rome, to suffer for a short time from slight diarrhœa. The usual Diarrhœa. English remedy is a glass of brandy; but this has the effect in Rome of increasing the complaint; the best specific is a mild aperient, such as a little rhubarb and salvolatile; but brandy or any other spirit should above all things be avoided. While writing of matters connected with health it may not be unnecessary to advise the traveller to be careful and purchase good medicine, should he unfortunately require any; and to secure this he cannot do better than send his prescriptions to be made up at Baker's Pharmacy, No. 497, Corso, The best chemist. the only English chemist in Rome, and, in fact, the only one thoroughly reliable. In choosing Apartments or Hotels. apartments those localities are best where there is plenty of sun. Many persons about to make a stay in Rome are at loss to decide between private apartments and hotels; but hotels will be found the most comfortable to all, except those who bring either first-rate couriers or their own men and maids with them. Private apartments are dear, and particularly so when considered with reference to the accommodation they afford and the insufficient manner in which the majority are furnished, and the Roman servants are anything but desirable. Taking into consideration the trouble and possible annoyance of housekeeping in a foreign country, without a sufficient knowledge of the language

and the prices of things, the greater comfort, and
even economy in the long-run, will be found in remaining in one of the hotels, of which now there
is ample choice. Those who do not care to remain
in hotels, and yet wish to avoid the trouble of
keeping house, cannot do better than take up their
quarters at the Misses Smith's boarding house, in
the Piazza di Spagna, if those ladies can receive
them; or at Miss Tellenbach's, also in the Piazza
di Spagna.

As regards money, the best thing people can do
is to carry either letters of credit or circular notes,
with a sufficient supply of *French* gold for immediate use.   A natural prejudice prevails among
English people that they cannot do better than
carry sovereigns, but this is a mistake. Sovereigns
not being current in Italy, and being more difficult
of transmission than paper, the same high rate of
exchange is not given for them. At the present
moment, in consequence of the financial difficulties
against which Italy has still to contend, the
value of sterling money is much above par, and
during the year 1874 an average of $2\frac{1}{2}$ francs
above the value of each English pound was given
in paper, and sometimes as much as four francs.
This, in the purchase of many things which have a
comparatively fixed value, is a great advantage to
the stranger; but it must not be forgotten that as
payment for every thing is taken in paper the
prices of all imported articles must necessarily rise
in proportion, for while the Englishman receives,
say twenty-eight francs for his pound, the Italian

has to pay the same, and even a trifle more, for every pound he has to remit to England in payment for goods imported from thence. It is not uncommon for an Englishman taking up a book which costs, say twenty shillings in England, to exclaim at the exorbitant profits charged by an Italian in asking thirty francs for it, forgetting that, through the rate of exchange, it has cost him twenty-eight francs, exclusive of carriage and Custom House duties.

Those who have already been in Rome, but have not visited it for the last four years, will at once be struck by the remarkable changes which have taken place since it became the capital of Italy. The streets now equal in scrupulous cleanliness those of any other city in Europe. It is no longer possible to encounter those dust heaps once found at almost every corner, with *Immondezzia* inscribed on the wall above them, where maids of all work deposited the daily sweepings of the house and kitchen, to be carted away at some indefinite period. All that look of dilapidation, so picturesque, but at the same time so mournful, has disappeared from the buildings of the modern city. The Municipality obliges every one to keep the exterior of his house in proper repair, and where any one neglects to do so, it is done for him at the public expense, and the bill sent in to him to pay. Hundreds of tons of lime have been expended in cleansing the dirty cobweb-hung house fronts of five years ago, with a proportionately purifying effect. The streets are well paved, and side walks have been laid down, so that it is no longer necessary to cripple one's feet upon the *opus reticulatum* of basalt upon which, until recently, all were condemned to walk.   Instead of a dispirited, impoverished population, of which the majority seemed to be formed of priests, monks, and foreign soldiers, there is now an active bustling people, thriving, working, and evidently prospering.

But it is not only in cleaning the outside of the platter that work has been done; numbers of old tumble-down houses have been thrown down, and handsome edifices erected in their stead, and a magnificent system of drainage, has not only been commenced, but nearly completed.   First one and then another of the main streets have been impassable for months, while enormous subterranean galleries, equal almost in size to the Cloaca Maxima, have been constructed beneath them; and through the excavations the Italian Government have carried out so extensively among the remains of the ancient city, the ancient drains—than which none finer were ever constructed—have in many places been discovered, cleared of the rubbish with which they were choked, and converted once more to use. These excavations, while of the highest scientific value from an historical and archæological point of view, have not only added immensely to those objects of interest which attract strangers from all parts of the world, but have contributed in no small measure to the health of the city.

A great portion of the modern level of the Forum was occupied by an extensive cemetery belonging to the Hospital of the Consolazione. It covered nearly half the area cleared since 1870, and was in use till a comparatively recent period. The bones were lying within eighteen inches of the surface, and were in thick layers, for a depth of many feet, in some places solid masses of corruption. All this has been swept away.

On another part of the Forum three yards of water were found, the consequence of an unknown spring pent up below the accumulation, but spreading beneath and continually sending forth noxious vapours during the hotter months. In the imme- *The Cloaca Maxima.* diate neighbourhood of this spring the ancient Cloaca Maxima, choked up with rubbish, was found. This has been cleared, the spring—to carry off the water of which was one of the original causes of its construction—has been turned into it, and thus from an evil has been converted into an advantage to the health of the city. A number of small drains passing *close* under the modern surface have been removed, and their course turned into the Cloaca Maxima.

But it would occupy too much space to enume- *New interests.* rate here the beneficial effects the extensive excavations carried out in all directions have had upon the health of the city. Some mention must be made of what they have done for science, and in contributing to the enjoyment of strangers, who, without going more than superficially into archæological matters, are all more or less desirous of visiting those spots rendered almost sacred to them through that most pleasant part of their early studies in school or college—the history of Rome. Twenty years ago a very considerable portion of those remains of ancient Rome, which now form the chief objects of interest to the visitor, were buried out of sight under thousands of tons of accumulation. First, Padre Marchi and Signor de Rossi, on behalf of the Commission of Sacred Archæology, commenced the excavations in the Catacombs, which have had such important results. Next, in 1855, H. H. Pius IX. commenced the excavations at Ostia; then nothing but a few unrecognisable ruins and mounds of rubbish, now a second Pompeii. In 1857, Father Mullooly discovered the original Basilica of St. Clement, by commencing that excavation, the results of which are of the deepest interest to all scholars, and to all Christians. In 1861, the late Emperor Napoleon III. bought the Farnese Orchards, on the Palatine, and, sweeping away vineyards and vegetable gardens, gradually restored to light the magnificent remains of the Palace of the Cæsars. In 1867, the guardhouse of the VII. Cohort of Vigiles, was excavated. In September, 1870, the Italian government, confirming Signor Rosa in the office he had so admirably filled in conducting the excavations for the Emperor Napoleon on the Palatine, recommenced the excavation of the Forum, which up to that time had not been extended further than for a very limited space around and in front of the Column of Phocas; the excavation of the Baths of Caracalla down to the original pavement; the excavation of the

Colosseum, now in progress; the excavation of the magnificent remains of the Villa of Hadrian, at Tivoli; and the energetic continuance of the explorations of the ancient city of Ostia.

The interest in the results of these important excavations far more than compensate for the discontinuance of those grand church ceremonies which once attracted so many visitors to Rome. When those sumptuous ecclesiastical pageants are likely to be renewed it is impossible to say, but in the meantime those who are interested in the majestic ritual of the Roman church can have their desire gratified by informing themselves as to what great Saints' days occur during their stay in Rome, and attending the ceremony at the principal church dedicated to him or her, as the case may be. Some of these formed great attractions in past times, on account of the music, which in some churches, and with the exception of the *Miserere*, was but little, if anything, inferior to that given during the great papal festivals. Of those, which are now performed with even greater ceremony than before, may be mentioned—

January 23rd, Feast of St. Agnes, at her Basilica, beyond the Porta Salaria.

January 25th, Feast of the Conversion of St. Paul, at his Basilica, outside the walls.

February 1st, Feast of St. Ignatius, at St. Clemente—the Subterranean Basilica illuminated.

4th Monday in Lent, Feast of the Santi Quattro Incoronati, at their Basilica.

March 25th, Feast of the Annunciation, at Sta. Maria Sopra Minerva.

C

April 25th, Feast of St. Mark, at his Basilica.

May 3rd, Feast of the Invention of the Holy Cross, at Sta. Croce, in Gerusalemme.

May 26th, Feast of St. Filippo Neri, at the Chiesa Nuova.

June 24th, the Nativity of St. John the Baptist, with fine music; also at the Vespers on the previous evening.

June 4th, Corpus Domini, at St. Peter's. This festa, although celebrated now on a much diminished scale, is well worth attending.

June 29th, Feast of St. Peter and St. Paul, at St. Peter's.

August 1st, Feast of St. Peter in chains, at St. Pietro in Vinculi.

August 15th, Feast of the Assumption, at Sta. Maria Maggiore.

August 25th, Feast of St. Louis, at St. Luigi dei Francese.

September 8th, Feast of the Nativity of the Virgin, at Sta. Maria del Popolo.

November 1st, Feast of All Saints, at St. Lorenzo, outside the walls, and at all the principal churches.

November 4th, Feast of St. Carlo Borromeo, at St. Carlo al Corso.

November 22nd, Feast of St. Cecilia—fine music; and also at the Vespers on the previous evening.

November 23rd, Feast of St. Clement, at his Basilica.

December 27th, Feast of St. John the Evangelist, at St. John Lateran; also Vespers the previous evening.

December 31st, Feast of St. Sylvester, at his church, in the Piazza San Sylvester; and in the afternoon a Te Deum, at the Gesu.

Jubilee.   While these pages were passing through the press His Holiness Pius the Ninth proclaimed the long-delayed JUBILEE, or Holy Year, which used to be celebrated every twenty-five years. Fifty years, however, have rolled by since the last Jubilee was held, in 1825, under the Pontificate of Leo XII. When the twenty-fifth anniversary came round, Pius IX. was in exile at Gaeta.

It has been generally supposed that Boniface VIII. instituted the Jubilee, in the year 1300—

that Jubilee which forms such an era in mediæval history, which has been so eloquently described by many authors, and which furnished a simile for Dante, when he wanted to describe a multitude in motion, and he alludes to the regulation for rendering the crossing of the bridge of St. Angelo possible by the crowds which flocked to Rome :—

> Even as the Romans, for the mighty host,
> The Year of Jubilee, upon the bridge,
> Have chosen a mode to pass the people over ;
> For all upon one side towards the Castle
> Their faces have, and go unto Saint Peter's ;
> On the other side they go towards the Mountain.*
> —*Inf.* xviii. 28, *Longfellow's Translation.*

But the Jubilee had been introduced into the Roman Church by far earlier Pontiffs, who drew the idea from the Sabbatical Year of the Mosaic Dispensation, as Boniface is recorded to have learned from manuscripts which were consulted in his days; and *Panciroli*, says an aged pilgrim, who came to the Jubilee of 1300, declared, in the presence of Boniface and his nephew, Cardinal San Giorgio, that he had been at Rome with his father a century previous, on the same occasion. But the earliest Bull existing on the Jubilee is that promulgated by Boniface VIII., beginning "*Antiquorum fides.*"

In past times the Jubilee was proclaimed by the Bull of Preparation issued on the previous Ascension Day, and the year commenced on Christmas Eve, with the grand ceremony of opening the

---

* The "mountain," *monte*, alluded to by Dante, was Monte Giordano, the slight elevation so named on the opposite side of the bridge from the Castle of St. Angelo.

Porta Santa, the Holy Door, at St. Peter's—a ceremony which the Pope has this time omitted; in fact, the present Jubilee was not proclaimed— or rather the Encyclicale announcing it was not signed by Pius IX. until the very moment when, under other circumstances, the vestibule of the great Basilica would have been crowded with the faithful, from the visible head of the Church to the poorest pilgrim.

The Holy Door.

All persons who have visited Rome will remember a walled up doorway, with a cross upon it, to the right as one enters the vestibule. The filling in of brickwork having been previously loosened, this door was approached by the Pope, who came down the *Scala Regia* in solemn procession, attended by the Papal Court and a number of Cardinals and Prelates. His Holiness first knelt down for a few moments in solemn prayer, and then, holding a lighted wax torch in his left hand, struck the Porta Santa thrice with a silver hammer, at the same time intoning the Psalm *Aperite mihi portas justitia*. Then the Grand Penitentiary took the silver hammer and beat other three blows upon the door. After whom the same ceremony was performed in turn by two of the penitentiaries, and then, with the assistance of the masons inside, down fell the door, crashing into pieces upon the pavement within, and over the ruin the Pope, followed by all present, entered the Basilica. The fragments were speedily removed—not, however, by persons appointed for the purpose, but carried off, piecemeal, by the thousands present, anxious to secure a relic. The door only remained open during vespers, after which it was again closed until the next year of Jubilee came round.

After the Pope had opened the *Porta Santa* at St. Peter's, he deputed three cardinals to perform the same ceremony at the other three great Basilicas— St. Paul's outside the walls, St. John Lateran, and Santa Maria Maggiore.

The principal devotion of the Jubilee consists in visiting the four great Basilicas on the same day, after having confessed and received the Sacrament, and for this liberal indulgences are granted. Three other Basilicas—St. Sebastian, Sta. Croce in Gerusalemme, and St. Lorenzo outside the walls—complete the mystical number—seven; and these the more devout visit, at the same time all laying offerings at the foot of the Pontifical Throne.

After having closed the *Porta Santa*, the Pope proclaimed the indulgences of the Jubilee, and the Holy Year commenced, to end at the ensuing Christmas.

According to the following chronology of Jubilees, or Holy Years (drawn from Manni's *Storia degli Anni Santi*, down to 1750), the current year makes the twenty-first Jubilee since that of Boniface VIII., in 1300:—

1st Jubilee.—The first Jubilee was celebrated by Boniface VIII., in 1300.

2nd.—Next followed the Jubilee of 1350, under Clement VI., who was sitting at Avignon, and the Eternal City was in her extremest ruin and loneliness. The pilgrims who streamed thither in thousands from all parts of Europe saw broken walls, falling houses, ruined temples. The Lateran Basilica was at that time roofless, exposed to wind and rain. The Romans sent an embassy to the Pope, at Avignon, imploring him to return; and adding supplications to reduce the space of time between the Jubilees from one hundred to fifty years. It was Petrarch who asked and obtained this last petition.

3rd.—The third Jubilee was celebrated in 1390, by Boniface IX., the Pope having returned to Rome, and further reduced the space between recurring Jubilees to 33 years (the years of Christ).

4th.—There is some confusion between the preceding Jubilee and that of 1400, but I find this latter recorded as granted by Boniface IX.

5th.—Much uncertainty also reigns as to the Jubilee said to have been celebrated by Martin V., in 1433.

6th.—Now we return to greater certainty. In 1450, the Jubilee was celebrated by Nicholas V. It was on this occasion that the throng of pilgrims was such as to cause the deaths of 200 persons on the bridge of St. Angelo, when some were trampled under foot, some pushed into the Tiber. This was a very rich Jubilee, and the funds amassed by it were expended by the Pontiff in rebuilding churches, repairing the city walls, fortifying the Castle of St. Angelo, and even the Vatican.

7th.—Pope Paul II. having further shortened the period between the Jubilees to twenty-five years, the Jubilee of 1475 was celebrated by Sixtus IV., and an inscription recording it is on his tomb in St. Peter's. It was towards the end of this Jubilee, in the month of November, that the Tiber rose so high as to prevent the pilgrims from reaching San Paolo fuori le Mura except by boats.

8th.—The Jubilee of 1500 was celebrated by Alexander VI., who, according to some authors, was the first Pontiff who opened the Porta Santa with the silver hammer.

9th.—Clement VII. celebrated the Jubilee of 1525, when the number of pilgrims was greatly diminished, owing to the Reformation in Germany.

10th.—Julius III. celebrated the Jubilee of 1550.

11th.—Gregory XIII. celebrated the Jubilee of 1575.

12th.—Clement VIII. celebrated the Jubilee of 1600.

13th.—Urban VIII. celebrated the Jubilee of 1625.

14th.—Innocent X. celebrated the Jubilee of 1650.

15th.—Clement X. 1675.

16th.—Clement XI. 1700.

17th.—Benedict XIII. celebrated the Jubilee of 1725.

18th.—Benedict XIV. celebrated the Jubilee of 1750.

19th.—The Jubilee of 1775, exactly a century ago, was celebrated by Pius VI. Between that and the twentieth Jubilee, under

20th.—Leo XII., in 1825—a period of fifty years—rolled the tremendous ocean of the French Revolution.

21st.—Another half century was to elapse before the Pope could find Europe sufficiently calm to render another Jubilee possible. Let us hope that His Holiness Pius IX. may be gratified by the concurrence of numerous pilgrims to Rome during this Anno Santo.

In addition to the religious festivals we have now the great National Festas, on which occasions all interested in the welfare and progress of Italy will find it well worth while to be in Rome. From the earliest hours in the morning the houses are decorated with flags; the day is generally celebrated in some manner especially arranged for the occasion, and in the evenings the principal streets and public buildings are illuminated, and bands play in the different Piazzas.

These National Fêtés are as follows:—

April 23rd, the Foundation of Rome.

First Sunday in June. Celebration of the Constitution; the Magna Charta of Italy granted by Charles Albert. The celebrated fireworks and GIRANDOLA, which used to be exhibited from the Pincio on Easter Monday, are given on this occasion from the Castle of St. Angelo.

September 20th. Anniversary of the Liberation of Rome. A procession is made to the spot, outside the Porta Pia, where the wall was breached; and in the evening, in addition to the customary illuminations, the inhabitants of the Trastevere, who claim to be direct descendants from the ancient Romans, generally illuminate their streets in a most picturesque manner, as a protest against the assertion made by the Ultramontanes, that the "real Romans" were opposed to the union between Rome and Italy.

Plebeian Illuminations.

October 2nd.   Anniversary of the Plebiscite, celebrated by the distribution of prizes to the 15,000 children of the national schools, opened for the first time after the change of government in 1870. The ceremony is held on the Capitol, and is one of the most interesting and charming sights it is possible to witness.   In addition to the usual illuminations, the inhabitants of the Monti, who claim to be the descendants of the Romans of the middle ages, generally take this occasion to illuminate their quarter, as the Trastevere do theirs on the 20th of September.   These "Plebeian illuminations" have a very distinctive character of their own, and are especially worth seeing.

Both the Author and Publishers of this *Guide* are altogether averse from distinguishing any Professional men, Bankers, Merchants, or Tradespeople, from others, as especially worthy of patronage or custom; and still more particularly so from following the course adopted hitherto in works of the same description with this, of quoting the rate of fees to be given to professional men, or the prices to be paid at Hotels for the accommodation they afford, or at shops for the goods they sell. For the most part these latter must necessarily fluctuate in accordance with the rise and fall of prices, and the financial condition of the country

Hotel charges and Tradesmen's prices.

at the moment.   Now that there are plenty of Hotels, affording different classes of accommodation, nothing is easier for the traveller than to change if he finds the prices charged to be higher than the accommodation and fare would seem to justify.   Scenes not very creditable to our countrymen sometimes occur, when, having received their bill, they take up a Guide Book, and accuse respectable Hotel-keepers of dishonesty, because the charges made do not agree with those quoted therein, and which, had the traveller the opportunity of

examining the past editions of the work, he would
see had been quoted at the same rate for a series,
and sometimes a long series, of years, during which
rent and the prices of commodities had risen considerably.

The same remarks apply to shops.

As, however, the traveller who is merely passing Professional
through Rome may be at loss for professional Fees.
advice, or as to where conveniently to supply himself with articles he may require, the following
names are mentioned, and they are necessarily
few, for this work is not intended to serve as a
directory.

English Physicians :—Dr. Gason, 81, Via della Croce ;
Dr. Grigor, 3, Piazza di Spagna; and Dr. Small, 56,
Babuino.

American Physician :—Dr. Gould, 107, Via Babuino.

German Physician :—Dr. Erhardt, 15, Via Maria di' Fiori.

Homœopathic Physician :—Dr. Liberali, 69, Via della
Frezza.

American Dentist :—Dr. J. B. Wasson, 107, Via Babuino.

Bankers :—Maquay, Hooker, and Co., 20, Piazza di
Spagna ; Spada, Flamini & Co., 20, Via Condotti ; Plowden
& Co., 50, Via della Mercede ; Theo. Linder, 9, Via Condotti.

Painters :—Penry Williams, 12, Piazza Mignanelli ;
Luther Terry, 8, Via degli Incurabile ; Arthur Strutt, 81,
Via della Croce ; Rollin Tilton, 20, Via San Basilio ; H.
P. Riviere, 68, Via Sistina ; Henry Coleman, 16, Vicolo
Zucchelli ; Achille Guerra ; Vertunni, 53, Via Margutta ;
Fattorini, 89, Via Margutta ; Carlo Possenti, 18, Passeg-
giata di Ripetta ; Keeley Halswelle, 36, Via de Greci ; Chas.
Coleman, 33, Via Margutta ; Cammerano, 72, Via San
Niccolo da Tolentino.

Sculptors :—Laurence Macdonald, 7, Piazza Barberini ;
Shakspere Wood, 504, Corso ; Holme Cardwell, 13, Via
Tordinona ; Arthur Pattisson, 7A, Vicolo San Niccolo da
Tolentino ; Randolph Rogers, 53B, Via Margutta ; Jos.
Swinnerton, Trinita di Monte ; Charles Summers, 72, Via
di San Niccolo da Tolentino.

Antiquities :—Depoletti, Via Leoncino, leading from the
Via Fontanella Borghese. People should be very careful

where they make their purchases under this head, so many spurious antiquities are imported.

Baker (English) :—88, Via della Croce.

Boarding House :—Misses Smith, 93, Piazza di Spagna.

Bookseller and Publisher :—Spithœver, 85, Piazza di Spagna.

Bookbinder :—Olivieri, 49, Piazza di Spagna.

Bronze Ornaments and Marble Tazze :—Rainaldi, 51A, Babuino.

Bronze Statuettes :—Röhrich, 104, Via Sistina; Chiapanelli, 92, Via Babuino.

Cameos :—Paolo Neri, 73, Babuino.

Carriages :—Fedeli, Piazza del Impresa.

Chemist and Druggist :—Baker, 497, Corso.

Cigars :—241, Corso.

Confectioner :—Spillman (Fratelli), 10, Via Condotti; sends out dinners, and furnishes ball suppers.

Gloves:—Anna Ugolini, 39, Piazza San Lorenzo in Lucina.

Grocer :—Lowe, 76, Piazza di Spagna.

Homœopathic Chemist :—Baker, 497, Corso.

Italian Masters :—A. Nalli, 63, Via della Purificazione; Pio Molajoni, 57, Piazza di Sora.

Lawyer:—Avocato F. Pifferi, 55, Via Fontanella Borghese, ult. po., for cases in the Roman courts and international legal business.

Library and Reading Room :—Piale, 1, Piazza di Spagna.

Milliners and Dressmakers:—Giovanetti, 50 to 53, Campo Marzo; Massoni, Palazzo Simonetti, Corso.

Monuments (Sepulchral) :—Giuseppe Sassi, 74, Via San Basilio.

Milkman :—Serafine, Via delle Virgine.

Old Lace :—Barni, 48, Corso.

Photographs :—Alessandri, 12, Corso.   Views of Rome and Cartes de Visite.

Printseller :—Raggi, 329, Corso.

Restaurants:—Morteo, 196, Corso; The Lepre, Via Condotti.

Roman Jewellery :—Civilotti, 94, Piazza di Spagna.

Roman Pearls : - Rei, 122, Babuino.

Roman Scarves :—Bianchi, 82, Piazza della Minerva.

Rosaries :—Canori Focardi, 94, Piazza di Spagna.

Shoemaker :—Luigi Lucketti, 11, Piazza St. Agostino.

Singing Master : - Professor Rotoli, 78, Via Borgognona.

Tailor :—Evert, 77, Piazza Borghese.

Terra-Cotta Statuettes :—64, Via del Seminario.

Watchmaker :—Carlo Ansorge, 72, Piazza di Spagna.

Wines (Italian):—Societa Vinicola, 32 and 33, Via della Croce.

PROTESTANT CHURCHES.

THE CHURCH OF ENGLAND, first edifice to the left outside the Porta del Popolo. Services: 11 a.m., 3 p.m. Protestant Churches.

THE AMERICAN CHURCH, the next edifice beyond he English Church, outside the Porta del Popolo. Services : 11 a.m., 3.30 p.m.

THE SCOTCH PRESBYTERIAN CHURCH, a little beyond the American Church. Services : 11 a.m., 3 p.m.

TRINITY CHURCH, in support of the Evangelical principles of the Church of England, Piazza San Sylvestro. Services : 11 a.m., 3 p.m.

AMERICAN CHURCH, on the basis of the Evangelical Alliance, 21, Via Condotti. Service : 11 a.m.

The REV. JAMES WALL'S APOSTOLIC CHURCH and Schools, Piazza San Lorenzo in Lucina. Service: 11 a m., 7.30 p m.

ITALO-AMERICAN HOME, Schools, Sunday Schools, Industrial Classes and Kindergarten, under the direction of Mrs. E. B. Gould, 106, Via in Arcione. Mrs. Gould is always happy to receive friends of her mission work at the above address daily (excepting Saturdays), from eleven to half-past one o'clock.

———

The British Embassy, Palazzo del Gallo, Foro Trajano. Embassies, &c.

The British Consulate, 378, Corso.

The American Embassy, 35, Via Fontanella Borghese.

The American Consulate, 64, Via Napoli.

English Club, 78, Via della Croce.

The British Academy of Fine Arts, Via Sistina.

POST OFFICE, Piazza Colonna. There are two mails for England each day; letters must be posted before 8 p.m. and 7.45 a.m.

TELEGRAPH OFFICE, 111, Piazza Monte Citorio. A message to London of 20 words, in which address and names are counted, costs 9 francs. There is an additional charge for messages sent to any other part of Great Britain.

ROUTES TO AND FROM ROME.

"ALL ROADS LEAD TO ROME," is a fact as literally true in this age of railways and steam communication, as it was proverbially correct in the times of the Cæsars, when "Roman roads" intersected the main lines of continents. But, during the reign of Pius IX., railways were very sluggish in their approaches to the "Eternal City," and there were few districts where travelling was more difficult, or attended with more inconveniences. Even the sea was, in a sense, but partially open for passenger traffic to Civita Vecchia, the Italian mail steamers not having access to that port.

After the railways connecting Florence with the Alps had been completed, it was still a difficult, protracted, and expensive journey from Tuscany through the "States of the Church" to their capital; and whilst suspicion of advancing encroachment continued, the impression prevailed that the railway works were intentionally retarded, and it was only by slow degrees, and bit by bit, that the Roman lines were eventually carried to completion. The coast line, intersected by a tedious and unpleasant diligence ride of six to eight hours, from Nunziatella to Civita Vecchia, was then the only railway route to Rome; and that route was barred by custom houses and police, to the annoyance of all civilized travellers. The completion of the central line, *via* Perugia, Foligno, and Terni quickened the action of the coast line contractors, and the completion of the two lines, succeeded by the annihilation of passport and custom house demands, placed Rome on a par with other cities of continental Europe. Foligno became a junction station for Ancona; at Ceprano an unbroken connection was effected with the Naples line, and now, from all sides, the approaches are completed, and it may be reiterated with truth "all roads lead to Rome."

A third connecting link, via the Northern chain, unites Orte with Empoli, and thus is shown another central through route, between Florence and Rome, passing through Siena, and other places of interest. The distance from Pisa to Rome has been abbreviated by a short cut separating the elbow at Leghorn, and ere these pages see the light, the Riviera line, from Spezzia to Genoa, will have been opened, thus completing a direct through line from Genoa to Rome—a line which must necessarily prove one of the most interesting tourist lines in the peninsula. There remains now but little to be desired in the through railway system of the Italian kingdom, and when the proprietary and management of the various divisions are satisfactorily arranged, no country will be able to show a better provision of railway accommodation than Italy.

The international roads to Rome are now nearly all that the tourist can desire, and the ways will be still more perfect on the completion of the St. Gotthard tunnel. From the north and the west travellers have choice of diligences by three Alpine passes—the Simplon, St. Gotthard, and Splugen; by the railway over the Semmering from Vienna, or over the Brenner from Munich and Innsbruck; under the Alps from Modane to Bardonnecche, for Turin; railway throughout from Paris via Lyons, Marseilles, Nice, Genoa; or thence from Marseilles to Genoa, Leghorn, Civita Vecchia, or Naples; all these four railway routes, three diligence roads, and the Mediterranean steamboat routes lead to Rome.

From the east there are equally direct facilities by the various lines of steamers to Italian ports, and thence by railways to Rome.

From Greece, Turkey, all the Levantine ports, and direct from India, China, Japan, Australia, and other parts of the Orient, by the Red Sea, overland from Suez to Alexandria, or by Suez Canal to Naples, Civita Vecchia, Leghorn, Genoa, Brindisi, Ancona, Trieste or Venice, and from all these ports by railway direct to Rome. All round the world, from any part of the vast circumference, coming eastward or westward, all roads lead to Rome; and, under the combined tourist ticket arrangements, mainly planned and perfected by THOMAS COOK & SON, through facilities are offered for coming to Rome on a single payment previous to starting. The routes from England, France, Switzerland, Belgium, Germany, and Austria may be shown in more minute detail.

From London to Paris by Dover, Boulogne, Brighton, Newhaven, or Southampton. From Paris by Mont Cenis, Turin, Florence, Foligno, Rome, the shortest and cheapest route, the entire journey from Paris to Rome being accomplished by Express Trains in about forty-six hours.

Going by Mont Cenis, other routes from Turin are by Genoa, Spezzia, Pisa, and Civita Vecchia; or from Pisa to Empoli, Siena, and Orte; or from Turin to Bologna, Ancona, and Foligno.

Another route from Paris is by Dijon, Macon, Lyons, Marseilles, Nice, San Remo, Genoa, and by coast or central routes to Rome.

There are also routes from Paris—by Paris, Lyons, and Mediterranean, or East of France Lines, to Switzerland; and from Switzerland by way of the Alpine diligence roads to Milan, and from Milan direct to Bologna, Florence, and thence by any of the previously-noted routes by Foligno, Pisa, or Siena, and to Rome. From Milan also, the Genoa and Pisa or the Ancona and Foligno routes are practicable.

In addition to these various routes through France, there is another connection of lines from London via Dover and Ostend, or by Harwich and Antwerp, by the Luxembourg Railway to Bale; or by the Rhine to the same point in Switzerland, and then by the St. Gotthard or Splugen to Milan. Another route by the Rhine is to Mayence, Darmstadt, Wurzburg, Munich, Innsbruck, over the Brenner to Verona, Padua (Venice or not at discretion), Bologna, and all other southerly routes as already indicated. Or a wider range may be taken from Munich to Vienna direct, or by Dresden, Prague, &c., over the Semmering to Trieste, or direct to Venice, and thence by the routes already indicated, by Ancona or Florence, and from Florence by way of three roads—Foligno, Siena, or Pisa to Rome.

Thus for English, American, and Continental travellers there is not a capital in the world that has more converging roads leading to it than the capital of Italy.

The facilities for travelling through and around Italy surpass in cheapness and completeness of arrangement those of any other country. The system of Excursions and Tours, inaugurated by Mr. Thomas Cook in 1863, has been extended and improved until it now covers nearly all tourist lines and attractive districts.

From Rome all the routes indicated above are just as practicable and easy as they are for going there, and it is not necessary to repeat their various details. But there are considerations of special interest to visitors and temporary or permanent residents in Rome. The geographical position, as well as the travelling facilities, are alike favourable for travellers and tourists desirous of visiting the East, after spending the greater part of the winter in Rome. From Rome to Egypt is but a journey of about six days; to Jerusalem of ten days; to Athens of seven or eight days; and to Constantinople about the same time. Nothing in circular arrangement can be better than to go from Rome to Egypt (by Naples or Brindisi), up the Nile, and back to Cairo; through Palestine to Beyrout; thence through Asia Minor to Constantinople, Athens, Corfu, Trieste, Austria, and Germany; or from Trieste by Venice and North Italy to Switzerland and France. Most travellers now going to the East avail themselves of the opportunity of including Rome in the outward or homeward journey. Americans can go from Rome to New York by the Austrian Steamers and their connections, from Naples, or Genoa, without the necessity of retracing their course through Europe; and when Spain is again settled, and free and safe for tourists and ordinary travellers, it will be very easy to get there from Rome. Excellent arrangements are now completed for connecting Rome with Sicily, Malta, Algeria, and nearly all the Islands of the Mediterranean. THOS. COOK AND SON issue tickets for all these combinations, from or to Rome. The old proverb may be reversed, and with equal truth it may be said, ALL THE ROADS LEAD FROM ROME.

ARRIVAL.

THE traveller enters Rome by the Central Railway Station, situated on the Esquiline Hill. The approach is through an aperture made in the wall of fortification—built by Aurelian—at a spot situated about midway between the gates called the PORTA MAGGIORE and the PORTA SAN LORENZO. After passing through the wall, a picturesque ruin, partly overgrown with ivy, is seen on the left. This is commonly called the Temple of MINERVA MEDICA, because of the discovery there of a very fine statue of Minerva, now in the Braccio Nuovo of the Vatican, No. 114.

As the train slackens its speed just before entering the station, a glance may be caught of a bit of the AGGER OF SERVIUS TULLIUS, of which a considerable portion, extending for several hundred yards, in a perfect condition, was discovered when the area was levelled for its present purpose—an operation which necessitated the almost entire destruction of this magnificent vestige of antiquity built by Servius Tullius between the years 564-560 B.C. The wall was so massive that in many places it had to be blown to pieces with gunpowder. One fragment, composed of great square blocks of *tufa* and *peperino*, was allowed to remain; and if the place is not too full of trains, it will be seen on the right-hand side.

On leaving the station—not yet entirely completed—we enter the PIAZZA DE TERMINI, once the great stadium of the THERMÆ OF DIOCLETIAN, the massive ruins of which, deformed by alterations made in past times, to convert them into haylofts, are seen on the right. The splendid jet of water rising to a great height is the FOUNTAIN of the AQUA MARCIA,

D

re-introduced into Rome by an English company in the year 1870. It is the finest water brought into the city, and was so considered in ancient times, when the inhabitants were supplied from many sources. Originally introduced by the Prætor Quintus Marcius Rex B.C. 146, it was used till the ninth century, when the aqueduct which conveyed it was broken. The source of the Aqua Marcia is situated near the thirty-sixth mile on the Valerian Way, but the aqueduct followed a course of more than sixty miles in length.

At the further extremity of the Piazza de Termini the FOUNTAIN OF THE AQUA FELICE, commonly called the FOUN- TAIN OF THE TERMINI, is passed. It was designed by Domenico Fontana, when Sixtus V. ordered the construc- tion of the aqueduct which brings in the water, called after him the Aqua Felice.* At that time the inhabitants were suffering through an insufficient supply, and one of the first acts of Sixtus was to provide a remedy. On the day of his coronation, April 12, 1585, he signed a decree for the purchase of the source from the Colonna family, and the commencement of the work. Between two and three thousand men were employed; considerable portions of the massive arcades of the Claudian Aqueduct were thrown down to provide the material; and on the 15th of June, 1587, the water issued through this fountain. The aqueduct constructed in so short a time is twenty-two miles in length, of which fifteen are subterranean and seven above ground.

The fountain is divided into three niches. That in the centre contains a colossal statue of Moses striking the rock, by Prospero Scavezzi of Brescia. This sculptor possessed so inordinate an idea of his own abilities that he boasted he

* The name of Sixtus V. was Felix Perotti.

would out-do Michael Angelo in his representation of the great law-giver; but on his work being uncovered to the public, it excited such an amount of ridicule that he died shortly afterwards of grief and vexation.

The lateral niches contain alto reliefs; that on the left, by Giovanni Battista della Porta, represents Aaron leading the people to drink of the long-desired water; that on the right, by Flaminius Vacca, represents Gideon watching his soldiers drink. The bason was formerly ornamented by two antique lions in black granite—now in the Egyptian Museum of the Vatican—which were found in front of the Pantheon. They have been replaced by four in Bardiglio marble of modern workmanship.

Proceeding along the Via Santa Susanna and the Via San Nicolo in Tolentino, the Piazza Barberini is reached, in the centre of which is the fountain of the Triton, by Bernini, erected by order of Urban VIII., 1623-44, and supplied by the Aqua Felice.

Thence, down the Via Tritone, and turning to the right along the Via de' due Macelli, brings us to the Piazza di Spagna, the centre of the English-speaking colony in Rome, and in or near which it is supposed the traveller will take up his abode.

THE PIAZZA DI SPAGNA

is generally believed to be the site of the Naumachia of Domitian, a maritime theatre, in which naval battles were given for the amusement of the people. In superficial measurement this Piazza is one of the largest in Rome; but it is ill-formed, and has but few pretensions to archi-tectural beauty. It is a long quadrangle of irregular form, extending from north to south, and terminating, as it were, almost in a point. The narrow end is bounded by the COLLEGE OF THE PROPAGANDA FIDE, instituted by Gregory XV. The building was founded in the year 1627, by Urban VIII., who entrusted its erection to Bernini, but it was finally completed by Borromino during the reign of Alexander VII., 1655-67. This is the great missionary establishment of Rome, and is now under the direction of the Jesuits. In it students from all parts of the world, even from the most remote, are educated, in order that they may be sent back to their own countries for the propagation of the Roman Catholic doctrines. The college possesses a remarkably fine library, and attached to it is a printing-office, in which works in all languages—not only European, but Oriental—are printed.

A short distance in front of this college stands the COLUMN OF THE IMMACULATE CONCEPTION, erected by order of Pius IX., in commemoration of the promulgation of that dogma on the 8th of December, 1854. The shaft, which is antique—a vestige of the magnificence of ancient Rome —is of that beautiful green and white marble of Carystus, commonly called Cipollino, from its resemblance to the onion. It supports a bronze statue of the Virgin, by Obici. The base is ornamented with bas reliefs, and four colossal statues—Moses, David, Ezekiel, and Isaiah. A flaw in the lower portion of the shaft necessitated the expedient of the bronze work to strengthen it.

Facing the column, and situated between Nos. 56 and 58, is THE PALAZZO DI SPAGNA, the residence of the Spanish ambassador, from which the Piazza takes its name. In the middle of the Piazza is the exceedingly quaint fountain in the shape of a boat, called THE BARCACCIA, erected in the time of Urban VIII., from the design of Pietro Bernini, the father of the celebrated sculptor. The idea is said to have been suggested by a barge stranded at this spot during one of the great inundations, possibly that which occurred on the 24th of December, 1598, during the reign of Clement VIII., when the Piazza di Spagna was entirely covered. How high the water rose on that occasion may be seen by entering the passage of the house No. 71, Via Condotti, close by, on the left wall of which is a tablet recording the event, and showing the height of the inundation. The inundation of December, 1870, reached as far as the door of the Hotel d'Allemagne, which is close to this spot. The fountain is supplied by the Aqua Vergine.

At the middle of the western side is the grand flight of steps called the SCALINATA, designed by Francesco de Sanctis, and completed in the year 1725, at the expense of M. Stefano Gueffier, Secretary to the French Legation at Rome. On these steps groups of painters' and sculptors' models, dressed in the costumes of their native villages, are often to be seen sitting and reclining about, waiting to be hired. At the summit of the Scalinata stands the church of the TRINITA DE' MONTI, and the Convent of the Nuns of the *Sacré Cœur*, in which is an educational establishment where the daughters of wealthy persons are received as boarders. The church was founded by Charles VIII. of France, in the year 1494, at the instigation of St. Francesco di Paola, and was consecrated by Paul V. on the 9th July, 1595. It contains, among other works of art, the celebrated fresco of THE DESCENT FROM THE CROSS, painted by Daniele da Volterra, and considered to be his masterpiece. Poussin pronounced it to be the third greatest painting in the world, ranking after The Transfiguration, by Raphael, and The

Communion of St. Jerome, by Domenichino. Unfortunately it was much damaged by the French when they detached it from the wall, and placed it on canvas, with the intention of removing it to Paris.

This church used to be much frequented by strangers, on Sundays and festivals, on account of the beautiful and devotional singing of the Nuns, but since 1870 it has been exceedingly difficult for any but well-known Catholics to obtain admission.

THE OBELISK in front of the church was erected by the architect Antinori in 1788, during the reign of Pius VI. It is believed to be that which ornamented the spina of the circus of Sallust. The height of the shaft is forty-three Roman feet, and from the ground to the top of the Cross one hundred feet. Cancellieri states that the Cross, which is of bronze, contains relics of the True Cross, of St. Joseph, St. Peter, St. Paul, St. Augustin, St. Pius V., and St. Francesco di Paola.

FROM THE PIAZZA DI SPAGNA TO ST. PETER'S AND THE VATICAN.

Proceeding along the VIA CONDOTTI—so called from the conduits of the Aqua Vergine which pass beneath it—and which opens from the Piazza di Spagna at a point immediately opposite the Scalinata, we pass on the right No. 68, the PALACE OF THE KNIGHTS OF MALTA, and on the left No. 40, the Monastery, with next to it the CHURCH, dedicated to the HOLY TRINITY, of the Spanish Trinitarians. The church, founded in the year 1741, was built from the design of Emmanuele Rodriguez de Santes, a Portuguese architect.

Traversing the Corso, the street takes the name of the Fontanella Borghese, on the right side of which, after passing No. 20, is

THE PALAZZO BORGHESE,

the residence of Prince Borghese. This enormous palace was commenced in 1590 by Cardinal Dezza, from the designs of Martino Lunghi, the elder. Before it was finished it was purchased by the great Borghese Pope, Paul V., who entrusted its completion to Flaminio Ponzio. The court or peristyle is particularly fine, being surrounded by double-storied porticoes, supported by 96 antique granite columns. The lower portico is of the Doric order, and the upper Ionic, with Corinthian pilasters. The court is ornamented with several antique colossal statues.

The picture gallery, one of the best private collections in Rome, is liberally thrown open to the public every day, except Saturdays and Sundays, between the hours of 10 and 3. It is on the ground floor, the door being under the left portico. In each room are hand catalogues of the works that room contains, printed in the Italian and French languages, for the use of visitors. The more important works in each room are as follows:—

Those marked with an asterisk are the gems of the collection.

FIRST ROOM.

1—Holy Family: *Sandro Botticelli.*

2—Madonna and Child: *Lorenzo di Credi.*

3—Holy Family: *Paris Alfani.*

4—Portrait—*Lorenzo di Credi.*

8—Vanity: *School of Leonardo da Vinci.*

27, 28—Petrarch and Laura.

30—A Nazzareno: *Perugino.*

32—St. Agatha: *School of Leonardo.*

33—The Young Christ: *School of Leonardo.*

34—Madonna: *School of Perugino.*

35—Raphael as a boy: *Raphael(?)*

36—Portrait of Savonarola: *F. Lippi.*

43—Madonna and Child: *Francesco Francia(?)*

44—The Crucifixion: *C. Crivelli.*
48—St. Sebastian : *Perugino.*
49, 57—Two curious paintings of the events of the life of Joseph, with the name written under each figure: *Pinturicchio.*
59—Presepio: Sketch said to have been taken by *Raphael* when a boy.

56—Leda and the Swan: *School of Leonardo.*
61—St. Antonio : *Francesco Francia.*
66—Presepio: *Mazzolino.*
67—Adoration of the infant Jesus : *Ortolano.*
68—Christ and St. Thomas : *Mazzolino (?)*
69—Holy Family : *Pollajuolo.*

Second Room.

6—Madonna with St. Joseph and St. Michael: *Garofalo.*
9—*The Deposition: *Garofalo.*
18—Portrait of Pope Julius II.: *Giulio Romano after Raphael.*
21—*Portrait of a Cardinal: *Bronzino(?)* attributed to *Raphael.*
24—*Holy Family : *School of Raphael.*
26—*Portrait of Cæsar Borgia: *Bronzino,* attributed to *Raphael.*
28—Portrait of a Woman : *Bronzino.*
36—Holy Family : *Andrea del Sarto.*

38—*The Entombment : *Raphael,* painted in his 24th year.
40—Holy Family : *Fra Bartolomeo.*
43—Madonna & Child : *Francia.*
44—Madonna & Child : *Sodoma.*
51—*St. Stephen : *Francesco Francia.*
59—Adoration of the Magi : *Mazzolino.*
60—Presepio : *Garofalo.*
65—The Fornarina : copy from Raphael by *Giulio Romano.*
69—St. John the Baptist in the Wilderness : *Giulio Romano.*

Third Room.

1—Christ bearing the Cross : *Andrea Solario.*
2—Portrait : *Parmigiano.*
4—Lucretia : *Vasari.*
5—"Noli me tangere:" *Bronzino (?)*
7, 8—Apostles : *Michael Angelo,* painted on panel in his early manner.
11—The Sorceress Circe : *Dosso Dossi.*
13—Mater Dolorosa : *Solario (?)*
18—Leda : *Vasari.*
24—Madonna and Child, with St. John and Angels : *Andrea del Sarto.*
28—Madonna and Child, with St. John : *Andrea del Sarto.*

29—Madonna and Child, with St. John and St. Elizabeth : *Andrea del Sarto.*
33—Holy Family : *Pierino del Vaga.*
34—The Saviour and St. Catherine : *School of Bronzino.*
35—Venus and Cupids : *Andrea del Sarto.*
40—*Danae : *Correggio.*
42—Portrait of Cosmo de Medici : *Bronzino.*
46—The Reading Magdalen : *School of Correggio.*
47—Holy Family : *Pomarancio.*
48—*The Flagellation.
49—Mary Magdalen : *Andrea del Sarto.*

Fourth Room.

1—Entombment: *Annibale Caracci.*
2—*Cumœan Sibyl: *Domenichino.*
10—The Rape of Europa: *Cav. d'Arpino.*
15—Sybil: *Guido Cagnacci.*
18—St. Francis: *Cigoli.*
20—St. Joseph: *Guido Reni.*

21—Lucretia: *Elisabetta Sirani.*
28—St. Francis: *Ann. Caracci.*
29—St. Domenic: *Ann. Caracci.*
37—Mater Dolorosa: *Carlo Dolce.*
42—Head of Christ: *Carlo Dolce.*
36—Madonna and Child: *Carlo Dolce.*
43—Madonna and Child: *Sassoferrato.*

Fifth Room.

5—Holy Family: *Scipione Gaetano.*
6—The Flagellation: *Cav. d' Arpino.*
11, 12, 13, 14—The Four Seasons: *Albani.*
15—*Diana with her Nymphs: *Domenichino.*

25—The Deposition: *F. Zuccheri.*
26—Madonna and Child with St. Anne: *Caravaggio.*
27—Venus Dressing: *Padovanino.*

Sixth Room.

1—The Madonna Adolorata: *Guercino.*
5—Return of the Prodigal Son: *Guercino.*
7—Portrait of G. Ghislieri: *Pietro da Cortona.*
10—*St. Stanislaus with the infant Christ: *Ribera.*
12—Joseph in Prison interpreting the Dreams: *Valentin.*

13—The Three Ages of Man: *Copy from Titian by Sassoferrato.*
18—Madonna: *Sassoferrato.*
22—Flight of Æneas from Troy: *Baroccio.*
23—Venus: *After Titian.*
24, 25—Landscapes: *Gaspar Poussin.*

Seventh Room.

Called the Stanza degli Specchi, from the mirrors with which the walls are covered. These mirrors, made at a time when large sheets of glass were difficult to obtain, are formed by a number of pieces being put together, and the joints hidden by festoons of flowers and Cupids exquisitely painted; the flowers by *Mario dei Fiori,** and the Cupids by *Ciro Ferri.* The result is to give the effect of a large sheet of glass with paintings upon it. In the centre of this room is a table formed of a great number of specimens of rare antique marbles.

Eighth Room.

1—Mosaic Portrait of Paul V.: *Marcello Provenzali.*
33—Landscape: *Salvator Rosa.*
82—Madonna and Child (Mosaic)

87—Orpheus (Mosaic).
91—Three Graces: *Vanni.*
96—Orpheus: *Brill.*

* The well-known street leading from the Via della Croce to the Condotti is named after this painter.

NINTH ROOM.

Frescoes.

1—The Nuptials of Alexander and Roxana.

2—The Nuptials of Vertumnus and Pomona.

3—Archers Shooting at a Target with the Arrows of the Sleeping Cupid.

The two first were painted from the designs of *Raphael* by some of his scholars; the third is said to have been designed by *Michael Angelo.* These frescoes were detached from the walls of a casino or summer-house, called after them the Casino of Raphael, in the grounds of the Villa Borghese, destroyed during the siege by the French in 1849.

The other frescoes in this room were painted by *Giulio Romano,* on the walls of the Villa Lante on the Janiculum, from which they were removed when it was converted into a convent.

TENTH ROOM.

2—*Cupid Blindfolded by Venus: *Titian.*

3—St. Cecilia: *Paul Veronese.*

4—Judith—*School of Titian.*

9—Portrait: *Pordenone.*

13—David with the Head of Goliath: *Giorgione.*

14—*St. John Preaching in the Desert: *Paul Veronese.*

16—St. Domenic: *Titian.*

19—Portrait of himself: *Bassano.*

21—SACRED AND PROFANE LOVE: *Titian.*

36—Madonna & Child: *Giovan Bellini.*

34—Saints Cosmo and Damiano: *Paul Veronese.*

ELEVENTH ROOM.

1—Madonna with Saints: *Lorenzo Lotto.*

2—St. Anthony Preaching to the Fishes: *Paul Veronese (?)*

3—Holy Family and St. John: *Titian.*

11—Venus and Cupid on Dolphins: *Luca Cambiaso.*

15—*Jesus and the Mother of Zebedee's Children: *Bonifazio.*

16—*Return of the Prodigal Son *Bonifazio.*

17—Samson: *Titian.*

18—Christ and the Woman taken in Adultery: *Bonifazio.*

19—Madonna and Saints: *Palma Vecchio.*

25—Portrait of himself: *Titian.*

27—Portrait: *Giovan Bellini.*

31—Madonna and St. Peter: *Giovan Bellini.*

32—Holy Family: *Palma Vecchio.*

TWELFTH ROOM.

1—Crucifixion: *Vandyke.*

7—*The Entombment: *Vandyke.*

8—Tavern Scene: *Teniers.*

19—Louis VI. of Bavaria: *Albert Durer (?)*

20—Portrait: *Holbein.*

21—Landscape and Horses: *Wouvermann.*

22—Cattle Piece: *Paul Potter.*

23—A Sea Piece: *Backhuysen.*

24—Portrait: *Holbein.*

26—Skating: *Berghem.*

27—Portrait: *Vandyke.*

35—Portrait: *Lucas von Leyden (?).*

44—Venus and Cupid: *Lucas Cranach.*

Turning to the right, on leaving the Borghese Palace, the street (which from this point bears a series of names—Piazza Borghese, Via del Clementino, Piazza Nicosia, Via di Monte Brianzo, Via dell Arco di Parma, and Via Tordinona), continues in a direct line to the Piazza in front of the BRIDGE OF ST. ANGELO. The large building on the right, before entering the Piazza, is the principal theatre of Rome—The Apollo—commonly called the Tordinona. On the site occupied by the Theatre there formerly stood a tower, built during the middle ages, to which condemned persons were taken the night before their execution, in order that they might be near the scaffold, which was erected on the area to the left of the bridge. The mournful procession, formed by the confraternity of the Penitents, conducting the prisoner to his last night's resting-place on earth, left the prison at nine o'clock: at the same moment the bell of the tower commenced tolling, to invite the prayers of the people; and hence from this fatal hour the tower took the name—which the Theatre retains—of, La Tor di Nona: the tower of nine. It was in this tower that Beatrice Cenci slept on the night of Saturday, the 11th of September, 1599, and in front of the procession which conveyed her thither was carried the banner on which Michael Angelo had, years before, painted *The Pietà*, on the condition that it was only to be used for such occasions. On the wall of the Theatre, immediately opposite No. 114, is a small marble tablet marking the extraordinary height to which the waters of the Tiber rose in December, 1870. Various other tablets may be seen in the streets of this part of the city showing the height of the inundation at those spots. Emerging from the street, we have before us a grand view of

THE BRIDGE AND CASTLE OF ST. ANGELO,

an imperial tomb, the MAUSOLEUM OF HADRIAN, turned into a fortress. The Mausoleum of Augustus, built to contain the ashes of the Imperial family, was full; the last niche had been occupied by those of Nerva. Trajan had formed a sepulchre for his ashes in the column still existing; and to provide a resting place for his own remains and those of his successors, Hadrian built the magnificent monument, which, as early as the time of Honorius, 393—403, was converted into a fortress, and became the centre for nearly all the faction fights for dominion, which have distracted the city from that day, nearly to our own. It was founded by Hadrian, together with the bridge, to give direct access to it—the same over which we pass—in the year 135 A.D. Two descriptions of the monument have come down to us— one written by Procopius, the other by Pope St. Leo. From these we learn that in its original form it was a grand circular mole 987 feet in circumference, standing on a square basement of considerable height, each side of which measured 247 feet.

It was entirely faced with massive blocks of the purest Parian marble. On the angles of the basement were groups of men and horses in bronze, of "admirable workmanship," and a range of marble statues ornamented the cornice. The summit was crowned by a colossal marble statue of the founder, the head of which is now in the Vatican Museum.* The gates were of gilt bronze, with gilded peacocks on the pilasters, two of which are also in the Vatican. Of this magnificent decoration nothing now remains. Of the ancient work all that is visible from the

---

* No. 549 in the Rotunda.

outside, is a portion of the circular wall of the mole, formed of great blocks of peperino, on which the outer casing of marble was placed. The rest, both above and below, is covered by the works of fortification constructed at various periods. The statues on the summit perished when the place was attacked by the Goths under Vitiges, in 537; they were flung down by the besieged upon their assailants.

The first whose ashes were placed within the monument was Ælius Cæsar, the first adopted son of Hadrian, who died A.D. 138. Then those of the founder. After him followed Faustina the elder, A.D. 141, and Antoninus Pius, A.D. 161, together with the ashes of their two sons and a daughter, Aurelia Fadilla, who died before them. Lucius Verus; Marcus Aurelius, 180; Commodus, 192; Septimius Severus, 211; and the last, Caracalla, in 217. After this the monument was closed, till Alaric, in the year 409, opened it in search of treasure. He rifled the different tombs and urns, dispersed the ashes, and carried off all that was valuable. Of the internal arrangement of this monument nothing was known till 1825, when excavations were made, and it was found that the principal door was in the centre of the square basement facing the bridge. It opens upon a corridor leading to a large niche, which, it is conjectured, contained a statue of Hadrian. The walls are constructed of large squared blocks of travertine, and bear evidence of having been panelled with Numidian marble; the pavement was mosaic, with a white ground. On the right side of the corridor, near the niche, commences an inclined spiral way, thirty feet high and eleven wide, leading up to the central chamber, which is in the form of a Greek cross. It is conjectured that the porphyry sarcophagus, which contained the ashes of Hadrian, occupied the centre of this chamber. About the year 1135 it was removed by Pope Innocent II. to the Lateran, in order that it might serve as his own tomb, and there it was destroyed by fire, in 1360. The cover, however, was saved, and was used for the tomb of the Emperor Otho II., in the Atrium of St. Peter's, until, on the building of the present Basilica, it was finally converted into the baptismal font, and is now in the first chapel on the left.

The Castle has for many centuries been also used as a state prison. A cell is shown in which it is said that Beatrice Cenci was confined. Napoleon III. was a prisoner for a short time in the Castle of St. Angelo, after the affair of 1830.

It received the name of the Castle of St. Angelo in consequence of a miraculous event which occurred in the year 590. In that year the city was stricken by the plague, which carried off an enormous number of victims. During its continuance St. Gregory was elected Pope. To appease Divine wrath, he instituted penitential processions, and while leading one of these across the bridge, then called the bridge of St. Peter, Gregory saw on the summit of the Castle an apparition of the Archangel Michael, sheathing a bloody sword, and from that moment the plague was stayed. In commemoration of this miraculous apparition, Boniface IV., 608-15, erected a chapel on the summit of the mole, which, from its lofty situation, was called St. Angelo *inter-nubes*. The bronze statue of the Archangel, placed where St. Gregory saw the apparition, was cast by order of Benedict XIV., 1740-58, by a Flemish sculptor named Peter Verschaffelt, to replace one of very inferior workmanship, in marble, by Raffaele da Monte Lupo.

A special permission is requisite to visit the Castle.

THE BRIDGE OF ST. ANGELO is not only a remarkable example of the solidity and perfection with which the edifices of ancient Rome were constructed, but is also a proof of how many would have remained entire to this day had they not been torn to pieces to supply building material for the modern City. After resisting the inundations of more than seventeen centuries, which have thrown down so many bridges built across the Tiber, it is still as perfect as the day when first opened. It was built by the Emperor Hadrian about 136 A.D., to afford the means of direct communication to his grand mausoleum, and was called after him the *Pons Ælius.* The only portions which are modern are the parapet and some of the travertine facing. The statues of St. Peter by *Lorenzetto,* and St. Paul by *Paolo Romano,* at the further extremity from the Castle, were placed there in 1530 by order of Clement VII. The parapet. with the ten statues upon it, was constructed in 1668 by order of Clement X. The statues — Angels with the instruments of the Passion—were designed by Bernini, and executed by his scholars, with the exception of that bearing the "inscription," which is by his own hand. The pedestal of the third angel on the right retains the mark of a cannon ball, which struck it full in the centre during the siege by the French in 1849.

Immediately after passing the Castle of St. Angelo a plain wall is seen on the right, leading across the moat, towards St. Peter's. This is the famous covered way or passage — from the Vatican to the Castle — which was constructed to afford the Pontiffs a ready means of escape to the fortress whenever it might be necessary. It was commenced by John XXIII., 1410-17; finished by Alexander VI., 1492-1503, and roofed over by Urban VIII. in

1630. It can be seen from place to place, crossing down the streets to the right on the way to St. Peter's.

The Via del Borgo Nuovo leads direct from the Castle of St. Angelo to St. Peter's. About half-way along the street, a small square piazza, with a fountain in the centre, called the Piazza Scossa-cavalli, opens on the left. Facing it on the right, and, in fact, forming one side of it, stands the PALAZZO GIRAUD, built for Cardinal Adriano da Corneto, by Bramante, in 1506. After the Cardinal's death it passed into the possession of Henry VIII. of England, and was for a short time the residence of the English Ambassadors, until Henry gave it to Cardinal Campeggio, on the occasion of his mission to England regarding the divorce of Katherine of Arragon. It takes its present name from the Giraud family, from which it was purchased by Prince Torlonia, who now owns it. At a recent Easter festival this palace was occupied by a large party of English tourists, conducted by Mr. Cook, for the use of which, for ten days, the sum of £500 was paid.

ST. PETER'S.

The first view of ST. PETER'S creates disappointment. This is not so much due to the mind being unable to comprehend the vast proportions of the structure, as to the changes made by Carlo Maderno in Michael Angelo's design, by which he altered the plan from a Greek to a Latin cross. To accomplish this he had to place the façade at three times the distance in advance of the dome originally intended, whereby its great height, intercepting the eye of the spectator, hides the whole of the drum and the spring of the dome. Great, comparatively, as is the distance between the spectator, as he enters the Piazza Rusticucci, and the Basilica, he is, in proportion to the height of the façade, too close under it to see the drum of the dome behind. This will be made perfectly clear by observing, that with each step made towards the Basilica, the dome gradually sinks out of sight. The effect produced by THE PIAZZA, with its magnificent semicircular colonnade on each side, its splendid fountains,* and the Egyptian obelisk† in the centre, is grand and imposing. The COLONNADES were built by Bernini, during the reign of Alexander VII., 1655-67. They are each formed by four rows of columns, equidistant, covering a width of 52⅓ feet. Each colonnade is formed by 142 columns and 45 pilasters. The columns, including base and capital, are 42⅓ feet in height. The height from the ground to the top of the balustrade is 59½ feet. On the balustrades are a number of statues, 236 in all, of Saints and Bishops, sculptured in travertine; each statue is 10 feet in height.

The space enclosed by the Colonnades measures 794¼ feet by 754½. The form—taking the line round the outsides and joining the ends—an ellipse measuring 913⅓ feet by 754½, or 226⅓ feet one way and 189⅓ the other larger than the Colosseum. To this area must be added that of the Piazza Rusticucci at one extremity, which measures 266¼ feet by 225; and the irregular square in front of St. Peter's at the other, which measures 372¾ palms by 367½.

In the pavement near each fountain a flat round stone will be found, marking the centre from which the line of the colonnade is drawn, and the point from which the columns radiate; standing on this stone, the colonnade

* Designed by Carlo Maderno: 1605-12; and supplied by the Aqua Paola.
† This obelisk occupied the centre of the spina of Nero's circus, on the site of which the Basilica was built. It remained standing erect in its original position till 1586, when it was placed, by order of Sixtus V., in the centre of the Piazza. A square flag in the pavement, on the southern side of St. Peter's, before passing under the arches which connect it with the sacristy, marks the site from which the obelisk was removed.

E

presents the effect of being formed by one line of columns only.   The colonnade is connected with the Basilica on the left, and with the Basilica and THE VATICAN on the right, by closed corridors, with galleries above them, each 238 feet in length and 17½ in width.   At the corners of the steps which lead up to the façade of St. Peter's are colossal marble statues : St. Peter, by Fabris ; and St. Paul, by Tadolini.

THE BASILICA OF ST. PETER marks two memorable sites : the spot where it is said the body of St. Peter was interred after his crucifixion on the Janiculum ; and the Circus of Nero—the foundation of the seats of which support the south wall of the Basilica—wherein occurred those fearful martyrdoms of the Christians, described by Tacitus.   Over the place of St. Peter's burial an oratory was erected A.D. 106, by St. Anacletus, fifth Bishop of Rome.   This oratory continued in use till the time of Constantine, who, at the suggestion of Pope St. Sylvester, founded a Basilica in its stead about the year 319, which was consecrated by St. Sylvester, on the 18th November, 324.*   Early in the fifteenth century, the Constantinian Basilica menacing ruin, Nicholas V., 1447-55, determined to rebuild it, or rather replace it by one of greater magnificence, and entrusted its construction to the architects, Leon Battista Alberti and Bernardino Rossellini.   With the death of Nicholas the work was suspended.   Paul II., 1464-71, advanced it somewhat, but no great progress was made till the time of Julius II., 1503-13.   This Pope entrusted the continuance of the work to the celebrated architect Bramante, who made an entirely new design on the plan of a Greek cross.   The

---

* The façade of this Basilica is represented in the background of Raphael's fresco of the *Incendio del Borgo* in the Stanze of the Vatican.

foundation stone was laid by Julius on the 18th of April, 1506, on the spot where stands that great pier of the dome, which is ornamented by the statue of St. Veronica. The deaths of the Pope and of the architect, in 1513 and 1514, again interrupted the work. Leo X. then appointed Giuliano da S. Gallo, Fra Giocondo da Verona, and Raphael Sanzio, the great painter, joint architects. By them, alterations were made in Bramante's design, and the plan changed to a Latin cross. Within seven years death had again carried off the architects, and Baldassare Peruzzi was appointed, who again made another design, and returned to the plan laid down by Bramante. During the reigns of Adrian VI., 1522-23, and of Clement VII., 1523-34, the works were suspended. Paul III., 1534-50, recommenced them, appointing Antonio Picconi di S. Gallo architect, who again altered the design; but his death occurring shortly afterwards, Paul sent for Michael Angelo, then in his 72nd year, and confided the work to him. Within fifteen days Michael Angelo had completed a new design, adhering to the plan of a Greek cross. He determined to give the building a façade like that of the Pantheon, to construct a double dome with a considerable space between the outer and inner walls, to carry it to the height of 450 feet, and, as he said, "raise the Pantheon in air." Michael Angelo set to work with that marvellous energy for which he was so remarkable, and at the time of his death, in 1564, had completed the building up to the top of the drum. Pius IV., 1559-66, then appointed Pirro Ligorio and Giacomo Barozzi di Vignola; but the former desiring to make alterations, Pius V., 1566-72, entrusted the continuance of the work solely to the hands of Barozzi, under whom it progressed slowly, for want of money.

On the death of Barozzi, Gregory XIII., 1572-85, appointed Giacomo della Porta.

On the accession of Sixtus V. 1585-90, a great stimulus was given to the work. This Pope, in his anxiety to see the dome finished, set apart the sum of 100,000 gold crowns annually for the purpose; 600 workmen were employed night and day, and in 22 months Giacomo della Porta had completed the work, with the exception of the lantern, which he constructed during the first seven months of the reign of Gregory XIV., 1590-91. During the reigns of Innocent IX., 1591-92, and Clement VIII., 1592-1605, he entirely finished the exterior of the dome, and ornamented the interior with mosaics. The ball and cross were placed in the year 1593. It was estimated that 30,000 pounds weight of iron were employed in the construction of the dome. On the death of Giacomo della Porta in 1601, the portico of the façade only was wanting to complete the design of Michael Angelo. Unfortunately, the foundations of the tribune had been laid considerably in the rear of the earlier Basilica, and hence, though the building, completed according to Michael Angelo's plan, covered infinitely more space, yet it did not enclose the whole of the site occupied by that which had given place to it. This was considered by Paul V., 1605-21, to be a grave error, and consequently he instructed Carlo Maderno to prolong the nave into the form of a Latin cross, so as to enclose the whole of the earlier church. The façade was carried forward to the point where it now stands, and that distortion of Michael Angelo's design accomplished, which has ruined the external aspect of the edifice from the Piazza. The foundation of the addition was laid on the 7th May, 1607; the nave was finished in 1612; the façade in 1614; and on the 18th

November, 1626, the Basilica was dedicated by Urban VIII.
During the reign of Alexander VII., 1655-67, Bernini
erected the colonnades, and finally Pius VI. laid the
foundation-stone of the Sacristy, on the 22nd September,
1776, and on its completion, consecrated the altar in it, on
the 13th June, 1784.

Calculating from the commencement of the work by
Nicholas V. in 1450, to the dedication of the Basilica by
Urban VIII. in 1626, no less than 176 years, extending
over the reigns of twenty-eight Popes, were occupied in its
construction, during which period no fewer than fifteen
architects succeeded each other in the direction of the
work. If the building of the colonnade and sacristy are
included, it covers a period of 334 years, and is in fact not
yet completed, for the pilasters of the nave, to which Pius
IX. has placed marble bases, are of stucco only.

According to the calculation made by the architect Carlo
Fontana, at the end of the 17th century, the expenditure on
the building, exclusive of the models, bell-towers, mosaic
pictures, sacristy, &c., had amounted to 46,800,498 Roman
scudi, equivalent to ten millions sterling. The buildings
occupy a space of 240,000 square feet. Bramante's
original plan, which comprised an area enclosed by an
outer range of buildings, would have covered 350,000
square feet, or about eight English acres. The sum annually expended in keeping the building in repair is 30,000
scudi, or £6,300 sterling.

The dimensions of the edifice are as follows : The façade
is $372\frac{3}{4}$ feet in breadth or frontage, and 154 in height; the
eight travertine columns which ornament it are 93 feet
in height, including base and capital, and $8\frac{7}{8}$ in diameter;
the thirteen statues on the summit are 19 feet high :

they represent the Saviour, in the middle, with St. John the Baptist and the Apostles, *exclusive* of St. Peter.

The Atrium, or vestibule, is 235 feet in length, 42 in width, and $66\frac{1}{2}$ in height. At each end of the Atrium there are wings, each 49 feet in length, beyond which are colossal equestrian statues of Constantine and Charlemagne. The extreme length between these statues is $466\frac{1}{2}$ feet. The interior of the Basilica is 619 feet in length, measuring from the door to the end of the tribune; and 449 transversely along the transepts.

The nave is 79 feet wide, and 148 high; but in the portion added by Paul V., to extend the Greek cross into the Latin form, it is 89 feet wide and 153 high.

The aisles are 207 feet long, $21\frac{1}{3}$ wide, and 48 in height.

The external measurement from the ground to the summit of the cross is 470 feet; from the pavement of the Basilica to the summit of the cross 453, and from the lower level of the *Confession* of St. Peter $462\frac{1}{3}$ feet. The internal diameter of the cupola is $141\frac{1}{4}$ feet.* The number of columns within and without the Basilica, including the colonnade, is 756, of which 245 are in the interior, the greater portion of which were taken from, or had belonged to, edifices of the ancient city. In 1828, the statues numbered 389: 40 of metal, 96 of marble, 161 of travertine, and 90 of stucco. Since that time at least nine colossal marble statues have been added, forming a total of not less than 396. There are 46 altars, and 121 lamps, the greater number of which are always kept burning. 132 Popes have been interred here, counting from St. Peter to Gregory XVI., 1831-46.

The external balcony, immediately over the central

---

* The internal diameter of the dome of the Pantheon measures $143\frac{3}{4}$ feet.

entrance, is that from which the Pope blessed the people three times each year—Holy Thursday, Easter Sunday, and St. Peter's Day. Three great entrances lead from the Atrium into the Basilica. The doors of bronze which close the central entrance belonged to the earlier Basilica, and were made by Antonio Filarete, called "Averulino," and Simone, brother of Donatello the sculptor, by order of Eugenius IV., 1431-39. There is a fourth door, of smaller size, to the right, which is walled up, and has a bronze cross upon it. This is the Porta Santa, or Holy Door, only opened for the Jubilee—nominally every twenty-five years—when the Pope breaks the wall with a silver hammer. Political events have prevented any Jubilee being held since 1825. After examining the bronze doors, let us turn round and look outwards and upwards at the celebrated Mosaic of the *Navicella*, placed inside the Atrium, and above the central entrance from the Piazza. It represents St. Peter walking on the sea, and was made by Giotto, in 1298, to ornament the old Basilica.

Entering the nave, a perception of the grandeur of the edifice begins to dawn upon the mind; but even here the first impression is somewhat mingled with disappointment. It is only after several visits that a full appreciation of its magnificence can be attained. This radical defect, arising through the alterations made by Carlo Maderno, is considered by some to be a proof of perfect proportions in the building. This has only been maintained around the dome, where alone an unqualified sense of magnitude is conveyed, and between the statues and the building, which are in perfect harmony with each other. On the great pilasters, to the right and left as we enter, are the holy-water fonts, supported by cherubs. At the first glance they appear to be of no more than natural size, but, on going up to them, they are found to be veritable Brobdignags. From these we can estimate the colossal size of the building, but that should be conveyed without the necessity for such comparison. Advancing up the nave, we have another evidence of size; the relative lengths of the six next largest churches in the world, marked upon the centre line of the floor by a brass star and the name of each. By as much as the distance of each star from the door, is St. Peter's longer than the church indicated; the exact length being given in the distance from the star to the tribunal wall. These are St. Peter's itself, 619 feet; St. Paul's, London, $516\frac{3}{4}$; the Duomo of Florence, 495; Milan Cathedral, 448; St. Petronio at Bologna, 440; St. Paul's, outside the walls, Rome, 423; Sta. Sophia, Constantinople, 364.

Against the last pilaster of the right side of the nave is the famous bronze statue of St. Peter, whose extended foot has been worn out of shape by the kisses of the devout. From this point there is a full view of the interior of the dome. The pictures which ornament it to the highest point, are all mosaic—as in fact are all the pictures throughout the Basilica with the exception of one.* Around the spring of the dome runs the text, "Tu es Petrus, et super hanc Petram ædificabo ecclesiam meam et tibi dabo claves regni Cœlorum," in letters of mosaic, 4ft. 10in. in height. The four great circular medallions, each 28 feet in diameter, above the piers which sustain the dome, represent the Evangelists Matthew, Mark, Luke and John. Below these medallions are balconies, with ornamented spiral

---

* That representing the fall of Simon Magus, immediately opposite the monument to Alexander VII. It is an oil painting, on slate, by Francesco Vanni, and will eventually be replaced by a mosaic.

columns on each side, which belonged to the old Basilica. From that on the left, above the statue of Sta. Veronica, as we look towards the tribune, the relics are exhibited on Holy Thursday and other great festivals. The chief of these are a piece of the True Cross; the head of the lance which pierced our Saviour's side; and the handkerchief of Sta. Veronica. Below the balconies, each pier is ornamented by a colossal statue, each $16\frac{1}{4}$ feet in height—excepting that of St. Longinus, which is $15\frac{1}{3}$ feet,—standing on pedestals 11 feet high. These statues represent Sta. Veronica holding the handkerchief in her hands, by Francesco Mocchi; St. Helena with the cross, by Andrea Bolgio; St. Longinus with the spear, by Bernini; and St. Andrew with his cross, by Francesco du Quesnoy, surnamed Fiammingo.

Immediately under the dome is the High Altar, above which stands the grand Baldacchino made by Bernini from the ancient bronze beams, taken by order of Urban VIII. from the Portico of the Pantheon. It measures $95\frac{1}{2}$ feet in height; 116,392 pounds of metal were employed in the casting, and the gilding alone cost 40,000 scudi, about £8,500.

In front of the High Altar is the CONFESSION of St. Peter —to which a double flight of steps descend—where, below the High Altar, and enclosed behind richly ornamented gilt bronze gates, is the shrine in which the remains of the Apostle are said to repose. The space in front, which is 10 feet below the floor of the Basilica, is surrounded by a handsome balustrade, around which, supported by gilt metal cornucopiæ, 89 lamps are kept burning night and day. On the floor of this CONFESSION, which is said to correspond with the ancient oratory of St. Anacletus, is the monumental statue of Pius VI. by Canova. The Pope is represented kneeling—as he was in the habit of doing at this spot—in prayer.

The north transept, and other portions of the Basilica contiguous to it, are enclosed off by screens made of canvas on light framework, painted to imitate marble. This was done when the transept was converted into the Council Chamber for the sittings of the Œcumenical Council.

Passing the High Altar, we enter the tribune, ascending by two steps of porphyry. In the centre is the great symbolical chair of Peter, supported by four colossal figures 17ft. 9in. in height, representing the Fathers of the Church —St. Augustin, St. Ambrose, St. Chrysostom, and St. Athanasius. It contains the ancient chair, which is said to have been used by the Apostle.

Above, is an oval window of stained yellow glass, with the Dove in the centre, surrounded by gigantic masses of gilt clouds, with cherubs among them, and great rays of glory as large as the beams of houses. The whole of this, together with the chair and the statues which support it, is of bronze gilt, the work of Bernini, and consumed no less than 219,161 pounds of metal. In the niche to the left is the monument to Paul III., by Giuglielmo della Porta; in that to the right the monument to Urban VIII., by Beruini. On the face of the piers within the tribune are four marble tablets, placed in commemoration of the promulgation of the dogma of the Immaculate Conception of the Virgin in 1854. On three, are inserted the names of the Cardinals, Archbishops, and Bishops present, among which are several English and American. Returning to the entrance, we shall now commence from the left side, and passing up the south aisle make the circuit of the Basilica, briefly noting the different chapels, mosaics, and monuments.

The first is the Baptismal Chapel. The porphyry four was originally the cover of the sarcophagus which contained the body of the Emperor Hadrian.—*Vide page* 46. The central mosaic is a copy of the Baptism of our Saviour, by Carlo Maratta.

On the left we pass the door which leads to the dome. Over it is the monument of Maria Clementina Sobieski, the wife of the old Pretender. She died in Rome in 1745, and is entitled Queen of Great Britain, France, and Ireland.

On the opposite pilaster is the monument to the Stuarts, by Canova, erected by order and at the expense of George IV. The inscription sets forth that the monument was erected to the memory of James the Third, King of Great Britain, and his sons, Charles Edward and Henry, who are styled by Lord Mahon Charles' the Third and Henry the Ninth. Had the latter attained the title, the Church of Rome would for the first time have had one of her Cardinals occupying an European throne, and that, the throne of England! James the Third, commonly called the Old Pretender, died in Rome on the 1st of January, 1766.

Chapel of the Presentation, so called from the mosaic copy of the Presentation of the Virgin in the Temple, by Romanelli. Against the right pilaster of the next arch is placed the bronze monument of Innocent VIII., 1484-92, by Pietro and Antonio Pollajuolo. This monument was originally in the old Basilica.

Above the door opposite to this monument is a plain plaster sarcophagus, painted in imitation of stone, and bearing no inscription. It awaits the body of Pius IX. This is the temporary sarcophagus in which the remains of each successive Pope are placed until the monument erected to him, whether in St. Peter's or elsewhere, is ready to receive them. The last who occupied it was Gregory XVI. Chapel of the choir. The mosaic over the altar is a copy of "The Conception," by Pietro Bianchi. In this chapel vespers are very beautifully sung every Sunday afternoon, commencing at two hours before sunset.

Against the right pilaster of the next arch is the monument of Innocent XI., 1676-89, by Etienne Monot : and against the left that of Leo XI., 1605, by Algardi.

Over the altar immediately opposite is a remarkably fine mosaic copy of the Transfiguration by Raphael.

Turning to the left, into what is called the Clementina Chapel, the first monument against the left wall is that of Pius VII., 1800-23, by Thorwaldsen. The altar of this chapel is ornamented with a mosaic copy of The Miracle of Gregory the Great, by Andrea Sacchi. Below the altar reposes, it is said, the body of Gregory the Great.

On the left the monument of Pius VIII., 1829-31, by Tenerani. The door in the lower part of the monument leads into the sacristy. The mosaic immediately opposite is a copy of the Ananias and Sapphira, by Roncalli.

We now cross the south transept, called that of Saints Simon and Jude, whose bodies are said to repose under the central altar, above which is a mosaic copy of the Crucifixion of St. Peter, by Guido Reni. The grand columns of Numidian marble, *giallo antico*, taken from some ancient Roman edifice, are well worthy of observation; as also the remarkably fine antique capitals which surmount them. The altar on the right is ornamented with a mosaic copy of The Incredulity of St. Thomas, by Camuccini, and that on the left with a mosaic copy of St. Francis receiving the *stigmata*, the wounds of our Saviour, by Domenichino. Below this altar reposes the body of Pope St. Leo IX.

Along the sides of the transept are ranged a number of confessionals for people of all nations, each bearing the name of the language spoken by the confessor who sits within.

Having crossed the transept we enter the chapel called that of the Madonna of the Column; passing on the left the monument to Alexander VII., 1655-67, by Bernini, with opposite to it an oil painting by Francesco Vanni, representing The Fall of Simon Magus.

This chapel takes its name from an ancient column belonging to the old Basilica, which on account of it bearing a representation of the Virgin Mary with the infant Saviour in her arms, was removed and placed above the altar. It is enclosed within an ornamental framework and glass, through which the painting can just be recognised. In an ancient sarcophagus beneath this altar repose the bodies of Popes Leo II., died 683; Leo III., died 816; and Leo IV., died 855.

The next altar, on the left, is that of Pope St. Leo the Great, beneath which his remains lie in an ancient marble sarcophagus. Above the altar is a magnificent alto relief, by Algardi, representing St. Leo forbidding the advance of Attila, King of the Huns, against Rome. Above the Pope's head are the figures of St. Peter and St. Paul, with drawn swords in their hands, who are said to have appeared in the heavens at the same time to warn back the invader.

Next, on the left, is the monument of Alexander VIII., 1689-91, with, opposite to it, the altar dedicated to the Apostles Peter and John, above which is a mosaic copy of the Apostles healing the lame man at the Gate of the Temple, by *Francesco Mancini*.

Passing across in front of the Tribune we find the corresponding angle to that just visited, closed by an artificial screen work. This was done at the time of the last Œcumenical Council, but entrance may generally be obtained by application at the Sacristy.

The first monument to the left is that of Clement X., 1670-76, by *Mattia Rossi;* above the altar opposite to which, on the right, is a mosaic copy of St. Peter raising Tabitha from the dead, by *Placido Costanzi.*   Above the next altar, on the left, is a mosaic copy, considered the finest mosaic in the Basilica, from *Guercino's* painting of Santa Petronilla, now in the Capitoline Gallery; and above the next altar, also on the left, a mosaic copy from *Guido's* painting of the Archangel Michael, in the Church of Cappuccini.

Next, also on the left, is the monument to Clement XIII., by *Canova;* and, above the altar, opposite to it, on the right, a mosaic copy of our Saviour saving St. Peter from sinking, by *Lanfranco.*

We then pass into the North Transept, which still remains in the condition into which it was transformed for the use of the Œcumenical Council.

Above the altar, at the end of the Transept, is a mosaic representing the martyrdom of Saints Processus and Martinianus, whose remains, it is said, repose beneath.

Above the altar, on the right of this, is a mosaic of St. Wenceslaus, King of Bohemia; and above the altar, on the left, a mosaic copy of the martyrdom of St. Erasmus, by *Poussin.*

Crossing the Transept from the monument of Clement XIII., we pass on the left the monument to Benedict XIV., 1740-58, by *Pietro Bracci,* and on the right, above the altar, a mosaic representing the Emperor Valens fainting in the presence of St. Basil.

Immediately opposite is the monument by *Amici*, recently erected to Gregory XVI., 1831-46, on the left of which is the altar dedicated to the *Madonna del Soccorso*, beneath which reposes the body of St. Gregory Nazianzenus.

Turning to the right, we find on the right hand side the altar dedicated to St. Jerome, and above it a mosaic copy of *Domenichino's* famous picture of that Saint receiving the last Communion.

Turning then to the left, between the piers we find the monument to Gregory XIII., 1572-85, by *Camillo Rusconi*, against that on the left, and the unadorned monument to Gregory XIV., 1590-91, against that on the right.

Next, upon the left, is the Chapel of The Holy Sacrament. Upon the altar is a magnificent tabernacle of gilt bronze and lapis-lazuli, and above it a fresco by *Pietro da Cortona*, representing the Trinity.

Above the altar, on the right, is a mosaic copy of Caravaggio's picture of the Entombment.

On the floor immediately in front of this altar, is the bronze monument to Sixtus IV., 1471-81, by *Pollajuolo*, and near to it a flat stone marking the grave of Julius II., 1503-13.

Turning from this chapel to the left, the niche on the right pier contains a very beautiful statue, by *Bernini*, of the Countess Matilda (died 1115), who founded the temporal power of the Popes; and on the left pier is the monument to Innocent XII., 1691-1700, by *Filippo Valle*.

Above the next altar is a fine mosaic copy of the Martyrdom of St. Sebastian, by *Domenichino;* after passing which we find on the right pier the monument to Christina, Queen of Sweden (died 1689), by *Carlo Fontana;* and above the door in the left the monumental statue of Leo XII., 1823-29, by *Fabris*.

The next, and last chapel, the *Cappella della Pietà*, is that dedicated to the dead. It takes its name more particularly from the group of the Virgin with the dead Saviour on her knees, called a *Pietà*, by *Michael Angelo.* Unfortunately it is placed in so bad a light that it is impossible for the spectator to form any just appreciation of its beauties.

THE VATICAN

is entered by the gate situated where the vestibule, on the left hand as we leave St. Peter's, joins the Colonnade. The entrance is kept by the Swiss guards, whose picturesque costume is said to have been designed by Michael Angelo.* Proceeding along the corridor we ascend the beautiful staircase called THE SCALA REGIA, one of the finest architectural works executed by Bernini. Alterations made in the Vatican during the Pontificate of Alexander VII. necessitated the construction of a staircase on this spot to give access to the great hall called the *Sala Regia.*† On account of the limited space great difficulties were experienced, which Bernini overcame by designing the staircase according to the principles of perspective, by which means he succeeded in giving it a much grander appearance than could otherwise have been obtained, and in making it worthy of the " Regal" name it bears.

Proceeding up a narrow staircase, which leads direct from the first landing of the Scala Regia, a small green baize door is found on the right, which leads into

---

* No persons are admitted without tickets, but those unprovided can obtain them at once by asking to be allowed to go up to the office of the Pope's Maggiordomo, Monsignore Pacca. His secretary gives each person (not members of the same party) two tickets, each admitting five persons, one for the Sculpture Gallery, the other for the Sixtine Chapel, the Loggie and Stanze of Raphael, and the Picture Gallery. The Vatican Galleries are closed on Sundays and Festas; and for Mondays and Thursdays, which are called public days, a separate ticket is required for each person.

† This hall, which contains the frescoes of the Massacre of St. Bartholomew, is now closed to the public.

THE SIXTINE CHAPEL,

so called from the Pope Sixtus IV., 1471-84, by whose orders it was built by Bartolommeo Pintelli. This chapel is famous throughout the world for the *Miserere* so wonderfully sung within it * on the afternoons of Wednesday, Thursday, and Friday, in Holy Week; and for the master pieces in fresco by *Michael Angelo*: THE LAST JUDGMENT, which covers the end wall, and the series of subjects from Genesis, with the majestic figures of THE PROPHETS, and THE SIBYLS, which decorate the ceiling. Michael Angelo was sixty years of age when he commenced the Last Judgment, by order of Clement VII. He spent seven years upon the work, completing it in 1541, during the reign of Paul III. In the centre, and occupying the chief position in the picture, is The Saviour, with His right arm upraised, in the act of saying, "Depart from Me, ye wicked, into everlasting damnation." Beside Him, on His right hand, is the Virgin "veiling herself with her drapery, and turning with a countenance full of anguish towards the Blessed." They are surrounded by the Saints, and the Martyrs holding the instruments of their martyrdom, by which they can be easily recognised: St. Catherine with the wheel, St. Bartholomew holding up his skin, and others. Below are the Angels sounding the last trumpet. On the left, looking towards the picture, are the dead rising from their graves: on the right are the damned, dragged down by devils to eternal punishment, and below them Charon, driving out of his boat a group he has ferried across the Styx. In the extreme corner, on the right, is the portrait of Messer Biagio of Cesena, whom Michael Angelo placed in hell and painted

---

* Now discontinued.

F

with asses' ears, for having criticized his work.   In the half circles above, arc Angels carrying the instruments of the Passion.

The fresco has suffered much by the smoke from the candles burnt in the chapel; through the draperies which were added to many of the figures, first by Daniel da Volterra and then by Stefano Pozzi; and from the blue back-ground, painted on at a later period, which throws the whole out of harmony.

THE CEILING is divided into nine compartments or pictures.   Commencing on the flat portion, immediately above the Last Judgment, the subjects are as follows :—

1—The Separation of Light and Darkness.	5—The Creation of Eve.
2—The Creation of the Sun and Moon.	6—The Temptation and The Expulsion from Paradise.
3—The Creation of Trees and Plants.	7—The Sacrifice of Noah.
4—The Creation of Adam.	8—The Deluge.
	9—The Intoxication of Noah.

On the arched sides of the ceiling arc triangular compartments, between which arc majestic figures of the Prophets and Sibyls alternately.   Commencing with that of Jonah, which occupies the compartment between the arches of the upper portion of the Last Judgment, and proceeding to the right, they will be found in the following order :—

1—Jonah.	7—Zachariah.
2—The Lybian Sibyl.	8—Joel.
3—Daniel.	9—The Erythræan Sibyl.
4—The Cumæan Sibyl.	10—Ezekiel.
5—Isaiah.	11—The Persic Sibyl.
6—The Delphic Sibyl.	12—Jeremiah.

In the spandrils between the Prophets and Sibyls, and in the arches above the windows, are a series of beautiful groups illustrating the genealogy of the Virgin.

The subjects in the four spaces which form the angles of the ceiling are :—Above the chief entrance—Judith and

Holofernes, on the left; David and Goliath, on the right. Above the Last Judgment—The Brazen Serpent, on the right; The Execution of Haman, on the left.

The walls are decorated with frescoes by the great masters of the 15th century; six on each side, and two on the end.

OVER THE CHIEF ENTRANCE.

The Resurrection of our Saviour, by *Ghirlandajo.*

On the left wall, looking towards, and commencing from, the chief entrance:

1—The Last Supper, by *Cosimo Rosselli.*

2—Christ giving the Keys to Peter, by *Pietro Perugino.*

3—The Sermon on the Mount, by *Cosimo Rosselli.*

4—The calling of Peter & Andrew, by *Domenico Ghirlandajo.*

5—The three incidents of the Temptation of our Lord, by *Sandro Botticelli.*

6—The Baptism of Christ, by *Pietro Perugino.*

The Archangel Michael, bearing away the body of Moses, by *Cecchino Salviati.*

On the right wall, looking towards, and commencing from, the chief entrance :

1—Moses blessing the Children of Israel before his death, by *Luca Signorelli:*

2—The Rebellion of Korah, and, The Punishment of Korah, Dathan, and Abiram, by *Sandro Botticelli.*

3—Moses receiving the Commandments on the Mount, The setting up of the Golden Calf, and, Moses breaking the Tables of the Law, by *Cosimo Rosselli.*

4—The Overthrow of Pharaoh in the Red Sea, and, Moses with the Children of Israel singing the song of deliverance, by *Cosimo Rosselli.*

5—Moses slaying the Egyptian; driving the Midianite Shepherds from the well; and, before the Burning Bush, by *Sandro Botticelli.*

6—The Journey of Moses and his wife Zipporah, into Egypt; Moses circumcising his son, by *Luca Signorelli.*

On the pilasters between the windows, are the portraits (?) of twenty-eight Popes, by *Sandro Botticelli.*

On leaving the Sixtine Chapel we turn to the right, and ascending the stairs, reach a closed door, at which we knock, and are admitted into the rooms leading into the Stanze of Raphael.   The first two contain paintings in oil by modern artists.   The walls of the third are covered with frescoes by *Podesti*, painted in commemoration of the Promulgation of the Dogma of the Immaculate Conception of the Virgin, by Pius IX., on the 8th December, 1854.

The beautiful mosaic pavement of this room is ancient; it was found at Ostia, a few years ago, in the course of the excavations still going forward.

THE STANZE OF RAPHAEL.

These three rooms (Stanze) are celebrated for the masterpieces of art painted by Raphael, in fresco, on their walls and ceilings, by order of Julius II.   He commenced them in 1508, being then in his 25th year.

First Room, called the *Stanza of the Incendio del Borgo.* The subjects on the walls are representations of events which took place during the Pontificates of Leo III., 795-816, and Leo IV., 847-55, and were intended to indicate the power of the Church, and its triumph over its enemies.

On the right wall (opposite the window), The Incendio del Borgo; a great fire which broke out in the neighbourhood of the Vatican, in the year 847, and, as it approached the Palace, was miraculously stayed by the Pope Leo IV., who is seen on the balcony making the sign of the cross, and forbidding the flames to advance.   In the background, is a view of the mosaic front of the old Basilica of St. Peter. *On the left wall* (over, and on the sides of the window), The Justification of Leo III. before Charlemagne, designed by *Raphael*, and painted by *Perino del Vaga.*

On the wall of Ingress, The Coronation of Charlemagne, partly painted by *Raphael*, and partly by *Perino del Vaga.*

The faces of the Pope and the Emperor, in both of these frescoes, are those of Leo X., and Francis I., King of France.

On the wall of Egress, THE VICTORY OF LEO IV. OVER THE SARACENS AT OSTIA, designed by *Raphael,* and painted by *Giovanni da Udine.* The Pope is a portrait of Leo X.

The ceiling is painted in imitation of mosaic, by *Pietro Perugino.* When the paintings by the earlier masters, in these rooms, were obliterated, to make way for those of Raphael, he would not allow this ceiling to be touched, out of respect to his master. The subjects are: The Almighty surrounded by Angels; The Saviour in Glory; The Saviour with the Apostles; and, The Glorification of the Saviour between Saints and Angels.

SECOND ROOM, called *The Stanza della Segnatura,* painted in illustration of the virtues of Theology, Philosophy, Jurisprudence, and Poetry, which are personified in the four circular, and illustrated in the four square frescoes, on the ceiling. Theology, by the Fall of Man; Philosophy, by the study of the Globe; Jurisprudence, by the Judgment of Solomon; and Poetry, by the Flaying of Marsyas. The paintings on the walls are illustrations of the same subjects.

On the wall of Ingress, THE DISPUTE OF THE SACRAMENT. Theology. This was the first of this series of frescoes painted by Raphael, and is by many considered to be his grandest work. In the lower portion, are ranged on each side of the altar, the Fathers of the Church, Popes, Bishops, and eminent Divines, whose writings have had reference to the "real presence." The upper portion represents the Heavenly Host. In the centre, The Three Persons of the Trinity, with The Virgin on one side and John the Baptist on the other. On the right, are St. Paul, Abraham, St. James, Moses, St. Laurence, and St. George. On the left, St. Peter, Adam, St. John, David, St. Stephen, and another.

On the wall of Egress, THE SCHOOL OF ATHENS. Philosophy. The great Philosophers, Mathematicians, and men of learning of antiquity, are represented as gathered together in the Poicile Stoa, at Athens.

On the right wall, Jurisprudence. Above the window are, Prudence, Fortitude, and Temperance. On the left side of the window, the Emperor Justinian delivering the Pandects to Tribonian, as illustrating civil law. On the right, Pope Gregory IX. (a portrait of Julius II.) delivering the Decretals to an advocate of the Consistory, illustrating canon law. The figures near the Pope are portraits of Cardinal de Medici, afterwards Leo X., Cardinal Farnese, afterwards Paul III., and Cardinal del Monte, who became Julius III.

On the left wall, MOUNT PARNASSUS. Poetry. Above the window, Apollo is seated surrounded by the Muses, and, on the left, Homer, Virgil, and Dante. By the side of the window, on the left are, Sappho, seated, Corinna, Petrarch, Propertius, and Anacreon ; on the right, Pindar, Horace, Sannazaro, Boccaccio, and others.

THIRD ROOM, called the STANZA OF HELIODORUS. The subjects on the walls are intended to represent " the Divine assistance granted to the Church against her foes, and the miraculous corroboration of her doctrine," with especial reference to events during the Pontificates of Julius II. and Leo X., reigning at the time they were painted.

On the wall of Ingress, POPE ST. LEO I. FORBIDDING ATTILA'S APPROACH UPON ROME, allusive to the expulsion of the French from Italy in 1513, through the victory gained by Leo X. in that year, over Louis XII., at Novara. On the left is St. Leo (a portrait of Leo X.) riding on a mule, and attended by two Cardinals. On the right, Attila, at the head of the Huns, starting back affrighted at the miraculous appearance in the heavens of Saints Peter and Paul with drawn swords in their hands.

On the wall of Egress, THE EXPULSION OF HELIODORUS FROM THE TEMPLE AT JERUSALEM (2 *Maccabees* iii.), "commemorative of the deliverance of the Ecclesiastical States from the foes of the Apostolic authority, under Julius II., and his preservation of the possessions of the Church." In the background is the High Priest Onias, kneeling at the altar in prayer for divine protection. In the foreground on the right, the spoiler, Heliodorus, lies prostrate beneath the feet of the "horse with the terrible rider;" on the left is Pope Julius II. being carried into the Temple in the *Sedia gestatoria;* an anachronism "intended to indicate the relation of the miraculous event to the circumstances of his time."

On the right wall, THE MIRACLE OF BOLSENA, designed to illustrate the infallibility of the Romish doctrines. A priest at Bolsena, having refused to believe in the real presence, is convinced by the miraculous bleeding of the Host. In this fresco, the portrait of Julius II. is again introduced, kneeling at one side of the altar.

On the left wall, THE DELIVERANCE OF ST. PETER FROM PRISON, painted in allusion to the captivity of Leo X. while Cardinal and Papal Legate, in Spain; and his delivery, the year before he was elected to fill the Papal chair. In the centre, over the window, the angel is awaking St. Peter in prison; on the right side of the window, the angel is leading him out between the sleeping guards; on the left, the soldiers are represented awaking from their sleep, to find their prisoner gone.

The ceiling is divided into four compartments, containing subjects from the Old Testament: The promise of God to Abraham, The Sacrifice of Isaac, Moses before the Burning Bush, and Jacob's Dream.

From this room we pass into THE HALL OF CONSTANTINE, the decoration of which Raphael had only commenced a short time before his death. His intention was to paint these walls in oil, but he only completed two of the allegorical figures—JUSTICE, on the right of the great picture of the Defeat of Maxentius; and CHARITY, near the angle to the left. They are easily to be recognised by the green draperies, and their darker tone. The decoration of the hall was continued, and completed, by his scholars. The great fresco on the wall, opposite the windows, represents THE DEFEAT OF MAXENTIUS BY CONSTANTINE AT THE MILVIAN BRIDGE—now called the *Ponte Molle*—about two miles from Rome, by *Giulio Romano*.

On the wall to the left of this: THE ADDRESS OF CONSTANTINE TO HIS TROOPS BEFORE THE BATTLE, AND THE VISION OF THE HOLY CROSS, by *Giulio Romano*.

On the wall to the right: THE SUPPOSED BAPTISM OF CONSTANTINE BY ST. SYLVESTER, by *Francesco Penni*.

On the space between the windows: THE DONATION OF ROME BY CONSTANTINE TO POPE ST. SYLVESTER, ascribed to *Raphaello da Colle*.

On the ceiling is a painting remarkable for its perspective and foreshortening. It represents a statue of Mercury, overthrown from its pedestal and broken, to give place to the Cross.

From this room we pass into The Loggie, and thence by a door, a few paces on the left, proceed upstairs to the Picture Gallery.

THE LOGGIE OF RAPHAEL

are the open balconies—recently closed in with glass—which form three sides of the great court-yard of the Vatican. That side of the middle Loggia, into which we turn immediately on the right after leaving·the Stanze, was painted by Raphael's scholars, from his designs and under his direction.* The walls are covered with arabesques and festoons of fruit and flowers, painted by *Giovanni da Udine.* This Loggia is divided into thirteen arcades, with vaulted ceilings, in each of which are four pictures representing subjects from the Old Testament,—with the exception of one of the arcades, on the ceiling of which there are four subjects from the New Testament—all easily recognizable. They were painted by *Giulio Romano, Francesco Penni, Pellegrino da Modena, Perino del Vaga,* and *Raphaello da Colle.*

THE PINACOTHECA,

the Vatican Picture Gallery, contains comparatively few works, but they are almost without exception of great excellence. After the battle of Waterloo, the French were obliged to restore the works of art they had carried off to Paris from the cities of Italy, and on the masterpieces taken from Rome, being returned, Canova and Cardinal Consalvi advised Pius VII. to ensure their better preservation, by forming them into a collection, instead of replacing them in the churches to which they had belonged. To those sent back from Paris, a few others have since been added.

The pictures in these rooms are not numbered, but they

---

* The other sides of this Loggia, which have recently been restored by *Signor Mantovani,* were finished in the time of Gregory XIII., 1572-85, and decorated after the same general design, by *Marco da Faenza, Paul Schnorr, Sicciolante da Sermonetta, Tempesta,* and *Sabbatini.*

are given below, in the order in which they will be found on the walls :

First Room.

St. Jerome, a sketch : *Leonardo da Vinci.*

St. John the Baptist : *Guercino.*

The Incredulity of St. Thomas : *Guercino.*

The Annunciation; the Adoration of the Magi; and the Presentation in the Temple : *Raphael.* These three charming little pictures originally formed the predella to the Coronation of the Virgin, by Raphael, in the third room.

Madonna and Child with St. Jerome : *Francia.*

Mary Magdalen and the Dead Christ : *Andrea Mantegna.*

The Dead Christ with the Virgin, St. John, and the Magdalen : *Carlo Crivelli.*

The Holy Family : *Benvenuto Garofolo.*

Faith, Hope, and Charity : *Raphael.* Originally formed the predella to his picture of the Entombment, now in the Borghese Gallery.

St. Benedict, St. Placidus, and Sta. Flavia : *Pietro Perugino.*

The Holy Family, with St. Catherine and St. Philip the Martyr : *Bonifazio.*

A Predella, with the story and miracles of St. Hyacinth : *Benozzo Gozzoli.*

The Marriage of St. Catherine of Alexandria with the Infant Christ : *Murillo.*

The Virgin : *Fra Angelico da Fiesole.*

The Story of St. Nicholas, of Bari : *Fra Angelico da Fiesole.*

The Adoration of the Shepherds : *Murillo.*

Second Room.

This room contains three pictures only, the gems of the Collection : The Transfiguration; The Communion of St. Jerome; and The Madonna da Foligno. The two former being among the very few which are ranked as the finest pictures ever painted.

The Transfiguration, on the left. This is Raphael's master-piece; his last work, left unfinished at his death; and it is conceded the supremacy over all other paintings existing. "The upper part of the picture is formed by an elevation to represent Mount Tabor. There lie prostrate the three disciples who went up with Christ, dazzled by the Divine light ; above them, surrounded by a miraculous glory, the Saviour floats in the air, in serene beatitude, accompanied by Moses and Elias." The lower portion, which Raphael had only drawn upon the panel, and which was completed by *Giulio Romano,* represents the Demoniac Boy, brought by his parents to the remaining nine disciples, who profess themselves powerless to cure him in the "Master's" absence on the Mount, up to which one of the disciples is pointing. The two small figures at one side of the upper portion, are St. Julian and St. Laurence; an anachronism, committed at the request of Cardinal de Medici, on account of their being the patron Saints of his father, Giuliano de Medici, and his uncle, Lorenzo, the magnificent. This picture was placed at the head of the bed on which Raphael was laid in state, and carried in the procession which accompanied his remains to the grave.

THE COMMUNION OF ST. JEROME, on the right, the master-piece of Domenichino. The Saint is represented, when, at the point of death, as he was carried, according to his desire, into the chapel of his Monastery, that he might receive the last Sacrament, which was administered to him by St. Ephraim of Syria. This picture was painted by Domenichino for the Monks of the Ara Cœli, who were so much dissatisfied with it, that they hid it away in a lumber room. Afterwards, having given Poussin a commission to paint them a picture, they brought out this, that he might utilize the canvas by painting over it, which he indignantly refused to do. It is now recognized as only second in merit to the Transfiguration.

THE MADONNA DA FOLIGNO, on the wall at the back, painted by Raphael for the high Altar of the Ara Cœli, but afterwards transferred to the Convent of St. Anna, at Foligno, whence its name. The kneeling figure draped in red, on the right, is a portrait of a certain Sigismondo Conte, a native of Foligno, the donor of the picture, and behind, St. Jerome recommending him to the Virgin's care. On the left are St. Francis and St. John the Baptist.

THIRD ROOM.

An Altar Piece: *Titian.* Called St. Sebastian and other Saints. The figures represent St. Nicholas in full episcopal costume, St. Ambrose, St. Catherine of Alexandria, St. Francis with the Cross, St. Anthony of Padua with the Lily, and St. Sebastian pierced with arrows; above is the Virgin and Child surrounded by Angels.

St. Margaret of Cortona: *Guercino.*

The Martyrdom of St. Laurence: *Spagnoletto.*

The Magdalen with Angels bearing the Instruments of the Passion: *Guercino.*

The Coronation of the Virgin: *Pinturicchio.*

The Resurrection: *Pietro Perugino.*

The Madonna di Monte Luco: *Giulio Romano and Francesco Penni.*

The Nativity: *Giovanni Spagna.*

The Adoration: *School of Perugino.*

The Coronation of the Virgin: *Raphael.* This is one of his earliest works.

The Madonna and Child enthroned, with St. Laurence and St. Louis of Toulouse, on one side, and St. Hercolanus on the other: *Pietro Perugino.*

The Virgin and Child, seated on a crescent moon, and surrounded by Cherubs: *Sassoferrato.* This picture was presented to Pius IX. by Queen Isabella of Spain.

The Entombment: *M. A. Caravaggio.*

Portrait of A. Gritti, Doge of Venice: *Titian.*

An Altar Piece, in three compartments: *Niccolò Alunno.*

Pope Sixtus IV. giving audience: *Melozzo da Forli.* All the figures are portraits.

An Altar Piece: *Niccolò Alunno.*

Fourth Room.

The Martyrdom of Saints Processus and Martinianus, the jailers of St. Peter: *Valentin.*	The Vision of St. Helena, the mother of Constantine, of the finding of the True Cross: *Paolo Veronese.*
The Crucifixion of St. Peter: *Guido Reni.*	The Madonna and Child with St. Thomas and St. Jerome: *Guido.*
The Martyrdom of St. Erasmus: *N. Poussin.*	
The Annunciation: *Baroccio.*	The Madonna della Cintola, with St. John and St. Augustine: *Cesare da Sesto.*
The Miracle of St. Gregory the Great: *Andrea Sacchi.*	
The Ecstacy of Sta. Michelina: *Baroccio.*	The Saviour: *Correggio.*
The Madonna and Child, with St. Francis and St. Bartholomew: *Moretto da Brescia.*	The Vision of St. Romualdo *Andrea Sacchi.*

The direct communication, from the Loggie to the Sculpture Galleries, having been closed to the public since September, 1870, it is now necessary to return to the Piazza of St. Peter's, and pass round the back of the Basilica, to where the Swiss Guards are standing sentry at the entrance to the Vatican on that side; then, passing under an archway on the left, we shall find, at the further extremity of the ascent before us, the entrance to

THE VATICAN MUSEUM OF SCULPTURE.*

This grand Museum of ancient sculpture was founded by Clement XIV., 1769-75. Acting on the suggestion of E. Q. Visconti, and Winkelmann, he set apart a series of galleries and chambers into which the various masterpieces of ancient sculpture, dispersed through the halls of the Pontifical Palace, were collected together and made accessible to the public. The nucleus thus formed, additions

* For fuller details regarding the masterpieces in this Museum, see *The Vatican Museum of Sculpture*, a lecture by Mr. Shakspere Wood, obtainable at all libraries.

have been constantly made to the collection, until it now contains nearly 1800 works.

Ascending the staircase we enter

THE HALL OF THE GREEK CROSS,

on each side of which is a magnificent Porphyry Sarcophagus. That on the right contained the body of the EMPRESS HELENA, the mother of Constantine. It was taken from her monument outside the Porta Maggiore, by Anastasius IV., 1150-54, who placed it in the Lateran, whence it was removed to the Vatican by Pius VI.

The Sarcophagus, on the left, contained the body of Constantia (died 354), daughter of Constantine. It was taken by Pius VI. from her monument—still existing on the Via Salaria, close to the Church of St. Agnes—and placed by him in this hall, as a pendant to that of her mother. The surface of both these Sarcophagi has been entirely worked over, and various parts restored.

On the floor are two ancient mosaics of great beauty: one representing a basket of flowers, found in the ruins called *Roma Vecchia*, four miles outside the Porta Maggiore ; the other, circular in form, and occupying the centre of the floor, was found in 1741, among the ruins of Tusculum.

574. THE VENUS OF CNIDOS, by *Praxiteles ;* an ancient copy, which has been partly covered with metal drapery.

600. THE TIGRIS. The head is a restoration by *Michael Angelo.*

Proceeding up the stairs, we find a small circular room, THE HALL OF THE BIGA, on the right, and a long gallery, THE GALLERY OF THE CANDELABRA, immediately before us.

THE HALL OF THE BIGA.

623. THE BIGA—in the middle of the room. A chariot drawn by two horses; possibly a votive offering made by a victor in the circus races. It is in great part a restoration, the only antique portions being the body of the chariot and the barrel of one of the horses.

608. The Indian Bacchus, commonly called Sardanapalus, from that name being cut along the border of the mantle.

610. Bacchus.

611. Alcibiades.

614. Apollo.

615. DISCOBOLUS, an ancient copy of the original, by *Naukides.*

616. Phocion.

618. DISCOBOLUS, an ancient copy of the original, by *Myron,* found in 1781 at the Villa Palombara on the Esquiline.

619. An Auriga. A charioteer; interesting as showing the dress.

609, 613, 617, 621. Four small Sarcophagi, the bas-reliefs on which represent the races in the circus.

HALL OF THE CANDELABRA.

This Gallery contains a number of objects, interesting from an archæological, rather than from an artistic point of view. Chief among them are, a number of Sarcophagi; Cinerary Urns of oriental alabaster and other materials; Marble Candelabra; richly ornamented Tazze and Vases; and Columns, portions of domestic architecture, of rare marble, richly variegated.

2 & 66. NESTS, in each of which are five Cupids, supported on pedestals sculptured in the form of trunks of trees.

20. Sarcophagus of a child, whose figure is recumbent on the lid.

31. Candelabrum.

35. Candelabrum.

48. Cinerary urn of Egyptian granitello.

49. Child plucking a bunch of grapes.

52. Recumbent Faun in green basalt.

69. Vase of rare jasper, called *Lysimaco.*

74. Satyr extracting a thorn from the foot of a Faun.

81. Diana of Ephesus, found at Hadrian's Villa.

82. Sarcophagus, with bas relief representing the murder of Ægisthus and Clytemnestra.

112. Sarcophagus, with bas relief representing the story of Protesilaus and Laodamia.

143A. The Genius of Death.

148A. Faun and Young Bacchus, found recently near the Scala Sancta.

194. Child playing with a goose.

204. Sarcophagus, with the story of the Children of Niobe.

208. Portrait statue of a boy wearing the golden bulla.

234. Candelabrum, found at Otricoli.

237. Idem.

253. Ceres, a statuette of considerable beauty.

Returning down the staircase, and crossing the Hall of the Greek Cross, we enter a large circular hall, called

THE ROTONDA.

PORPHYRY TAZZA of colossal dimensions, in the centre of the room; found in the time of Julius III., 1550-55, among the ruins of the Baths of Trajan. It measures 44½ feet in circumference.

MOSAIC PAVEMENT of great beauty, found among the ruins of the Baths at Atricoli.

539. JUPITER: Colossal bust, supposed to have been copied from the Jupiter Olympus, *by Phidias.*

540. Antinous: colossal statue found in 1733, at Palestrina.

541. FAUSTINA THE ELDER, wife of Antoninus Pius, found at Hadrian's Villa.

542. Ceres. Colossal statue.

543. HADRIAN. Colossal bust, found in his mausoleum; now the Castle of Saint Angelo.

544. COLOSSAL HERCULES of gilt bronze, called the Hercules Mastai, from Pius IX., who purchased it at the price of 50,000 scudi, (£10,000) from its discoverer, Sig. Righetti, and placed it in the Museum. It was found in 1864, 20 feet below the level, in the courtyard of the Palazzo Biscione, near the Campo di Fiore. This Palace stands above the ruins of Pompey's Theatre.

545. ANTINOUS: colossal bust.

546. The BARBERINI JUNO: colossal statue; found on the Viminal near the Church of St. Lorenzo in Panisperna.

548. NERVA: colossal seated statue.

549. Jupiter Serapis: colossal bust.

550. CLAUDIUS DEIFIED: colossal statue, found at Civita Lavinia in 1865; it was purchased for the Museum by Pius IX.

551. Claudius, bust.

552. Juno Sospita, the preserver.

553. Plotina, wife of Trajan, colossal bust, found on the Cœlian.

544. JULIA PIA, wife of Septimius Severus: colossal head.

556. PERTINAX: colossal bust.

HALL OF THE MUSES.

The statues of Apollo Musagetes and the Muses, from which this hall takes its name, were, with the exception of two (Euterpe, No. 520, and Urania, No. 504), found in the olive wood near Tivoli, among the ruins of an ancient villa, supposed to have been that of Cassius.

499. Melpomene, the Muse of tragedy.
502. Thalia, the Comic Muse.
504. Urania, from the Lancelotti Palace at Velletri. This statue has been restored, with the attributes of the Muse of Astronomy, to complete the nine, but it is doubtful if it was originally a muse.

506. Clio: the Historic Muse.
508. Polyhymnia: the Muse of Memory.
511. Erato: the Lyric Muse.
515. Calliope: the Epic Muse.
516. Apollo Musagetes.
517. Terpsichore: the Muse of Lyric Song and Dance.
520. Euterpe: the Muse of Music, from the Lancellotti Palace at Velletri.

THE HALL OF ANIMALS.

The contents of this hall have been graphically described as a "menagerie done into marble." The subjects are so obvious that it is unnecessary to specify them.

Turning to the left through this hall, on leaving the Hall of the Muses, we enter that portion of the Museum called

THE GALLERY.

In the middle of the room, opposite the door, is a cinerary urn of oriental alabaster, of large size and great beauty, which it is believed contained the ashes of Livilla, daughter of Germanicus; and further on to the right, a magnificent bath of oriental alabaster.

250. The Genius of the Vatican, a fragment of very great beauty, supposed to be the remains of an ancient copy of the celebrated Cupid of *Praxiteles;* that which Phryne chose and presented to her native town of Thespis.
255. Paris.
261. Penelope.
264. Apollo Sauroktonos; the lizard killer. An ancient copy from the celebrated bronze by *Praxiteles;* found on the Palatine in 1777.

265. Amazon: an exceedingly fine ancient copy from one of the fifty bronze statues of the conquered Amazons which adorned the Temple of Diana at Ephesus. Five of these statues were adjudged superior in merit to the others, and it is believed that the different Amazons found among the ruins of ancient Rome, are copies made from them. Another very fine copy from the same original from which this was taken, is in the Capitoline Museum.

271. Posidippos : Greek comic poet.

390. Menander : the Prince of Greek comedy.

These magnificent portrait statues have come down to us in so wonderful a state of preservation, through their having been preserved from injury in the Church of St. Lorenzo, in Panisperna, where, during the dark ages, they were reverenced as Christian saints. On the revival of letters, the name of Posidippos was read upon the base, the subjects recognised, and, by order of Sixtus V., they were removed to his villa on the Esquiline—now the Villa Negrono. The rivets of the metal plates, with which the feet were covered, to prevent their being worn away by the kisses of the devout, still remain.

393. Dido.

396. The wounded Adonis.

401. Hemon and Antigone.

405. One of the daughters of Danaus, filling the sieve.

406. Faun. One of the many ancient copies of the celebrated masterpiece of *Praxiteles.*

414. Ariadne : bought from Girolamo Maffei by Julius II., 1503-13. This is one of the gems of the Vatican collection. It is perfect as a composition, the drapery is a masterpiece of art, and the restless sleep in which the nymph is lying is most admirably rendered. Ariadne is represented at the moment when, sleeping on the island of Naxos, she was deserted by Theseus. For a long time this was supposed to be a statue of Cleopatra, on account of the armlet in the form of a small snake.

THE RESERVED CABINET,

the door of which is in the recess opposite the entrance to the Gallery.

Mosaic Pavement of great beauty, found at Hadrian's Villa in 1780.

429. The Crouching Venus, found in some ruins on the Roman Campagna, near the farm called *Salone.*

431. Diana Lucifera.

433. Faun, of *rosso antico*, the companion statue to that in the Capitoline Museum, and found at the same place, Hadrian's Villa, near Tivoli.

435. Mithraic Genius.

436. Tazza of *rosso antico* of great beauty.

439. A Sella Balnearia, or bath chair, of *rosso antico.* It is supposed by some to be an example of the *Sella Stercoraria* used at the coronation of the Popes during the middle ages; and recent discoveries tend to show that this name is a correct indication of the purpose those marble chairs served, in the more sumptuous houses and villas of ancient Rome.

442. Ganymede.

443. Adonis.

Alto reliefs on the walls representing the labours of Hercules.

G

Returning through the Hall of Animals, we enter the courtyard, with a small fountain in the centre, around which are four cabinets.

THE FIRST CABINET,

on the right, contains the celebrated group of LAOCOON, No. 74. This magnificent work was discovered in 1506, near the ruins of the Baths of Trajan, commonly called the Baths of Titus, by a certain Felix de Freddis, from whom it was purchased by Julius II. It was at once recognised as being the group mentioned by Pliny, in his Natural History, as the work of three Rhodian sculptors, Agesander, Athenodorus, and Polydorus. It illustrates the story of the tragic death of Laocoon and his sons, described in the 2nd Book of Virgil's Æneid. Laocoon, the priest of Neptune, having incurred the wrath of Minerva, by flinging a lance at the wooden horse to expose the deception, the goddess sent two serpents, who, entangling the old man and his sons in their folds, killed them on the altar on which they were about to sacrifice.

The three raised arms are restorations. That of Laocoon should have been bent back so as to rest upon the head.

THE SECOND CABINET

contains the APOLLO BELVEDERE, No. 92, the *chef d'œuvre* of the collection, and for long considered the grandest example of ancient sculpture which has come down to us; and although it is now recognised as but a copy from some still finer work, whose author's name even is unknown to us, it yet stands a marvel of the unsurpassed excellence of the great sculptors of antiquity.

It was found at the end of the 15th century, among the ruins of the Palace of Nero, at Porto d'Anzio, the ancient Antium. It is supposed by some that the god is represented at the moment when he slew the Python; by others, that he has discharged his arrow at the children of Niobe; or again, that it is a copy from the celebrated bronze by Calamides, mentioned by Pliny, representing Apollo, the Averter of Evil, erected at Athens on the cessation of the great plague.

A small bronze, discovered a few years ago, would lead to the supposition that it represents Apollo holding the Ægis, the emblem of thunder, lightning, hail, and earthquake, and with it repelling the Gauls, who attacked Delphos, B.C. 278, and when, according to the legend, the deity came to the assistance of the Greeks.

The hands are restorations.

THE THIRD CABINET

contains three works by *Canova*. In the centre PERSEUS with the head of the Gorgon, No. 82. On the right hand, the boxer DAMOXENUS, No. 33; and on the left, the boxer CREUGAS, No. 34.

When the great masterpieces of ancient sculpture were carried off to Paris by Napoleon I., the Perseus was bought from Canova by Pius VII., who placed it on the pedestal of the Apollo, and called it the *Consoler*.

The subject of the two boxers is taken from Pausanius, who relates, that, rival champions, they fought for supremacy, or, as we might say, for "the belt." Victory remaining doubtful, it was decided that each should, without defence, withstand a blow from his opponent, standing in the attitude in which he placed him. Lots were drawn. The first fell to Creugas, who struck his adversary upon the head without injuring him ; whereon Damoxenus, having placed his man in the position represented by Canova, drove his hand with fearful force into his side, and killed him on the spot. The Athenians were so much disgusted with the want of fair play that they decreed the wreath of victory, posthumously, to Creugas, and banished Damoxenus from the city.

THE FOURTH CABINET

contains the MERCURY OF THE BELVEDERE, No. 53. There can be little doubt that this statue, though possessed of less "subject" than the Apollo, in point of art surpasses it. It is sculptured in Parian marble of the very finest quality, and was found in the time of Paul III., 1534-50, near the Church of St. Martino ai Monti. For a long time it was called THE ANTINOUS of the Belvedere, from its bearing some resemblance to Hadrian's favorite, a supposition which was strengthened by the fact of its having been discovered in the ruins of the Adrianopolo, a place built by that Emperor on the Esquiline. The mistake was rectified by Visconti. The palm-tree which gives support to the leg was sacred to Mercury.

The right ankle has the appearance of being somewhat distorted. This is due to the unskilful manner in which the broken pieces were put together, and to the sculptor employed for the purpose, having rasped away some of the marble to make the edges even.

Having made the circuit of the Cabinets, and returned to the entrance of the Hall of Animals, we must now cross the courtyard, and entering a small vestibule, we find, in a recess on the left, another of the masterpieces of the collection, MELEAGER, the slayer of the Caledonian boar, No. 10.

Though ancient sculpture generally suffers through restoration, this statue would probably have gained, had the wanting hand been replaced. It held the lance on which the hero was represented as leaning, the absence of which causes the figure to appear somewhat off its balance. The marble also, which is that from Mount Hymettus, detracts from the effect of the statue, through its cold blueish tint and opaque quality. It was found in the 15th century, in a vineyard outside the Porta Portese.

Continuing onwards, we come to one of the great treasures of the collection, the celebrated TORSO, No. 3. This magnificent fragment was found near the Campo di Fiore, in the time of Julius II., 1503-13. It was an object of continued study by Michael Angelo, and has been a source of admiration from all artists, from his day to our own. It is, however, too much injured to obtain a full recognition of its beauties by the general public. On the base is the name of the sculptor, Apollonius, the son of Nestor; but as this name is unknown in the records of art, it is presumed to be that of the artist who copied it, from, in all probability, the Hercules deified, by *Lysippus*. It is believed that the statue represented Hercules seated at the table of the gods, his right hand resting on the club, and holding the wine cup aloft in his left.

Against the wall, is the SARCOPHAGUS, No. 2, of the stone called peperino, which contained the body of SCIPIO BARBATUS, who took Taurisia and Samnium, and conquered Lucania. He was the great-grandfather of Scipio Africanus. This sarcophagus was found in the tomb of the Scipios, on the Appian Way, in the year 1780, together with a number of inscriptions, now on the walls around it, all relating to the same family.

Descending a few steps, we enter the long

CHIARAMONTI GALLERY,

which contains a number of works, chiefly interesting from an archæological point of view only.

62. Hygeia.
112. VENUS; worthless in point of art, but interesting as being a copy from the celebrated Venus of Cnydos, by *Praxiteles*.
121. Clio, the Muse of History.
176. NIOBID. This magnificent fragment is the finest representation of drapery in marble to be found in the museum. The subject is doubtful. It is supposed by some to be one of the daughters of Niobe flying from the shafts of Apollo and Diana ; by others, to be Diana descending from her chariot to visit Endymion.
179. Sarcophagus, with the story of Alcestis.
197. Minerva, colossal bust.
240. Britannicus.
352. Venus.
399. Tiberius ; colossal head.
400. TIBERIUS ; semi - colossal statue, seated.
416. THE YOUNG AUGUSTUS, one of the most beautiful heads in the collection. It is perfect as a work of art, and bears undoubted evidence of being a most truthful portrait of Augustus, at about the age of fifteen. It was found in 1808, at Ostia, by Robert Fagan, then English Consul.
417, 419. CAIUS and LUCIUS, the grandsons of Augustus, children of Julia and Agrippa; found in 1859, near the Church of Sta. Balbina.
422. Demosthenes ; bust.
493. Diadumenianus, son of the Emperor Macrinus.
494. TIBERIUS ; semi - colossal statue, seated.
495. CUPID; believed to be an ancient copy from the celebrated Cupid by *Lysippus*.
497. Fragment of a large sarcophagus, on which is the representation of a corn mill turned by horses ; found outside the Porta San Giovanni, in 1836.
510A. Cato.
512. Caius Marius (?)
544. Silenus.
546. Sabina, the wife of Hadrian.
547. Isis ; colossal bust.
635. Hercules holding Telephus in his arms.
682. ANTONINUS PIUS; found at Hadrian's Villa.
698. Cicero (?) bust, found at the Villa of the Quintilii, on the Appian Way.
701. Ulysses.
732. Hercules recumbent.

Just before reaching the end of the Chiaramonti Gallery, we turn to the right, into the

BRACCIO NUOVO,

which contains some of the finest works in the collection.

5. Caryatid, supposed to have belonged to the Temple of Pandrosia at Athens. The head and fore arms are restorations, by *Thorwaldsen*.
8. Commodus.
11. SILENUS WITH THE INFANT BACCHUS.

14. Augustus; this magnificent statue was found in 1863, at Prima Porta, about eight miles from Rome, among the ruins of a Villa, Livia had at that spot. It is without exception the finest imperial portrait statue which has come down to us. The small figures sculptured on the cuirass are exceedingly beautiful; the statue bears very distinct traces of colouring.

23. Pudicizia; Modesty; evidently a portrait statue of some imperial or noble Roman lady. The head and right hand are restorations.

26. Titus; evidently an exact portrait, both of face and figure. Found near the Lateran in 1828.

39. Colossal vase of black Egyptian basalt; found in fragments in the Quirinal.

44. Wounded Amazon.

50. Diana; supposed to be looking upon Endymion.

53. Euripides.

62. Demosthenes. This grand portrait of the great Athenian orator was found among the ruins of ancient Tusculum, and, it is thought, may possibly have belonged to Cicero. Both hands, with the roll held by them, are restorations.

67. The Athlete, with the Strigil, called The Apoxyomenos. This fine statue was discovered in 1849, in the Vicolo della Palme, in the Trastevere. It was at once recognised to be an ancient copy of the celebrated bronze Athlete by *Lysippus*, described by Pliny, who relates that it was brought from Greece by Marcus Agrippa, and placed by him in the portico of his Thermæ.

71. Amazon.

77. Antonia, wife of the elder Drusus; found at Tusculum.

83. Ceres; found at Ostia in 1856.

86. Fortune; found at Ostia in 1798.

92. Venus Anadyomene.

109. The Nile. This grand group was discovered near the Church of Sta. Maria sopra Minerva, in the time of Leo X., 1513-22. It is believed to be an ancient copy from a group in basalt, described by Pliny as having been placed by Vespasian in the Temple of Peace.

111. Julia, daughter of Titus; found, together with that of her father, No. 26, immediately opposite, in 1828, near the Lateran.

114. Minerva Medica; sculptured in Parian marble of the finest quality; but it has been worked over and the original surface entirely removed. It was found in the ruin near the Porta Maggiore, called the Temple of Minerva. (See page 33.)

120. Faun, an ancient copy of the celebrated Faun by *Praxiteles;* the same as No. 406 in "The Gallery."

123. Lucius Verus.

129. Domitian.

132. Mercury.

Turning to the right, on leaving the Nuovo Braccio, we

find, at the end of the Chiaramonti Gallery, a closed gate, which leads into the GALLERY OF INSCRIPTIONS, and through this gate admission is given, to small parties at a time, to

THE LIBRARY,

in which, notwithstanding the value of its contents, especially in MSS., no books are visible, beyond a few choice editions, and an example or two of the rarer illuminated MSS., placed in show cases, which will be opened by the *custode* if he is not pressed for time, through other visitors waiting for entrance. The contents of the Library are contained in closed cupboards round the sides of the rooms. It is, however, well worth visiting, if only on account of the grand Hall, which forms its chief feature. The first two rooms are devoted to the use of the librarians and persons admitted to study. We then enter the Great Hall, which is 230 feet in length by 56 wide. It has a double vaulted ceiling, supported by pilasters, and is richly decorated with frescoes and arabesques. Between the pilasters are placed a number of handsome presents, sent to the Popes of this century; among which are some Sevres vases and candelabra given by Napoleon I. to Pius VII.; the baptismal font of the Prince Imperial, sent to Pius IX. by Napoleon III.; and a magnificent tazza of Scotch granite, presented by the late Duke of Northumberland.

At the end of the great Hall, the Library branches off to the right and to the left. In the wing to the right, there are no objects of interest, but in the rooms to the left, there is an interesting collection of Christian antiquities, chiefly from the Catacombs; and at the end, a small collection of pictures, of the early Italian schools. In a room to the side is the celebrated NOZZE ALDOBRANDINI, with some other ancient Roman frescoes; and also a choice collection of .brick stamps.

THE ETRUSCAN MUSEUM,

founded by Gregory XIV., contains a number of Etruscan antiquities, discovered in the excavations made at Toscanella, Cervetri, Corneto, Volterra, Tarquinii, Vulci, and other places, and is well worth visiting.

THE EGYPTIAN MUSEUM,

founded by Pius VII., contains little of interest for those who have visited the collections of Egyptian antiquities in the British Museum and the Louvre, beyond a number of statues sculptured in Rome, in the Egyptian style, for the Emperor Hadrian, to ornament the Canopus in his villa, near Tivoli, among the ruins of which they were found.

FROM THE PORTA DEL POPOLO TO THE CAPITOL.

The modern PORTA DEL POPOLO supplies the place of the celebrated Porta Flaminia, though there is reason to believe that the ancient gate was somewhat higher on the side of the Pincio. It was built in the time of Pius IV., 1559-66, by *Giacomo Barozzi da Vignola*, from, it is said, the designs of *Michael Angelo*. The statues of St. Peter and St. Paul on the outside are by *Mochi*, and the columns, between which they stand, originally belonged to the ancient basilica of St. Peter. The frontage of the gate toward the city was constructed by *Bernini*, in the time of Alexander VII., 1655-67.*

---

* Immediately outside the gate, on the right, is the VILLA BORGHESE. The extensive grounds, through which there is a charming drive, are open every day, excepting Monday. The Villa contains an interesting collection of sculpture, but is only open to visitors on the afternoons of Saturday.

It opens upon one of the finest piazzas of the city—THE PIAZZA DEL POPOLO, from which radiate three principal streets—the Via Babuino, leading to the Piazza de Spagna, on the left; the Via Ripetta, on the right; and the Corso intersecting the city, between them. Handsome fountains, adorned with sculpture, ornament the sides, and on the left rises the Pincian Hill—the fashionable drive—richly planted, and divided into terraces, each supported by an architectural frontage, ornamented with statues and rostral columns. THE OBELISK, in the centre, was brought from Egypt by Augustus to adorn the Circus Maximus, from whence it was removed to its present position by Sixtus V., in 1589. The shaft measures 78 feet, and, from the level of the Piazza to the summit of the cross, 120 feet.

To the left of the gate, on entering, stands the

CHURCH OF STA. MARIA DEL POPOLO,

built, according to the legend, on the site where Nero was buried, in the sepulchre of the Domitii. On this spot grew a tree which, being infested by evil spirits, was uprooted by Paschal II., 1099-1118, who erected a chapel, in order to purge the place from the baneful influence surrounding it. To maintain the memory of this event, the Roman people, in 1227, built a church on the site of the chapel, placing it under the invocation of St. Mary of the People. This church was rebuilt in its present form by Sixtus IV., 1471-84. It contains many objects of interest, particularly several paintings by *Pinturicchio*, and a number of fine examples of the richly carved monuments of the 15th century.

First Chapel, commencing on the right. Over the altar, the Nativity, by *Pinturicchio*. On the vaulted ceiling are lunettes, containing subjects from the life of St. Jerome, by

Pinturicchio.   On the left, is the monument of Cardinal Christoforo della Rovere ; and on the right, that of Cardinal di Castro—both fine examples of 15th century work.

Second Chapel, of the Cibo family, richly decorated with columns of *Sicilian jasper*, and panellings and pilasters of *verde antique*.   Over the altar is the Assumption, by *Carlo Maratta*.

Third Chapel; painted by *Pinturicchio.*   The picture over the altar represents the Virgin and Child, with St. Joseph and St. Augustine.   That on the left wall, the Assumption. The lunettes on the vault, incidents from the life of the Virgin.   Under the painting, on the left, is an interesting recumbent bronze figure of an unknown bishop.

Fourth Chapel, has a very fine 15th century altar-piece, in marble, the figures on which represent St. Catherine between St. Anthony of Padua and St. Vincent.   The frescoes in this chapel are also by *Pinturicchio.*   On the wall of the right transept is a fine 15th century monument, erected to Cardinal Podocantharus of Cyprus.

Over the high altar is a miraculous picture of the Virgin, one of those attributed to St. Luke.

In the Choir behind the altar, are two exceedingly beautiful 15th century monuments by *Sansovino*, erected to Cardinal Ascanio Sforza and Cardinal Girolamo Basso, nephews of Julius II.   The vaulting was painted by *Pinturicchio.*

The Chapel, to the left of the high altar, has over the altar an Assumption by *Annibale Caracci*, and paintings on the side walls by *Michael Angelo da Curavaggio.*

In the left transept is another fine 15th century monument, erected to Cardinal Bernardino Lonati.

Continuing along the left aisle; the last chapel but one, is that of the Chigi family.   It was built from the design made by *Raphael*, who also made the drawings for the mosaics in the Cupola, executed by *Aloisio della Pace*, and for the picture over the altar, representing the Nativity of the Virgin; but in consequence of his premature death, the painting was entrusted to *Sebastiano del Piombo*, and finally completed by *Francesco Salviati*. The statue of Jonah, in the further corner to the left, was also modelled by *Raphael*, and executed in marble by *Lorenzetto*. The statue of Elijah is by *Lorenzetto*, and those of Daniel and Habakkuk by *Bernini*.

In the last Chapel, on the left, are two fine 16th century Ciboria, and a monument of the same period, erected to Cardinal Antonio Pallavicini.

Relics of The Seven Sleepers are said to be preserved in this church; and it was in the Augustine Monastery, attached to it, that Luther abode while in Rome.

The twin Churches, one on each side of the entrance to The Corso, are dedicated—that on the right to Santa Maria de Miracoli; that on the left to Santa Maria di Montesanto. They were commenced by Alexander VII., 1655-67, and finished at the expense of Cardinal Gastaldi.

Proceeding along the Corso, which follows the line of the ancient Flaminian Way, in the first street, on the left, the Via della Fontanella, was the studio of the great sculptor, John Gibson, Nos. 4, 5, 6, and 7. It is now turned into coach houses.

No. 518, on the right of the Corso, is the palace of the Russian Embassy. In the courtyard, there is an unfinished work of Michael Angelo's, rejected by the sculptor.

In the house opposite, No. 18, the great German poet, Goethe, lived while in Rome.

The little studio, in the first courtyard of No. 504, was occupied by the great American sculptor, THOMAS CRAWFORD, at the commencement of his career. In it he modelled his Flora.

On the left, after passing No. 44, is the CHURCH OF THE GESU E MARIA, founded about 1640, from the plans of *Carlo Maderno*. The façade was designed by *Rainaldi*.

Almost immediately opposite, is the CHURCH OF SAN GIA-COMO DEGL' INCURABILE, designed by *Francesco Ricciarelli da Volterra*, and completed by *Carlo Maderno*. The adjoining Hospital, to which this church belongs, was founded in 1339, by Cardinal Pietro Colonna.

In the street by the side of the Hospital, the Vicolo di San Giacomo, is a range of low buildings, in the wall of one end of which a number of fragments of ancient sculpture have been inserted. This was the studio of the great sculptor, CANOVA. It will be additionally recognised by the tablet upon the wall.

After passing No. 468, on the right, we turn into the Via dei Pontefici, and entering through the gateway of the Palazzo Corea, No. 57, find the ruins of

THE MAUSOLEUM OF AUGUSTUS,

very much hidden among the houses surrounding it, and transformed into an open air theatre for equestrian per-formances. A considerable portion, however, of the outer wall is still visible, and the cavea and arena of the modern circus will convey a sufficient idea of its size, and of its cir-cular form, which was the same as that of the Mausoleum of Hadrian, now the Castle of St. Angelo. It measured 255 feet in diameter. By application to the *custode*, entrance can be obtained into some of the lower chambers. They will be found exceedingly interesting, their original formation being unchanged.

It was founded by Augustus, in the year of his sixth consulate, 28 B.C. Five years later the ashes of Marcellus—"*Tu Marcellus eris*," were laid in it. Then followed: Marcus Agrippa, who was married to Julia, the daughter of Augustus, B.C. 13; Octavia, sister of Augustus, and wife of Mark Antony; Drusus, the elder brother of the Emperor Tiberius, B.C. 8; Caius and Lucius, the children of Julia and Agrippa —the Emperor Augustus, A.D. 14; Germanicus, A.D. 19; Drusus the younger, son of Tiberius, A.D. 23; Livia, the widow of Augustus, A.D. 29; the Emperor Tiberius, A.D. 37. Then, the ashes of Agrippina, the widow of Germanicus, and of her two sons, Nero and Drusus, were placed in the monument by her son, the Emperor Caligula. Next followed Antonia, the widow of Drusus, and mother of Germanicus. Then the ashes of the Emperor Caligula were removed hither; followed by the Emperor Claudius, A.D. 54; Britannicus, son of Claudius, A.D. 55; and lastly, the Emperor Nerva, A.D. 98.

The Mausoleum remained intact until 409 A.D., when Alaric broke it open, and rifled the sarcophagi and urns in search of treasure. During the middle ages it was turned into a fortress by the Colonna family, and ultimately became a ruin, through the damage it received during the faction fights of that period. In the year 1354 it finally served as the funeral pyre of the great Tribune, Cola de Rienzi. After his murder, his body, having been hung by the feet for two days in front of the Church of St. Marcellus, was dragged through the streets, to the ruins of the Mausoleum of Augustus, where, being thrown upon a heap of dried thistles, it was burnt till not a vestige remained.

Returning to the Corso. After passing on the right No. 444, the street widens into a small piazza, in which is the CHURCH OF ST. CARLO, the national church of the Lombards. It was originally dedicated to St. Nicolò del Tufo, but having fallen into a ruinous condition, it was given by Sixtus IV., in 1471, to the Lombards, who rebuilt it from the foundations, and dedicated it to Saint Ambrose. It was again rebuilt in 1612, and, on the canonisation of St. Carlo Borromeo, Archbishop of Milan, his name was included in the dedication, and it is now known by his alone. It is a handsome church, richly decorated, with a fine dome, but does not contain any objects of particular interest.

Passing where the Via Condotti and its continuation, the Via della Fontanella Borghese, intersect the Corso, we find on the right, the noble PALACE OF THE RUSPOLI family, built in 1586 by *Ammanati*, filling the space between the Via della Fontanella Borghese, and the Piazza San Lorenzo in Lucina.

Opposite is the PALAZZO BERNINI, No. 151, built by the great sculptor, and where he resided. In a recess in the entrance is a statue of Truth, " the naked truth," by him— not in his best style—allusive to the calumnies through which he suffered.

Nearly opposite the Palazzo Bernini, is the PIAZZA, which takes its name from the church on the further side, dedicated to ST. LORENZO IN LUCINA, so called, because, according to some, it was built on the ruins of a temple to Juno Lucina, or, according to others, on the site of the house or land belonging to Sta. Lucina, a Roman matron, niece of the Emperor Gallienus. The church is said to have been originally founded by Sixtus III., 432-40. In 1650 it was in great part rebuilt, and assumed its present form. Over the high altar is a painting of the Crucifixion, by *Guido*

Reni, one of his finest works; and against one of the pilasters on the right, the monument erected by Chateaubriand to Nicholas Poussin, who is buried here.

In the courtyard of the PALAZZO FIANO, which forms the corner of the Piazza and the Corso on that side, are some magnificent colossal fragments of the marble cornice of a grand edifice, on the ruins of which the Palace was founded in the 14th century. Those ruins went by the name of the Palace of Domitian.

· Close to this spot, the Via Flaminia was spanned by a TRIUMPHAL ARCH ERECTED TO ANTONINUS PIUS. It remained standing, though in a somewhat ruined condition, till 1665, when it was thrown down by Alexander VII., for the greater convenience of the races along the Corso, during Carnival. The position of the arch is marked by a tablet to commemorate this act of vandalism, inserted in the wall of No. 167. It was ornamented with sculptures in alto relief, and columns of the rarest *verde antique*. The alto reliefs were removed to the Capitol, and are now on the wall of the staircase of the Palace of the Conservatori, Nos. 49 and 50; of the four columns, two are in the Church of St. Agnese, and two are above the altar of the Corsini Chapel in St. John Lateran.

We next reach the magnificent PALACE OF THE CHIGI FAMILY, commenced in 1526, by *Giacomo della Porta*, continued by *Carlo Maderno*, and completed by *Filippo della Greca*. The flank of this palace forms one side of THE PIAZZA COLONNA; the side along the Corso is formed by the PALACE OF PRINCE PIOMBINO, in front of which are a number of shops; the third side, opposite to the Palazzo Piombino, is occupied by the POST OFFICE; and on the fourth, is the small church of San Bartolommeo de Bergamaschi, and some private houses. In the centre stands

THE ANTONINE COLUMN,

erected to Marcus Aurelius, A.D. 174.   It is covered, from
the base to the summit, with sculpture in bas relief, illustrating the war against the Marcomanni.   One of the
events represented, is that recorded by Eusebius, of the
miraculous rain which followed the prayers of the—
thenceforth called—thundering legion.   The army was
suffering through want of water.   The Emperor was told
that the soldiers of one of the legions, who were Christians,
believed that everything was attainable through prayer.
" Let them pray, then," he replied.   They fell upon their
knees, and immediately the heavens became overcast, a peal
of thunder was heard, and down came the long desired
rain.

The statue of Marcus Aurelius is believed to have been
torn from the summit by Constans II., who, during his visit
to Rome in 663, pillaged the city of all the bronze he could
obtain.   In 1589, Sixtus V. cleared away a number of
wretched habitations which had been built around the
column, and confided its complete restoration to *Fontana*.
The pedestal was entirely refaced with marble, and the
bronze statue of St. Peter, which originally was gilt, placed
upon the summit.*

The column is formed of 28 blocks of marble, and measures
125 feet in height.   The ascent to the summit is made by
190 steps, lighted by 41 loopholes.   The massive base, 12
feet in height, on which the pedestal stands, and in which

---

* On this work Sixtus spent 9640 scudi, or rather more than £2000, of which 250
scudi were paid to Constantino de Servi for the model of the statue; 1942 scudi to
Bastiano Torregiani for the casting; and 165 scudi to Tomasso Moneta for gilding it.
The statue originally faced towards the Piazza del Popolo, but the Pope, not approving
of this, 300 scudi were expended in turning it towards the Vatican.   The amount of
metal employed was 12,777 lbs., valued at 1597 scudi.

is the original door into the column, is hidden below the modern level of the Piazza. The statue of St. Peter is fourteen feet in height.

Behind the Post Office is the PIAZZA DI MONTE CITORIO, one side of which is formed by the palace of the same name, built in 1650, from the designs by *Bernini.* It is also called the CURIA INNOCENZIANA, from its having been set apart by Innocent XII. to serve as law courts for the trial of civil causes. In 1871 it was converted into the

CHAMBER OF DEPUTIES

to the Italian Parliament.

The Chamber itself is a temporary construction, erected within the enormous courtyard of the Palace, the rooms of which have been adapted to serve as committee-rooms, library, reading rooms, and other purposes connected with the business of the Lower House. We are admitted by ticket into the Gallery,* one part of which is reserved for ladies, and another for gentlemen. The seats for the Deputies are arranged in a semicircle, opposite to which is a raised platform for the President, and the officials of the House. On the floor, in front of this platform, and facing the Deputies, is a long table, covered with blue, at which the Ministers sit. At the table, in the form of a segment of a circle, opposite to the Ministers, sit the members of the Commission on the bill under discussion. The little square table in the middle of the floor is for the official stenographers. The seats of the Deputies are divided by steps into eight radiations. The two immediately below us, and to the left of the President, are occupied by the members of

* One portion of the Gallery is open to the public, but it is generally crowded by the lower orders.

H

the extreme left—the Opposition. The next division, by the Left Centre; the next two, by the Centre; the next one, by the Right Centre; and the two at the end of the half circle furthest from us, by the Right—the supporters of the Government. Above, and behind the President, and on the same level with the Gallery, is a range of tribunes. The large square tribune nearest to us, is for the members of the Senate; the corresponding one on the further side, is for the Diplomatic body. Those between, and somewhat further back, are for ex-Deputies, members of the Royal household, and Government officials. The first division of the Gallery furthest from us, is reserved for Municipal officials; the next five, for the Press; the two in the centre, facing the President, are open to the public; the next one is reserved for members of the National Guard; the remainder, where we are sitting, are for ladies and gentlemen admitted by ticket. On the wall behind the President, are inscribed the different Plebiscites which united the Italian States into one kingdom, and on the bracket in the middle is a bust of the King.

The best time to visit the Chamber, for those who do not desire to listen to the debate, is half-an-hour before dusk, in order to see the lighting up, which is very effective.

In the middle of the Piazza is THE OBELISK, mentioned by Pliny as having been brought from Heliopolis by Augustus, and erected by him in the Campus Martius, to serve as the gnomon to an enormous sundial. Portions of the gigantic bronze circle and radiations were found, from time to time during the 15th and 16th centuries, in the neighbourhood of the Church of St. Lorenzo in Lucina; and at the commencement of the 16th century, the obelisk, broken into several pieces, was discovered below the level of the Via del

Impresa.   It was not excavated, however, till 1748, when
it was found to be so much injured, through breakage and
the effect of fire, that nothing was done with it till 1792,
when it was put together by order of Pius VI., and erected
in its present position.   It was repaired with the fragments
of the colossal granite column of Antoninus Pius, found
entire in 1704, but which had been split to pieces by the
people lighting a fire against it, during the cold winter of
1705.*   The obelisk is $72\frac{1}{2}$ feet in length, and the height
from the ground to the summit $96\frac{1}{2}$ feet.

Continuing along the Corso, as far as No. 335 on the
right, we turn down the Via de Pietra into the PIAZZA DI
PIETRA.   On the left side are the magnificent remains of
an ancient edifice, supposed by some to have been THE
BASILICA OF ANTONINUS PIUS; by others, THE TEMPLE OF
NEPTUNE.   The spaces between the eleven Corinthian
columns, which measure 4ft. 2in. in diameter, and 39ft. 6in.
in height, were walled in by Innocent XII. in 1695, to form
part of the Custom House of modern Rome.

Returning to the Corso, and continuing along the Via
delle Muratte, immediately opposite, we come to the
grandest of the many fountains of Rome,

THE FOUNTAIN OF TREVI.

It was commenced by order of Clement XII., 1730-40,
but was not completed till 1762, in the time of Clement XIII.

It is supplied by the Aqua Virgine; first brought into
Rome by Marcus Agrippa.   According to the legend, some
of his soldiers passing across the Campagna, tired and faint

---

* This column was 57 feet in height and 6 in diameter.   The beautiful sculptured
base of white marble on which it stood is now in the garden of the Vatican.

with thirst, were shown the source by a young virgin, hence the name. During the 5th or 6th century the aqueduct was broken, and the flow of the water interrupted for a thousand years, till, in 1560, it was again introduced by Pius IV., who erected a fountain, close to this spot, with three large apertures through which the water passed, and from which the name Trevi *(Trivio)* was derived. In the centre is a grand figure of Oceanus, on a car drawn by two sea horses led by tritons, the work of *Pietro Bracci.* In the niches behind are statues of Fertility and Salubrity, and above them bas reliefs—one representing the maiden pointing out the source to the soldiers, the other, Agrippa, examining the plan for the aqueduct. On the attic above are statues of the Four Seasons.

Returning to the Corso, No. 239 is

THE PALAZZO SCIARRA,

built in 1603, by *Flaminio Ponzio.* The doorway was designed by *Antonio Labbaco,* or some say by *Vignola.* The Gallery, which contains an interesting collection, numbering 284 works of art, is open to the public on Saturdays from 10 to 4.

FIRST ROOM.

4. The Virgin and infant Jesus, with St. Laurence and St. John: *Pietro Perugino.*
5. Death of St. John the Baptist: *Valentin.*

13. Holy Family: *Innocenzo da Imola.*
15. Rome Triumphant: *Valentin*
20. Madonna & Child: *Titian.*
23. Sta. Francesca Romana: *Carlo Veneziano.*

SECOND ROOM.

16. Landscape: *Salvator Rosa.*
17. The Flight into Egypt: *Claude Lorrain.*

18. Sunset: *Claude Lorrain.*
36. St. Matthew: *Nicholas Poussin.*

THIRD ROOM.

6. Holy Family: *Francia.*
9. Boar Hunt: *Garofolo.*
11. Holy Family: *Andrea del Sarto.*
17. The Introduction of St. Andrew of Padua into Heaven: *Gaudenzio Ferrari.*
23. "*Noli me Tangere:*" *Garofalo.*
26. The Vestal Claudia drawing the galley, bearing the statue of Cybele, up the Tiber with her girdle: *Garofolo.*
29. Tavern Scene: *Teniers.*
33. The Fornarina: *Copy from Raphael by Julio Romano.*
36. Repose of the Holy Family during the Flight into Egypt: *Lucas Cranach; dated* 1504.

FOURTH ROOM.

1. HOLY FAMILY: *Fra Bartolommeo.*
5. St. John the Evangelist: *Guercino.*
6. THE VIOLIN PLAYER: *Raphael*
7. St. Mark: *Guercino.*
8. Herodias receiving the head of St. John the Baptist: *Guercino.*
12. Conjugal Love: *Agostino Caracci.*
16. THE GAMBLERS: *Michael Angelo da Caravaggio.*
17. MODESTY AND VANITY: *Leonardo da Vinci.*
19. MAGDALEN: *Guido Reni.*
24. A Family Portrait: *Titian.*
25. Portrait: *Bronzino.*
26. ST. SEBASTIAN: *Perugino.*
24. Martyrdom of St. Erasmus: *Poussin.*
29. THE BELLA DONNA: *Titian.*
31. The death of the Virgin: *Albert Durer.*
32. THE MAGDALEN: *Guido Reni.*

Directly opposite to the Sciarra Palace is the NEW SAVINGS BANK, built by *Cipolla.*

At this spot, the Via Flaminia was spanned by a TRIUMPHAL ARCH erected to the EMPEROR CLAUDIUS. Nothing is known as to the period of its destruction, but a considerable portion of its remains were discovered beneath the level of the Corso, in 1565. The bas relief, No. 41, on the staircase of the Palace of the Conservatori, on the Capitol, belonged to this arch.

No. 307, on the right, is THE SIMONETTI PALACE, and opposite to it is

THE CHURCH OF ST. MARCELLUS.

It was originally the private house of a Roman matron, Lucina, and was given by her to Pope St. Marcellus, about

the year 305, that he might convert it into a Christian church.
Immediately afterwards, it was profaned by Maxentius, who
turned it into a stable, making the Pope serve as ostler, and
die a lingering death. Shortly after the triumph of Christianity, the church was rebuilt, and dedicated to the martyred Pope. In 1375 it was restored by Gregory XI. On
the 22nd May, 1519, it fell down; but the great crucifix of
wood, now in the fourth chapel, on the right, remaining
uninjured in its place, with the lamp burning before it
unextinguished, religious enthusiasm was sufficiently aroused
to cause plentiful subscriptions to pour in to rebuild it.

The architect employed was *Giacomo Sansovino*, who
transposed the direction of the church, making it face upon
the Corso. The façade was added somewhat later, from
the designs of *Carlo Fontana*.

The *Third Chapel*, on the right, belongs to the Clifford
family, and contains the monument of Cardinal Thomas
Weld, who died 1837.

The *Fourth Chapel*, on the right, in which is the miraculous
crucifix, has, on the vault, some frescoes commenced by
Pierino del Vaga, and completed from his cartoons by
Daniello da Volterra. The Creation of Eve, in the centre,
and the picture of the Evangelists St. Mark and St. John,
on the right, are by the former.* This chapel contains the
monument of Cardinal Gonsalvi, the famous Secretary of
State to Pius VII., who is buried beneath.

The *Fourth Chapel*, on the left, belonging to the Frangipani, has an altarpiece representing the Conversion of St.
Paul, by *Federico Zuccheri*. Of the monumental busts

---

* There are passages in *Vasari* and *Lanzi*, quoted in all guide books to the present
day, lauding the beauty of the colouring of these frescoes, but it has long faded past
recognition.

ranged on each side, three are by *Algardi*; the others are of earlier date.

The great fresco of the Crucifixion, above the door, was painted by *Giovan Battista Ricci*.

To the right of the door, on leaving, is the fine 15th century monument of Cardinal Michieli.

This church has recently been restored.

On the right we find the Via Lata, and, at the further corner, the Church of

SANTA MARIA IN VIA LATA,

built upon the remains of "*his own hired house*," in which "*Paul dwelt two whole years.*"

Descending by a staircase, on the left of the portico, we enter a series of three rooms, grievously transformed by *restorations*, and encumbered by modern altars, but yet showing sufficient evidence of their original construction. In these rooms, or in rooms of the house of which these form the ground floor, St. Paul taught and ministered. Here he wrote his epistles to the Ephesians, Philippians, Colossians, Hebrews, Philemon, and the second epistle to Timothy. Here were gathered around him Onesiphorus of Ephesus, Epaphras of Colosse, Timothy, Hermas, Aristarchus, Marcus, Demas, Luke the physician, and Onesimus, "*whom I have begotten in my bonds.*"

It is said, that in this house St. Luke wrote the Acts of the Apostles, and painted the portrait of the Virgin Mary.

The earliest record of the church above, dates from the time of Pope St. Sylvester, 314-35, when it was dedicated to St. Cyriacus. It was rebuilt by Sergius III., in 700, and by Innocent VIII., in 1485, who at the same time destroyed the remains of a triumphal arch which spanned the Via

Flaminia at this spot, supposed to have been erected to Gordian.   The façade was built by Alexander VII., 1655-67, from the designs of *Pietro Berrettino da Cortona*, and at the same time the interior was modernized, the columns, which were of *Cipollino*, being removed and replaced by others of *Sicilian jasper*.   Over the altar is a miraculous portrait of the Virgin, said to have been painted by St. Luke.

At the end of the right aisle is the monument of Edward Dodwell, the distinguished scholar, who died 1832.

The grand palace, almost regal in its dimensions and decoration, which adjoins the Church of Sta. Maria in Via Lata, is

THE DORIA PALACE.

It has two façades; that upon the Corso was designed by *Valvasori*, that upon the Piazza of the Coleggio Romano is said to be by *Borromino*.

The Picture Gallery, in which also are a few pieces of sculpture, contains 793 works of art.   It is open to the public on Tuesdays and Fridays, from 10 to 2.

FIRST ROOM.

5. The Deluge : *Scarsellino.*
8. The Angel Teaching St. Augustine the lesson that it would be easier to empty the sea into a hole in the sand than to understand the mystery of the Trinity. *Gaspar Poussin.*
23. Landscape : *Poussin.*

Sculptures, &c.

Sarcophagus, with Meleager, hunting the Caledonian boar.
Sarcophagus, with the Story of Marsyas.
Statue of the Indian Bacchus.
Bust of Innocent X. : *Bernini.*
Sarcophagus, with Diana and Endymion.
Ulysses escaping from the Cave of Polyphemus by clinging below a sheep.

SECOND ROOM.

4. Roman Charity: *Valentin.*
   The Madonna of the Swallow: *Rondinello.*
15. Temptations of St. Anthony: *Andrea Mantegna.*
19. St. John the Baptist in the Desert: *Guercino.*
   Marriage of the Virgin: *Pisanello.*
23. Pope St. Sylvester before Maximin II.: *Pisellino.*
27. The Virgin (a triptyque): *Taddeo de Bartolo da Siena.*

28. The Annunciation: *Filippo Lippi.*
   Birth of the Virgin: *Pisanello.*
33. St. Agnes on the Pile: *Guercino.*
37. The Magdalen: *A copy from Titian.*
THE MADONNA: *Sasso Ferrato* —(not numbered).
WOMAN WITH A BOOK: *Murillo.* —(not numbered).

Sculpture, &c.

Mithraic Sacrifice.
Centaur, found at Albano.

Three Chandeliers of old Venetian glass.

THIRD ROOM—*Closed.*

FOURTH ROOM.

5. Erminia and Tancred wounded: *Guercino.*

Sculpture, &c.

Bust of Innocent X., 1644-55, in porphyry, with bronze head.
Bronze water vessel of the 4th century, with subjects upon it representing the story of David and the Shunamite woman.

The Nile, in basalt.
Mask of a Faun, in bronze.
Two glass cases, containing antique statuettes, strigils, mirrors, rings, buckles, fibulas, &c.
Two tables of *verde antique.*

FIFTH ROOM.

25. St. Joseph: *Guercino.*
22. Holy Family with St. Catherine: *Titian (early manner).*

In the middle, a group of Jacob wrestling with the Angel: *School of Bernini.*

SIXTH ROOM.

13. Madonna and Child: *Carlo Maratta.*
30. Portrait of a Boy (unfinished) *Vandyke (?)*

34. Conflagration in the hay-lofts near S. Maria in Cosmedin: *Alexis de Marchis.*

CABINET.

A Stag Hunt: *Breughel.*
Table covered with Fruit and Flowers: *Breughel.*
The Terrestrial Paradise: *Breughel.*

Bust of Donna Olympia Pamphili Maldacchini: *Algardi.*
Bust of Prince Philip Andrew Doria Pamphili.

SEVENTH ROOM.

1. The Falls of Terni: *Orizzonte*
3. Rocks on a Seashore: *Salvator Rosa.*
8. Belisarius in the Desert: *Salvator Rosa.*
19. Massacre of the Innocents: *Mazzolino.*
25. Ruins of a Temple, with the Pyramid of Caius Cestius: *Viviani.*

29. View of the Campo Vaccino (the Forum) in the 18th century, looking towards the Palatine: *Viviani.*
30. View in the 18th Century, taken from near the Colosseum: *Viviani.*

The Infant Bacchus, statue in Rosso antico.

EIGHTH ROOM.

14. Deposition from the Cross: *Cecchino Salvati.*

22. St. Sebastian: *Ludovico Caracci.*

NINTH ROOM.

6. Fruit Piece: *Zenardi.*

11. Fruit, Flowers, and Dead Game: *Spadino.*

TENTH ROOM

Contains a number of paintings of fruit and game.

GALLERY OF THE MIRRORS.

On the left, is the third Gallery of Pictures (see page 108), but it will be found more convenient to continue through the Gallery of the Mirrors and directly onwards.

This Gallery, lighted on both sides, is ornamented with a number of mirrors in richly gilt frames, with an antique statue between each, but none possessed of any particular merit.   Over the fireplace, about the middle on the right side, is a curious piece of tapestry, representing the Rape of the Sabines.

THE CABINET

contains a few of the gems of the collection, but they are not numbered.   Commence to the left:

TWO HEADS: *Raphael.*
PORTRAIT OF ADMIRAL ANDREA DORIA: *Sebastiano del Piombo.*

THE MISERS: *Quintin Matsys.*
THE DEPOSITION: *John Memling.*
PORTRAIT OF INNOCENT X., 1644-55: *Velasquez.*

The First Gallery.

In these three galleries, the paintings on the right walls have different sets of numbers from those between the windows.

1. Assumption of the Virgin : *Annibale Caracci.*
5. Mercury stealing the oxen of Apollo : *Claude Lorrain.*
6. The Flight into Egypt : *Annibale Caracci.*
10. Portrait of his wife : *Titian.*
11. Portrait of Macchiavelli : *Bronzino.*
12. THE WATER MILL : *Claude Lorrain.*
18. A Pietà : *Annibale Caracci.*
23. The Temple of Apollo: *Claude Lorrain.*

26. Portrait : *Mazzolo.*
27. Portrait: *Giorgione.*
28. Adoration of the Magi : *Annibale Caracci.*
29. Portrait of Lucretia Borgia : *Paolo Veronese.*
33. Diana hunting: *Claude Lorrain.*
34. The Entombment: *Annibale Caracci.*
35. Portrait of Catherine de la Vannozza : *Dosso Dossi.*

Between the windows.

5. The Mystic Marriage of Sta. Catherine of Alexandria : *Garofolo.*
8. St. Louis, King of France,

giving alms : *Mantegna.*
11. A Battle: *Borgognone.*
17. The Temptations of St. Anthony : *Mantegna.*

Second Gallery.

6. The Virgin and Child, with St. Francis of Assisi and St. Paul : *Francia.*
21. Portrait of a Widow : *Vandyke.*
25. "Air," one of the Four Seasons (see Nos. 30, 60, 65): *Breughel.*
26. Abraham's Sacrifice : *Titian.*
30. "Earth" : *Breughel.*
33. Portrait of a Prince Pamphili: *Vandyke.*
37. Portrait of his wife: *Rubens.*
40. Herodias with the head of St. John the Baptist: *Pordenone.*
50. The Preacher of the Apostolic Chapel: *Rubens.*

53. PORTRAIT of Jane II., Queen of Naples : *Leonardo da Vinci.*
56. The Magdalen : *Titian.*
60. "Water :" *Breughel.*
61. Birth of our Lord, with St. John the Baptist, St. Joseph, St. Francis of Assisi, and St. Madelaine : *Benvenuti.*
65. "Fire :" *Breughel.*
69. Glory crowning Valour ; a sketch : *Correggio.*
70. The Garden of Eden: *Breughel.*
76. A Village Wedding : *Teniers.*
80. Portraits of Titian and his wife : *Titian.*

Between the windows.

4. Passage of the Red Sea, painted on alabaster by *Tempesta.*

22. Judith, with the head of Holophernes: *Giorgio Vasari.*

THIRD GALLERY.

2. Holy Family, with (below) St. Francis of Assisi and St. Bernardino of Siena: *Garofolo.*

3. The Magdalen: *Annibale Caracci.*

9. Holy Family: *Sassoferrato.*

14. Portrait of Marco Polo: *Titian.*

15 HolyFamily: *Andrea delSarto*

19. The Three Ages of Man: *Titian.*

21. Return of the Prodigal Son: *Guercino.*

25. Rest, on the Flight into Egypt: *Claude Lorrain.*

26. THE MEETING OF ELIZABETH AND MARY: *Garofolo.*

31. Cupids Wrestling: *Francesco Gessi.*

38. The Aldobrandini Marriage (copy from the fresco in the Vatican): *Nicholas Poussin.*

45. The Child Jesus sleeping: *Guido Reni.*

49. Angel playing on a tambourine: *Paolo Veronese.*

Opposite to the Doria Palace is the PALAZZO SALVIATI, between numbers 274 and 276, originally built by *Rinaldi* for the Duke de Nevers.

A few steps further brings us to where the end of the Corso opens upon THE PIAZZA DI VENEZIA. *(See page 113.)*

Turning to the left, along the Via San Romualdo, we find, immediately opposite, in the Piazza S.S. Apostoli,

THE COLONNA PALACE,

standing back, on three sides of a large courtyard, closed on the fourth towards the street by a row of two-storied shops, with entrance gates, Nos. 66 and 53, at each end. It was commenced by the Colonna Pope, Martin V., 1417-31, and has since been enlarged and embellished, by successive members of this ancient and once powerful family. Here Julius II., 1503-13, lived. The building possesses no external features worthy of notice.

THE PICTURE GALLERY

is open to the public every day from 11 to 3. In past times it was one of the richest and most valuable collections in Rome, containing as many as 1362 pictures, but the chief of these have been dispersed. There are now only 194 works, including sculpture.

Two of the ante-rooms, before entering the gallery, are hung with very curious old tapestry.

First Room.

The pictures are not numbered, but each bears the name of the artist; and the portraits, the name of the person.

The principal works, *commencing, in each room, to the left,* are as follows:—

The Virgin of the Cherries: *Lippi*
The Virgin and Child: *Botticelli*
Landscape: *Albani.*
The Virgin and Child, with St. Elizabeth and St. John the Baptist: *Luini.*
Portrait of a young man: *Giovanni Sanzio* (the father of Raphael).
Landscape with Sheep: *Albani.*

Portrait of Maria Mancini Colonna: *Netscher*
Meeting of Jacob and Esau: *Rubens.*
Holy Family: *Parmeggianino.*
Moses with the Tables of the Law: *Guercino.*
The Resurrection of Christ and of the Dead: *Pietro da Cortona.*

The Throne Room.

Portrait of Pius IX.

Two beautiful Venetian lustres.

Third Room.

The Virgin giving the Scapular to St. Simon Stock: *Scarsellino.* (Over the door.)
Portrait of Panvinius, the Historian: *Titian.*
The Rape of Europa: *Francesco Albani.*
The Guardian Angel: *Guercino.*
St Jerome praying in the Desert: *Spagna.*
Man Playing on the Clavecin: *Tintoretto.*
Man Eating Soup: *Annibale Caracci.*

Resurrection of Lazarus: *Salviati.*
Portrait of Lorenzo Colonna: *Holbein.*
Portrait: *Paolo Veronese.*
St. Carlo Borromeo: *Daniel Crespi.*
Holy Family and St. Jerome: *Bonifazio da Venezia.*
On the ceiling; the Apotheosis of Martin V. (Colonna),1417-31.

Fourth Room.

Vestibule to the grand hall. On the left is a cabinet of the seventeenth century, of great beauty, ornamented with twelve columns of rock amethyst, and inlaid with precious stones and bouquets of flowers in Florentine mosaic, upon a ground of lapis-lazuli. The balustrade is surmounted by statuettes of the Muses, with Apollo seated on a laurel.

On the right, a very handsome ebony cabinet, of the seventeenth century, with bas reliefs carved in ivory, representing subjects from the Old and New Testaments, and, in the centre, the Last Judgment, from Michael Angelo.

The Grand Hall.

This magnificent hall measures 70 metres in length by 12 in width and 10 in height. The vault was painted in fresco by *John Paul Scor*, assisted by *Bernascona*, and by *Giovanni*, and *Francesco da Luca*. The five subjects represented are: the Doge of Venice sitting in council, on the war against the Turks; St. Pius V., 1566-72, giving the command of the fleet to Marc Antonio Colonna; the battle of Lepanto; the triumph of the conqueror on his return to Rome; the erection of his statue in the Capitol.

There are a number of antique statues, much restored, in this hall, but none worthy of particular notice.

The mirrors, made of several pieces, are painted with cupids and garlands of flowers, by *Mario de' Fiore*.

St. Jerome studying the Scriptures: *Spagnoletto*.	The Colonna Family, 1581, portraits: *Scipione Gaetani*.
A Family Group, portraits: *Annibale Caracci*.	Our Saviour at supper with Simon the Pharisee: *Bassano*.
Assumption of the Virgin: *Rubens*.	St. John the Baptist preaching in the Desert: *Salvator Rosa*
Portrait of Federico Colonna: *Subtermans*.	St. Irene removing the Arrows from St. Sebastian: *Cantarini*.
St. Jerome in the Desert: *Guercino*.	Telemachus in the Island of Calypso: *Nicholas Poussin*.
The Roman Daughter: *Bernardo Strozzi*.	The Virgin protecting a Child against the Devil: *Niccolo Alunno*.
Descent of our Saviour into Hades, and the Last Judgment: *Allori*.	St. Francis of Assisi praying: *Guido Reni*.
The Temptation: *Salviati*.	Martyrdom of St. Catherine of Alexandria: *Salmeggia*.
"Ecce Homo:" *Francisco Albani*	
Portrait of Charles Colonna on horseback: *Vandyke*.	

On one of the marble steps which give ascent into the next room, is a ball, which struck there and fell, during the siege of Rome by the French in 1849.

SIXTH ROOM.

The vault, painted in fresco about the year 1700, represents the Apotheosis of Marc Antonio Colonna, and his introduction into Olympus by Hercules.

Portrait of Marc Antonio Colonna *Novelli.*

Portrait of Marc Antonio Colonna *Scipione Gaetani.*

Portrait of Victoria Colonna, the Poetess : *Muziano.*

Portrait of Cardinal Pompeo Colonna : *Lorenzo Lotti.*

Portrait of Stephen Colonna : *Cagliari.*

Tobias and the Fish : *Tintoretto.*

Portrait of Isabella Colonna : *Novelli.*

Virgin and Child, with St. Peter presenting the Donor : *Palma Vecchio.*

Portrait of Lucretia Colonna : *Vandyke.*

Virgin and Child with St. Jerome and Sta. Lucia : *Titian.*

Temptations of St. Anthony : *Kranach.*

Venus and Cupid surprised by a Satyr : *Bronzino.*

Portrait of a Page with a Dog : *Moretto da Brescia.*

Adoration of the Holy Spirit : *Tintoretto.*

Portrait of Pope St. Pius V. : *Scipione Gaetani.*

Portrait of Francesco Colonna : *O'Hale.*

In the middle of the room is a spiral column of *rosso antico*, with figures sculptured upon it representing the grades of the Roman army.

There are two charming little rooms, which a small additional fee will induce the custode* to open. The walls of one, are entirely lined with glass, on which are cupids and arabesques, most delicately painted. The walls of the other are covered with exceedingly curious embroideries.

On the same side of the Piazza with the Colonna Palace, and to the right as we leave it, is

---

* The custode, Cesare Magni, has some very good copies for sale, at reasonable prices.

THE BASILICA OF THE SANTI APOSTOLI,

now under restoration. It takes its name, not from "the twelve," but from Saints Philip and James, whose relics are said to be those recently found under the high altar. A grand "*confession*" is in course of construction, which will expose to view the level, and the bases of some of the columns of the primitive Basilica, in which St. Gregory I. pronounced his 36th Homily. Popularly attributed to Constantine, it was founded by Pelagius I., 555-59, and completed by his successor, John III. Restored, in the 8th century, by Paul I., and Adrian I.; by Stephen V., in 886; by Martin V., 1471-31; and by Sixtus IV., about 1475; it was entirely rebuilt at the commencement of the last century from the design of *Francisco Fontana*, with the exception of the portico, built by *Baccio Pintelli*, for Sixtus IV. The first stone was laid by Clement XI., in 1702, and the new edifice was dedicated by Benedict XIII., in 1724. The façade above the portico was erected in 1827, at the expense of John Torlonia Duke of Bracciano. At the end of the portico, on the right, is an ancient bas-relief of an eagle holding a crown of oak leaves, an ornament, supposed to have belonged to the Forum of Trajan; opposite to it, at the end, on the left, is a monument to the engraver, Giovanni Volpato, sculptured and dedicated to his memory by *Canova*.

The nave measures 281 feet by 59 feet. At the end of the left aisle is the monument of Clement XIV., 1769-75, by *Canova*, one of his finest works, executed while in his 26th and 27th years. It is difficult to say which is most worthy of admiration, the mourning female extending her arm over the sarcophagus, or the figure of Meekness seated on the right.

Opposite, is THE ODESCALCHI PALACE, No. 314. Its façade was built in the time of Alexander VII., 1655-67, from the design of *Bernini.*

At the end of the Piazza, on the right, No. 49, is THE PALAZZO SAVORELLI, in which the Old Pretender, commonly called in Rome James III., King of England, lived, and where he died in 1769.

At the end of the Piazza, on the left, is the Palazzo Valentini.

Returning by the Via San Romualdo, we come to

THE PIAZZA DI VENEZIA.

The grand mediæval building with machiccolated battlements, which occupies the entire side on the right, is THE PALAZZO VENEZIA. It was built with stone taken from the Colosseum, for Paul II., 1464-71, by *Guiliano da Majano.* For some time it was used as the Pontifical Palace. The Popes, Paul III., 1534-49, Julius III., 1550-55, and Paul IV., 1555-59, lived here; and here Charles VIII. sojourned, in 1494, when marching against Naples. Finally, it was given by Pius IV. to the Venetian Republic, as the residence for its ambassadors to the Holy See. Thus it passed into the possession of Austria, and was especially reserved when the Venetian territory was ceded to Italy in 1866. It is now the residence of the Austrian ambassador.

Opposite is THE TORLONIA PALACE, No. 135, originally built by *Carlo Fontana* for the Bolognetti family.

The Palace, No. 130, which forms the corner of the Corso, with the Piazza, is THE BUONAPARTE PALACE, built for the Aste family, by *Giovan Antonio de Rossi.* It was here that Madama Letizia, the mother of Napoleon the First, died.

I

Passing into the narrow street at the further end from the Corso, called the Ripresa de' Barberi. The Via San Marco on the right leads to the Basilica of St. Mark (*see* page 115). The continuation in a straight line from the Ripresa de' Barberi leads direct to The Forum, and here, a few steps on the left side, is THE TOMB OF BIBULUS. The street on the left leads to

THE FORUM OF TRAJAN.

Up to the commencement of the present century this area was in great part covered with houses, which were thrown down in 1812, and the excavation commenced, which has restored to light about 55,000 square feet of the 330,000 occupied by Trajan's Forum. The grey granite columns are those which supported the roof of its great basilica, THE BASILICA ULPIA, so called from the family name of Trajan. The line formed by the nave and aisles can be accurately traced; the ends are still hidden under the modern level. On the northern side stands TRAJAN'S COLUMN, covered with bas-reliefs, in spiral series, from base to summit, representing the incidents of the Dacian war. The construction of this column is in itself a marvel. It is composed of 32 great masses of marble, 8 of which form the pedestal, one the base, 21 enormous circular blocks, one upon the other, form the shaft, one the capital, and one the pedestal which supported the statue of Trajan, now replaced by a statue of St. Peter. The ascent to the summit is made by 185 steps, worked in the solid marble, and lighted by 45 loopholes. The bas-reliefs were sculptured after the column was erected. It measures 128 feet in height. The inscription records that Trajan, in order to obtain a sufficient area for his Forum, cut away a neck of land, which united the

Quirinal and Capitoline hills, equal in height to that of the column. The statue of St. Paul, which originally was gilt, was placed on the summit by order of Sixtus V., iu 1589. It was modelled by *Leonardo Sorman*, assisted by *Tommaso della Porta.**

At the end of the Piazza are two churches. That with the highest dome is St. Bernardo alla Colonna Trajano, built in the time of Clement XII., 1730-40. The other, nearer to the Corso, is Santa Maria di Loreto, built by *Antonio di San Gallo*, in 1507. It contains a beautiful statue of St. Susanna, by *Fiammingo*.

Recrossing the end of the Via della Ripresa de' Barberi, by the Via del Foro Trajano, and passing along the Via San Marco, we enter a small piazza with a garden in the centre, at the right hand side of which is

THE BASILICA OF ST. MARK,

originally built by Pope St. Mark I., 336-37. It was re-stored by Adrian I., 772-95; and rebuilt by Gregory IV., 828-44, who ornamented the apse with the mosaic still existing. It was again rebuilt by Paul II., in 1468 (from the tribune, which he left intact outwards), at the same time, when he built the adjoining Palazzo di Venezia; and finally, in 1744, Cardinal Quirino placed the columns of *Sicilian jasper* in front of the pilasters which divide the aisles from the nave, and within which the original columns are probably hidden.

Over the first altar on the right, is The Resurrection, by *Palma' Giovane*.

---

* On this work Sixtus spent 2837 scudi, in addition to 10,000 scudi—4000 of which was paid by himself and 6000 by the Roman people—for the purchase and demolition of a number of houses to form a space round the column. The amount of metal employed in casting the statue was 13,530 lbs., valued at 1691 scudi.

Over the third, The Adoration of the Magi, by *Carlo Maratta*.

· In the fourth chapel, a Pietà, by *Gugliardi*.

In the Chapel of the Sacrament, Pope St. Mark, by *Carlo Crivelli*.

On each side of the Tribune are two columns of porphyry.

The Ciborium, in the Sacristy, is a very fine example of fifteenth century sculpture. It was made for Cardinal Barbo, afterwards Paul II., 1458-64, for the reception of the holy oils.

Beneath the high altar repose, together, it is said, with relics of St. Mark the Evangelist, the remains of Pope St. Mark, to whom also the Basilica is dedicated; and of the Persian martyrs Abdon and Sennen. These martyrs were condemned to fight with wild beasts in the amphitheatre, but the animals refusing to touch them, they were dispatched by the gladiators. It was Pope St. Mark who introduced the Nicene Creed into the canon of the Mass.

The doorway is a good example of 15th century work; above it is a bas-relief of the 14th century, representing Pope St. Mark.

To the left of the door of the church stand the mutilated remains of a colossal statue of Isis. This fragment is called by the people, MADAME LUCREZIA, and is one of the interlocutors with Pasquin in his satires.

Continuing along the street from the further corner (No. 23) of the Piazza, the second turning on the left leads direct to

THE CAPITOL,

at the base of which are three ascents. The winding road on the right, and the incline in the middle, lead to the

Piazza of the Capitol. The lofty flight of 125 steps on the left leads up to THE CHURCH OF THE ARA CŒLI, but we shall find it more convenient to enter it by the lateral door from the Piazza of the Capitol.

Proceeding, then, up the central incline. At the corners of the summit are the semi-colossal statues of Castor and Pollux, with their horses, found in the Ghetto, in the time of Paul IV., 1555-59. On the balustrade are statues of the sons of Constantine, and on that to the right is the first milestone of the Appian Way, found outside the Porta San Sebastiano.

The buildings, which form three sides of the Piazza of the Capitol, were designed and commenced by Michael Angelo, for the use of the Roman Municipality. The edifice in the centre is called the Palazzo dei Senatori; that on the right the Palazzo dei Conservatori; that on the left is the Capitoline Museum of Sculpture.

In the middle of the piazza stands the magnificent gilt bronze EQUESTRIAN STATUE OF MARCUS AURELIUS. Originally placed before the arch of Septimius Severus, on the Forum, it was removed by Clement III., about the year 1187, to the front of the Basilica of St. John Lateran, from whence it was again removed to its present position by Michael Angelo.

THE CAPITOLINE MUSEUM OF SCULPTURE.*

In the courtyard, and in the corridors leading from it to the right and left, are a number of works, but none of any special interest except the colossal recumbent statue of OCEANUS—the *Marforio* of the Roman Pasquinades—over the fountain; and the semi-colossal statue of THE CYPRIAN

* For detailed information regarding the contents of this museum, see THE CAPITOLINE MUSEUM OF SCULPTURE, by Mr. Shakspere Wood. It must be obtained, at any library, before visiting the Museum, as no catalogues in any language are allowed to be sold there.

MARS, No. 31, at the foot of the staircase. On the walls of the staircase are a number of panels containing the fragments of the celebrated PIANTA CAPITOLINA—an ancient plan of the city of Rome, made, it is believed, in the time of Septimius Severus—found in the 16th century behind the Church of SS. Cosma and Damiano.

After ascending the staircase we cross the long gallery, which extends to the right, and enter

THE HALL OF THE GLADIATOR.

1. THE DYING GLADIATOR (in the middle of the room). Although it has been clearly proved that it is an error to suppose this to be a statue of a gladiator, it is unlikely that it will ever be known by any other name, than that it has borne so long. Gladiator, or vanquished Gaul, it is equally a representation of a wounded man, heaving his last breath, so marvellously true to nature that we might expect to see him fall back dead before us. Gaul, or Gladiator, Byron's magnificent lines in *Childe Harold* are equally applicable to it. It was found in the vicinity of the Villa Ludovisi, together with the group in the Ludovisi collection, of a Gaul supporting a dying woman on one hand, and stabbing himself with the other. There can be no doubt that this group, and the Dying Gladiator, formed parts of a grand composition of many figures, illustrating some event glorious to the Roman arms.

2. Lycian Apollo, found near the sulphur stream on the road to Tivoli.

4. ARIADNE; a bust of great beauty.

5. AMAZON; antique copy from one of the fifty statues of Amazons which adorned the Temple of Diana at Ephesus. The same from which No. 265 in the "Gallery" at the Vatican was copied. (*Vide* page 80.)

6. ATYS, the Sun God; bust: popularly called Alexander the Great.

7. JUNO.

9. BUST OF BRUTUS, who slew Cæsar.

10. Isis.

11. FLORA (?); portrait statue of a Roman lady, found in 1744, at Hadrian's Villa.

13. ANTINOUS; found at Hadrian's Villa in the time of Clement XII., 1730-40.

15. FAUN;* an ancient copy from the celebrated statue by Praxiteles. (*Vide* pages 81 and 86 for other copies in the Vatican.)

16. Girl Protecting a Dove; portrait statue.

Zeno, the Founder of the Stoic School of Philosophy.

* This statue is the hero of Hawthorn's novel of "The Marble Faun, or Transformation."

THE HALL OF THE FAUN.

1. FAUN OF ROSSO ANTICO, in the middle of the room; found at Hadrian's Villa in 1736.
11. Sarcophagus, with the story of Endymion.
13. BOY WITH A SCENIC MASK.
21. BOY PLAYING WITH A GOOSE.
23. Bacchante; head.

25. Ariadne; head.
26. SARCOPHAGUS; with the battle between the Amazons and the Athenians, led by Theseus. Found in 1744 on the Campagna, near the source of the Aqua Virgine.

THE HALL OF THE CENTAURS.

BOY EXTRACTING A THORN FROM HIS FOOT;* bronze statue of great beauty; recently brought here from the Hall of the Conservatori opposite.
1. Jupiter, in black marble.
2. YOUNG CENTAUR; found in 1736, together with the companion statue, No. 5, among the ruins of Hadrian's Villa.
3. COLOSSAL INFANT HERCULES, sculptured in a rare and valuable variety of green basalt, which has the qualities of touchstone; found in the 15th century on the Aventine.
4. AGED CENTAUR. (*Vide* No. 2)
5. Æsculapius, in black marble.
THE BRONZE WOLF,* believed to be the wolf mentioned by Cicero as having been struck by lightning. The twins are a restoration, made in the 15th century.
10. Wounded Amazon; ancient copy from one of the fifty Amazons of the Temple of Diana at Ephesus.

11. Venus and Mars; portrait group in the semblance of these deities.
14. Faun.
15. Pythian Apollo.
17. Trajan; colossal bust.
19. Ceres.
21. Hadrian.
24. HERCULES, of bronze gilt; found in the time of Sixtus V., 1585-90, near the Church of Sta. Maria in Cosmedin.
25. Wounded Amazon; ancient copy from the same statue as No. 10. The head, evidently a portrait, did not originally belong to the statue.
27. Pancratiast, found at Hadrian's Villa in 1742.
28. Prefica; a hired mourner at funerals.
31. Antoninus Pius; colossal bust.
33. A HUNTER; monumental portrait statue, found in 1747, among the remains of a tomb on the Latin Way.
34. HARPOCRATES: found at Hadrian's Villa in 1744.

---

* *The Bronze Wolf,* and *The Boy extracting a Thorn from his Foot,* are placed temporarily in this Hall, during the preparation of a room especially destined for the Capitoline bronzes, in the Palazzo dei Conservatori opposite. The reader will find them there if they have been removed from this Hall.

THE HALL OF THE PHILOSOPHERS.

MARCUS MARCELLUS, seated statue in the middle of the room, believed to be a portrait of Marcus Claudius Marcellus, the conqueror of Syracuse.

On the shelves around the room is a series of portrait busts—more or less verified—of celebrated philosophers, poets, historians, and other illustrious men.

1. Virgil (?).	37. Hippocrates (?).
4, 5, 6. Socrates.	41, 42, 43. Euripides.
9. Aristides (?).	44, 45, 46. Homer.
16. Marcus Agrippa.	49. P. Cornelius Scipio Africanus
19. Theophrastus (?).	51. Pompey the Great.
20. Marcus Aurelius.	52. Cato of Utica.
21. Diogenes the Cynic (?).	53. Aristotle.
23. Thales.	60. Thucydides.
25. Theon of Smyrna.	61. Æschines.
26. Apuleius (?).	63. Epicurus and Metrodorus ; a
27. Pythagoras (?).	double Hermes.
30. Aristophanes.	70. Antisthenes.
31. 32. Demosthenes.	72. Julian the Apostate.
33. 34. Sophocles.	75. Cicero (?).
35 Aulus Persius Flaccus.	76. Terence.
36. Anacreon (?).	82. Æschylus.

THE HALL OF THE EMPERORS.

On the shelves are a number of busts of the Roman emperors, empresses, and other imperial personages, arranged in chronological order.

AGRIPPINA (seated statue in the middle of the room), wife of Germanicus, daughter of Agrippa, granddaughter of Augustus, mother of Caligula, and grandmother of Nero.

1. Julius Cæsar.	15. 16. Nero.
2. Augustus.	17. Poppea Sabina.
3. Marcellus.	18. Galba.
4, 5. Tiberius.	19. Otho.
9. Germanicus.	20. Vitellius.
11. Caligula.	21. Vespasian.
12. Claudius.	22. Titus.
13. Messalina.	23. Julia, daughter of Titus.

24. Domitian.	50, 51. Septimius Severus.
26. Nerva (modern).	53. Caracalla.
27. Trajan.	57. Heliogabalus.
31, 32. Hadrian.	60. Alexander Severus.
35. Antoninus Pius.	62. Maximinus.
37. Marcus Aurelius	64. Gordian I.
41. Lucius Verus.	65. Gordian II.
43. Commodus.	80. Diocletian.
45. Pertinax.	82. Julian the Apostate.

Turning into the GALLERY from the Hall of the Emperors, the door of the small cabinet, containing the celebrated VENUS OF THE CAPITOL, will be found on the left, between Nos. 55 and 58. This beautiful statue was found walled up in a niche of an ancient house, discovered about the middle of the last century. As an embodiment of the goddess, this Venus ranks third after the Venus of Milo at Paris, and second after the Venus de Medicis at Florence. As a work of art it is superior to the Venus de Medicis; and looking upon it simply as a statue of an exceedingly beautiful woman, it would be difficult to overstate its merits.

THE GALLERY.

1. Marcus Aurelius.	is antique, and was part of an ancient copy of the Discobolus by *Myron*.
2. Faustina, wife of Antoninus Pius.	
3. Septimius Severus.	53. Psyche.
5. Silenus.	70. Marcus Aurelius.
13. CUPID; antique copy from that by *Lysippus*.	71. Minerva.
20. DRUNKEN OLD BACCHANTE.	76. Large vase, found in 1680, near the tomb of Cecilia Metella.
36. Gladiator. The torso only	

HALL OF THE DOVES.*

So called from the celebrated mosaic representing three doves on the edge of a vase, No. 89, on the wall to the left. It was found in the middle of an ancient pavement at

* The door of the Hall of the Doves will be found between Nos. 14 and 17 in the Gallery.

Hadrian's Villa, in 1739, and was supposed at the time to be that described by Pliny in his Natural History *(Lib.* 36, c. 60). Pliny's " Doves" formed the centre of the pavement ·of a temple at Pergamos, from which, the probability is, this was copied for Hadrian.

On the shelves are a number of unrecognised busts.

25. The Iliac Table.
36. Diana of Ephesus.
58. MOSAIC; the central ornament of a pavement, representing two scenic masks, found in the Aventine about the time of Leo XII., 1823-28.
60. Sarcophagus of a young girl, named *Gerontia*, orna-mented with the story of Endymion.
88. Sarcophagus, ornamented with a number of figures in alto relief, crowded together, representing the incidents of the story of Prometheus.
89. MOSAIC, PLINY'S DOVES (*see above*).

On Pedestals at the end of the Room.

CUPID DISGUISED in the attributes of Hercules; found in 1872, in enlarging the Cemetery at St. Lorenzo, outside the walls.
FOOT (fragment) of a colossal statue of Venus, found in 1872, opposite the Church of St. Cesario on the Appian Way.
MITHRAIC SACRIFICE, found in 1870.

Descending the staircase, we turn to the left into three small rooms, called THE HALLS OF THE INSCRIPTIONS. They contain a few busts and sculptures, interesting chiefly from an archæological point of view, the most noticeable being the SARCOPHAGUS, No. 1, in the second room, found in the Vigna Amendola, on the Via Appia, in 1829; and the LARGE SARCOPHAGUS, with two recumbent figures on the cover, No. 1, in the third room, found outside the Porta San Giovanni, in 1594.

At the opposite end of the corridor, passing the entrance, are three other rooms, called THE HALLS OF THE BRONZES. In the first, No. 1, a mutilated bronze horse (the remains of an equestrian statue). No. 2, foot, supposed to have belonged to the rider; and No. 16, the remains of bronze bull: were found in 1849, in the same excavation with the Athlete, No. 67, in the Nuovo Braccio of the Vatican.

6. Sacrificial tripod.
8. A surveyor's measure.
9. Two wine or oil measures.
10. Colossal foot.
13. Diana Triforme.
14. LARGE FLUTED VASE, found at the beginning of last century, at the bottom of the harbour of Porto d' Anzio, the ancient Antium.

15. A CAMILLUS; an assistant at the sacrifices.
17. Colossal hand.
19. Globe of Sovereignty, held in the hand of the bronze statue of Trajan, which originally stood on his column.

The only objects of general interest in the second and third rooms are, a LARGE SARCOPHAGUS, opposite to the window in the second room; and in the third, also opposite to the window, a MONUMENTAL CIPPUS, erected to the memory of a boy poet of the name of Quintus Sulpicius Maximus.

Crossing to the wing, called THE PALAZZO DEI CONSERVATORI, on the opposite side of the Piazza, in the courtyard there are a number of FRAGMENTS OF COLOSSAL STATUES of extraordinary size.

On the walls of the first landing of the staircase, as we ascend to the Picture Gallery, there are FOUR VERY FINE ALTO RELIEFS. Of these, No. 41 belonged to the Arch of Claudius on the Via Flaminia (*vide* page 101), and Nos. 42, 43, 44, to a triumphal arch erected to Marcus Aurelius, the site of which is not known.

On the second landing we shall find the entrance to the Picture Gallery on the left; and a little further on, a corridor, containing a small collection of ETRUSCAN ANTIQUITIES; beyond which again is a small room, *the eighth room* of the Halls of the Conservatori (*vide* page 125); the only one now generally accessible to the public. It was originally the chapel, and has, on the wall facing the window, a fine fresco by *Pinturicchio*, of the Virgin with the Infant Jesus adored by Angels.

THE PROTOMOTHECA* AND THE PICTURE GALLERY.

On each side of the long gallery are a number of busts of illustrious Italians, including a few foreigners, who attained eminence either in Rome or through studies made here, viz., Angelica Kauffmann, Nicholas Poussin, Winckelmann, and others. The busts have been recently placed here, without any attempt at chronological arrangement. They are not numbered, but the names will be found on the bases of most of them.

A staircase on the left leads up to the two rooms (the first, in front of the stairs, the second, to the left), which contain the Capitoline Collection of Paintings.

First Room.

2. L'Anima Beata: *Guido.*
4. Joseph Sold into Egypt: *Pietro Testa.*
6. St. Cecilia: *Romanelli*
7. Triumph of Bacchus: *Pietro da Cortona.*
9. Magdalen: *Albani.*
11. The Meeting of Jacob and Esau; *Raffaellino del Garbo.*
13. St. John the Baptist: *Guercino.*
14. The Triumph of Flora: *Nicholas Poussin.*
16. The Magdalen: *Guido.*
20. The Cumæan Sibyl: *Domenichino.*
21. David with the Head of Goliath: *Romanelli.*

26. The Magdalen; *Tintoretto.*
27. The Presentation in the Temple: *Fra Bartolommeo di San Marco.*
30. The Holy Family: *Garofalo.*
34. The Persic Sibyl; *Guercino.*
35. Judith with the Head of Holophernes: *copy by Carlo Maratta from Guido.*
36. The Expulsion of Hagar: *Francesco Mola.*
38. The Holy Family: *Schiavone.*
47. Rape of the Sabines: *Pietro da Cortona.*
52. Madonna and Child, with St. Nicholas and St. Martin: *Sandro Botticelli.*
58. The Sacrifice of Iphigenia: *Pietro da Cortona.*

* This Gallery has been recently arranged to serve as entrance to some large halls now in course of preparation, in which the bronzes and a collection of terra cottas and other antiquities are to be placed. It is in one of these halls that the bronze Wolf will be found, if it has been removed from the Sculpture Gallery.

63. The Adoration of the Magi:
    Scarsellino.
70. Madonna and Child, with St.
    Francis of Assisi, St. Jo-
    seph, St. Jerome, and St.
    Catherine of Alexandria:
    copy from Paul Veronese.
78. The Virgin Enthroned be-
    tween St. Peter, St. Paul,
    St. John the Baptist, St.
    Andrew, and St. John the
    Evangelist: *Francia.*
79. St. Sebastian: *Giovan Bel-
    lini.*
81. Circe and Ulysses: *Elizabetta
    Sirani.*
87. St. Nicholas (Bishop): *Gio-
    van Bellini.*
89. ROMULUS & REMUS: *Rubens.*

SECOND ROOM.

100. Portraits: *Vandyke.*
106. Portraits: *Vandyke.*
108. Baptism of Our Lord: *Tin-
     toretto.*
117. Cleopatra in the Presence of
     Augustus: *Guercino.*
119. St. Sebastian: *L. Caracci.*
128. The Fortune Teller: *M. A.
     da Caravaggio.*
130. A WITCH: *Salvator Rosa.*
131. The Infant Jesus and St.
     John the Baptist (sketch):
     Guido.
132. Portrait of himself; *Giovan
     Bellini.*
134. Portrait of himself: *Michael
     Angelo.*
142. Birth of the Virgin: *Albano.*
143. SANTA PETRONILLA: *Guer-
     cino.*
145. The Holy Family: *Guercino.*
146. A Fair: *Breughel.*
160. St John the Baptist: *Par-
     migiano.*
161. The Annunciation: *Garo-
     falo.*
164. THE MADONNA IN GLORY;
     and, below, in a very
     beautiful landscape, St.
     Francis of Assisi, and St.
     Anthony of Padua: *Garo-
     falo.*
190. Defeat of Darius: *Pietro da
     Cortona.*
196. The Assumption: *Cola della
     Matrice.*
199. Death of the Virgin, sur-
     rounded by the Apostles,
     St. Thomas Aquinas, St.
     Catherine of Siena, and
     St. Dominic: *Cola della
     Matrice.*
201. The Virgin, surrounded by
     the attributes of the four
     Doctors of the Latin
     Church: *Garofalo.*
202. The Rich Man Feasting
     Sumptuously: *Cario.*
207. Portrait of Petrarch's Laura.
     Giovan Bellini.
217. The Temple of Vesta: *Van-
     vitelli.*
223. Madonna: *Paul Veronese.*
224. THE RAPE OF EUROPA:
     Paul Veronese.

Returning to the head of the staircase we shall find,
opposite to it, the door of THE HALLS OF THE CONSERVATORI,
not now always open to the public without an order.

FIRST ROOM.—The walls are decorated with paintings in fresco, by
Cav. d'Arpino, illustrating the Regal period of Roman History; The
finding of Romulus and Remus; The Foundation of Rome; The Rape
of the Sabines; Numa with the Vestals performing Sacrifice; The

Battle of the Horatii and Curiatii; around the room are statues in marble of Leo X., 1513-22; and of Urban VIII., 1623-44, *Bernini;* and a bronze statue of Innocent X., 1644-55, *Algardi*.

SECOND ROOM.—Decorated with subjects painted by *Laureti*, illustrating the Republican Period of Roman history; Mutius Scævola putting his hand in the fire; Brutus pronouncing sentence of death on his two sons; Horatius Cocles defending the Bridge; and The Battle of Lake Regillus. Around the room are statues of celebrated military leaders of the 16th and 17th centuries.

THIRD ROOM.*—The frescoes on the walls were painted by *Daniele da Volterra*, in illustration of the wars with the Cimbri.

FOURTH ROOM.—Contains the FASTI CONSULARES of ancient Rome.

FIFTH ROOM.—Audience Chamber.

SIXTH ROOM.—The Frieze, representing the triumphs of Scipio Africanus, was painted by *Annibale Caracci*.

SEVENTH ROOM.—Decorated with subjects, painted in fresco, by *Daniele da Volterra*, taken from the history of the Punic Wars.

EIGHTH ROOM.—The Chapel. (See page 123.)

Recrossing the Piazza. The incline on the right of the Sculpture Gallery leads up to the side door of

THE CHURCH OF THE ARA CŒLI,

built, it is believed, on the site of the famous TEMPLE OF JUPITER CAPITOLINUS. The interior is the most picturesque in effect of all the churches in Rome. Built somewhere about the 10th century; altered, and in part rebuilt, in the 13th and 15th; altered again in the 16th; and recovered with a magnificent ceiling in 1571, to commemorate the victory of Lepanto; it bears visible evidence of every period, and seems imbued with the atmosphere of each blended with the others. The pavement inclines gradually upward from the great door, and is formed of most varied materials. Sepulchral slabs with half obliterated inscrip-

* As changes are now being made in the arrangement of the moveable works of art, which have been preserved for a long period of time in this and the following rooms, it becomes impracticable to mention what may have been removed elsewhere while these pages are at press.

tions, and monumental effigies in relief worn almost smooth, break up the design of the original *Opus Alexandrinum*, which has been rudely repaired from time to time, and patched with slabs, richly inlaid with *Cosmati* mosaic; remains of the marble choir, long since removed. The aisles are divided from the nave by 22 columns, varying in size and material, taken from ancient edifices. The third to the right bears the inscription, A . CVBICVLO AGVSTORVM. At the corners, where the nave joins the transepts, are the pulpits, richly ornamented with *Cosmati* mosaic, which belonged to the ancient choir, removed from the nave by Pius IV., 1559-66, and of which we have seen the fragments in the pavement.

The walls of the first chapel on the right, dedicated to St. Bernardino of Siena, are covered with frescoes by *Pinturicchio*, illustrating the life of the saint.* The vault was painted by his scholars, *Francesco di Castello*, and *Luca Signorelli*. In the chapel of the Savelli family, at the end of the right transept, are some very fine thirteenth century monuments, richly ornamented with *Cosmati* mosaic. That on the left was erected to Luca Savelli (died 1266), father of Pope Honorius IV., 1285-87, with, opposite, that of his wife, Vana Aldobrandesca, over which the recumbent figure of the Pope, her son, originally in old St. Peter's, was placed by Paul III., 1534-50.

Opposite, at the end of the left transept, is another fine monument of the same period, but much damaged, and with most of the mosaic removed, erected in 1302, to Cardinal Matteo d'Aquasparta, who is mentioned by Dante in the Paradiso; and at the bottom of the wall, to the left, facing

---

* To see these frescoes, properly, the Visitor must get one of the monks to draw the curtain from the windows.

this, is the monumental inscription to the memory of Felix de Freddis (died 1529), who discovered the celebrated group of the Laocoon, as recorded on the slab.

In the middle of this transept there is the celebrated chapel in the form of an altar, covered with a ciborium, called THE HOLY CHAPEL.   According to the early legends of the church, it marks the spot where Augustus is said to have erected, in the temple of Jupiter Capitolinus, an altar to the FIRSTBORN OF GOD, *Ara primogeniti Dei*, and from which the church takes its name of Ara Cœli — the Altar of Heaven.   All that is positively known upon the subject is, that it is one of the earliest altars in the church—probably erected anterior to the 12th century.   At the commencement of the 17th century, a magnificent ciborium was erected over it, which was destroyed during the disturbances in 1798, and replaced at the beginning of this century by that now above it.

The pavement of the left aisle, down which we now turn, is almost entirely formed by curious sepulchral slabs, with quaint figures in bas relief, of the persons whose graves they cover, or whose death they record.   The chapels along this aisle were once decorated with frescoes, by *Benozzo Gozzoli*, *Filippo Evangelisti*, and *Niccolò da Pesaro*, but all have disappeared except some by the latter, now in a very damaged condition.

Fourth Chapel, dedicated to the Ascension.   Frescoes on the vault, by *Niccolò da Pesaro*, much injured.   The arabesques on the pilasters are very beautiful.

Fifth Chapel, dedicated to St. Paul.   On the left side, the monument of Philippo de Valle is a very fine example of fifteenth century work.

Seventh Chapel, dedicated to St. Anthony of Padua.   The

frescoes on the vault are by *Niccolò da Pesaro.* St. Anthony is the saint whose aid is invoked in moments of peril through wayside and other accidents, and the front of the chapel is covered with a complete picture gallery of *ex-votos*, representing dangers, from the fatal consequences of which the Saint has preserved the donors. The subjects are worthy of a chamber of horrors, and the fearful nature of the events depicted would be enough to make one's blood creep, were they treated in a manner less calculated to provoke laughter. There are masons precipitated from scaffoldings; persons thrown out of carriages; others being run over; a man and a horse gored by a bull; a child falling headlong from a window into a well beneath; a nun dropping through a hole in a floor; a lady with a fashionable bonnet and parasol, going headfirst down a flight of steps, &c. But, hung up in the chapel, are things of a more distinctly suggestive character. Crutches, needed no longer; firearms; and knives and daggers, encrusted with very suspicious-looking rust.

Eighth Chapel is that of *the Præsepio*, and is closed, except at Christmas, when the Nativity is represented by groups of life-sized figures, of wood, draped; with smaller groups of the other events of the birth of our Lord, represented among the scenery behind. THE CELEBRATED BAMBINO, richly bedizened with jewels, then forms part of the exhibition. This is a quaint figure of the infant Jesus—said to have been carved out of olive wood by a pilgrim, and painted by St. Luke—to which miraculous powers of healing the sick, when past all other aid, are attributed. To see it, application must be made in the Sacristy.

Gibbon tells us, that it was while sitting meditating in this church, that he conceived the idea of writing "The Decline and Fall of the Roman Empire."

K

Leaving the church by the door we entered, and descending to the Piazza, we shall see, on the opposite side, another flight of steps, leading up to that part of the Capitol now called Monte Caprino.   Passing through the archway on the summit, and continuing onwards to a row of modern buildings on the left, enquiry at the first door, No. 130, will produce the *custode* of The Tarpeian Rock.   There is but little now recognisable of this celebrated spot, covered as the cliff is by houses built on and against it.   The height also looks insignificant, but it must be borne in mind that the modern level is some thirty feet above that of ancient Rome.

FROM THE CAPITOL TO THE PALACE OF THE CÆSARS.

Descending from the Piazza of the Campidoglio, by the road which leads from the foot of the steps of Monte Caprino, we see, spread out before us, all that remains of

THE FORUM ROMANUM,*

and the magnificent edifices which surrounded it, hemmed in by the meaner buildings of modern Rome.

As we descend, we look down to the left, upon the remains of three temples, a small portico, and the grand triumphal arch of Septimius Severus (*see* page 133); passing which,

---

* The object this book has to serve, being merely that of "a Guide," to enable the stranger, and particularly one pressed for time, to find, and to visit, the many places of interest, of both ancient and modern Rome, with the least possible difficulty, *and in the order in which they come*, it would be outside its purpose, and interfere with its object, if the Author were to depart from the plan laid down, and enter into archæological dissertations.   The existing remains of the Roman Forum will be separately noticed, in the order in which they will be found, but no attempt will be made to reconstruct the Forum, or to indicate the sites of edifices and places that have disappeared, or the situation of which are subject of conjecture and controversy.   These remarks will apply also to the Palatine, and some other portions of the ancient city.

and turning directly to the left, we come to a little church, with a small bas relief on the front, representing St. Peter and St. Paul in prison. It is THE CHURCH OF S. GIUSEPPE DE' FALEGNAMI, St. Joseph of the Carpenters, built, in 1639, over

THE MAMERTINE PRISON.

This is the most ancient, and, at the same time, the best verified edifice belonging to ancient Rome. It is the old prison at the corner of the Forum, minutely described by Sallust. It consists of two chambers, one beneath the other, the lower being in the form of a truncated cone, with an almost flat roof of peculiar construction, held together without any keystone. In it there is a circular opening, through which the condemned were precipitated to die of cold and hunger. Among those who suffered death here were, Jugurtha; Cethægus and Lentulus, the accomplices of Catiline; Vercingetorix; Sejanus; and Simon Bar Gionas, the defender of Jerusalem. Tradition relates that St. Peter and St. Paul were confined in the lower chamber, being bound to the column enclosed in an iron grating, and that here they baptised the jailers, Processus and Martinianus, with forty-seven others, to the faith of Christ, miraculously creating for the purpose the well in the middle of the floor. Above the modern staircase, also, which leads down into the chamber, a depression, protected by iron bars, resembling the mould of a human profile, is said to be the impress made by St. Peter's head, when the jailer struck it against the wall. There is nothing improbable in the apostles having been confined here; but doubts arise through the column, which is a mediæval addition; the impress on the wall, where no man's head (granting the possibility) could have touched it in that position; and the miraculous origin ascribed to the well, of the existence of which there is historical evidence anterior to the time of St. Peter. In the lower chamber is a bas relief, representing St. Peter and St. Paul baptising the jailers, and opposite to it an iron door closing the mouth of a branch drain leading to the Cloaca Maxima. The upper chamber has been so much changed by the introduction of altars, the cutting of the stairs leading down into it, and from it into the chamber below, and the wide modern opening from the church, that it is difficult for the stranger to form a just estimate of its original appearance. The communication into it was originally through the opening above. It is said that the upper prison was built by Ancus Martius, and the lower afterwards added by Servius Tullius, and from him called THE TULLIANUM; but there is evidently some mistake in the records, for the construction of the lower chamber indicates a much earlier period.

Immediately to the left, on leaving the Prison, is THE CHURCH OF STA. MARTINA AND ST. LUKE, of considerable antiquity, the earliest record being its restoration in the 8th century, by Adrian I. In 1588 it was given by Sixtus V. to the artists, painters, sculptors, and architects, who added the name of their patron, St. Luke, to the dedication. It was rebuilt from the foundations in its present form by *Pietro da Cortona*, in the time of Urban VIII., 1623-44. It contains the original model of Thorwaldsen's statue of our Saviour. The crypt is exceedingly beautiful, and well worth visiting.

A few steps further, on the left, is THE CHURCH OF ST. ADRIANO, with the perfectly unadorned front. It was built by Adrian I., about the year 630, and has been restored at several periods subsequently, but contains nothing of general interest. The great bronze doors of St. John Lateran originally belonged to this church ; they were taken away by Alexander VII., 1655-67.

In front of these churches stands

THE ARCH OF SEPTIMIUS SEVERUS,

built in the year 204. It has three openings, those on the sides being smaller in size, and having internal communications with the central arch. It is ornamented on each face with four columns of the composite order, and a series of bas reliefs, illustrating the Parthian, Arabian, and Adiabenian victories, in honour of which it was erected. The inscription is repeated on each side of the attic, and contains interesting evidence of the truth of the record that the remorse felt by Caracalla, after having murdered his brother, A.D. 212, was such as compelled him to obliterate the name of Geta from every public monument. The fourth line, which originally contained the words, ET P . SEPTIMIO . L FIL · GETAE . NOBILISS . CAESARI. has been erased, and the words P . P . OPTIMISQVE . FORTISSIMISQVE . PRINCIPIBVS inserted.

The mass of shapeless ruin, immediately behind the arches, is all that remains of the once splendid TEMPLE OF CONCORD, built by Camillus B.C. 386, to commemorate the accord established between the Patricians and Plebeians, regarding the election of the Consuls. It was in this temple that Cicero convoked the Senate, B.C. 63, and delivered his second oration against Catiline. It was entirely rebuilt by Tiberius A.D. 7. There is no communication whatever, from either the cella or the crypt of this temple, to the Tabularium behind.

The three Corinthian columns to the left are the remains of THE TEMPLE OF VESPASIAN, erected by Titus to his deified father, and afterwards restored by Septimius Severus, to which, the fragment of the inscription, E S T I T V E R, still remaining on the cornice, relates.

Behind these temples there is a massive wall of great squared stones, surmounted by a portico, walled up during the middle ages, but of which one arcade has been lately opened—the whole serving as substruction to the modern offices of the Roman municipality. This was THE TABULARIUM, the great Record Office of ancient Rome, built by Q. Lutatius Catulus, B.C. 78. The interior of what remains of this massive edifice is well worth visiting. The door is at the left end of the building, at the summit of the descent we have just made.

The eight Ionic columns to the left, are the remains of the TEMPLE OF SATURN,* from the earliest times the public treasury. Originally dedicated by A. Sempronius Atratinus and M. Minucius B.C. 497, it was rebuilt several times. The last restoration, as shown by the defective construction, was made at a late period, under the Empire, but at what exact date the inscription remaining on the pediment gives no information.

Further back, and between the temples of Saturn and Vespasian, there is a range of small columns—THE PORTICO OF THE DII CONSENTES—the twelve great deities—reconstructed by Vettius Agorius Prætextatus, A.D. 367, in front of a series of offices for the use of the public scribes and notaries, believed to be THE SCHOLA XANTHA.

---

* As an English archæologist, in a work recently published, has transposed the names of the temples of Saturn and Vespasian, it becomes necessary to state, that the identity of these three temples, at the base of the Capitoline, as given in this Guide, has been established beyond the possibility of contradiction.

By the side of the Arch of Septimius Severus are the remains of THE OLD ROSTRUM, a platform of convex projection, with the base moulding, and some portions of the marble facing still remaining; and at the end, nearest to the arch, is the base of one of the Rostral columns, which bounded it.

Turning now in the opposite direction, we have immediately before us THE COLUMN OF PHOCAS—Byron's "nameless column with a buried base"—erected by the Exarch Smaragdus, A.D. 607, in honour of the Emperor Phocas. The area around the base of this column was excavated in 1816, at the expense of the Duchess of Devonshire,* and to this, and a small portion of the nearest corner of the great Basilica Julia opposite, was the excavation of the Forum limited up to the end of the year 1870.

Immediately after Rome became the capital of Italy, the works were recommenced, under the able direction of Signor Rosa, and since then the extended area before us has been cleared of the enormous mass of accumulation which covered it. The discoveries made have entirely set at rest the many contending theories regarding the direction of the Roman Forum, and the names of the different edifices of which remains were visible, anterior to the commencement of the excavations at the beginning of this century.

Extending away to the right is the enormous area covered by THE BASILICA JULIA, founded by Julius, and completed by Augustus, on the site of the Basilica Sempronia. The many square brick pedestals are restorations of the pilasters of the arcades which formed the external porticoes around the grand central hall. These have been erected on the remains

---

* The Duchess of Devonshire had nothing to do with the excavation of the temples and edifices already mentioned.

of the ancient foundations, and at the west side, and north-
west corner, are several of the original pilasters *in situ*,
with some portions of the vaulting. Along THE VIA SACRA,
which divides the Forum in its length, and THE VICUS
TUSCUS, which turns from it at right angles at the further
end, the ancient steps which led from these streets into the
Basilica can be traced from place to place; and in the porticoes are considerable remains of the large white marble
slabs, and in the great hall, of the richly coloured slabs of
rarer marbles, with which they were paved. The great
drain—cleared and restored to use since its discovery at
this point—visible beneath the pavement of the portico, at
the further end, is a portion of THE CLOACA MAXIMA, built
by Tarquinius Priscus, to drain the marshy ground of the
Forum and the Velabrum.

Beyond the Basilica Julia stand three splendid Corinthian
columns, the remains of the TEMPLE OF CASTOR AND POLLUX,
originally dedicated, B.C. 484, in commemoration of the
victory gained at Lake Regillus. Rebuilt and enlarged at
different times, the three columns still standing are the
remains of the temple as restored by Domitian.

Directly under the modern level, in front of the Arch of
Septimius Severus, and between the Column of Phocas and
the Church of St. Adriano, are TWO MARBLE BALUSTRADES,
sculptured on both sides. On the inner sides of each are
the animals—a pig, a sheep, and a bull—offered in the
sacrifice of expiation called the *Suovetaurilia*. On the outer
side, towards the Capitol, is an alto relief commemorating
the great act of—one might say Christian—charity, performed by Trajan, in the establishment of a number of
orphan asylums throughout the Roman dominions; and
on that towards the Palatine, the burning of the public

records of the arrears of taxes, remitted by the same Emperor.

On the side of the Via Sacra, opposite to the Basilica Julia, are the pedestals of a number of HONORARY COLUMNS; and in the middle of the flagged area, the fragmentary nucleus of the pedestal of the colossal gilt bronze equestrian STATUE OF DOMITIAN, described by Statius; the key to the topography of the Forum, and the discovery of which definitely settled all controversy on the subject.

Proceeding along the modern level, at the edge of the excavation, we reach, on the left, THE TEMPLE OF ANTONINUS AND FAUSTINA, dedicated to the Empress Faustina, A.D. 138. After the death and deification of Antoninus Pius, his name was included in the dedication, and added to the inscription, still remaining, above that of his wife. The portico, formed by ten monoliths of Carystian marble, a considerable portion of the marble cornice, and the walls of the cella, are still entire; and we are indebted for their preservation to a church, dedicated to ST. LORENZO IN MIRANDA, having been constructed within them at a very early period. It is mentioned as being a collegiate church in the time of Martin V., who, in 1430, gave it to the confraternity of apothecaries, or, as we might say, to the College of Surgeons of that time.* The church was rebuilt in its present form by *Torriani*, in 1602.

Turning from the temple and church to the excavation below, we see, between them and the Temple of Castor and Pollux, a great mass of concrete. This is the nucleus of the podium of THE TEMPLE OF THE DEIFIED JULIUS, erected by

---

* This neighbourhood would seem to have been the head-quarters of the medical profession from the days of the Empire. It was close to this spot that Galen had his shop on the Via Sacra, which was burnt down during the great conflagration when the Temple of Peace was destroyed; and the ancient church, a little further on, upon the left, is dedicated to the martyred physicians, Cosmas and Damian.

Augustus, on the spot where Cæsar's body was burnt.   It was a small temple on a lofty platform, and in front is the lower platform of the Rostrum, erected in connection with the temple, and decorated by Augustus with the prows of the galleys taken at the victory of Actium.

Somewhat to the left, and immediately under the cliff of the accumulation, is a shapeless mass of concrete, which can be recognised as having originally been circular.   This is all that remains of the famous TEMPLE OF VESTA, originally founded by Numa Pompilius; the abode of the vestal virgins during life, and after death; the shrine in which they preserved the Palladium, veiled from sacrilegious eyes; and where, typical of the social hearth of the Roman people, they kept the sacred fire for ever burning.   Adjoining, are fragments of ruined walls jutting out from the accumulation.   These, in all probability, are the remains of THE REGIA, but we must await the continuation of the excavations, before anything certain can be known regarding them.

The little Church, close to the three columns of the temple of Castor and Pollux, is dedicated to SANTA MARIA LIBERATRICE.   Of early origin, and originally dedicated to *S. Salvatore in Lacu*, it was rebuilt in its present form in 1617.

Continuing onwards, we find, on the left, a small church, with an ancient door of bronze, flanked by small columns of porphyry, dedicated to the martyred physicians, SAINTS COSMA AND DAMIANO.   (*See* page 142.)

The hurried traveller may proceed direct to this Church, but the reader, desirous of forming a clear conception of the topography of the ancient city, is advised to make a divergence to

THE FORA OF AUGUSTUS AND NERVA,

taking the Academy of St. Luke on the way, and back to

the Temple of Antoninus and Faustina, in front of which we are supposed to be standing.

Returning to the Arch of Septimius Severus, turn to the right, into the Via Bonella. The first edifice on the left, No. 44, is

THE ACADEMY OF ST. LUKE,

where the Picture Gallery is open every day from 9 to 5.

We ascend the stairs, on the walls of which are plaster casts of some of the sculptures on the Column of Trajan; and passing through the ante-room, where there are some old engravings, enter the Gallery. The pictures are not numbered, but each bears the name of the painter, and the subjects will be easily recognised in the following order, omitting those of lesser importance :—

FIRST ROOM.
Turn to the left on entering.

A Storm : *Tempesta.*
The Flight into Egypt : *Barocci.*
The Mystic Marriage of St. Catherine of Alexandria : *Memling.*
Deposition from the Cross : *Unknown.*
The Three Graces (a sketch) : *Rubens.*
A Pastoral Scene : *Orrizonte.*
The Virgin with the Infant Christ and Angel Musicians : *Vandyke.*
Landscape with Ancient Monuments : *Orrizonte.*
St. Jerome Praying in the Desert : *Titian.*
Portrait of Innocent XII. : *Velasquez.*
Sea Piece : *Vernet.*
Landscape : *Poussin.*
Cascade with Peasants Fishing : *Salvator Rosa.*

Mountain Scene with Fishers : *Salvator Rosa.*
Idem : *Poussin.*
St. Jerome Expounding the Scriptures : *Spagnoletto.*
A Seaport : *Vernet.*
VANITY : *Paul Veronese.*
Portrait of a Lady with a Lace Collar : *Vandyke.*
Cumæan Sibyl Chanting the Oracles : *Gherardo della Notte.*
Cardinal Wolsey receiving his Cardinal's Hat : *G. H. Harlow.*
Portrait of a Man : *Titian.*
VANITY, semi nude, Lying on a Couch : *Titian.*
Angels Announcing the Nativity to the Shepherds : *Bassano.*
A Seaport : *Claude Lorrain.*
A Bust with floating hair : *Bernini.*
DOLORE ; a bust.

Passing the pilasters which divide the third room from the first; on the last:

Heads of Cats: *Salvator Rosa.*	St. Agatha: *Bonifazio.*
Bust of SALVATOR BETTI.	Cupid and Psyche: *Luti.*
Bust of TENERANI.	Portrait of a Lady with a Lap
Bust of THORWALDSEN.	Dog: *Titian.*

SECOND ROOM.

Commencing from the right.

BACCHUS AND ARIADNE: *Guido.*	Musicians (unfinished): *Titian.*
Susanna and the Elders: *Paul Veronese.*	Venus and Cupid (fresco transferred to canvas): *Guercino.*
The Virgin Suckling the Infant Jesus: *Albani.*	TARQUIN AND LUCRETIA: *Guido Cagnacci.*
Sea Piece: *Vernet.*	CUPID (transferred from a vaulting in the Vatican): *Raphael*
THE TRIUMPH OF GALATEA; copy by *Julio Romano;* from Raphael's fresco in the Farnesina.	FORTUNE: *Guido.*
Triumph of Bacchus: *Poussin.*	The Mystic Marriage of St. Catherine of Alexandria: *Paul Veronese.*
Hebe: *Pellegrini.*	CALLISTO AND THE NYMPHS:*Titian*
View on the Tiber: *Vanutelli.*	Perseus and Andromeda: *Cav. d'Arpino.*
St. Bartholomew Flayed: *Bronzino.*	An Architectural Elevation: *Canaletto.*
ST. LUKE PAINTING THE PORTRAIT OF THE VIRGIN: *Raphael.*	PORTRAIT OF CLAUDE GELLEE— called Lorrain; painted by himself in 1862.
The Tribute Money: *Titian.*	
St. Andrew: *Bronzino.*	

On the upper part of the walls are arranged 136 portraits of members of the Academy of St. Luke.

THIRD ROOM

chiefly contains portraits of Academicians of St. Luke. On the wall to the right, as we face the window, and on the right of a frame containing medals, is The Death of St. Cecilia, by *Pozzi;* and, the second in the second row above it is a portrait of THORWALDSEN. On the left, a Servant, by *Subleyras;* and above it, the portrait of ANGELICA KAUFFMANN. On the wall, under the window to the right, is a small portrait of JOHN GIBSON, wearing a red cap, by *Penry Williams;* and in the middle of the end wall, to the left, is another portrait of him, in a grey coat, leaning on his modelling stool and holding a white handkerchief, by *Boxall.* On the pilasters, facing the windows, are a portrait of VIRGINIA LEBRUN, and a picture of Iris, by *Head.*

On the lower floor there are three rooms, containing chiefly paintings, models, and drawings, to which the prize medals have been awarded. In the first room are the original models of Gibson's " Hunter," and of a fine statue of an " Athlete," by *Kessells.* In the third is the model of Thorwaldsen's " Graces," by no means one of his best works; and a number of casts of the Egina marbles, sent by King Louis of Bavaria to Pius IX.

At the end of the Via Bonella stands a massive wall of ancient masonry, with a low arch, called the *Arco dei Pantani,* leading through it, and on the left, three grand columns of the Corinthian order. The wall is the boundary of THE FORUM OF AUGUSTUS,* and the columns the remains of the TEMPLE OF MARS ULTOR—Mars the Avenger—built by Augustus within the limits of his Forum, and dedicated to the deity who had aided him in taking vengeance on the murderers of his uncle.

Turning through the arch to the right, and again taking the first turning to the right, we find, on the left, two Corinthian columns, half buried, supporting an entablature, and standing outwards from a wall of large squared stones. These are remains of the boundary wall, and inner portico of THE FORUM TRANSITORIUM. Within its area stood a grand temple to Minerva, of which considerable remains were in existence to the time of Paul V., 1605-21, who threw them down to use the materials elsewhere. On the entablature is a figure of Minerva in alto-relief, from which this ruin is popularly supposed to be the remains of a temple dedicated to that goddess. The frieze is ornamented with a number of small figures in alto-relief, illustrating the arts protected by her.

Turning now, to the left, and then taking the second street to the right, brings us back to the Temple of Antoninus and Faustina; beyond which, to the left, we find the bronze doors of

---

* The construction of this wall affords the clearest evidence that it is a great mistake to suppose that it ever formed part of the fortifications of the regal period.

THE CHURCH OF S.S. COSMA AND DAMIANO.

It is built in and among the remains of three ancient
edifices, believed to be temples. The first, forming the
circular vestibule, was THE TEMPLE OF ROMULUS, erected by
Maxentius to his son of that name, who was deified immediately after death. The second edifice, forming the body
of the church, and the third, the posterior portion, have not
been satisfactorily recognised. The church was originally
constructed by Felix IV., 526-59; and it is presumed that
the ancient mosaic in the apse, dates from that period. In
subsequent alterations made, the lateral portions of the
mosaic were cut away, so that the design is incomplete;
and it has been altered and restored in parts. The floor,
also, was raised by Urban VIII., in 1632, considerably
above the ancient level, which has now become the floor of
the crypt.

Next to the church, is THE ORATORY OF THE CONFRATER-
NITY OF THE LOVERS OF JESUS, and, in front of it, two half
buried columns of Carystian marble, of uncertain pertinence.
A little further, on the left, are the magnificent ruins of THE
BASILICA OF CONSTANTINE. Three colossal arches, forming
one aisle, are standing almost entire; while portions of the
great piers, which supported the remainder of the building, show the ground plan complete. This Basilica was
founded by Maxentius, the last of the pagan emperors, and
completed and dedicated by Constantine. It stands on, or
near, the site of the celebrated Temple of Peace, erected by
Vespasian, on the site of the Atrium of Nero's Palace. It
measures 320 feet in length by 235 feet in width, and the
span of each arch is 80 feet.

The vaulting of the nave was supported by eight grand

columns of the Corinthian order, the last of which was still erect in its place at the commencement of the year 1613, when Paul V. spent 10,996 scudi (about £2,200), in removing it to the piazza in front of Santa Maria Maggiore, to support a bronze statue of the Virgin and Child.

Directly opposite is the entrance to

THE PALATINE AND THE PALACE OF THE CÆSARS.*

The excavations made upon the Palatine, and chiefly at the expense of the late Emperor of the French, Napoleon III., since 1861, have rendered it a centre of the deepest interest to all strangers visiting Rome, and second only in importance to the Forum itself.

Up to a comparatively recent period, this hill, which, by the time of Alexander Severus, had become entirely covered by the grand series of palatial edifices which constituted the Palace of the Cæsars, was divided into a number of private vineyards, beneath which the remains of the imperial residence lay buried. All that was visible of the magnificent structure, which covered no less than $62\frac{1}{2}$ acres, were some picturesque fragments of ivy-clad walls, jutting up here and there from among the vines and vegetables, and, at the north-west and south-east corners, great masses of ruin, almost unrecognisable, so entirely were they filled by accumulation and overgrown by vegetation.

In 1861 the Emperor of the French bought that portion of the Palatine known as the Orti Farnesiani—the Farnese orchards—from the ex-Royal family of Naples, into whose possession it had passed, and commenced the excavations which have had such important and interesting results.

---

* Open to the public on Thursdays and Sundays only.

The greater part of the remains of the Imperial Palace have been laid bare; the portions erected by succeeding emperors clearly ascertained; and the uses and purposes of the various halls, chambers, and galleries, fully made out.   At the same time, together with these discoveries, others, connected with the earlier history of the Palatine, have been made; remains of the republican houses, and temples, that stood upon the hill before the palace was commenced, and some portions of the wall of fortification of the time of Romulus.

But it is altogether beyond the bounds of possibility, for a stranger, Guide-book in hand, to make his way through the multitude of ruins, so as to recognise and understand them.   To do so would have been difficult enough when the whole was entire, and each portion had its distinctive aspect, but, when each clump of ruin bears a more or less general likeness to those around it, the task becomes hopeless. Were each traveller an archæologist, versed in the language of stones, and able to recognise at a glance, each separate mode of construction,—for each has its distinct characteristic, like the paintings of different schools—then the path through the labyrinth might be indicated, with some degree of certainty of the directions being understood; but as this is impracticable, all that can be attempted will be to give a general indication of the localities, and refer the student to archæological lectures for further information.

The reader must bear in mind what vicissitudes and changes this gigantic edifice, or congregation of edifices, has undergone.   The building of the palace was commenced by Augustus.   It was enlarged by Tiberius, and still further extended by Caligula.   Cut down in size by Claudius, its extent was more than doubled by Nero, who continued its buildings away on to the Esquiline, as far as the central railway station.   It was partly burnt down in his time, and rebuilt with greater splendour.   Its extent was restricted again by Vespasian, to the limits of the Palatine.   In the time of Titus it was burnt a second time, and was rebuilt, and added to, by Domitian.   Commodus made other additions; his immediate successors, changes and alterations. Septimius Severus built a great wing towards the south, which Heliogabalus and Alexander Severus extended still further to the south-east.   With the removal of the seat of empire to Constantinople, it fell into ruin; the Goths and Vandals—much maligned people—are said to have stripped its remains to the condition in which we find them, but, strangely enough, the materials are recognised in the many churches and marble palaces of mediæval Rome.

Such being, in brief, the history of the palace, the reader will easily comprehend that several volumes would be required to furnish an exact guide to the remains, and that it is no discredit to this little book to decline attempting, except in a general, and necessarily imperfect manner, what every Guide to Rome yet written has utterly failed to accomplish.

Ascending the incline, we find before us a chamber containing a picturesque cascade fountain.   This was made by the Farnese family, and forms no part of the Imperial Palace.   Turning to the left, as far as the angle near the Arch of Titus, we come to the remains of an ancient road, the *Summa Nova Via*, which, after skirting the side of the Palatine, joined the Via Sacra at the Arch of Titus, and then, turning to the right, led—at a lower level than that it now follows — to the *Porta Vetus Palatii*, the later name for the PORTA MUGONIA of the wall of Romulus. Considerable remains of this gate were found, but the

L

stones—*tufa* of a very friable quality—have crumbled almost entirely to dust, and only a few of the lower range can be recognised.   The shapeless mass of concrete on the right is the remains of the celebrated TEMPLE OF JUPITER STATOR, founded by Romulus, on the spot where the tide of battle turned against the Sabines.   It was in this temple that Cicero summoned the senate to meet, and pronounced his first oration against Catiline.   The great pile of ruins immediately in front are the remains of the grand suite of STATE ROOMS BUILT BY DOMITIAN—the *Ædes Publicæ* of Nerva.   The central opening leads into THE GREAT AUDIENCE CHAMBER, with, on one side, the LARARIUM, and on the other the BASILICA—the Judgment Hall.   It was believed to be that mentioned in the Acts of the Martyrs S.S. Silvester and Lawrence; but there is no ground whatever for the supposition that it was here St. Paul was brought before Nero.   The evidence of the date when this portion of the palace was built, obtained in the course of the excavations, precludes all possibility of such having been the case.   Nor can the arguments be sustained which would seek to prove that it was an earlier Basilica, rebuilt on the same spot by Domitian, or that in some other way it marks the site of that in Nero's Palace.

Behind these three chambers is the great PERISTYLIUM— believed to be that called *Sicilia* by *Capitolinus*, and if so, it was here that Pertinax was murdered.   It has a range of small rooms on the right.   The left side is partly encroached upon by the grounds and buildings of the Monastery of the Nuns of the Visitation.

From this Peristyle a subterranean passage, originally paved with mosaic—of which some portions remain—passes under the AREA PALATINA, to a long CRYPTO-PORTICUS, and connects the buildings of Tiberius and Caligula with those of Domitian.

A flight of narrow steps leads down from the area of the Peristyle, to some small chambers of the early imperial period, with considerable remains of coloured decoration of great beauty on the ceilings. These were excavated and left open to visitors, long before Napoleon's excavations were commenced, and are popularly known as THE BATHS OF LIVIA; but there are no traces of baths within them, nor are there any indications, from which it can be ascertained, if they formed an adjunct to the House of Augustus in this direction, or if they are rooms belonging to a private house of the same period.

From the Peristyle we pass into THE GREAT TRICLINIUM, believed to be the *Jovis Cœnatio* mentioned by Capitolinus, with THE NYMPHÆUM, and the remains of its great fountain, on the right. It is conjectured that a corresponding Nymphæum will be found on the opposite side, when the excavations are continued in that direction.

Passing beyond the Triclinium, we find the remains of a small portico of columns of Carystian marble of the Corinthian order, which probably formed one side of an Atrium, and beyond it, the remains of two halls, to which the designations of Library, and Academy, have been given, on conjecture.

Turning to the right, we come to the platform of a large temple, supposed to be that of JUPITER VICTOR (?), built in commemoration of the victories over the Samnites gained by Fabius Maximus, B.C. 295 ; and next to it the foundations of a smaller temple, supposed to have been that of JUPITER PROPUGNATOR.

Continuing along the same side of the hill, we reach a

deep cutting, where a Clivus has been discovered, leading
down from this corner towards the Velabrum.   It was
formed by steps of travertine, interrupted from place to
place by short paved inclines, and on each side are the
remains of the ancient wall of fortification, in some parts
distinctly showing the construction of the regal period.
Signor Rosa would identify this Clivus with that, up which
Virgil describes Æneas and Evander ascending.   It answers
the description exactly, and in all probability is the locality
indicated by Virgil, but it would be absurd to suppose, nor
does Signor Rosa intend to imply, that any of the constructions belong to so remote a period, or even to the time of
the first kings of Rome.   On the other side of the Clivus,
and at its summit, are foundations and architectural fragments of large size, belonging to edifices and temples of the
Republican period, but regarding which nothing has yet
been ascertained.   The lofty mass of ruin, overgrown with
shrubs, somewhat further on, was conjectured to be the
remains of THE AUGURATORIUM ; but its particular form, and
the STATUE OF CYBELE, found close by, lead to the supposition
that it was the temple of that goddess, which is known to
have stood in this vicinity.

The range of vaulted chambers of small size, immediately
before us, are a portion of the substructions of THE HOUSE
OF TIBERIUS, above which the accumulation has not been
touched.   On the right we look down into a series of
chambers, with richly coloured fresco paintings on the
walls, in a wonderful state of preservation.   This—one of
the most important and interesting discoveries made in the
course of the excavations — belongs to the period immediately preceding the foundation of the Imperial Palace.   It
is believed to be THE HOUSE OF TIBERIUS CLAUDIUS NERO, the

father of the Emperor Tiberius.* The Vestibulum is almost perfect, its vault is entire, and the painting on the walls, and the mosaic pavement, are scarcely damaged. Considerable remains of the mosaic pavement of the Atrium, which belongs to the class described by Vitruvius as *Atria Testudinata*, are still remaining, and sufficient of the decoration of its walls, to convey an exact conception of what its appearance must have been. Three large rooms open off from the Atrium. The walls of that in the centre—the Tablinum—are painted with subjects from classical mythology. On the right, the fable of Io guarded by Argus, and on the end wall, the story of Acis and Galatea. In the corner is a view of a part of a Roman house, divided into terraces; and above are two smaller pictures. The rooms on each side of the Tablinum, called the right and left wings, are decorated with richly coloured panels, figures of genii, and wreaths of fruit and flowers, painted in a most masterly manner.

A doorway at the corner of the Atrium, to the right on entering, opens into another room, supposed to have been the Triclinium, also richly painted. Close to this is a narrow staircase, leading to the posterior portion of the house, which is divided by a long passage. On the right side are the bath rooms, store room, and, at the further end,

* A solitary opinion has been given, that these are the remains of the House of Hortensius, in which Augustus lived for forty years. It is supported on arguments in direct contradiction and misinterpretation of the many passages in the classic authors, which allude to the House of Hortensius, and the Domus Augustana which succeeded it. Those passages mention in detail the surroundings of the house of Hortensius as rebuilt by Augustus, of not one of which is there the slightest indication in this locality. The entire topography is altogether different from that described. Suetonius distinctly tells us, that the house of Hortensius was destroyed by fire; but in opposition to this, it is argued that, being built of stone, it could not have been destroyed, and that the Domus Augustana was nothing more than the "House" of Hortensius re-roofed and repaired. An examination of the friable tufa with which the house is built —the material in use at the end of the Republic—will convince any one that, subjected to the action of fire, it would crumble to dust. The construction is that called *opus reticulatum*, formed of small stones cut square, placed diamond-wise, and of pointed wedge shape, entering from six to eight inches into the body of the wall.

two shops, fronting upon an ancient street; on the left, a number of small rooms, surrounding the Peristyle, in the middle of which are the remains of the staircase which led to the upper floor.   From the further end a subterranean passage opens, and leads direct to the site of THE HOUSE OF AUGUSTUS, the remains of which lie under the cypresses we see before us on emerging from the passage.

Crossing now to the side of the hill, facing towards the Aventine, we descend the inclined path, and turning to the left, pass in front of a number of unrecognised constructions, and then reascending, find some grand masses of ruin in front, and on the left.   Turning to the left, we enter an immense area in the form of a parallelogram.   This was the great STADIUM OF DOMITIAN, still encumbered with many feet of accumulation, except a small space in front of the IMPERIAL PULVINAR—the great semicircular niche—which was excavated in 1871.

Passing to the further end, and round the back of the Pulvinar, through the remains of halls, of which portions are standing to a considerable height, we see before and below us, the colossal substructures built by Septimius Severus, to support the enormous extension of the palace made by him on this side of the hill.   A portion of its grand frontage, the SEPTIZONIUM, was standing till the sixteenth century, when it was destroyed by Michael Angelo for building purposes.   A little causeway on the right, leads to a platform on the more projecting ruin, from whence there is a magnificent view on all sides.   Returning from this spot, and passing some great fragments of vaulting, coated with mosaic, we shall find, on the side overlooking the Coelian, a modern staircase, very much out of repair. This leads down below the Porticoes of Septimius Severus, from whence we return towards the north. Repassing the end of the Stadium of Domitian, we descend to the lowest level, and find the remains of a richly sculptured cornice of a portico—of which only one of the small granite columns was found—supported on pilasters of modern brickwork, with, behind it, a number of small chambers of irregular form, still bearing considerable remains of the stucco facing, and traces of colouring. These are believed to be part of the Domus Gelotiana, incorporated into the Imperial Palace. The intonaco on the walls is covered with graphites, rude scratchings made by soldiers and schoolboys, from which it would seem that there was an entrance to the palace from this side, guarded, as the graphites show, by veterans of the foreign legions called *Peregrini*, and, that it led to the school of the imperial pages. It was on one of these walls, that the celebrated graphite of the crucifixion of a man with an ass's head, was found, with the inscription, Αλεξάμενος σέβεται θεὺν. It was cut out from the wall, and removed to the Museum of the Roman College.

Passing through the door at the further end, and turning sharply round to the right, a few paces up the ascent, we see the remains of a wall, formed by large blocks of tufa. This is a section of the original Wall of Fortification of Romulus, preserved, as will be seen, by having been incorporated into later constructions.

Returning to the lower level, and continuing onwards, we reach the west corner of the hill, and the remains of a private house, which, from its construction, may be attributed to the time of Hadrian, or Trajan. A few yards in front of it is a curious altar, found here in 1820, bearing the inscription:

SEI. DEO. SEI. DEIVAE. SAC.
C. SEXTIVS. C. F. CALVINVS. PR.
DE. SENATI. SENTENTIA. RESTITVIT:

supposed to have been re-erected, near the Temple of Vesta, by the son of Caius Sextus Calvinus, who was Consul, B.C. 122, in commemoration of the mysterious voice of warning heard in the Forum, before the invasion of the Gauls.

Turning along the north-west side of the hill, we find, immediately on the right, another portion of the original WALL OF FORTIFICATION BUILT BY ROMULUS. It is massive in construction, formed of large parallelograms of tufa, imperfectly squared, and rudely put together. Along this side of the hill we pass the flank of the houses of Tiberius and Caligula, behind which are walls of *opus reticulatum*, remains of the earlier edifices of the Republic, and beneath them buttresses of large squared blocks of tufa, supposed by some to be a continuation of the wall of fortification, but the perfection of the masonry indicates a much later period. In all probability they were substructures of one of the grand palatial residences of the later Republicans, which gave place to the Imperial Palace.*

The circular brick edifice at the bottom of the valley, on the left, is THE CHURCH OF ST. THEODORE, built, it is believed, on the remains of an ancient edifice, possibly a temple. The church dates from a very early period, for the first record we have regarding it, is its restoration, by Adrian I.,

---

* It must not be supposed that because a wall is built of square blocks of tufa, it necessarily belongs to the time of the kings; the greater probability is that it does not. Tufa being the native stone of the country, has been used in various forms, from, anterior to the foundation of Rome, to our own day; and as long as temples, basilicas, and other great edifices were being erected, portions of them were built of great squared blocks of tufa, peperino, Gabine stone, or other primitive materials, at the discretion of the architect. *Vide* the great blocks of tufa in the walls of the Colosseum. Their position shows them to be integral parts of that edifice, and not walls of earlier buildings incorporated into it.

in 774; and the mosaics in the tribune are supposed to belong to that time.

Having reached the northern corner of the Palatine, we turn to the right, into an ancient street, called THE CLIVUS VICTORIÆ (?), with ruined walls on each side, and vaultings above it, towering to a great height. These mark the site of that portion of THE HOUSE OF CALIGULA, which was thrown down by Claudius, and rebuilt again at a later period. Some arches, lined with ornamental stucco work, will be seen on the right, which probably formed the front of the Domus Caligulæ, as restricted by Claudius. A very narrow staircase, immediately on the right after turning, leads up to a series of chambers, above the lower range of arches, in which there are remains of the mosaic pavements, and of the fresco painting on the walls. A kind of balcony passes in front of these chambers, protected by a marble balustrade, of which a portion remains *in situ;* and it is supposed that this gave communication to THE BRIDGE, which Caligula threw across the Forum, to the Capitoline Hill. A little further, on the right, is another staircase, wide and lofty, leading to the imperial apartments on this side. Further, on the left, we find a few steps, which lead to a small modern building at the corner, one of the edifices of the Farnese, now converted into

THE MUSEUM

for the reception of things found in the course of the excavations. The contents are not all numbered, but the principal objects will be recognised in the following order, commencing to the right against the wall :

A number of fragments of bas reliefs and statuettes in terra cotta.

A very fine terra-cotta double lamp (injured), standing on a small column of *peperino*.

Glass case (*under the window*) containing a number of ancient brick stamps.

Glass case (*between the windows*) containing a number of fragments of ancient glass.

Glass case (*under middle window*) containing a number of silver and bronze coins.

Glass case (*between the windows*) containing a number of implements in bone, such as hair pins, bodkins, styles, &c.; and fragments of ancient glass, terra-cotta, and bronze.

Glass case (*under the window*) containing a number of fragments of ancient fresco painting.

On the end Wall.

Two squares of inlaid marbles—*opus sectile*, in gilt frames—being angles of wall panelling formed of a number of small pieces arranged in very beautiful designs; found in the House of Tiberius, and carefully restored.

Against the Wall facing the Windows.

Shelf, holding a number of specimens of the ancient marbles —found on the Palatine— which were used for the decoration of the walls of the Palace.

Pyramidal glass case, containing a number of objects in bronze, marble, and terra cotta.

Four Shelves — On the upper two are various fragments of sculpture, &c., in rare and very richly variegated marble. On the lower two are a number of specimens of the ancient marbles used in the Palace—as above.

Pyramidal glass case, containing a quantity of terra cotta vases, lamps, balsamaries, and other objects.

Two frames—One containing a number of hair pins, knife handles, spoons, and other objects in bone; and the other, a variety of implements in bronze.

In the middle of the Room.

1. Torso seated.
2. Head of Venus (*mediæval*).
3. Head of dying Persian Soldier
4. Fragment of the lower portion of a Statue of Æsculapius.
6. Head of a Faun.
7, 13, 16. Three Caryatides in black marble—*nero antico*, found, together with the head of Claudius, No. 18, on the edge of a lime kiln, near the *Piscina*, in front of Signor Rosa's house.

8. Plaster cast of a fragment of an ancient copy of the celebrated Faun of Praxiteles; found on the edge of a lime kiln. *The marble was sent to Paris.*
9. Head of Atys, coloured red; found in the Domus Transitoria, beyond the Arch of Titus, on the right.
10. Leg of an Apollo.
11. Bust of a Girl; the face has much beauty.

13. *Vide* No. 7.
14. Head of Æsculapius, belonging to No. 4.
15. Head of Agrippina (?) or of Antonia (?) the younger, the wife of Drusus.
16, *Vide* No. 7. In front is a fragment of *Spato fluore*, supposed by some to be a piece of the celebrated *Murrhine Stone*.
17. Head of Nero.
18. Head of Claudius. *Vide* No. 7
19. Head of Marcus Aurelius.
21. Infant Bacchus, seated on the hand of a Faun.
25. Head of Seneca; this was not found in the Palatine.
26. Fragment of a statuette sculptured in green basalt;

found at the same place with No. 7, &c.
27. Torso of a statuette of a Boy Bacchus.
28. Torso of a statue of Venus Vectrix, draped in a thin veil, of great beauty.
31. Head of an old Woman, dressed in a style which would indicate the commencement of the Empire.
32. Female head.
33. Head of Cupid.
34. Plaster cast of a head of Julia, daughter of Titus; *sent to Paris*.
38. Plaster cast of Head of an Imperial Lady, probably one of the Flavian family; *sent to Paris*.

FROM THE PALACE OF THE CÆSARS TO ST. JOHN LATERAN.

Immediately on the right, after leaving the Palace of the Cæsars, stands

THE ARCH OF TITUS,

erected to him, posthumously, A.D. 81, in honour of the conquest of Judea, and the taking of Jerusalem. Having fallen into a very ruinous condition, it was entirely restored by *Valadier*, in 1822; but the portions added, being of travertine, are easily distinguishable. It was built of white Pentelic marble; a single archway, with four engaged columns, fluted, and of the composite order, on each front—two on each side of the archway, divided by large panels—and the whole surmounted by an attic, bearing an inscription on each face, of which only that towards the Colosseum remains. The inscription towards the Forum records the restoration

made by order of Pius VII.   The alto-reliefs on the inside
of the arch represent two scenes from the triumphal entry
of Titus, after the war.   On one side, Titus in his triumphal
chariot, drawn by four horses, preceded by a personification
of Rome, and surrounded by senators, and lictors carrying
the fasces.   On the other, soldiers bearing the chief trophies
brought from Jerusalem—the golden table, the silver trum-
pets, and the seven-branch candlestick.   The vault of the
arch is ornamented with rosettes and sunk panels, and, in
the centre, is a representation of the Apotheosis of Titus.

The mass of ruins, with the great wall behind them, on
the right, after passing through the arch, formed part of the
Palace of the Cæsars, where it extended to the eastern corner
of the hill; possibly the commencement of THE DOMUS
TRANSITORIA OF NERO.   From the presence of walls of a
much later date, built in among the original construction, it
is evident that in the course of the fourth century, this part
of the palace was either appropriated for, or given up to,
private uses.   Among these later additions, are some interesting remains of baths.

On the left of the Arch of Titus and in a line with it, are
some of the white marble steps still remaining, which gave
ascent, from this side towards the Forum, into the great porticoes which surrounded

THE TEMPLE OF VENUS AND ROME.

This magnificent edifice was designed by the Emperor
Hadrian, and founded by him A.D. 121.   For its support he
constructed the immense artificial platform of concrete,
which extends from the ridge of the Velia in the direction of
the Colosseum.   It measures about 500 feet by 300, and, at
the end facing the Colosseum, forms a terrace 28 feet in

height above the ancient level. The temple was double, formed by two *cellæ*, placed back to back, the one fronting towards the Forum, the other towards the Colosseum.

The Proneos of each front was formed by four Corinthian columns of white marble, and the whole was surrounded by a double portico. The inner, had ten Corinthian white marble columns, of six feet in diameter, at each end, and twenty on each side, counting the corner columns both ways. The outer, was formed by a double range of grey granite columns, of four feet in diameter, but extending along the sides only; and of these a number of great fragments are still lying on the platform.* The ascent to the area of the porticoes from the end towards the Colosseum, was by flights of steps, of which only the shapeless foundations remain at each corner. Of the temple itself, nothing is left but the two great apses, and part of the walls of the cellæ; but only that towards the Colosseum is entirely visible, the other being enclosed within, and to a great extent hidden by, the buildings of the Monastery connected with

THE CHURCH OF SANTA FRANCESCA ROMANA,

which is not only built on the platform of the temple, and among its ruins, but to a great extent was constructed of the materials belonging to it. The Church is supposed to date from the time of St. Sylvester, 314-335, and to mark the spot where Simon Magus fell to the ground and was carried off by demons. It was first dedicated to Sts. Peter and Paul.† It was restored by John VII., in 705. About

---

* Murray states that the columns of this outer portico were about 200 in number; but I cannot find his authority for saying so.

† There is reason for believing that the Church of S.S. Peter and Paul, built where Simon Magus fell, was a different edifice, situated in the immediate vicinity, but having been destroyed at an early period, its memory has become confused with this.

850 St. Leo IV. gave it the title of Sta. Maria Nuova, in consequence of having transferred to it the sacred articles belonging to a neighbouring church, called Sta. Maria Antica, which had fallen down. About 860 it was rebuilt, almost from the foundations, by St. Nicholas I., to whose time the mosaics on the vault of the apse are attributed. About 1216 it was injured by fire, and restored by Honorius III., and again it was entirely restored under Paul V., by *Carlo Lombardi*, who built the present façade in 1516.

Between the stairs leading up to the higher level of the tribune and transepts, is a group of Santa Francesca, recently executed by *Mele*.

In the right transept is the tomb of Gregory XI., 1370-78, and above it, a curious and interesting bas relief, by *Olivieri*, representing his entry into Rome in 1377, and the return of the Papal court, after 72 years' banishment in Avignon. On the end wall is a block of basalt, protected by iron bars, which is said to bear the impress made by the knees of St. Peter on the Via Sacra, when he knelt to invoke the Almighty aid against the arts of Simon Magus. At the end of the left transept there is a fine marble Ciborium of the fourteenth century.

Repassing under the Arch of Titus, and down the incline —the ancient Via Triumphalis—we see before us the Colosseum, and on the right,—

THE ARCH OF CONSTANTINE,

dedicated to him in honour of the great victory gained over Maxentius at the Pons Milvius, now called the Ponte Molle, situated about two miles beyond the Porta del Popolo. Seen from a short distance, and taken as a whole, it presents the appearance of a grand work of art and architecture combined; but examined in detail, it is found to be a most remarkable piece of architectural patchwork. The inscriptions relate to Constantine, but the greater part of the sculptures belong to the time of Trajan, and illustrate events in his reign; some also belong to an intervening period—possibly to the time of the Gordians.

It has three archways, that in the centre being larger than the others; and is ornamented on each front by four Corinthian columns of Numidian marble—*giallo antico*—above each of which is a statue of a Dacian prisoner,* and between the statues are the inscriptions over the central, and two alto-reliefs over each side archway. These statues and alto-reliefs belonged to an arch erected to the Emperor Trajan, as did also the circular bas-reliefs over the side arches, and the upper reliefs on each end. These latter originally formed one piece of sculpture, which was cut in two to adapt it to the ends of this arch. Whether the arch erected to Trajan was destroyed to afford materials for this, or through some other cause, we have no means of ascertaining, but the beauty of the architectural proportions would suggest, that in addition to the materials being utilised, the original design by Apollodorus was closely followed. The bas-reliefs on the inside of the central arch are conjectured to be of the time of the Gordians. The remainder of the sculptures are of the time of Constantine, and those immediately over the side arches illustrate events during his reign. The lower portion of the column, at the angle towards the Temple of Venus and Rome, has been repaired with white marble.

* The heads of these statues were broken off, it is said, by Lorenzino de Medici, and were restored by Clement XII., in 1734, who also replaced the statue on the right of the central arch towards St. Gregorio—of which all the upper portion had been destroyed —by one in white marble, placing the ancient fragment, which, like the others, was sculptured in Phrygian marble, in the Atrium of the Capitoline Museum. (See No. 11.)

In front of the arch are the remains of an ancient fountain, called THE META SUDANS, vulgarly supposed to have been for the gladiators to wash the perspiration from their bodies. The name was given from the central portion being in the form of the *Metæ*, which stood on the goals of the circus. It was called Sudans, because the water trickled, like drops of perspiration, over the sides from a small orifice on the top. A little further on, between the Colosseum and the end of the platform of the Temple of Venus and Rome, are the remains of a square construction. This was the base of the colossal bronze STATUE OF NERO.

We now enter the magnificent ruins of

THE FLAVIAN AMPHITHEATRE,

commonly called THE COLOSSEUM, a name it received in the middle ages, from the enormous proportions, which make it a Colossus among buildings. It was called the Flavian Amphitheatre, from the three Emperors of the Flavian family—Vespasian, Titus, and Domitian. It was founded by Vespasian, about the year 72, on the site of the ornamental lake in Nero's garden. In the year 80, Titus dedicated it with games which lasted 100 days, and during which 9000 wild animals were slain on the arena; and it was completed by Domitian, who added the shields and ornaments which surmounted the cornice.

According to the traditions of the Church, thirty thousand Jewish prisoners of war were employed in building it; and an inscription discovered in the Catacomb of St. Agnes—now in the crypt of the Church of Sta. Martina—has led to the supposition that the architect was a certain Gaudentius, who became a Christian, and himself suffered martyrdom on the arena.

In form it is an ellipse, measuring 1848 feet in circumference. Externally it is divided into three series of arcades, one above the other, surmounted by an attic. The arcades are supported by great piers, with engaged columns on the exterior. The lowest, 35ft. 6in. in height, is of the Doric order; the second, 39 feet in height, is of the Ionic; the third, 39ft. 5in. in height, is of the Corinthian order; and the attic, which has Corinthian pilasters, measures 46ft. 7in. in height, with an entablature above of 4ft. 6in.—the total height being 165 feet. The extreme length from the external walls is 629ft. 6in., and the extreme width 527ft. 6in. The arena measures 288ft. 6in. long, by 182ft. 6in. wide. The height of the Podium from the arena is 22ft. 4in.

The *Cavea*, which was capable of giving accommodation to 87,000 spectators, was divided into four belts of seats, ranging upwards from the arena. First, the *Podium*— a platform on which were the seats for the Imperial family, the Vestal Virgins, Magistrates, and other members of the Government of the day. Second, the first *Præcinctiones*, formed of 24 rows of seats one above the other, for persons of Senatorial rank. Third, the second *Præcinctiones* of 16 rows of seats, for persons of the Equestrian order. Fourth, the *Menianum* of 25 rows of seats, the upper 16 of which were of wood, for the Plebeian order. The entrance to the seats was through the 80 arches of the external portico, each fourth arch admitting to one of the four belts of seats in regular rotation. Each arch—with the exception of the four which formed the principal entrances, one at each end of the greater, and one at each

M

end of the lesser axis—is numbered on the key-stone, the numbers remaining being from XXIII. to LIIII.

In the arches over the two main entrances, at the end of the greater axis, were bronze chariots drawn by four horses; and marble statues stood in all the other arches of the second and third tiers. The spectators were protected from the sun's rays by a great *Velarium*, extended from 240 masts, which were passed through holes, 18 inches square, in the cornice, and stepped on the corbels below.

The great number of holes in the walls were made during the dark ages, for the purpose of extracting the metal bolts used in the construction,* with the exception of a few in the lower arcade, which were made for the supports of the partitions, when, first Sixtus V., 1685-90, converted the Colosseum into a woollen manufactory, and afterwards Clement XI., 1700-21, turned it into a saltpetre manufactory, for the supply of his gunpowder mills, established among the remains of the Baths of Trajan.

There is reason to believe that the outer wall remained entire until it was rent by the great earthquake in September, 1349. The earliest record of the materials being employed for other purposes is found in a letter written shortly after that event, *i.e.*, in 1362, by the Bishop of Orvieto to Urban V., at Avignon, stating that he had met with little success in raising money by the sale of the stones of the Colosseum. During the middle ages it served as a great stone quarry. The Venetian Palace, the Cancelleria, the Farnese, and Barberini Palaces, and the Quay

---

* It is an absurdity to suppose that these holes were caused by the rusting of the bolts cracking the stones and forcing the portions outwards. The marks of the tools employed for the purpose are visible in many places. The same thing was done at the Janus Quadrifrons, in the interior of the Column of Trajan, and other places, on the harder material of the marble blocks of which the marks of the pointed tools can be still more distinctly seen.

at the Ripetta, to say nothing of a host of smaller edifices, were built of the great blocks abstracted from it. This spoliation continued till Benedict XIV., 1740-50, arrested the further destruction of the building by dedicating it to the blood of the Christian martyrs who suffered within it, and erected stations* around the Podium on the modern level. Finally, as portions of the outer wall at the fractured ends menaced ruin, Pius VII., in 1805, built the great buttress on the side towards St. John Lateran, and, in 1828, Leo XII. completed that on the side towards the Forum.

It is an error to suppose that the Amphitheatre was constructed for the purpose of giving gladiatorial shows. It was a place built for the exhibition of wild animals, and wherein the spectators could see them fight together, or with men, without the danger to which they were subjected when such games were given in the Circus. In all the earliest records, the Colosseum is called a hunting theatre; but, as it was admirably adapted for gladiatorial combats, many were given within it, together with every other variety of exhibition of a kindred nature, which, through the shedding of blood, whether of men or beasts, held the spectators under an overpowering fascination. Many Christians suffered martyrdom in the arena: not that they were absolutely brought here for execution, but, as it often happened that the number of the men called *Bestiarii*, who devoted themselves to the fighting with animals as a profession, was insufficient for the purpose, malefactors were given by the Government, or refractory slaves by their owners, to supply the deficiency, and among such malefactors were Christian men and women, condemned for the crime of superstition, and neglecting, or inciting to the

* The excavations now in progress have necessitated the removal of these stations.

neglect, of the service of the gods. It is possible that distinguished persons, such as St. Ignatius, Bishop of Antioch, were sometimes sent into the arena to give greater zest to the enjoyment of the spectators, and to serve as a greater warning.

Excavations are now being carried on within the Colosseum, for the purpose of removing the many feet of accumulation under which the original level of the arena has hitherto been hidden. A portion of it has already been laid bare.

Leaving the Colosseum by the end furthest from the Forum, we see two streets running parallel from us. That on the right, called *Via San Giovanni Laterano*, leads direct past the Basilica of St. Clement, to the Basilica of St. John Lateran; but we shall take that on the left, called the *Via Labicana*. A short distance on the left side, a doorway in the wall leads up an incline to the ruins miscalled THE BATHS OF TITUS, but which are in reality the remains of a portion of

THE GOLDEN HOUSE OF NERO.

These lofty chambers and corridors were filled in with rubbish by Trajan, in order to convert them into a platform to support his Baths* and give them a magnificent aspect towards the city. At the same time, a number of transverse walls were built, to give the platform greater strength, and others obliquely from the front, to serve as foundations for the open air theatre of the stadium above.

---

* Some magnificent and most picturesque clumps of ruin—the remains of these Baths—are to be seen in the vineyard above, but, being private property, the place is not easy of access. It is very extraordinary, that notwithstanding that these ruins were verified as long ago as 1818, as being the remains of the THERMÆ OF TRAJAN, all the guide books, Murray included, continue to call them the Baths of Titus, jumbling up the Baths of Titus, of Trajan, these remains of the Golden House of Nero, and the Villa of Mæcenas, into a mass of confusion, suggestive of the blind guiding the blind.

The difference between the constructions of Nero and of Trajan can easily be recognized. The former show traces throughout of the marble panellings and pavements, and of the fresco painting on the upper part of the walls, and on the vaultings : the latter, bear no traces of ornamentation of any kind, and have panels of *opus reticulatum* in the brickwork. This portion of the Palace consists of a rectangular court, or internal garden, having a fountain in the centre, with ranges of chambers on three sides, and a long crypto-porticus on the fourth. On some of the vaulted ceilings are considerable remains of fresco painting, which we may reasonably suppose to have been either the work of *Amulius** or executed from his designs. At the entrance to the crypto-porticus some mosaics have been discovered at a lower level. They are pavements of small private houses which occupied the site anterior to the building of the Golden House.†

The custode show two pedestals on which they state that the group of the Laocoon, and the statue of the Meleager, both in the Vatican Museum, were found ; but neither of these works of art were found here. The Laocoon was discovered in the Vigna de Freddis, at some short distance from these remains, and on the higher level of the vineyard above, near the ruins of the great reservoir of the Baths of Trajan, called the Sette Sale ; and the Meleager was found on the other side of Rome, outside the Porta Portese. Before these chambers were filled up, everything of value

---

* These chambers were first discovered in the time of Raphael, when the paintings were in a much better state of preservation, and it is related by Vasari, that they served as models for the Arabesques in the Loggie of the Vatican, painted by Giovanni da Udine, under Raphael's direction.

† It is vulgarly supposed that these pavements formed part of the Villa of Mæcenas, but that Villa was on the further side of the Esquiline, near where now stands the Basilica of Sta. Maria Maggiore. That it was on the outskirts of the city is proved by the fact, that Horace was buried in the grounds of the Villa, and intermural sepulture was forbidden by law.

was removed; nothing of any importance was discovered during the clearance of the portions excavated, nor is there the least probability of anything being found in the parts which are still full of rubbish.

Although these chambers were first discovered at the end of the fifteenth century, it was not till 1811-14 that the parts now accessible were entirely cleared, and the nature of the edifice to which they belonged ascertained.

Turning to the left, along the Via Labicana, the first street on the right takes us into the Via San Giovanni Laterano, by the end of

THE BASILICA OF ST. CLEMENT,

the door of which will be found by turning again to the right, and proceeding a few steps, in the direction of the Colosseum. Until recently this Basilica was believed to be that which, according to the testimony of St. Jerome, preserved *the memory* of St. Clement—that memory, according to tradition, being the house in which he had lived, and wherein he ministered to his Christian brethren. Of a church dedicated to St. Clement we have a continuous series of records, from the end of the fourth century to our own day, and as the records from the twelfth century distinctly apply to this Basilica, it was supposed—in the absence of any other church bearing the same dedication—that those of the earlier centuries did so equally. In the year 1857, however, Father Mullooley, the learned Prior of the Irish Dominicans, to which order the church belongs, commenced excavations, and discovered an earlier Basilica, of which no record remained, exactly beneath, what, by comparison, must now be called the modern church. At some period, anterior to the twelfth century, it was abandoned—filled up, as the chambers of the Golden House were—and turned into a sub-structure for the church above. It is probable that the necessity for this arose through the ruin and devastation caused throughout this region, by the soldiers of Robert Guiscard, when he entered Rome by the Lateran Gate, in 1084, on behalf of Gregory VII., and that, as the building of the upper was contemporaneous with the abandonment of the lower church, the memory of the one became merged in the other. The columns * dividing the aisles from the nave are still standing in their places; the intercolumnia-tions filled in with a rude wall of foundation for the church above. The walls are seen to have been covered throughout with paintings in fresco; some irreparably damaged, and scarcely recognisable, others in a most remarkable state of preservation. The mosaic pavement is in many places entire, and the foundations of the marble choir and ambones removed into the upper church†—at the time it was built, are distinctly recognisable.

The following are the more important of the frescoes found :—

<table>
<tr><td>On the wall of the right aisle, at the back of a niche :
The Virgin with the infant Saviour on her lap.
On the Vault.
A head of our Saviour.
On the sides.
Fragments of what is supposed to have been a representation of the sacrifice of Abraham.</td><td>Two groups of heads, on the upper part of the wall, looking from opposite points to one centre, and which formed the corners of a large picture, supposed to have been a representation of one of the Councils held in St. Clement's
Mutilated figure of our Saviour, life size.</td></tr>
</table>

* Excepting some on the south side, which had been injured and replaced by brick pilasters, covered with fresco painting, some time anterior to the building of the upper church.

† The evident antiquity of the marble choir in the upper church, was regarded as evidence of its being the same mentioned by St. Jerome ; but it is now clear, that when the lower church was abandoned, the choir was removed, and placed in the new church above.

On the south side of the nave.
Pier : St. Clement officiating at the altar, and, above, his installation by St. Peter. Below, is a scene representing some slaves moving a column under the direction of a centurion.
Pier : The story of St. Alexius; above, a seated figure of our Saviour between the archangels Michael and Gabriel, and St. Clement and St. Nicholas.
On wall and pilaster at corner.
The Crucifixion.
The Marys at the Sepulchre.

The Descent of our Saviour into Hades.
The Marriage at Cana in Galilee.
On walls between the columns of the Narthex.
Translation of the relics of St. Clement from the Vatican to this Basilica.
The Miracle at the shrine of St. Clement.
Our Saviour blessing according to the Greek rite, between two angels ; and St. Cyril and St. Methodius.
At the end of the left aisle.
Fragments of the Crucifixion of St. Peter.
St. Cyril baptising by immersion.

But, in addition to these discoveries, it was found that the Basilica, which shows the construction of the fourth century, was built upon the walls of an edifice of the first century, which further explorations have proved to be the remains of

ST. CLEMENT'S HOUSE.

Of this several rooms have been excavated. A Vestibulum, leading into a chamber with a vaulted ceiling, adorned with beautiful stucco ornaments, and, through this, another chamber, beyond which is a staircase communicating with the south aisle of the Basilica. Beyond these, towards the west, a triple arch, divided by columns, opens upon a kind of corridor, from whence a door leads into a large room, which, towards the end of the third century, as shown by the construction, was converted into a MITHRAIC TEMPLE ! ! There can be little doubt that this was the *Memoria* mentioned by St. Jerome.

THE ORATORY,

wherein he, and whomsoever among the apostles may have

been in Rome, ministered to the first Christian converts, and that it was converted to the service of the Persian deity, when, in all probability, the property was confiscated during the fearful persecution in the time of Diocletian.

In the course of these excavations, walls of still earlier edifices were discovered below the floor of the primitive Basilica. One, of large blocks of *tufa*, supposed to be a portion of the agger of Servius Tullius, and upon it, a course of blocks of travertine, the remains of an edifice of the Republican period, for which it had served as foundation.*

As we have record of the Church of St. Clement having been rebuilt by Paschal II., 1099-1118, and as this was shortly after the taking of Rome by Robert Guiscard, in 1084, we must attribute the building of the upper Basilica to him. It is one of the purest and most complete models of the Basilican form that has come down to us, and was entered, as were all the early Basilicas, through an Atrium still existing.† There was no doubt a *Narthex*, although its line can no longer be traced. The marble Choir and Ambones originally belonged, as we have seen, to the primitive Basilica. There is reason to suppose, from the curious monogram on the panels, which is read—*Johannes*—that they were erected by John II., 522-35, who, anterior to his elevation to the Pontificate, was Cardinal titular of St.

* The author of this Guide desires to direct the attention of the Visitor to the extraordinary difficulties under which this remarkable excavation has been made beneath the flooring of the upper church, resting as it did only on the filling in, which had to be removed. As the work progressed, it became necessary to throw arches across and build pilasters to support the weight above. The whole of this arduous undertaking has been accomplished by the untiring energy and perseverance of one man—Father Mullooley—unaided, except by the contributions of friends interested in the work. The excavation of St. Clement's house has still to be completed. The works will be recommenced when there are sufficient funds, towards which all who can appreciate—and who cannot?—the importance and interest of the subject, will gladly contribute, in recognition of the advantage they have derived through Father Mullooley's labours. A book for subscriptions is kept in the Sacristy.

† The original entrance is from the side street connecting the Via St. Giovanni Laterano with the Via Labicano.

Clement's; more particularly, also, as there are two other records of him, on materials utilised in this upper church, which originally belonged to the lower. On one of the marble slabs used for the foundation of the ambones, there is the inscription, "*Salvo Hormisda Papa Mercurius presbyter cum sociis offert*," which is supposed to indicate a restoration of the altar by him, during the pontificate of his predecessor, Hormisdas, 514-23; and on the rim of one of the capitals of the delicately carved columns of the monument of Cardinal Venerio (*obit* 1479), at the tribune end of the left wall, his name again appears—"*Mercurius presb. S. Clementis.*" There can be no doubt that these columns, thus curiously utilised, belonged to the lower church, and it is conjectured that they formed part of the support of the Ciborium.

The walls of the little chapel of the Crucifixion, to the left on entering, are entirely covered with frescoes by *Masaccio*, chiefly illustrative of the life of St. Catherine of Alexandria. The subjects, commencing from the left, are: St. Catherine refusing to worship Idols; Converting the wife of the Emperor Maximin from the window of her prison; The Execution of the Empress; Catherine disputing with the Heathen Philosophers; Her Delivery from Martyrdom on the Wheel; Her Decapitation; The Crucifixion (over the altar); An Inundation at Alexandria, in punishment for the death of the Martyrs, with St. Catherine praying at a window. The subject of the next painting is not known.

In the Chapel of the Sacrament, at the end of the right aisle, are two good fifteenth century monuments, and a statue of St. John the Baptist, by *Simone*, the brother of Donatello.

The Church, which is 170ft. 6in. long, by 70ft. 9in. wide,

was restored in the upper portion by Clement XI., in 1715, to whose time the ceiling, and the paintings on the walls illustrative of events in the lives of St. Servulus, St. Ignatius, and St. Clement—belong.

Turning to the left, on leaving by the side door, we continue up the ascent of the Via San Giovanni Laterano, to where it opens on a large piazza, in the middle of which is a grand Egyptian Obelisk. At the right hand corner, and on the left side, before we enter the Piazza, are the buildings which form the Hospital of the Santissimo Salvatore, for females, capable of giving accommodation to 578 patients. It was founded by Cardinal Giovanni Colonna, in 1316. On the further side of the Piazza are THE LATERAN PALACE, the side entrance to THE LATERAN BASILICA, and THE BAPTISTRY OF THE LATERAN.

THE OBELISK

is the largest, and the most ancient of those brought from Egypt to Rome. It was erected by Thotmes IV., in front of the great temple at Thebes, 1740 years before the Christian era. It was brought as far as Alexandria by Constantine the Great, and from thence to Rome by his son, Constantinus, who erected it on the spina of the Circus Maximus.* It was found in 1587, among the ruins of the Circus, broken in three pieces, and so injured at the base, by fire, that it was necessary to shorten it by about three feet. The original height of the shaft was 109ft. 7in.; it now measures 106ft. 7in. The mass contains 11,256 cubic feet, and weighs 440 tons. It was erected where it now stands, by *Fontana*, for Sixtus V., the same year it was found. The Pope in fact

---

* The Obelisk in the middle of the Piazza del Popolo, brought to Rome by Augustus, also stood on the spina of the Circus Maximus.

had it disinterred for the purpose, expeuding on the excavation, restoration, erection, &c., 24,716 scudi, or about £5200,
besides 2858lbs. of metal for the bronze cross and ornaments. The cross is 6ft. 6in. high.

As we look towards the Obelisk from the portico of the
lateral entrance to the Basilica, we see two ancient brick
arches, towering above the modern buildings—the *Osteria
del Cocchio** —on the opposite side of the Piazza. They
form a fragment of THE AQUEDUCT OF NERO, a branch built
by him from the Claudian, to convey water for the supply of
the Imperial Palace.

THE BASILICA OF ST. JOHN LATERAN

is the Cathedral of Rome: "*Sacrosancta Lateranensis ecclesia
Omnium urbis et orbis Ecclesiarum Mater et Caput*"—Mother
and head of all the churches in the city, and throughout the
world. It is in this church the Pope is crowned, when he per-
forms one of his first acts as supreme Pontiff—that of taking
possession of the Lateran Basilica. It is called San Giovanni
in Laterano, from its having been built on the site of the
house of a Roman senator named Plautius Lateranus. Constantine first gave the house to Pope Melchiades as his
episcopal residence, and afterwards, at the request of his
successor, St. Sylvester founded the Basilica. It was consecrated by St. Sylvester, in the year 319, and dedicated to
The Saviour, which name, together with that of the Constantinian Basilica, it retained till 1144, when Lucius II.,

---

* The weary sightseer can get simple and thoroughly good, though roughly served,
refreshment in this Osteria. They have an unlimited supply of fresh eggs for omelettes
frittate ; and the wine, the ordinary wine of the country, is excellent. There is a clean
little room for *foresticri* up stairs: or, if the leaves are on the trees, the best place is
the open air under the shade of the *Cocchio* behind the house. A speciality of this
Osteria is SNAILS, which they cook most exquisitely; but, unfortunately for the majority of travellers, they only come into season on St. John's Day, the 24th of June,
when the place is crowded with the lovers of this delicacy.

having instituted here a special worship to the Saints John the Baptist and the Evangelist, the name was changed to that it now bears. It was also called the *Basilica Aurea*, on account of the immense value of the offerings, in the shape of lamps and sacred vessels, by which it was enriched.

It was first restored by St. Leo I., 440-61 ; then by St. Zachariah, 741-52. In 896 the columns of the south aisle were seriously damaged by the great earthquake of that year, when, in consequence of the discord regarding the elections of the Pontiffs, it fell into so neglected a condition that grass and thistles grew in the nave. In 905, restorations were commenced by Sergius III. It was re-roofed by Innocent II., 1130-43. The vault of the tribune was decorated with the mosaic still existing, and a new façade built, by Nicholas IV., 1287-91. In 1308 it was, with the exception of the tribune, almost entirely destroyed by fire, through the workmen employed in repairing the lead covering of the roof, upsetting a pan of lighted charcoal. Clement V., who then occupied the papal chair in Avignon, sent a small sum of money to commence the rebuilding of the church, but the work proceeded very slowly till Petrarch influenced Benedict XII., 1334-42, who sent 50,000 florins. In 1360 it was again injured by fire, and restored by Urban V., 1362-70, who erected the Gothic tabernacle over the high altar, which has recently been restored by Pius IX.; and finally it was completed by Gregory XI., 1370-78, who made the lateral doorway which opens towards the Obelisk. The beautiful pavement of *opus Alexandrinum* was laid by Martin V., 1417-31, and other embellishments commenced by him were finished by Eugenius IV., 1431-47, who also strengthened the columns and architraves. Sixtus IV., 1471-84, repaired the Campanile, and Innocent VIII., 1484-92, or, according to others, Alexander VI., 1492-1503, built the great arch, supported by columns of grey granite, at the end of the nave. The magnificent carved wood ceiling was made by order of Pius IV., 1559-66, from, it is said, a design by *Michael Angelo.* It was gilt by his successor, Pius V., and was restored at the end of the last century, by Pius VI. Sixtus V., 1585-90, erected the portico and loggia in front of the side door, and placed, as we have seen, the Obelisk in the middle of the Piazza. About the commencement of the seventeenth century, Clement VIII., 1592-1605, altered the basilican plan into the cruciform, by the construction of the transepts, which he embellished with marble panelling and paintings in fresco, as we now see them, covering them with a ceiling of wood, richly carved, but very inferior in style to that of Pius IV., over the nave.

Notwithstanding, however, all these additions, alterations, and repairs, made through a long succession of years, it was found that the condition of the building was insecure, through the injuries the columns had received, first from the earthquake in 896, and afterwards from the effects of the fire in 1308. Consequently, in 1650, Innocent X. gave orders to *Borromino* to rebuild the church, instructing him at the same time, to preserve all that was possible of the earlier edifice. The work of *Borromino* was chiefly confined to the nave and aisles, leaving the transepts and tribune untouched, and preserving the floor of Martin V., and the ceiling of Pius IV. However completely his alterations may have ensured the stability of the building, they have had the effect of depriving it of its original grandeur, and its Basilican characteristics. It must be remembered that, up to this time, the two aisles on each side were divided from the nave by lines of columns. The arrangement was that which can be seen in the Basilica of St. Paul's, outside the walls. Borromino enclosed each column of the outer aisles in a great square pilaster, and each *two* columns of the lines which bounded the nave, in massive piers, which almost obliterate from view the double aisles on the one side and the other, and diminish the apparent size of the church to that of the nave. Finally, the façade was built by *Alessandro Galilei*, for Clement XII., 1730-40. Standing within the great doors and looking along the nave, we see, at the further extremity, the apse, decorated with mosaic by Nicholas IV., in 1287; in front of it, the tabernacle, erected by Urban V., in 1362, in which are said to be preserved the heads of St. Peter and St. Paul. Below our feet, the *opus Alexandrinum* pavement, laid down by Martin V., in 1417; above us, the ceiling made by Pius IV., in 1559; and on each side, the piers of *Borromino*, 1650, in which the ancient columns are imprisoned. In each pier is a large niche, ornamented with two small ancient columns of beautiful *verde antique*, and containing a statue of one of the twelve Apostles. These statues are a little more than fourteen feet in height, executed by sculptors of that day, in the prevailing style, introduced by Bernini. The alto-reliefs above the statues are in stucco, modelled by *Algardi* for execution in bronze, an intention which has never been carried out. On the floor of the *Confession*, at the end of the nave, is the monument of Martin V., by whose orders the floor was laid. It is a bronze slab, with an effigy of the Pope in bas relief, the joint work of *Simone*, the brother of Donatello, and *Filarete*, the sculptor of the bronze doors of St. Peter's.

Passing along the inner aisle, to the right, commencing from the door, we find, on the first pier of the nave, a portrait, in fresco, of Boniface VIII., 1294-1303, standing between two cardinals, by *Giotto.* It represents him in the act of publishing the first Jubilee of 1300, and originally formed part of a great fresco which ornamented the ancient portico. On the second pier is the monument of the Magician Pope, Sylvester II., 990-1003, whose bones are said to rattle in his coffin when a Pope is about to die ; and on the third pier is the monument of Alexander III., 1159-81, who held the third great Lateran Council within the Basilica, when the doctrines of the Waldenses and Albigenses were condemned. On the fourth pier is the monument of Sergius IV., 1009-12. Passing into the transepts, which were made by *Giaccmo della Porta,* for Clement VIII., on the occasion of the Jubilee of 1600, we see, at the end of the right, the great organ, built at the same time, and which bears the name of the maker, *Lucas Blasii Perusinus, fecit anno. D.* 1599. The great flag hanging from the corner was that of the Porcupine, the flag-ship of the Turkish fleet, defeated by the Knights of Malta, near the island of Gozo, on the 23rd of May, 1721. It was sent to Innocent XIII., by Fra Marcantonio Zondadari, the 64th grand master of the order.

On each side of the doorway below the organ, is a beautiful column of Numidian marble—*giallo antico*—27 feet in height, spoils of the magnificence of ancient Rome ; but it is not positively known from whence they were taken. The grand mosaic on the vault of the apse, executed for Nicholas IV., 1287, bears the names of its authors. On the left, at the spring of the vault, are the words, *Jacobus Torriti pictor hoc opus fecit ;* and on the right, *Fra Jacobus de Camerino socius magistri.* In the centre of the vault is a head of our Saviour. It is said that during the dedication of the Basilica by St. Sylvester, an apparition of the face of our

Lord appeared above the altar. This miraculous event was represented in the original mosaic of the apse, made in the time of Leo I., 440-61, of which the upper portion, as we see it, preserved during all the vicissitudes the building has undergone, was incorporated in the work of *Torriti* and *Camerino*, before us. The lower part of the mosaic was made by *Gaddo Gaddi*, in 1292.

A low vaulted portico, called the Leonine Portico, after St. Leo I., passes behind the apse. Against the wall, on the right on entering, there is a curious kneeling figure of Pope Boniface VIII., originally in old St. Peter's.

Over the altar, at the back of the apse, is an ancient crucifix, of wood, with rude marble statues of an early period, representing St. Peter and St. Paul, on the sides.

Through this portico we pass into the left transept, at the end of which is the richly decorated

ALTAR OF THE SACRAMENT,

erected in the time of Clement VIII., 1592-1605, by *Olivieri*. It is ornamented in front by four magnificent bronze columns, gilt, the spoil of some imperial edifice, but nothing positive is known regarding them. According to the legends of the Church, they belonged to the Temple at Jerusalem, and were brought to Rome by Titus. Some archæological authorities state that they were cast by Augustus, from the bronze prows of the galleys of Anthony and Cleopatra's fleet, taken at Actium, and were erected by him in the Temple of Jupiter Capitolinus; others say that they formed part of the Temple of Jupiter at Athens, and were brought to Rome by Sulla; and others, again, that they belonged to the Temple of Nemesis. All that can be affirmed with certainty is, that they are antique. They are said to be full of earth, brought from the Holy Land.   The Ciborium is richly adorned with *pietra dura* of the rarest qualities, and precious stones, part, it is said, of the confiscated wealth of the *Cenci*.   Behind the bas-relief of the Last Supper, the top of the table at which our Saviour and His disciples sat, is said to be preserved.*

On the right of this altar is the chapel of the choir, built by *Girolamo Rainaldi*. at the expense of Cardinal Ascanio Colonna.   It contains a fine portrait of Martin V., by *Scipione Pulzone*.

Of the chapels—five on each side, which open from the walls of the Basilica—two are especially worthy of notice. THE TORLONIA CHAPEL, the second on the right from the entrance, lately reconstructed by the Torlonia family, who have richly ornamented it with monumental sculpture, and placed above the altar a fine deposition from the cross, by *Tenerani;* and, the first upon the left,

THE CORSINI CHAPEL,

built for Clement XII., 1730-40, by *Alessandro Galilei.* Over the altar is a portrait in mosaic—one of the finest examples of this art in Rome—of St. Andrew Corsini, to

---

* The list of relics connected with our Saviour, said to be preserved in this church, is something marvellous.   *Panciroli* enumerates the following : Some portions of the manger in which our Saviour lay at His birth ; The shirt, and the seamless coat, worn by Him, both made by the Virgin Mary; Some of the barley loaves and two fishes, miraculously multiplied ; The table of tLe Last Supper; The linen cloth with which He dried the feet of the apostles ; The purple robe with which He was invested ; The reed with which He was smote upon the head; The veil given by the Virgin to the crucifiers to bind about His loins ; Two vessels filled with the blood and water which flowed from His side; The handkerchief with which His face was covered in the sepulchre.   *In the Cloisters:* The marble slab (*porphyry*) on which the soldiers cast lots; The well of the woman of Samaria ; A marble slab, supported on four columns, marking His height ; Two of the columns which were rent in twain.   And, in the building close by (*vide* page 195), called the Sancta Sanctorum, are the steps up which He ascended to the judgment hall in Pilate's house.   Besides these, a number of other relics, too numerous to mention, are preserved at the Lateran, such as Aaron's thurible and his rod which sprouted ; The rod with which Moses divided the Red Sea, and struck the rock, &c. ; and so on, in chronological order, down to the mediæval saints.   The exhibition of many of the chief of these relics on Easter eve is a curious sight to witness.

whom the chapel is dedicated. On the left, is the monumental seated statue of Clement XII., in bronze, by *Maini*. The porphyry sarcophagus in front, is, with the exception of the cover, antique. It was a bath belonging to the Thermæ of Agrippa, and was found in clearing away the accumulation from the front of the Pantheon, in 1523. Opposite to this, on the right, is the monument of Cardinal Nereus Corsini, by *Maini*. The columns of porphyry at the sides, of *verde antique* at the altar, and the profusion of richly coloured variegated marbles employed in the panelling of the walls of this chapel, are all antique.

A winding staircase takes us down into the mortuary chapel below, in which are the tombs of many members of the Corsini family; and over the altar an exceedingly beautiful *Pietà*, by *Andrea Montauti*, commonly attributed to *Bernini*.

In the third chapel, on the left, is a very fine Crucifixion, the size of life, attributed by some to *Stefano Maderno*, and by others, to *Aurelio Cicoli*.

The garden of THE CLOISTERS is entered through the fifth chapel on the left. It is surrounded by a beautiful Gothic portico, formed by small columns, in pairs,—plain and twisted shafts—inlaid with the exquisite Cosmate mosaic of the 12th century, and supporting a beautiful frieze of the same work. Unfortunately, the mosaic is very much damaged. In this portico a number of interesting fragments belonging to the primitive basilica are preserved, and among other things, an episcopal throne, of marble, said to have been that of St. Sylvester. There are also a number of curiosities for the credulous. (*Vide note to page* 178.)

Leaving the church by one of the main entrances, we pass into the Vestibule, at the right end of which is a statue of

Constantine the Great, found in the remains of his baths on the Quirinal, and placed here by Clement XII., 1730-40.

The grand façade was built in 1734, by *Alessandro Galilei*, and from the central balcony the Pope used to give the Papal benediction, on St. John's day, to the multitude assembled in the Piazza.   Above the cornice is a statue of the Saviour, 22 feet in height, with 14 statues of different saints, each 20 feet in height, all sculptured in travertine.

The mosaic on the vault of the large niche, a short distance beyond the Basilica on the left, is that which ornamented the end of the papal dining hall, THE TRICLINIUM, built by Leo III., 795-816, in the old Palace of the Lateran. The remains of the Triclinium were still standing when the façade of the Basilica was built, but Clement XII., desiring to increase the size of the Piazza, had them thrown down, and the mosaic stored away in pieces in one of the rooms of the Palace, where it remained till Benedict XIV., for its better preservation, had it put together, restored, and erected on this spot in 1743.* The building a little further to the left is the SANCTA SANCTORUM, where the HOLY STAIR-CASE from Pilate's house is preserved.   (*Vide* page 195.)

Returning through the Basilica of St. John Lateran, to the side door through which we entered, we shall see, on the right, THE PALACE OF THE LATERAN, adjoining the church, and on the left, a small octagonal building,

THE BAPTISTRY OF CONSTANTINE,

dedicated to *St. Giovanni in Fonte*.   It is said to have been originally built by Constantine, at the same time with the Basilica, but the edifice, as we see it, dates from the time of

---

* It is very curious that, notwithstanding the plain record on the inscription placed here by Benedict XIV., all the guide books state this to be a copy from the fragments of the original, preserved in the Vatican.

Sixtus III., 432-40, since when it has been restored at different periods, and finally assumed its actual appearance in the time of Urban VIII., 1623-44. The font—an ancient bath, of green basalt—is surrounded by eight porphyry columns, supporting a cornice, on which are eight smaller columns of white marble, sustaining the dome. The entrance, on the further side towards the Basilica, is formed by two other porphyry columns, sustaining a richly wrought cornice, of the same design as that over the columns around the Font. These columns, and the cornice, belonged to some ancient edifice of considerable importance, and are particularly worthy of observation. The font is that in which Constantine is said to have been baptised by St. Sylvester, and in it Rienzi bathed on the night of the 1st of August, 1347, previous to the grand ceremony in the Basilica, when he assumed the insignia of knighthood, and was crowned with the seven crowns of the Holy Spirit.

The frescoes in the cupola are by *Andrea Sacchi*, and those on the walls, illustrating the life of Constantine, are by *Carlo Mannoni, Carlo Maratta, Gimignano,* and *Andrea Camassei.*

The vaults of three of the chapels which open from the Baptistry, are ornamented with very interesting mosaics.

THE LATERAN PALACE.

The ancient Palace of the Popes, given to Pope Melchiades, 311-14, by Constantine, having fallen into neglect and ruin, through age, through the injuries it had received by fire—notwithstanding subsequent restorations—and through the removal of the papal residence to the Vatican after the return from Avignon, Sixtus V., 1585-95, had the remains of the ancient edifice removed, and employed *Domenico*

Fontana to build an entirely new palace.   Directly it was finished, Sixtus took up his abode within it, but since his death, it has never been inhabited by any pontiff.   It is now converted into a Museum of Pagan Antiquities and Christian Art.

THE SCULPTURE GALLERY

contains a valuable collection of ancient sculpture, but, as it chiefly consists of fragments of statues and architectural ornament, the mere sightseer will find comparatively little that is attractive.   For artists, architects, and archæologists, however, its contents possess an interest beyond even that of the Vatican and Capitoline collections, for the objects it contains have, with few exceptions, been left in the condition in which they were found, unadulterated by meaningless restorations.   The contents of the Museum are not numbered.

First Room.
Turn to the left on entering.

2nd bas relief on the wall : Helen and Paris.

4th. Two Boxers, in alto-relief.

5th. A Poet reciting his verses to an audience. *In front of this*, a fine bust of Marcus Aurelius.

5th. A FRAGMENT OF A PROCESSION; the Emperor Trajan (the first head in high relief on the right), attended by Senators and Lictors.   Found in Trajan's Forum.

7th. The Nymph Leucothea feeding the infant Bacchus.

On the opposite wall are three fronts of Sarcophagi.   On pedestals around the room are torsos and fragments of statues.

On the floor : A portion of the mosaic pavement of the great niche of the north-west Palæstra of the Baths of Caracalla ; found there in 1828.

Second Room,

Contains a number of architectural fragments, richly sculptured.

Around the room is a series of Capitals, most marvellously wrought and deeply undercut, but for the greater part overloaded with ornament.

On the right wall : A large fragment of a very fine frieze.

Two Cupids pouring water, with a large vase between them ; and,

On the left wall, opposite : A Cupid giving drink to a Griffin.   These are said to have belonged to the Forum of Trajan.

On the end wall : A large frieze of scroll work.

Third Room.

On the right : Statue of Æsculapius.
In the Niche : Statue of Antinous.

Fourth Room,

Contains a number of monumental Cippi and cinerary urns, found in the excavations at Ostia and on the Appian Way.

Turning to the right : Vestals sacrificing ; fragment of a bas relief.

Statue of Germanicus.
Statue of Mars.
Ancient copy of the Faun of *Praxitiles*.

These three statues are said to have been found at Frascati.

Fifth Room.

Turning to the right :

Small terminal figure of Silenus, with the infant Bacchus. It is not improbable that it was from this figure Retsch took the idea of Mephistophiles, which has become the received type.

Statue of Æsculapius.
Silenus seated on a Leopard.
The Muse Urania.
Small terminal figure of Silenus, with the infant Bacchus ; companion to the above.

Cinerary Urn—found at Cervetri—covered with most delicately carved ornaments. On the front is represented the end of a cock fight. The backers are Cupids, one of whom is blubbering loudly as he carries away his dead bird.

In the middle of the Room.

Mithras sacrificing the Bull ; discovered near the Scala Sancta
A short-horned Cow.
A Stag, in basalt ; part of a colossal group, found outside the Porta Portese.

Sixth Room,

Contains a number of Imperial statues, found at Cervetri in 1839, together with several inscriptions relating to them. *Turning to the right :*

Britannicus (?)
Augustus (?) These two statues were found without the heads, which are additions made in plaster.
Tiberius, wearing a civic crown ; torso of a colossal seated statue.
Agrippina, the wife of Germanicus, in the attire of a priestess.

Claudius, wearing a civic crown ; torso of a seated statue.
Drusus
Germanicus.
Livia.
Colossal Head of Caligula (?) erroneously called Augustus.
In the middle of the room are two recumbent statues of Silenus.

SEVENTH ROOM.

Turn to the right.

Female figure, draped.
Fragment of a bas relief, with colossal figures (in the corner)
DANCING FAUN; supposed to be a copy of the statue of Marsyas, by *Myron*; found in the Via S. Lucia in Selce, on the Esquiline.
Fragment of a large Sarcophagus (in the corner).

Statue of Ceres.
SOPHOCLES. This grand statue was found at Terracina; and after having been restored in some parts, was presented to the Museum by Cardinal Antonelli.
Torso of a Statue of Diana.
Statue of the Young Apollo.

EIGHTH ROOM.

STATUE OF NEPTUNE, found at Porto. The legs and arms are restorations. To the left of the door, on entering, is a curious bas relief, representing a vendor of masks, with an actor making his selection.

NINTH ROOM,

Contains architectural fragments. On each side is a column covered with very delicate scroll work in low relief.

TENTH ROOM.

Turn to the right.

A very curious bas relief, representing an enormous crane, with ropes and pulleys; and below, a tread-wheel with a number of figures; a remarkable illustration of the means employed by the Romans to raise large masses of stone It formed, together with the portrait busts of a man and a woman on each side, part of a sepulchral monument found in 1848, at the Cento Celle, on the Via Labicana.

On the opposite wall, is a bas relief, found at the same place, on which are represented the façade of a temple, of the Corinthian order, believed to be that of Jupiter Stator, and four triumphal arches. One bears the inscription, ARCVS . AD . ISIS . ; and another, evidently that of Titus, ARCVS . IN . SACRA . VIA . SVMMA .

Above this are heads of Mercury, Ceres, Jupiter, and Juno, in high relief, on one slab.

At the end of the room; a curious sepulchral monument, representing a female figure lying on a lofty funeral couch, with a number of small figures of mourners and musicians around and below it.

In the middle of the room; a figure of Cupid on a Dolphin.

ELEVENTH ROOM,

Contains a number of Sarcophagi, found in the painted tombs on the Via Latina, in 1857 and 1858.

<table>
<tr><td>

Turn to the right.

Sarcophagus : Triumph of Bacchus.

Sarcophagus ; the Four Seasons.

Bas relief ; Pugilists.

Diana of the Ephesians.

</td><td>

Sarcophagus ; a Boar Hunt, and, a man, possibly the occupant, who has been gored, having his wound tended.

Sarcophagus ; Hyppolitus and Phædra.

In the middle : Sarcophagus ; The Triumph of Bacchus.

</td></tr>
</table>

TWELFTH ROOM.

Among the contents of this room are three Sarcophagi, marked *, discovered in an ancient tomb in the Vigna Lozzano Argoli, near the corner of the Prætorian Camp, in 1839.

<table>
<tr><td>

Turn to the right.

Sarcophagus, with a representation of the occupant.

*Sarcophagus, with Orestes and the Furies.

Statue of a young Patrician, wearing the golden bulla.

*Sarcophagus, with heads of Medusa and garlands of fruit.

Head of Britannicus (upon the sarcophagus).

</td><td>

Terminal figure of a Faun (in the corner).

Statue of a young Patrician, wearing the golden bulla.

*Sarcophagus ; Slaughter of the Children of Niobe.

Statuette of a Roman Lady, seated (on the sarcophagus).

In the middle : A circular cinerary urn, with bacchanalian figures beautifully sculptured in low relief.

</td></tr>
</table>

THIRTEENTH ROOM.

<table>
<tr><td>

Curious semi-nude recumbent monumental portrait of a certain ULPIA EPIGONI, found in the Appian Way.

Statue of a Senator named DOGMATIUS (see name on plinth)

A number of large fragments of statues, sculptured in porphyry.

Sarcophagus of GALLIA PRIMITIVA, ornamented with allegorical figures of the Seasons ; and portraits in the centre.

</td><td>

Statue of a Consul.

Five portraits in alto relief ; part of the monument of the Furia Family ; found on the Appian Way.

In the middle : Sarcophagus of CECILIUS VALLIANUS, representing the deceased reclining on a couch, with musicians playing, and servants carrying in viands.

</td></tr>
</table>

FOURTEENTH ROOM.

Opposite the door is an unfinished statue of a barbarian prisoner, discovered in 1840, in digging a cellar in the Via de' Coronari, interesting as still preserving the sculptor's "points." Against the walls are several circles of marble, the ends of unfinished columns, found in the state in which they were sent, roughly wrought from the quarries. These ends were sawn off, and placed in the Museum on account of the quarry marks and inscriptions found upon them. By the sides of the further door, are two plaster casts, one from the statue of Sophocles, in the Seventh Room, the other from the statue of Aristides, in the Museum at Naples.

FIFTEENTH ROOM.

This room and the next contain, exclusively, objects found in the course of the excavations made at Ostia, during the reign of Pius IX.

Turn to the right.

Head of Trajan.
Recumbent monumental figure, in low relief.
Female statue, draped.
Sarcophagus of RUBRIUS THALLUS
Statue of an Empress, or Priestess (?)
Statue of a Patrician boy, wearing the golden bulla.
Sarcophagus, with marine divinities.

On this Sarcophagus :
Head of a girl, of great beauty.
Head of Atys, the Sun God.
Head of a youth, with a flat cap.
In front of the windows :
Two glass cases, containing a number of small objects, in glass, bronze, and terra cotta
Between the windows :
A niche of mosaic — the back of a domestic altar—with a figure of SYLVANUS, to whom it was dedicated.

SIXTEENTH ROOM.

In the middle of the room is a recumbent statue of Atys, on which are traces of the original gilding.　Against the wall are a number of leaden water pipes, bearing inscriptions; and on the wall, several fresco paintings, found in the course of the excavations.

THE CHRISTIAN MUSEUM

is entered from the further right hand corner of the courtyard.*　It was founded by Pius IX., for the reception of sarcophagi and inscriptions, either found in the Catacombs during the excavations in progress, or in churches to which they had been removed from the Catacombs, in past times. Its arrangement was confided to the late celebrated *Padre Marchi*, who has been succeeded in his duties by the *Commendatore Giovanni Battista De Rossi.*

We enter by a small VESTIBULE, in which there are a few small sarcophagi, of no great interest.　At the further end is an ugly modern statue of our Saviour, and on the wall behind, three mosaics.　That in the middle is a copy, made

---

* The custode is sometimes obliged to admit the Visitor by the door at the head of the staircase, which opens into the last room of the Picture Gallery—called the Council Chamber—into which, in the usual course, we pass from the Christian Museum.　In this case, it will be necessary either to walk through the rooms to the entrance at the other end, or to turn to page 195, and take the rooms in the inverse ratio.

in 1709, from one—now in the Crypt of St. Peter's—which originally belonged to the monument of the Emperor Otho II., in the Atrium of the old Basilica; the other two, representing *our Saviour blessing*, and *the new born Jesus washed by Salomé*, are ancient (of the 8th century), and formed part of the decoration of the Chapel of John VII., in old St. Peter's.

The Vestibule leads to the foot of the grand staircase and passage leading to the pontifical apartments. It is now converted into a gallery for Christian sculptures. Along its sides are ranged a series of remarkably fine and interesting sarcophagi, intact, and in the walls are encased a number of the ornamented fronts of sarcophagi of smaller size. The subjects sculptured upon them are taken from the Old and New Testaments, and in many instances are very curiously mingled together.

At the foot of the staircase, is A LARGE SARCOPHAGUS—one of the most important—found under the floor, and near the high altar, of the Basilica of St. Paul outside the walls, in the course of digging the foundations for the new Baldacchino. The front is ornamented with a double row of alto-reliefs, and, in the centre, two unfinished heads, intended to be portraits of the occupants. The subjects, commencing from the left of *the upper row*, are—The Creation of Adam and Eve; Adam and Eve condemned to labour, indicated by a bunch of ears of corn in the hand of Adam, and a lamb by the side of Eve; The Tree of Knowledge; The miracle of changing the water into wine; The multiplication of the loaves and fishes; The raising of Lazarus. *On the lower row*—The adoration of the Magi; The restoration of sight to the blind; Daniel in the lions' den; The prediction of Peter's denial; Our Saviour led away by two Jews wearing round caps;* and Moses striking the rock.

On each side of the Sarcophagus are statuettes of the Good Shepherd; and on the left, a Sarcophagus, on which is represented the passage of the Red Sea.

We now proceed up the stairs, on the sides of which the Sarcophagi and other objects are ranged exactly opposite to each other, in the order given :—

---

* This subject, almost identically treated, is found on many of the Sarcophagi, and is considered by Catholic authorities to be the arrest of St. Peter.

ON THE LEFT SIDE.

1. SARCOPHAGUS—The raising of Lazarus; Moses striking the rock; Our Saviour led away; A pastoral scene; History of Jonah.

2. SARCOPHAGUS—Restoration of sight to the blind; The woman touching our Saviour's garment; The paralytic taking up his bed; The entry of our Saviour into Jerusalem.

3. SARCOPHAGUS—*On the left end:* Shadrach, Meshach, and Abednego in the fiery furnace. *On front:* The temptation of Adam and Eve; The miracle at the marriage at Cana; Restoration of sight to the blind; The raising of the widow's son; "Thou shalt deny me thrice;" The paralytic taking up his bed; Sacrifice of Abraham; Our Saviour led away; Moses striking the rock. *On right end:* Daniel in the lion's den; Noah in the ark.

4. SARCOPHAGUS — The sacrifices of Cain and Abel; Temptation of Adam and Eve; The occupant; The paralytic taking up his bed; The restoration of sight to the blind; Miracle at the marriage at Cana; The raising of Lazarus.

5. SARCOPHAGUS—*Upper row:* Entry of our Saviour into Jerusalem; Adam and Eve condemned to labour; Moses breaking the tables of the law; Portraits of the occupants; Sacrifice of Abraham; Raising of the widow's son; Multi-

ON THE RIGHT SIDE.

1. SARCOPHAGUS—Christ and the Apostles; Raising of the daughter of Jairus; Figure of the occupant; The raising of the widow's son; Our Saviour led away; The sacrifice of Abraham.

2. SARCOPHAGUS — The occupant, with a Phœnix, at one end; Moses striking the rock, at the other; The miracle at the marriage at Cana.

3. SARCOPHAGUS—The defunct between the Genii of the Four Seasons, with a musician at each corner.

Above, on the wall.

Noah in the ark; Shadrach, Meshach, and Abednego in the fiery furnace.

Moses striking the rock; Daniel in the lions' den; The sacrifice of Abraham.

4. SARCOPHAGUS—Our Saviour and six Apostles under an arcade.

Above, on the wall.

The Good Shepherd and the defunct.

A pastoral scene.

5. SARCOPHAGUS—The raising of Lazarus; The temptation of Adam and Eve; Multiplication of the loaves and fishes; The restoration of sight to the blind; The paralytic taking up his bed.

plication of the loaves and fishes. *Lower row:* Moses striking the rock; Our Saviour led away; "Thou shalt deny me thrice;" Daniel in the lions' den; The paralytic taking up his bed; The restoration of sight to the blind; The woman touching our Saviour's garment; The miracle at the marriage at Cana.

Above, on the wall: Adoration of the Magi; Birth of our Lord, and oxen looking into the manger; Daniel in the lions' den; The defunct, CRISPINA; Multiplication of the loaves and fishes; Our Saviour led away; Moses striking the rock.

6. SARCOPHAGUS—*Upper row:* Multiplication of the loaves and fishes; "Thou shalt deny me thrice; Moses receiving the tables of the law; Portraits of the occupants, in a circle; Sacrifice of Abraham; Restoration of sight to the blind; The raising of Lazarus. *Lower row:* Susanna and the elders (?); Our Saviour led away; Genii of the Seasons; Daniel in the lions' den; Miracle at the marriage at Cana; The paralytic taking up his bed; Moses striking the rock.

7. SARCOPHAGUS—The Vintage, in the middle; The Good Shepherd, at each corner; and on the ends, The Four Seasons.
Above, on the wall: Our Saviour taken before Pilate; Adoration of the Shepherds, with two asses' heads over the Infant

On the wall, above.
The raising of Lazarus; Multiplication of the loaves and fishes; Miracle at the marriage at Cana; The occupant; The woman touching our Saviour's garment; Our Saviour led away; Moses striking the rock.

Jonah thrown into the sea; Daniel in the lions' den; The sacrifice of Abraham; Jonah under the gourd.

6. SARCOPHAGUS — A pastoral scene, with a number of goats, bearing distinct traces of colour. On the left, The Good Shepherd; and on the right, The occupant.

Above, on the wall.
Elijah ascending to Heaven.

Our Saviour before Caiaphas; On the way to Calvary; The Resurrection; Our Saviour being taken before Pilate; Pilate washing his hands.

7. SARCOPHAGUS—*On the end:* Temptation of Adam and Eve. *On the front (each subject is in a niche divided by columns):* The sacrifice of Abraham; Moses receiving the tables of the law; Restoration of sight to the blind; "Thou shalt deny me thrice:" The

Christ, who is swaddled like a mummy; Baptism of our Lord; The raising of Lazarus.

8. SARCOPHAGUS—*Upper row :* The raising of Lazarus; Multiplication of the loaves and fishes; Portraits of the occupants in a shell; The sacrifice of Abraham; Restoration of sight to the blind; " Thou shalt deny me thrice ;" Adam and Eve condemned to labour. *Lower row :* Moses taking his shoes from off his feet; The woman touching our Saviour's garment ; The miracle at the marriage at Cana; Jonah thrown into the sea ; Daniel in the lions' den; Our Saviour led away; Moses striking the rock.

9. SARCOPHAGUS—*Upper row :* The raising of Lazarus; " Thou shalt deny me thrice ;" The restoration of sight to the blind; Moses receiving the tables of the law; Portraits of the occupants, in a shell ; The sacrifice of Abraham; The raising of the widow's son ; Our Saviour teaching (the sermon on the mount ?). *Lower row :* Moses striking the rock; Our Saviour led away; The miracle at the marriage at Cana ; The woman touching our Saviour's garment; Daniel in the lion's den; Multiplication of the loaves and fishes; The paralytic taking up his bed.

woman touching our Saviour's garment; Multiplication of the loaves and fishes; Moses striking the rock.   *On the cover :* Shadrach, Meshach, and Abednego in the fiery furnace; History of Jonah.

8. SARCOPHAGUS—The front is strigiled, with in the centre the prediction of the denial by St. Peter.   On the cover : The temptation of Adam and Eve ;   The occupant, and the history of Jonah.

On the wall, above.

Multiplication of the loaves and fishes ; " Thou shalt deny me thrice ;" Our Saviour between St. Peter and St. Paul; The miracle of the marriage at Cana; The paralytic taking up his bed.

9. SARCOPHAGUS, strigiled—At the left corner is a man fishing with a hook and line ; and, in the middle, The sacrifice of Abraham. The right corner is lost.

On the wall, above.

Portion of the cover of a sarcophagus, on the corner of which is a curious head (like the masks at the corners of the covers of Pagan sarcophagi), with rays like the sun.   The subjects are—The woman touching our Saviour's garment, and The Multiplication of the loaves and fishes.

10. Sarcophagus, over which is a tabernacle, supported by two columns of Phrygian marble, with spiral flutes, to show the manner in which sarcophagi, or tombs, were erected in the Atria, or Vestibules, of the primitive churches. On the front of the sarcophagus, in a kind of portico, supported by eight columns, are three subjects: The sacrifice of Abraham; Our Saviour surrounded by the Apostles; and Pilate washing his hands. *On the ends*, in front of a curious background, representing the buildings of a city, are: The prediction of the denial by St. Peter; Moses striking the rock; and The woman touching our Saviour's garment. *Above, on the wall*, is a fresco, copied from one in the Catacombs; and a slab, on which two peacocks are represented, perched on a vase.

11. Sarcophagus — Our Lord carrying His cross; Our Lord crowned with thorns; Our Lord being taken before Pilate; Pilate washing his hands. In the centre is The Labarum, guarded by two soldiers.

10. Sarcophagus of Sabinus—Moses striking the rock; Our Saviour led away; The miracle at the marriage at Cana; The occupant; The restoration of sight to the blind; The multiplication of the loaves and fishes; The raising of Lazarus. *Upon the cover:* The occupant, on the left; and a wild boar hunt on the right.

Above, on the wall.

The Good Shepherd; and the defunct, between St. Peter and St. Paul.

The entry of our Saviour into Jerusalem; The Resurrection; Daniel in the lions' den; The raising of Lazarus.

11. Sarcophagus—Abel offering a lamb; Our Saviour led away; Pilate and his wife. In the centre is the Labarum, guarded by two soldiers.

On the wall, between the two small flights of steps, is a bas-relief, representing Elijah ascending to heaven, and leaving his mantle to Elisha; and, on the landing above, is a seated statue of St. Hippolitus—the head is a restoration—found at St. Lorenzo, outside the walls. On the left side of the chair is engraved the Calendar, composed about A.D. 223, to regulate the date of Easter; and on the right, a list of the works written by the Saint.

Through the door to the left, we pass either directly onwards, into THE PICTURE GALLERY (see next page), *or first turn to the left*, into THE LOGGIA, on the walls of which a very remarkable and important collection of CHRISTIAN INSCRIPTIONS, chiefly found in the Catacombs, has been classified by the Commendatore De Rossi. They are arranged in a series of numbered compartments as follows:—

I. and II —Public inscriptions relating to Christian worship.

    III.—Elegies of martyrs written in verse, by POPE DAMASUS, and engraved by *Filocalus*.

    IV.—Epitaphs, bearing consular dates from the year 70 to 359.

    V.—*Idem* from the year 360 to 392.

    VI.—*Idem* from the year 392 to 409.

    VII.—*Idem* from the year 425 to 557.

VIII. & IX.—Inscriptions concerning dogmas.

    X.—Epitaphs of Popes, Priests, Deacons, and other ministers of the Church.

    XI.—Epitaphs of virgins, widows, pilgrims, neophytes, catechumens, &c.

    XII.—Epitaphs of illustrious men and women, soldiers, artizans, and divers officials.

    XIII.—Epitaphs of relationship; family, nation, and country.

XIV. & XV.—Figures and symbols of Christian dogmas. The faces of St. Peter and St. Paul, No. 42, are curious.

    XVI.—Figures and symbols of arts, and civil and domestic occupations.

    XVII.—Epitaphs distinguished by singularity of form.

    XVIII.—Inscriptions painted on brick, in red and white, found in the Catacomb of Sta. Priscilla, on the Via Salaria Nuova.

    XIX.—Inscriptions found in the Catacomb of St. Prætextatus, on the Appian Way.

    XX.—Inscriptions found in the Catacomb of St. Agnes, on the Via Nomentana.

    XXI.—Inscriptions found at Ostia.

    XXII.—Inscriptions found in the Catacombs of the Vatican.

    XXIII.—Inscriptions found in the Catacomb of St. Cyriacus, at St. Lorenzo, outside the walls.

    XXIV.—Inscriptions found in the Catacomb of St. Pancratius, on the Janiculum.

    XXV.—Inscriptions found in the Jewish Catacombs.

THE PICTURE GALLERY.
First Room.

This room and the next contain copies, the size of the originals, from paintings found in the Catacombs.

Commencing to the left.

Painting on the vault of a chapel in the Catacomb of *St. Callixtus*, with the Good Shepherd in the centre.

The Good Shepherd, from the Catacomb of *S.S. Trason* and *Saturninus.*

Various subjects on one canvas, from the Catacomb of *St. Callixtus.*

Idem.

Vault of a chapel, with the Good Shepherd, from the Catacomb of *St. Prætextatus.*

Various renderings of the Adoration of the Magi, from the Catacombs of *Sts. Callixtus; Agnes; Nereus & Achilleus;* and *Peter & Marcellinus.*

Susanna and the Elders (*over the door*), symbolised by a Lamb between two Wolves.

Second Room.

Turn to the right.

Painting on a side wall over an *arcosolium* with figures of the persons buried. The names — Zoe; Eliodoro; Procopi; Nemiesi; Dionysas — beside each figure, with, "*in pace,*" after each name.

Our Saviour, with the Apostles.

Our Saviour, St. Peter, St. Paul, and others, with the Lamb on a mound, from the Catacomb of *St. Peter and Marcellinus.*

Our Saviour, St. Urban, and St. Cecilia, from the Catacomb of *St. Callixtus.*

Policamus, Sebastianus, and Curinus, from *St. Callixtus.*

Third Room,

Contains a number of frescoes of the fourteenth century, removed from the wall of a room in the Monastery attached to the Basilica of St. Agnes, outside the Porta Salaria; and others, of the ninth century, representing the Prophets, and birds, brought from the crypt of St. Niccolo in Carcere, which has been recently restored.

Fourth Room.

To the left.

The Martyrdom of St. Sebastian, cartoon by *Julio Romano.*

Mosaic, in separate squares, part of the pavement of a *Triclinium,* found in the Vigna Lupi, near the Porta San Paolo, on which are represented the unswept fragments of a banquet, such as oyster shells, fragments of lettuce leaves, fish-bones, claws of crayfish, &c., believed to be a copy of the *Asoratos Œcos,* by *Sosus,* mentioned by Pliny.

Mosaic. A series of Scenic Masks, with the name of the artist, *Heraclitus,* found on the Aventine.

Mosaic, Egyptian divinities and animals.

The Incredulity of St. Thomas: *Camuccini.*

The Descent from the Cross: Cartoon by *Danielli da Volterra.*

Mosaic on the floor — found near the Sora Palace.

O

Through the door on the right, we pass into the

Fifth Room.

Turn to the right.

The Annunciation: *Cav. d' Arpino.*

King George IV. of England: *Sir Thomas Lawrence.* Sent by His Majesty to Pius VII., in return for the portrait of himself the Pope had sent to the King, then Prince Regent, on the occasion of the return of the works of art which Napoleon had taken away to Paris, and toward the expense of carriage and re-placing of which the Prince had voluntarily contributed 200,000 francs.

The Assumption of the Virgin: *Guercino.*

Proceeding up a narrow staircase, we enter a kind of balcony in

The Sixth Room,

and look down upon the pavement, which is entirely formed by the ancient mosaics discovered in 1828, on the floors of the two large niches in the Palæstræ of the Baths of Caracalla. It consists of a number of figures and heads, evidently portraits, of celebrated athletes, wrestlers, boxers, and the like. On the right wall, are drawings showing the condition of the mosaics when found, and their position on the floors of the palæstræ.

Returning through the fourth room we enter

The Seventh Room.

Turn to the left.

The Madonna and Child, with St. Laurence, St. John the Baptist, and St. Francis of Assisi, on the left, and St. Peter, St. Anthony, and St Thomas Aquinas, on the right: *Marco Palmezzano di Forli. Signed and dated* 1537.

Madonna and Saints: *Carlo Crivelli*, 1482.

An Altar Piece. The Madonna giving her girdle to St. Thomas: *Fra Angelico da Fi·sole*, with a Predella, by *Benozzo Gozzoli.*

The Madonna and Child, with St. John the Baptist and St. Jerome: *Marco Palmezzano.*

Eighth Room.

Turn to the left.

Portrait: *Vandyke.*

The Madonna and Child: *Carlo Crivelli, signed and dated* 1482.

Portrait of Sixtus V. when Cardinal Montalto: *Sassoferrato.*

Tapestries made in the Hospital of St. Michael at Rome.

Our Saviour and the Tribute Money: *Michael Angelo da Caravaggio.*

Ninth Room.

Turn to the left.

Baptism by immersion, according to the Greek rite: *Pietro Nocchi*, 1840.

Assumption of the Virgin: *Cola della Matrice*, 1515.

Holy Family: *Andrea del Sarto.*

The Entombment: *Lombard School.*

Tenth Room.

Baptism of Our Lord: *Cesare da Sesto.*

The Magdalen and St. Dorothea (?) *Luca Signorelli.*

The Annunciation: *Francia.*

St. Lawrence and St. Benedict: *Luca Signorelli.*

The Coronation of the Virgin; on the sides, the donors with their patron saints: *Filippo Lippi.*

St. Jerome seated on a throne, and robed as a Cardinal: *Giovanni Sanzio* (the father of Raphael).

Eleventh Room.

Turn to the left.

A Pagan Sacrifice: *M. A. da Caravaggio.*

An Altar Piece: *Antonio da Murano*, 1464.

The Supper at Emmaus: *M. A. da Caravaggio.*

Twelfth Room.

The Martyrdom of St. Andrew: *copy from Domenichino by Silvagni,* 1835.

Thirteenth Room,

Called the Great Hall of the Council, from its replacing that in the old Palace, in which sat the five Œcumenical Councils held in the Lateran. This room contains a number of statues and busts in *terra cotta* of North American Indians, modelled from life by *Pettrich of Dresden.*

Leaving the Lateran Palace, we turn the corner to the right, and see before us the building which contains

THE SCALA SANCTA,

the Holy Staircase, of 28 steps of marble, believed, by devout Catholics, to be those ascended by our Saviour, on his way to the Judgment Hall in Pilate's house. They are said to have been brought from Jerusalem by St. Helena, the mother of Constantine, a tradition which would seem to receive support from the fact, that they are formed of the veined white marble of Tyre. When Sixtus V. threw down the ruins of the old Lateran Palace, in order to erect the present edifice, he had this staircase removed to where it now stands, in front of an ancient oratory, originally connected with the Lateran edifices, and then dedicated to St. Laurence. In it were preserved the more important relics belonging to the Basilica, and Panciroli says, it was the private chapel of the Popes.   In placing the staircase here in 1589, Sixtus had it enclosed, by *Domenico Fontana*, in a kind of portico—recently altered by Pius IX.—with five openings; that in the centre, giving upon the holy stairs, and the others, on two flights of steps at each side, by which the faithful can return, after having made the ascent of the Holy Stairs on their knees—no one being permitted to walk up them—or up which people can walk to the oratory above.

It was while Luther was ascending the Holy Stairs upon his knees, to gain the indulgence of nine days, for each stair, granted to those who perform the penance, that midway, struck by the reflection that " The just shall live by faith," he rose to his feet, and descending, left the place.

The Oratory at the summit of the stairs is called the SANCTA SANCTORUM, from an epigraph on some stone boxes, in which the Pontiffs, Leo II., 682-84, and Leo IV., 847-55, deposited a quantity of relics.   It is now chiefly venerated for a miraculous picture of our Saviour, said to be have been finished by supernatural hands, while St. Luke, who, with the assistance of the Virgin, had commenced it, slept. Women are not permitted to enter the Oratory, nor any men except the clergy.

The groups of The *Ecce Homo*, and The Kiss of Judas, on each side of the Holy Stairs, are by *Giacometti*.   A very fine statue of our Lord bound to the column, by *Mele*, has just been placed at the left end of the vestibule, by order of H.H. Pius IX., by whom it was purchased from the sculptor, at the price of 30,000 fcs.

For the *Triclinum* adjoining, on the right, *see page* 180. The lofty arches of ancient brickwork, on the left, are the remains of THE AQUEDUCT OF NERO, a branch from the Claudian, built by him, to supply the Imperial Palace with water. Its remains can be traced, from place to place, in a continuous line to where it crosses the valley between the Cœlian and the Palatine. We have already noticed (*page* 172) two of its arches, as we stood on the steps of the side entrance to the Lateran, and, turning down the lane to the right, we shall see the Arcade continuing onwards through the grounds of THE VILLA WOLKONSKY, till it joins the Claudian Aqueduct at the Porta Maggiore. Above the arches, the *Specus,* or conduit for the water, is distinctly visible.

BEYOND THE LATERAN.

The view from the front of the Lateran, on a clear day, and particularly towards evening, is very fine. Immediately on the right are the ruins of the ancient PORTA ASINARIA of Honorius, 393-403, with, a little further on, the modern PORTA SAN GIOVANNI, built by *Giacomo del Duca* for Gregory XIII., in 1574. The arches continuing onwards from it, form the inner arcade of the ancient wall of the city; and the low continuous line of arches, somewhat more distant, at a right angle from the wall, belong to THE AQUEDUCT OF THE AQUA FELICE, built by Sixtus V. (*see page* 34). In the distance, in front are, THE SABINE, and on the right, the ALBAN, HILLS.

The Church at the further end of the open space before us is THE BASILICA OF SANTA CROCE IN GERUSALEMME.

On our way to it, along the inside of the wall, we come to a great semicircular projection, the remains of

THE AMPHITHEATRUM CASTRENSE,

which were incorporated into the wall of fortification by

Aurelian, and project on both sides. Very little is known regarding this small amphitheatre; but its name, and the style of its construction, prove that it was built for the amusement of the Prætorian Guard, at some period between the reigns of Tiberius and Nero. What remains on the outside of the wall is in a very fine state of preservation, and it is only through seeing it from thence, that a correct idea of its appearance can be formed. It is an ellipse measuring 300 feet by 250, and was surrounded by two tiers of arcades, formed by 48 arches,—built entirely of brick. The lower were ornamented with engaged columns and the upper with pilaster's, both of the Corinthian order. A few steps further brings us to

THE BASILICA OF SANTA CROCE IN GERUSALEMME.

It was founded by Constantine, about the year 330, within the precincts of the Sessorian Palace, the residence of his mother St. Helena, in honor of the Cross, sent by her from Jerusalem, a large fragment of which is said to be still preserved within it. Interesting as this Church is through its historical associations, it has, like all the Constantinian Basilicas, undergone so many vicissitudes and changes, that nothing of its primitive appearance remains, and but little of its original construction. In 1144, it was rebuilt by Lucius II., who exactly reversed the direction of its front, and, in 1744, under Benedict XIV., it was entirely modernized and a new façade built by *Pietro Passalacqua* and *Domenico Gregorini*, some of the columns dividing the aisles from the nave, being enclosed within pilasters, after the fashion of St. John Lateran.

The fresco, recently restored, on the wall of the apse, representing the incidents of the discovery of the Cross, though attributed to *Pinturicchio*, is in all probability the work of his scholar, *Benedetto Bumfiglio.*

The high altar is supported upon an ancient bath of ferruginous coloured basalt, with lions' heads, containing the relics of Saints Cesarius and Anastatius, and above it is a baldacchino, supported on four beautiful little columns, two of *Breccia-corallina*, and two of *Porta Santa.*

We descend by the left side of the tribune, into a portion of the primitive edifice called the Chapel of St. Helena, the floor of which is said to rest on a quantity of earth sent from Jerusalem. The vaulting is covered with mosaic work of the 11th century, restored in the 16th, it is believed by *Baldassare Peruzzi.* In this Chapel—into which women are not permitted to enter—a number of important relics are preserved, and among others, a small wooden panel, said to be the veritable "TITLE" placed upon the Cross.

It is related that in 1492, some workmen engaged in making repairs, discovered a closed niche at the summit of the apse, with above, the words *Titulus Crucis* in mosaic letters, which had become almost illegible. Within the niche they found a leaden box, hermetically sealed, containing a small panel bearing the inscription, *Jesus Nazarenus Rex Judeorum.*

Within the vineyard of the Cistercian Monastery attached to the Church, considerable remains of the Sessorian Palace are visible. It is believed to have been built by Heliogabalus. The ruin is popularly known by the name of the TEMPLE OF VENUS AND CUPID.

Passing onwards along the lane, we come to some grand remains of the AQUEDUCT OF NERO, under which it passes, and of which we have already seen portions near the Lateran.

The arches are in a very fine state of preservation, and are remarkable as showing the wonderful state of perfection to which building with brick had attained in the time of Nero.

Turning to the right, we have before us

THE PORTA MAGGIORE,

in reality two arches of the great Claudian Aqueduct, which, like the Amphitheatre Castrense, and other edifices, were incorporated into the wall of fortification, and made to serve the purpose of a gate, or rather, in fact, of two gates. That on the right, as we leave the city, was called the *Porta Prænestina*, and that on the left the *Porta Labicana*, from the two roads which leave Rome at this point, and on which they respectively open.

On the attic are three inscriptions. The upper, of four lines, relates to Claudius, in whose reign the Aqueduct, commenced by Caligula, was completed: that, of three lines, in the middle, relates to Titus; and the lowest of four lines, to Vespasian, who restored the Aqueduct. It brought in a supply of water from two different sources, and by turning somewhat to the left, after passing through the gate, we shall obtain a view of the section of the attic and of the two great conduits along which the waters flowed; the lower being that of *Claudian*, the upper, that of *Anio Novus*.

A few yards from the gate, on the same side, *i.e.*, the right, looking towards it, we shall see the remains of an arcade which carried three other aqueducts, and intersected the wall at right angles. Nothing is left but the mere section of a pier, flush with the wall, and above it, sections

of the three channels, or conduits, of—counting from below
—the *Marcian*, *Tepulan*, and *Julian* waters.

The square ruin directly in front of the gate is the
remains of THE TOMB OF THE BAKER, EURYSACES, and Atistia,
his wife, discovered in 1838, through the demolition of a
tower of fortification, built by Honorius in front of the
archway on the right, and in which it had been incorporated.

The form of the monument is exceedingly curious, and
from the hollow cylinders of travertine placed endways,
of which it is formed, it is supposed that the worthy baker
desired to imitate one of the arks, or receptacles for bread
called *panarii*—bread baskets, in fact—in which the
Romans kept their family supply. They were perforated
at the sides and covered on the top, in order to allow the
bread to cool slowly.

On the frieze above are sculptured—also in travertine—
the various operations of the baker's trade. From the
material employed, and the archaic spelling in the inscription, it evidently belongs to the republican period: in all
probability to the commencement of the century before
Christ. There were no bakers in Rome anterior to 173
B.C.

A little to the left of the gate, as we look towards it,
the Claudian Aqueduct turns at right angles, and forms
part of the wall of the city, the arches being filled in.
Following its line for a short distance, we turn to the right
under one of the arches which has been left open, and continuing along the walls, re-enter the city by the PORTA
SAN GIOVANNI LATERANO (*see page* 197), passing on the way
the external portion of THE AMPHITHEATRUM CASTRENSE
(*see page* 197), and parts of other edifices incorporated at

the same time into the straight line of the walls.   Of some
of these the doors and windows are distinctly visible.

THE CŒLIAN HILL.*

Re-entering the city by the Porta San Giovanni, we pass
round the Lateran Palace as far as the opening of the Via
San Giovanni Laterano, which leads to the Colosseum.   To
the left there is a narrow lane, along which our road lies.
At a short distance it bifurcates, and we must first continue
along the lane to the right as far as

THE CHURCH OF THE QUATTRO CORONATI,

and thence returning follow that on the left.   We enter
this quaint old Church through the gateway of the half
palace, half fortress of the middle ages, within the precincts
of which it stands.   Though entirely rebuilt, by Paschal
II., 1099-1118, and restored thronghout, in the time of
Martin V., 1417-31, it retains much of its original characteristics.   The six columns of plain and fluted shafts, and
different materials, on the right, and the double range before
us, as we traverse the second court-yard before reaching the
door, are vestiges of the Atrium and Narthex of the primitive building.   The aisles are divided from the nave by four
granite columns on each side, standing on bases far too
large for them, and above the aisles are clerestories.   Any
epigraphist fond of deciphering impossible inscriptions, will
find ample employment in studying the pavement which is
in great part formed of sepulchral slabs, both pagan and

---

* Instead of following the route laid down, it may be taken in exactly the contrary
direction.   Passing through the Arch of Constantine, from the Forum, or from the
Colosseum, we shall find the CHURCH OF SAN GREGORIO on the left, standing on the
summit of a flight of steps, and after visiting it, proceed up the ascent, to the right as
we leave it.

christian, taken from other places. Worked into the pavement of the tribune, are some good bits of *Opus Alexandrinum* and *Cosmati* work. The latter, in all probability, belonged to the old altar.

The frescoes on the wall and vault of the tribune, characterised by vigorous drawing and brilliant colouring, are the work of *Giovanni Mannozzi*, called *Giovanni de S. Giovanni*. They represent the martyrdom and glorification of "the four crowned Painters, and five martyred Sculptors," to whom the church is dedicated. The painters are called crowned, from the manner of their martyrdom. Iron circlets, armed with points, were driven down upon their temples.

The original Church, said to have been built by Pope Melchiades, 310-14, was destroyed when Robert Guiscard took Rome in 1084, for it was at this fortress that the soldiers of the anti-Pope Clement made their last stand. The conclave for the election of Popes Leo IV., 847-55, and Stephen VI., 896-97, met within it. The door at the further right hand corner, from the entrance of the first court-yard, leads into a chapel dedicated to St. Sylvester, in which are some very interesting frescoes of the eighth century, illustrating events in the life of Constantine.

We now retrace our steps to the bifurcation, and turn to the right, along the lane we first entered. It is skirted throughout the entire length, first on the right and then on the left, by continuous fragments of THE AQUEDUCT OF NERO; the same, of which we have seen portions, over the *Osteria del Cocchio*, by the side of the Scala Sancta; and at the Porta Maggiore, from whence, in fact, its course can be traced direct to the Palatine.

After proceeding a short distance, we reach

THE CHURCH OF ST. STEFANO ROTONDO,

a circular edifice, on the left, standing back somewhat from the lane.

Before us is a little portico, but the doors of the Church are closed, and we enter by one on the right, and passing through a small court-yard, with a picturesque mediæval well-head in the middle, find ourselves in an edifice, 198 feet in diameter, which bears no resemblance to any other Christian Church. It is an open space, surrounded by an interminable circular wall, covered with paintings of the most fearful martyrdoms, and in the area, " a perfect forest " of columns. In the middle, are two of great height, supporting the centre of the roof, with around them, a double circle of fifty-six of smaller size,—twenty in the inner, and thirty-six in the outer, range. Up to the time of Nicholas V., 1447-65, there was, where the outer wall now stands, a third range of columns, the original wall being at a distance from them, equal to that between the present wall and what is now the outer range. It is evidently an ancient edifice, dedicated at an early period to christian worship, but nothing is positively known of the purpose for which it was originally built. The archæologists of the fifteenth century say it was a temple of Faunus, but there seems more probable reason for believing that it was THE MACELLUM MAGNUM, the great meat market, known to have been built by Nero, on the Cœlian.

It is believed to have been dedicated by Pope Semplicius, 408-83, and there is positive mention of a Marcellus, titular of St. Stefano al Monte Cœlio; as it was anciently called, sitting in the council held by Pope Symmacus, 498-514. In the middle ages, it was one of the most richly ornamented churches in Rome; the walls were panelled with the rarest marbles, and the vaultings encrusted with brilliantly coloured mosaic. But early in the fifteenth century, the roof was destroyed, and it remained some time in a neglected condition, until Nicholas V. restored (?) it, by taking down the original wall with its panelling of variegated marbles, restricting the building in size, and reducing it to the condition we see.

The paintings on the walls, by *Pomarancio*, represent, with most horrible reality, the fearful tortures inflicted upon the martyrs, from the time of Herod, to Julian the Apostate. The series commences, on the left as we enter, with the Massacre of the Innocents; then The Crucifixion; next The Stoning of St. Stephen; and so on in chronological order, depicts the sufferings of the Confessors of the Faith. The pictures of the Martyrdom of Saints Primus and Felicianus, inside the chapel dedicated to them, and the Massacre of the Innocents, and, Our Lady of Sorrows, outside, were painted by *Tempesta*. The landscapes are by *Matteo da Siena*. The tabernacle of bizarre design, in the middle of the church, was made by a Swedish baker! as an offering to the Jesuit directors of the German College, to whom the Church belongs.

A little further on, the lane opens into a wide piazza to the left, on the right side of which is

THE CHURCH OF SANTA MARIA IN DOMINICA,

sometimes called *Sta. Maria della Navicella*, from the marble galley in front of the portico, a copy, made in the time of Leo X., from an antique original which occupied the same position. The Church dates from the time of Sta. Cyriaca, a pious Roman widow, who suffered martyrdom under the Emperor Valerianus, 253-60. It was originally part of her house, which she had devoted to the use of her Christian brethren. In 817 it was entirely rebuilt by Paschal I., who ornamented the apse with the mosaic still existing. At the beginning of the sixteenth century it was in great part rebuilt by Leo X., then Cardinal titular of the Church. *Bramante*, and afterwards *Raphael*, were the architects, and finally the façade and portico were completed by *Michael Angelo*. The frieze in chiaro-scuro was painted by *Pierino del Vaga*, from the designs of *Giulio Romano*.

Turning to the left, on leaving this Church, and continuing to the left, we pass under THE ARCH OF DOLABELLA; an arch of transit, of which nothing is positively known, beyond the fact, that it bears an inscription to the effect, that it was erected during the Consulate of Publius Cornelius Dolabella, and Caius Junius Silanus, A.D. 10, and that, as we see, it was incorporated into the Neronian Aqueduct.*

On the left, before passing under the archway, is the door of the abandoned Church of the Redemptorists—an order formed for the emancipation of Christians carried off into slavery—called S. TOMMASO IN FORMIS, from its opening from one of the arches of the Aqueduct.

Above the door, is a curious mosaic, representing a Vision seen by Innocent III. of an angel between two slaves, by *Jacobus Cosmati*, whose name, and the date, 1260, are inscribed on the arch.

A little further on we come to

---

* It will be observed, that here the line of the Aqueduct bends at a sharp angle and then continues on. These angular breaks in the direct line—*vide* the Claudian Aqueduct at the Porta Maggiore, and also on the Campagna, at the Porta Furba, and other places—were purposely made to check the force of the stream flowing through the specus.

THE CHURCH OF SAN GIOVANNI E PAOLO,

built in the fourth century by St. Pammachius, on the site of the house and martyrdom of these Saints. They were officers of distinction who held important posts in the household of Constantia, the daughter of Constantine, and suffered under Julian the Apostate, 361-63. Notwithstanding its antiquity, this Church has been so much changed and modernised, that it presents little of interest beyond the ancient portico with its quaint cornice of brickwork, and the exterior of the apse with its picturesque gallery formed of small arches, divided by miniature columns.

The Church originally fronted in exactly the contrary direction.

Towards the middle of the nave, to the right, is a raised slab, enclosed in a railing, said to mark the spot where the Saints were decapitated. It bears the inscription, *Locus martyrii S.S. Joannis et Paoli in ædibus propriis.*

Immediately within a wooden gateway—which the sacristan will open—between the Church and the campanile of the Passionist Convent, are the remains of a massive portico of the Imperial period, built of travertine, within which are extensive caverns, ancient stone quarries, supposed to be THE VIVARIUM, where the wild animals, for the supply of the neighbouring Colosseum, were kept. These quarries are well worth examining, but it is not safe to go far into them without torches, on account of the deep water. The Portico is supposed by some to be the remains of THE TEMPLE OF CLAUDIUS.

Continuing down the incline, commonly called THE CLIVUS OF SCAURUS, and passing under the arched buttresses built to support the side of San Giovanni and Paolo, we see on the left

THE CHURCH OF SAN GREGORIO,

standing on the summit of a flight of thirty-two steps. What appears to be the façade is one of those architectural vagaries which characterise the works of the Roman architects of the 17th century. It is nothing more than a sham front, built before the Atrium, and at some distance from the Church itself. On this site stood the paternal mansion* of Saint Gregory the Great, 590-604, a large portion of which he converted into a monastery, and built a Church in connection with it, dedicated to St. Andrew. After his death the monks deserted both the monastery and Church, but in the eighth century St. Gregory II., 715-31, brought them back to it, and rebuilt the Church, dedicating it to his sainted predecessor. Of the ancient edifice nothing remains but the plan. In 1633, the sham front and steps were constructed by *Gio. Battista Soria*, and in 1725 the entire Church and Atrium were rebuilt by *Giuseppe Serratini* and *Francesco Ferrari*. Finally, it was restored and redecorated in the time of the late Pope, Gregory XVI., by Cardinal Zurla, the General of the Camaldolese Order, to which the Church and Monastery were transferred in 1573.

The altar of the chapel at the end of the right aisle is ornamented with three beautiful bas-reliefs of the fifteenth century: that in the centre represents the miracle of St. Gregory, the Host bleeding in his hands to convince an unbeliever; and the others, the masses performed by him for the liberation of souls from purgatory. The nude figure of

---

* The ruins of an edifice, built in that mode of construction called the work of the *Decadence*, visible in the vineyard on the left, are believed to be the remains of St. Gregory's house.

a man rising with his hands joined in prayer is supposed to be intended for the Emperor Trajan. Above the altar is a painting of St. Gregory, by *Sesto Badalocchi*, a scholar of Annibale Caracci's. A door on the right leads into a small Chapel, reputed to be the monastic cell of St. Gregory. An inscription marks the situation of his bed, and the marble chair is supposed to have been his episcopal throne. Behind a grating are a number of relics.

Above the high altar is a fine painting of St. Andrew, by *Antonio Balestra.*

A door in the wall of the left aisle leads into the Salviati Chapel, in which there is an exceedingly fine marble Ciborium of fifteenth century work, dated 1469.

On the walls of the Atrium are a number of monuments, among which are several erected to English Catholics of the sixteenth century. One to Sir Edmund Carue (written *Carno*)—erected by *Galfridus Vachanus* (Vaughan) and *Thomas Fremannus*—who acted, together with Cranmer, on the famous commission, appointed by Henry VIII. to take the opinion of the foreign universities as to the validity of his marriage with Catherine. He was afterwards ambassador to Charles V.; then envoy to Rome, and finally died here in 1561. Another monument is that of Robert Pecham, who died in 1569, erected by Thomas Goldwell and Thomas Kirton.

Detached from the Church on the left are THREE CHAPELS, said to have been erected by St. Gregory, but restored in the sixteenth century, as we see them, by the celebrated Cardinal Baronius. That on the right is dedicated to St. Sylvia, the mother of St. Gregory. Over the altar is a statue of the saint by *Niccolo Cordieri*, a pupil of Michael

P

Angelo's, and on the vault a fresco by *Guido*, of the Almighty, with angels below playing on musical instruments.

The middle Chapel is dedicated to St. Andrew, and is celebrated through the frescoes painted on the walls. On the right, The Flagellation of St. Andrew, by *Domenichino*, and on the left St. Andrew adoring the cross on which he was about to suffer, by *Guido*. Unfortunately, they are both much damaged, and particularly the Flagellation, which was restored by Carlo Maratta.

The Chapel on the left, dedicated to Sta. Barbara, is called the *Triclinium Pauperum*, from the marble slab preserved in it, said to have been the table at which St. Gregory daily fed twelve poor pilgrims. On one occasion, thirteen sat down, the additional guest proving, it is said, to be an angel. The statue of St. Gregory in this chapel is by *Niccolo Cordieri*.

From the summit of the steps leading up to the church there is a fine view of the south east side of the Palatine, covered by the ruins of the Palace of the Cæsars; and of a magnificent fragment of the Aqueduct of Nero stretching across the valley between the Cœlian, on which we stand, and the Palatine, before us. Descending from the church to the road at the bottom of the valley, and turning to the left, we can continue our course as below.

FROM THE FORUM TO THE BATHS OF CARA-CALLA AND THE APPIAN WAY.*

Those triumphal processions, which entered the city from the south, traversed the three celebrated ways, the VIA

* This section may be taken up, either from the Forum, as headed, or after the Palace of the Cæsars, or the Colosseum, or direct from the Church of St. Gregory, where the last section ends.

Appia, the Via Triumphalis, and the Via Sacra, and we shall now follow the line in the contrary direction. We see the Via Sacra dividing the Forum along its length, from the base of the Capitoline Hill to the Temple of Castor and Pollux. There it turns to the left, in front of the Temple of the Deified Julius, and then turning to the right in front of the Temple of Antoninus and Faustina, continued on past the Temple of Romulus, now the Church of S.S. Cosma and Damiano, to the Basilica of Constantine, from whence, winding up the ascent of the Velia, it terminated—*according to the course we are following*—at The Arch of Titus. Passing under the arch we enter the Via Triumphalis, which followed the descent towards the Colosseum, and passing under the Arch of Constantine led between the Cœlian and Palatine Hills, past the Church of St. Gregory, till it reached the southern corner of the Palatine. Here it turned to the left (the first turning to the left after passing the Church of St. Gregory), and terminated at The Porta Capena, in the ancient circuit of the wall of Servius Tullius. At the distance of a few yards, after turning to the left, we reach the gate of a vineyard on the left. Beneath this spot the remains of the Servian Wall are still existing, traversing the line of the modern road at right angles from the Cœlian towards the Aventine, and here The Appian Way commenced.* Just outside the Porta Capena stood the tomb of the unfortunate Horatia, and from this spot to the Alban Hills, and far beyond, the road was lined on each side with a series of magnificent sepulchral monuments, of which, with the exception of the

---

* Although in general terms it may be sufficient to consider the gate of the vineyard as marking the position of the Porta Capena, and the modern road, the line of the Appian Way, the ancient road in reality lay somewhat to the left, and the actual site of the Porta Capena is just on the further side of the farm-house we see through the gate.

Tomb of the Scipios, and the Columbaria in the Vigna Codini, nothing remains within the circuit of the Aurelian Wall, save, here and there, an almost unrecognisable fragment. The road, as far as the Gate of San Sebastian, is now called the VIA DI PORTA SAN SEBASTIANO.

In the vineyard behind the ropewalk, on the right, are the ruins of THE PISCINA PUBLICA, the great reservoir, originally constructed by Appius Claudius, 312 B.C.

On the summit of the elevation on the right, called the false Aventine, stands the fortress-like CHURCH OF SANTA BALBINA, reached by turning up the first lane to the right. According to tradition, this Church, originally dedicated to the Saviour, was built by Pope St. Mark, 336-37, but we have no authentic record of its existence until the time of St. Gregory, 590-604. The monument of Stefano di Surdis is a fine example of Cosmati work, and bears the name of the master. The adjoining monastery has recently been converted into a reformatory for boys.

The second lane on the right bears the name VIA ANTO-NINA. Opposite to it, on the left, is the brook called THE MARRANA, in ancient times THE WATER OF MERCURY. Behind the angle formed by the wall at this spot, we see a small brick edifice, within which is a copious spring of clear fresh water, THE FOUNTAIN OF EGERIA.

Turning up the Via Antonina, a narrow winding lane, we come to the magnificent ruins of

THE BATHS OF CARACALLA,

almost surpassing the Colosseum in grandeur, and scarcely inferior in interest to the Palace of the Cæsars and the Forum, from the remarkable illustration they afford of the degree of luxury to which the Roman people had attained

when this sumptuous establishment was opened in the year
216 A.D. It covered an area measuring a quarter of a mile
on each side, and consisted of a grand central edifice—that
we are about to enter—measuring 750ft. in length by 500ft.
in width, surrounded, on three sides, by gardens planted
with trees and shady alleys, and ornamented with statues
and fountains, and, on the fourth, by the extensive stadium;
the whole being enclosed by an outer range of buildings, of
which we see some lofty remains on the right. The inner
edifice was devoted exclusively to the use of the bath; the
outer range was designed for intellectual purposes. It was
divided into Libraries, Lecture-rooms, Halls for Philoso-
phic disputation, Exedræ, where poets and authors could
for the first time read in public their latest works, Picture
Galleries, and great Halls, filled with masterpieces of
sculpture; with, on the south-west side, the great reservoir
for the supply of the Baths, hidden behind the rising range
of seats of an open air theatre, from whence the people
could witness the athletic games in the Stadium.

The manner of bathing was the same as that in the so-
called Turkish Baths of the present day; the hot air bath,
the warm water bath, and the cold water plunge bath.
From Vitruvius especially, and from other authors, so much
information has come down to us regarding the manner of
the bath, and the formation of the edifices devoted to it,
that no difficulty was found in recognising the various
parts among the ruins; and the fuller light thrown on the
subject, through the excavations carried out by the Italian
Government since 1871, has proved the exactness of the
accounts left us, and the accuracy with which they had
been applied by archæologists, who have too lightly been
accused of amusing themselves by identifying the different

chambers. It seems almost impossible to believe, had we
not the proof before us, that these lofty walls were panelled
with the rarest marbles from end to end, and from floor
to ceiling, and the vaults decorated with the richest mosaic.
Before the excavations were commenced, the accumulation
was full of glittering cubes of smalt, and on almost
every wall we see fragments below and indications above,
of the wealth of marble expended upon them. The
niches in the walls were filled with statues and bas-
reliefs, and many magnificent works of art have been
discovered during excavations made in past times. The
celebrated Farnese Hercules ; the Farnese Flora ; and
the magnificent group, called the Toro Farnese, were
found here. · The pavements — of which considerable
portions, in a more or less fine state of preservation,
have been uncovered—were formed of mosaic made of
porphyry, serpentine, giallo antico, and other marbles, for
the most part arranged in geometric designs, in scroll work,
and like the scales of a fish ; but, in the two enormous niches
of the Palæstræ, on the one side and the other, they were
composed of a series of portraits—some heads, some full
length figures, of celebrated athletes. These pavements were
discovered in 1828, and removed to the Lateran Museum
(*vide page* 194), with the exception of some fragments
which were overlooked, and are still to be seen on the
floor of the great niche towards the south. In examining
these Baths, which were capable of accommodating 1,600
bathers, it should be borne in mind, that by the time of
Constantine, they formed but one of eleven other establishments of the same kind, some of which were larger, others
no doubt smaller in size. Those built by Diocletian gave
accommodation to double the number of bathers. To

supply the Baths with water, Caracalla built a branch aqueduct from the Claudian, carrying the specus over the Arch of Drusus (*vide* page 219). Although opened to the public in 216, the outer range of buildings were not completed till the time of Alexander Severus, 222-35.

Shelley narrates, in the preface to his " Prometheus Unbound," that he wrote that poem "upon the mountainous ruins of the Baths of Caracalla."

Returning to the Via San Sebastiano, and continuing onwards we reach, on the right, THE CHURCH OF SAINTS NEREUS AND ACHILLEUS, the martyred chamberlains of Flavia Domitilla. Until recently it has been supposed that this Church was originally founded about the year 425, on the site of an ancient Temple of Isis, and that falling to ruin in the eighth century, it was rebuilt by St. Leo III., 795-816. The recent discovery, however, of the Basilica of Santa Petronilla, where the remains of Nereus and Achilleus were interred, shows that some confusion had arisen between the church where those martyrs were buried, and this dedicated to them at a later period. All that we know with certainty is, that it was rebuilt by Sixtus IV., 1471-84; that it fell to ruin, remained desolate for some time, and was finally restored as we see it, in 1597, by the celebrated Cardinal Baronius, who evidently did all that was possible to preserve the ancient characteristics of the church, for he left an inscription praying his successors not to alter or remove any portion of them. The Church is interesting as being one of the few remaining examples of the internal arrangement anterior to the abolition of the simpler ritual of the earlier ages of Christianity; and for the beautiful cosmati mosaic with which the choir is ornamented. At the back of the tribune is a marble episcopal throne, on which

Cardinal Baronius had a portion of St. Gregory's 28th Homily inscribed, in the belief, entertained until recently, that it was seated in this chair, within this church, where the remains of Saints Nereus and Achilleus *now* lie, that it was delivered by the sainted Pontiff. The ancient records, however, state that St. Gregory spoke it to the people in the *cemetery* of those martyrs, that is, in the Catacombs where their bodies were lying at the time when he lived; and their remains were not removed to this church till much later. The recent discovery of the Basilica of Santa Petronilla (*see page* 225), within the Catacomb of Flavia Domitilla, has restored to us the spot where the homily was delivered.

A few steps further on, upon the same side, is the Gate to the VIGNA GUIDI, which is situated in the area between the central edifice and the outer range of buildings of the Baths of Caracalla, and where, below the level of the platform, made by Caracalla for the Baths, very interesting REMAINS OF A ROMAN HOUSE, of the second century, have been discovered. Considerable portions of the mosaic pavements of both the ground and first floor are still existing, and when the excavation was first opened, the walls were entirely covered with fresco paintings, of the most brilliant colours, which unfortunately are rapidly becoming obliterated.

Immediately opposite is THE CHURCH AND MONASTERY OF ST. SISTO VECCHIO, originally built, at some period unknown anterior to the year 499, by a pious matron of the name of Trigida. It was first restored by Innocent III., 1198-1216, and given by the next Pope, Honorius III., to St. Dominick, who founded the Dominican order here; again, in the time of Sixtus IV., 1471-84, when the façade was built by *Baccio Pintelli*; and lastly, by Benedict XIII., 1724-30.

A short distance further, on the right, stands THE CHURCH OF ST. CESARIO. Writers in past times, having confounded this church with the Oratory of St. Cesario, in the Lateran, the erroneous supposition has arisen that the Popes St. Sergius, 687-701, and Eugenius III., 1145-50, were elected here. There is no historical record of the church anterior to the 12th century, to which period the cosmati mosaics belong, with which the pulpit and altar are decorated. This Church and the Church of S.S. Nereus and Achilleus we have just passed, will be found especially worth visiting by all interested in this beautiful style of mosaic work. Having fallen into a ruinous condition, it was rebuilt in the form we see by Clement VIII., 1592-1605. The mosaic in the apse belongs to this period, and was made by *Francesco Zucchi*, from a design by the *Cav. d'Arpino.*

The bifurcation of the road to the left shows where the once grand VIA LATINA, now a miserable lane, branched off from the Via Appia. At the end of this lane, just inside the Porta Latina, now closed, is the ancient and almost deserted CHURCH OF SAN GIOVANNI A PORTA LATINA. The date of its foundation is not known. It was rebuilt by Adrian I., in 772; and in 1190 was restored throughout and reconsecrated by Celestine III., since when it has been partially restored at various periods, without any material alteration in its form.

Opposite to it is a little octagonal Chapel, called SAN GIOVANNI IN OLIO, said to mark the spot were St. John the Evangelist was immersed in a caldron of boiling oil, from which he came forth as from a refreshing bath. The Chapel was restored in 1509, by a certain Benedict Adam, French auditor of the Rota, in the reign of Julius II.

Continuing our way along the Via San Sebastiano, we

reach a small door in the wall on the left, with above it the words—

SEPVLCHRA SCIPIONIVM.

Here, in the month of May, 1780, the tomb of the great family of the Scipios was discovered, in the form of a kind of catacomb, cut in the living rock. Within it were found the sarcophagi of Scipio Barbatus, the great grandfather of Scipio Africanus, and various other members of the family, together with several inscriptions, and a bust sculptured in peperino, supposed to be a portrait of the poet Ennius. The sarcophagus of Scipio Barbatus, the separate inscriptions, and the bust of Ennius (?) were removed to the Vatican exactly as they were found. (*See page* 84). From the other sarcophagi, which were entirely unornamented, the inscriptions were sawn off, and, together with those on slabs, inserted into the wall around where the sarcophagus now stands. The monument fronted on a cross road leading at this spot from the Appian to the Latin Way.

A little further on, upon the same side, we reach another door in the wall with a flight of steps leading up to it, and above, the word

COLOMBARIVM.

This is the entrance to the Vigna Codini, where first one, as the title indicates, and then two other Columbaria were discovered in the year 1853, in a remarkably fine state of preservation. These monuments, or sepulchres, will be found exceedingly interesting, and particularly by the stranger unacquainted with the ancient method followed by the Romans in preserving the ashes of the dead. They were called Columbaria from the ranges of small semicircular niches, resembling dovecotes, wherein the *ollæ*, or vases containing the ashes, were placed. Of this class of monument there were three kinds ; those built by private individuals, for the members of their family ; those erected by persons of distinction or wealth, to receive the ashes of their freedmen ; and those made at the expense of associations, burial clubs in fact, formed by individuals whose means being insufficient to permit of their purchasing separate or family places of burial, subscribed together to erect a kind of joint-stock sepulchre, each receiving a number of pigeon holes, in proportion to the amount of his subscription. It is to this last named class that these three monuments in the Vigna Codini belong. Over each niche is a small marble slab bearing the names, ages, and sometimes the occupation of the persons whose ashes rest within them, and from the inscriptions in these Columbaria, a great deal of interesting information has been obtained regarding what may be described as the committee of management and officers, by whom the affairs of these associations were managed. The first of these three monuments contains the ashes of persons who died during the reigns of the first Emperors, from Augustus to Nero. The second the ashes of freedmen of Tiberius, and of the *Gens* Pompeia. The third, of persons who died during the reigns from Augustus to Claudius. The custode never recognises the gratuity given as sufficient, and least so when it is ample.

We now see before us THE ARCH OF DRUSUS, or rather the ruins of a TRIUMPHAL ARCH, believed to be that, erected on the Appian Way, to Drusus, the brother of the Emperor Tiberius, in the year 2 A.D. It is a single archway, solidly built of travertine, once entirely faced with white marble, of which some portions remain, and had four columns of Numidian marble on each front, two of which are standing in their places on the further side. Above this arch, Caracalla carried the conduit for the supply of water to his Baths, as can still be seen.

Immediately beyond is the PORTA SAN SEBASTIANO, built, it is supposed, by Belisarius; and here, according to the modern naming of the roads and streets,

THE APPIAN WAY

commences. We descend by what in ancient times was THE CLIVUS OF MARS, and pass, on the left, the site of the Temple and Field of Mars,* where victorious generals drew up their legions and waited the decree of the Senate to enter the city in triumph. After reaching the level, we cross, on the left, the little stream of THE ALMONE, which bounded one side of this Campus Martius, and see before us the remains of THE TOMB OF GETA, the murdered brother of Caracalla, now a shapeless mass of concrete of enormous size, on which the guardian of the vineyard where it stands has perched his house. It is what the Romans call the *ossatura*, or bones of the monument, and of such *ossaturæ* we shall now see many examples of different sizes, on both sides of the road. Each of these was a magnificent monument, externally faced with marble, ornamented with columns, and richly carved cornices, and often adorned with statues, but they have long been stripped to the inner construction of concrete, to supply materials for the modern city, whether to the architect or the lime-burner.

A little further, on the right, behind a roadside wineshop, are the remains of the splendid tomb—described by Statius—erected by Abascantus, a favourite freedman of

---

* This must not be confounded with the celebrated Campus Martius, on the north side of the Capitoline.

Domitian's, to his wife Priscilla. The ruin is surmounted by a rude circular tower, built some time during the middle ages. Nearly opposite is the little Church of Santa Maria delle Piante, commonly known as Domine Quo Vadis. According to the legends of the church, it was here that St. Peter, flying from Rome, met an apparition of our Saviour: "*Domini quo vadis ?*" "Lord, where goest thou ?" asked Peter, "*Venio Romam iterum crucifigi,*" "I go to Rome to be crucified again," was the reply. Peter understood the reproof, and returned to the city. The Church was built to commemorate this miraculous event, but according to *Panvinius*, *Severanus*, and other authors, the exact spot is marked by the little circular chapel a few yards further on, and which on that account was restored by the English Cardinal, Reginald Pole, in 1536. The church is called Sante Maria delle Piante, from the impressions said to have been made by the feet of our Saviour on the stone where he stood,—that we see on the pavement of the church being a copy from what is said to be original stone, now preserved in the Church of St. Sebastian (*see page* 225). It is also called Santa Maria delle Palme, from the palms of martyrdom received by 4,000! Christians said to have been burnt to death here in the time of the Emperor Hadrian. The Church was rebuilt in 1610, and the façade renewed in 1637. The statue of our Saviour is a plaster cast from that by Michael Angelo, in the Church of Santa Maria sopra Minerva.

At this spot the road bifurcates; that on the left is the continuation of the Via Appia, that on the right is the Via Ardeatina, now called the Via della Madonna del Divin' Amore, and leads direct to the newly discovered Basilica of Santa Petronilla (*see page* 225). Continuing up the ascent we go some little distance along the road, till we find a small door in the wall on the right, with above it the words, CEMETERIO DI S. CALLISTO.   It is the entrance to

THE CATACOMB OF ST. CALLIXTUS.

While waiting for the custode we have time to observe the remains of two Pagan monuments directly within the wall; one is constructed of brickwork; of the other, and originally the most important, somewhat to the right, nothing remains but a lofty slender mass of concrete.

Beneath the whole of this district lies an extensive net-work of Christian Catacombs, extending on all sides, and formed of two, three, and sometimes even four and five *piani* or galleries, one beneath the other, crossing and intersecting each other in every direction.   It was for sometime supposed that there was a direct communication between all these Catacombs, that the names, in fact, were merely indications of the different localities in one bewil-dering labyrinth of galleries, but it is now found that they are separate and distinct.   Stripped of their contents during past ages, from the mouldering bones of the dead, to every scrap of marble by which the bodies were en-closed in their long horizontal shelf-like resting places, the Catacombs revealed nothing, but an interminable series of weird tunnel-like galleries; but within the last twenty years a fresh interest has sprung up in these last resting places of the early Christians.   New explorations have been made, and through the labour and erudition of the celebrated Christian archæologist, *Giovanni Battista De Rossi*, we can now see portions of the Catacombs, sufficiently uninjured to enable every one to form an idea of what they were, before they became the prey of the curiosity seeker and the relic monger. This Catacomb of St. Callixtus is especially interesting from the discovery, recently made, of a chamber or crypt wherein a number of the early Popes were buried. On the walls are the remains of fresco paintings, and enclosing four of the recesses are —though in a shattered condition—the marble slabs bearing the names in Greek of four martyred Popes—entitled simply Bishop and martyr—St. Anteros, 236; St. Fabianus, 236-51; St. Lucius, 253-55; and St. Eutychianus. There is reason for believing that the other niches contained the bodies of St. Urbanus, 224-31, and of St. Sixtus II., martyred in 258. The crypt has also been discovered in which St. Cecilia was buried, and whence her remains were removed by Paschal I., in 820, to the Church dedicated to her, in the Trastevere. On its walls are several paintings; a Roman lady richly attired, supposed to be St. Cecilia; a large head of our Saviour, with the nimbus arranged like a Greek cross; and figures of St. Urban, and three Saints, Polycamus, Sebastianus, and Curinus.

In addition to these, several *cubiculi*, or chapels as some call them, with the walls and ceilings covered with paintings, have been cleared of the earth with which they had been filled in. On entering this catacomb, the stranger may perhaps be disappointed by the newly-constructed look some parts have; but the *tufa* rock, through which the galleries are cut, is of so friable a nature, that these restorations have been requisite to strengthen portions which had given way during the lapse of time.

A little further, on the opposite side, we come to a modern castellated kind of house. Here

THE JEWISH CATACOMB

is situated.   It is particularly interesting from the circumstance that, no reverence being attached to the relics of the persons buried here, the bones have been allowed to remain untouched, and consequently the place has all that evidence of reality the Christian Catacombs seem to want.   The galleries are much wider and more lofty, and have more the appearance of having originally been a sand pit, than expressly cut for the purpose they were to serve, as the Christian Catacombs were.   In every other respect they bear a strong resemblance to them.   There are the same kind of chambers—*cubiculi*—opening off from the galleries from place to place, and some are covered with very interesting fresco paintings.   Among the many inscriptions found here, there has not been one of a Christian or Pagan character, and on several of those still in their places we recognise the seven-branch candlestick and other Jewish emblems.   There is no evidence of the date beyond that afforded by one of the inscriptions, which bears the Consulate of Avienus, A.D. 502.

A little further, on the right, we come to a lane called the VIA DELLE SETTE CHIESE, and immediately after it

THE BASILICA AND CATACOMB OF SAINT SEBASTIAN.

The history of this Church, anterior to the building of the actual edifice by Cardinal Scipio Borghese, in 1611, is involved in great uncertainty.   According to some it was founded by St. Sylvester, 314-36 ; and rebuilt by St. Damasus 366-85.   According to others it was founded by Innocent I., 401-17.   It is only certain that a Basilica, dedicated to San Sebastian, existed in this vicinity from a very early period, and had been in a ruined condition for some time before Cardinal Borghese rebuilt it, either on the same spot or near where it originally stood. In the Chapel of St. Sebastian, on the left, is a fine recumbent statue of the saint, designed by *Bernini* and sculptured by *Giorgetti*. The relics of St. Sebastian repose under this altar. They had been removed from the Catacombs to St. Peter's, and were returned to this Basilica by Honorius III., in 1218, enclosed in a stone coffin, in which they still remain.

In a Chapel opposite, a number of relics are preserved, and are shown to visitors by one of the monks, after he has duly lighted the candles. There is the stone with the impress of the Saviour's feet, removed here from the Church of *Domine quo Vadis;* an arm of St. Sebastian and one of the arrows with which he was shot; an arm of St. Andrew the Apostle; the head of St. Callixtus; and many others. A door, on the left of the Chapel of St. Sebastian, leads down into the Catacomb. In its general aspect it is more impressive than that of St. Callixtus, and from the almost entire absence of restoration, conveys at first sight a more distinct idea of what the Catacombs were. About midway in the circuit visitors make, there is a long stairway leading down to a second and third tier, well worth descending.

Before continuing our route along the Appian Way, we might proceed a few hundred yards along the adjacent *Via delle Sette Chiese*, already mentioned, and visit the newly discovered

BASILICA OF SAINT PETRONILLA.

Signor de Rossi, in the course of his explorations in the Catacomb of Flavia Domitilla, the niece of the Emperor Vespasian, made his way into what at the time, now nearly 20 years ago, appeared to be a crypt of more than

Q

usual importance. Two marble columns and some sarcophagi, richly carved, were found, but unfortunately at this moment, before the nature of the discovery could be ascertained, an accident happened; the earth above gave way, and the works had to be suspended, and through various impediments were not resumed till 1873. In the month of November Signor De Rossi recommenced the excavation, and speedily found that what he had supposed to be an important crypt, was in reality a Basilica, built down on the floor of the second of the three ranges of galleries of which this Catacomb is formed. The outer walls are complete to a considerable height; the bases of the columns which divided the aisles from the nave are in their places, the majority of the columns lying prone from them; and the foundations of the choir and ambones, situated like those of St. Clemente, distinctly recognisable. It is evident, however, that at some period the Church was abandoned, for, with the exception of the columns, all the marble decoration had been removed, and through the apertures in the denuded floor a number of marble sarcophagi are visible where they were originally placed; and through where the floor has further given way, we look down into the lowest of the three galleries into which the Catacomb was divided.

In the course of the excavations, some fragments of an enormous slab of marble, bearing portions of an inscription, cut in the well-known Damascene characters, were discovered. Reference to the copies, handed down to us by the pilgrims of the sixth and seventh centuries, of the many inscriptions placed by Pope Damasus in the Catacombs, at once verified these fragments as part of those relating to the martyrs Nereus and Achilleus, and identified the Basilica

as that dedicated to Santa Petronilla; a Basilica of which
so shadowy a record remained, that its having had an
existence was looked upon as a fable. This discovery has
removed many uncertainties regarding the Basilica dedicated to Saints Nereus and Achilleus inside the walls; and
establishes the fact, that it was from his episcopal chair,
placed in the apse before us, that St. Gregory delivered his
28th Homily.

Returning to the Appian Way, we next pass on the left
the remains of a circular edifice—in front of which a
modern house, now deserted, has been built—standing in
a large quadrangular area surrounded by a ruined portico.
This is supposed by some to have been the Temple, but was
more probably THE TOMB, OF ROMULUS, the son of Maxentius.
A few steps further, and we see the extensive ruins of

THE CIRCUS OF ROMULUS

stretching along the valley. This was the last built and the
smallest in size of the nine Circuses Rome contained. It was
built by Maxentius, about the year 311 A.D., and dedicated
by him to his son Romulus, then recently deceased and
deified. The inscription of dedication, found in fragments
during the excavations made in 1825, has been placed within
the arch of the triumphal gateway at the further end.

These remains are especially interesting, from the circumstance, that ruined as they are, sufficient is left to illustrate
and show the construction of every component part of the
Roman Circus; the general plan, the gates, the arrangement
of the seats, the spina dividing the arena along its length
to form the course, the carceres, from whence the chariots
started, the magisterial tribune, the Emperor's pulvinar,
and, in fact, every detail. The arena measures 1,620 feet

in length by from 240 to 250 in width, varying according to the divergence of the outer walls at the *Metæ.* The spina is 1,000 feet in length, and the seats were capable of accommodating 15,000 spectators. The obelisk, which stood on the centre of the spina, was removed by Innocent X., in 1650, to ornament *Bernini's* fountain in the Piazza Navona.

On the summit of the ascent before us stands

THE TOMB OF CÆCILIA METELLA,

the "stern round tower of other days," so magnificently described by Byron. It is only necessary to look at this, in order to form a sufficiently correct idea of what the monuments along the Appian Way were like. Large as it is, there were many of more colossal dimensions, and very many equal to it in size; and in point of decoration the many architectural fragments lying further on along the road, give sufficient evidence that it was far from being one of the most magnificent. A mere glance at the further side, where the fractured wall reveals the concrete core within, will show the condition to which this monument would be reduced if the outer casing of travertine were stripped away, and the exact resemblance it would then bear to the concrete masses we have passed. It was erected to contain the body of Cecilia, the wife of Crassus, and daughter of Quintus Metellus, surnamed Creticus, from his conquest of Crete B.C. 86; but whether she was the wife of the wealthy Crassus, who perished in Parthia, or the wife of his son; whether, as Byron asks, "she died in youth" or "with the silver grey on her long tresses," nothing remains to tell. We owe its preservation to its having, in the beginning of the fourteenth century, been converted into the stronghold of the GAETANI FORTRESS, by which that family dominated the Appian Way, levied black mail on all travellers and traffic, and led to its abandonment as a public road. The walls of the house and the fortifications of the Gaetani are still standing, and within these the picturesque ruin of the Gothic CHURCH OF ST. NICHOLAS OF BARI, curiously suggestive of the convenience of an arrangement by which the victim could be shriven, and the slayer absolved, without unnecessary loss of time.

From a short distance beyond this point, we can look along the road stretching in a direct line to the Alban Hills, and intersecting the declivity like a white ribbon; and from thence we shall find frequent remains of sepulchral monuments, until, after passing a kind of tollgate, the ruins continue in unbroken succession on each side of the way. There are masses of concrete varying in size and formation, remains of brick tombs, with delicately-wrought mouldings and capitals of terra cotta; ground plans, as it were, of monuments, of which the walls have been razed to the very foundations; and piles of brick and stone where others stood. A mantle of vegetation is spread over the whole, and reveals here and there broken capitals, masses of richly carved cornices, fragments of statues, and fractured inscriptions, for archæologists to glean, where builders and lime burners have reaped a harvest of spoil.

Passing many unrecognised remains, or of which the inscriptions found relate to persons unknown to history, we come to a brick wall on the left, built for the purpose of preserving the architectural fragments encased in it. On the upper part, in front, is a long bas-relief illustrating the story of Atys and Adrastos, and on the side a mutilated bust. These are the remains of

THE TOMB OF SENECA;

and behind stood the villa, where he was at supper, when the Tribune arrived with Nero's command that he should commit suicide.

On the same side, after passing the concrete core of a large circular monument—unknown—we come to the ruins of THE TEMPLE OF JOVE, where Valerian, the husband, and Tiburtius, the brother, of St. Cecilia, and other Christians, suffered martyrdom.

On the right are the remains of the monuments of PLINIUS EUTYCHUS, erected by CAIUS PLINIUS ZOSIMUS, the favourite freedman of Pliny, the younger; of a certain CAIUS LICINIUS; of a certain HILARIUS FUSCUS, with a marble slab containing five portraits; of the family of THE SECUNDINI; of RABIRIUS HERMODORUS, RABIRIA DEMARIS, and USIA PRIMA, a priestess of Isis, with their portraits in one slab; and others.

Passing these, we come to a CIRCULAR TUMULUS, on the right side, surmounted by a rude circular tower, built upon it during the middle ages, and some few yards further on, TWO OTHER TUMULI of the same form and size. These are believed to be THE TOMBS OF THE CURIATII, and to mark the spot where the celebrated battle between the Horatii and Curiatii was fought.

Turning off from the road through the gate by the side of the first Tumulus, we find some massive remains of a wall built of great squared blocks of stone, and the indication of the lines it followed in enclosing a rectangular area, 340 feet in length, by 200 in width. This was THE GREAT USTRINUM, where the bodies were burned.

On the opposite side to the Tumuli is an enormous mass of concrete, like a colossal mushroom, the remains of an unknown tomb, which, from the architectural fragments found, must have been of great magnificence; and opposite to the third Tumulus are the remains of an interesting PRIVATE COLUMBARIUM of small size. Care must be taken here of the holes opening into the subterranean portion—the *hypogeum*—of the adjoining sepulchre.

A little further on, we come to a modern wall, with a door opening on a court-yard paved with flag-stones, in front of an immense niche, partly encumbered with constructions of the middle ages. This is a portion of the frontage of the magnificent

VILLA OF THE QUINTILII,

which extended along the Via Appia for a considerable distance, and back, as far as the modern road to Albano, called the Via Appia Nuova. Ascending to the higher ground on our right, we see two enormous square masses of ruin with windows like those of a cathedral. These, with other smaller ruins around them, formed the chief portion of the villa in that direction, and for those who have time to walk across the field, are exceedingly well worth visiting. The ancient and powerful family of the Quintilii consisted, in the time of Commodus, of two brothers, Maximus and Condinus, and a son of the latter. For some offence they had given the Emperor, or he had conceived against them, they were put to death, partly, it is believed, through the desire Commodus had conceived to obtain possession of this villa. He laid out an extensive hippodrome; spent much of his time here in the amusements of chariot racing and hunting, and finally was murdered here A.D. 193. Between the years 1787 and 1792, and again in 1828, extensive excavations were made among these ruins, and many statues and other works of sculpture found.

About a quarter of a mile further on we reach the ruin called CASALE ROTONDO, an enormous circular mass of concrete, on which stands a farm house and a grove of olive trees. It is the remains of the TOMB OF COTTA, and was originally a colossal mole, 342 feet in diameter, with a pyramidal roof, covered with slabs of marble, laid like gigantic fish scales, and surmounted by a kind of circular lantern. Of the marble facing of this lantern, and of the slabs which covered the roof, considerable fragments were found in excavations made in 1852. They have been encased in a wall built for the purpose alongside, and a very slight examination will enable any one to understand what the decoration was like. The COTTA, whose name is on the fragment of the inscription found, is believed to be VALERIUS MESSALINUS COTTA, second son of the celebrated historian and poet, MESSALA CORVINUS, the friend of Augustus and Horace, and it is possible that his remains may have been deposited within the monument. In the middle ages this tomb was fortified by the Savelli family. Many faction fights were fought around it, and on the 30th November, 1485, it was attacked by the Orsini, and taken by assault. Further than this, which corresponds with about the sixth mile along the Appian Way, few persons are able to go.

Returning, on the opposite side, not quite midway to the Villa of the Quintilii, are the remains of baths, with mosaic pavements rapidly disappearing, built by some speculator for the convenience of travellers going to Rome.

Taking the *Via della Propaganda*, to the right of the College of the Propaganda Fide, we pass, on the left the CHURCH OF ST. ANDREA DELLE FRATTE, built in 1612, upon the site of an earlier church of the fifteenth century. It was commenced by *Gio Battista Guerra*, and finished by *Borromini*, with the exception of the façade, built in 1826, by *Pasquale Belli*.

Continuing in a straight line to the end of the short *Via St. Andrea delle Fratte*, we turn to the right, and following the curve to the left, pass through the *Piazza Poli*, and the little *Piazza dei Crociferi*, in a straight line onwards, to the side of THE FOUNTAIN OF TREVI (*see page 99*).

The left side of the Piazza Poli is formed by THE PALAZZO POLI, No. 91, and opposite to it is THE ORATORY OF SANTA MARIA IN VIA. At the corner of the *Via Poli* and the *Piazza dei Crociferi* is THE CHURCH OF SANTA MARIA IN TRIVIO, built in 1573, by *Giacomo del Duca*, on the site of one of very ancient date, rebuilt, according to tradition, by Belisarius, in expiation for having deposed Pope Silverius, A.D. 537.

At the further corner, opposite the fountain of Trevi, stands THE CHURCH OF S.S. VINCENZO AND ANASTASIO, rebuilt in 1600, by *Martino Lunghi*, the younger, at the expense of Cardinal Mazzarin. Up to the time of Leo XII., 1823-29, this was the parish church of the Quirinal Palace, and it is remarkable as the place where the *pre-cordi*—the portions removed previous to embalment—of the Popes who died in the Quirinal Palace, from Sixtus V., 1585-90, to Pius VIII., 1828-31, were interred. Their names are registered on a marble slab on the wall of the tribune.

Passing along the street, to the right of the Church, we take the first main turning to the right, and ascending the side of

THE QUIRINAL HILL,

enter the region where NEW ROME is rapidly springing into existence, on the high table-land, from which the promontories of the Quirinal, Viminal, and Esquiline project. This district has always been considered the healthiest portion of the city. In the days when ancient Rome had become a desert, and the modern city was restricted to the Campus Martius; when the inhabitants were compelled to drink the water of the Tiber, and even to purchase it from water carriers, who conveyed it to their houses; when it was even a luxury to the extent that Pius III., 1503, and Clement VII., 1523-34, when on their journeys to Loreto, Bologna, and as far as Marseilles, had a supply of it carried with them; the Quirinal Hill was a country suburb to the Rome of that day. We read how Bernardo Tasso, the father of the great Torquato, received the loan of a villa belonging to the Colonna, on the Quirinal, that he might have a pleasant place with good air, where to spend the summer with his children. Bartolommeo Carrari, in his life of Paul IV., 1555-59, says:—

"The Pope was in the habit of using the Caraffa Palace on the Quirinal, often going there to reside, and to enjoy the amenity of the place, and the salubrity of the air. At that time, the Pontiffs possessed no habitation on that Hill, and it was only after some years, when, taking into consideration that Cardinal Oliveri had selected the best site in Rome, they bought those edifices, and, with sumptuous magnificence, made them their residence."

On the site of these buildings Gregory XIII., 1572-85, founded

THE QUIRINAL PALACE,

employing the Lombard architect, *Flaminio Ponzio.* The work was continued by *Dominico Fontana*, under Sixtus V., 1585-90, and Clement VIII., 1592-1605. Paul V., 1605-21, increased the size of the Palace by building a splendid chapel, with a grand hall and noble suite of rooms, under the direction of *Carlo Maderno*, and, taking up his residence here on the 4th of January, 1614, commenced to date the Papal Bulls, *Apud S. M. Majorem*, in place of *Apud S. Marcum.* Urban VIII., 1623-45, isolated the building, and surrounded the gardens with a high wall, and Alexander VII., 1655-67, employed *Bernini* to erect that long wing extending in the direction of the Via Venti Settembre, called the *Manica lunga*, for the use of the Pontifical household. The building which forms this portion of the Palace was extended during the following pontificates, and finally completed, as we see it, by *Fuga*, in the time of Clement XII., 1730-40. It is this wing of the Quirinal Palace which for many years was, on the death of the Pope, set apart for the Conclave, and it was from the balcony above the chief entrance from the piazza, that the name of the newly-elected Pope was announced to the people. The Quirinal Palace was the favourite residence of Pius VII. Here he was taken prisoner by Napoleon I., here he died in 1823, and from here, in 1849, Pius IX. made his escape to Gaeta. It is now the Royal Palace of the King of Italy, but is chiefly inhabited by the Prince and Princess of Piedmont—Prince Humbert and the Princess Margherita—to whom are deputed the duties of presiding over the regal hospitalities in Rome. The State Rooms, except on very rare occasions, can always be seen, and also the private apartments of the Prince and Princess, when they are absent from Rome.

Traversing the portico, by the side of the great courtyard, which measures 303 feet in length by 162 in width, we ascend the grand staircase, and enter

The Sala Regia,

150 feet in length, built by Paul V. The vault is covered with frescoes by *Lanfranco* and *Carlo Saraceni.* Along the frieze, the arms of the cities of Italy have recently been painted. At one end of the hall is a painting of Frances de Valois and Maria Giovanni Battista, the two wives of Charles Emanuel II. of Savoy, on horseback, by *De'fino.* On the wall facing the windows are two pictures, one from Dante's Inferno, the other of the Lombard League, by *Arienti.* Over the door leading into the Pauline Chapel is a fine alto-relief, with figures the size of life, of our Saviour washing the feet of the Apostles, by *Taddeo Landini.*

The Pauline Chapel,

built by *Carlo Maderno,* for Paul V., from whom it takes its name. It was in this chapel that the election of the Popes chosen in the Quirinal was completed. The Cardinal chosen being asked by the Cardinal Deacon if he accepted the Pontifical dignity, and replying in the affirmative, he was invited to declare his name, in accordance with the usage established by Sergius IV., 1009-12, that " the Pontiff elected shall leave his baptismal name and assume another." Having been invested with the Pontifical robes, by the two senior Cardinals, he gave from the altar his first benediction to the Cardinals present, and then seating himself upon the Pontifical throne—which stood on the daïs to the left—received the homage of the members of the Sacred College, in the manner directed by the ceremonial, as follows:—" One at a time the Cardinals shall leave their places, and kneeling before the Pontiff kiss his right foot and hand, then rising on their feet shall give him the kiss on both cheeks, which is called the *osculum pacis.*" He then received the fisherman's ring from the Cardinal Chamberlain, and his permission was asked that his election might be announced to the people. On the eve of the taking of Rome, by the Italian army, on the 20th September, 1870, this chapel was formally deconsecrated. On the walls are now hung some fine Gobelin tapestries, recently brought from Florence—Our Saviour driving out the Money Changers ; The Last Supper; Our Saviour washing the Apostles' feet; The Miraculous Draught of Fishes; The Stoning of St. Stephen. Turning to the left, on leaving the chapel, we enter a series of ante-rooms leading to the state apartments.

First Ante-room.

The paintings are—David and Goliath, *Guercino.*
The Triumph of David, *Guercino.*
David going forth against Goliath, *Guercino.*

Second Ante-room.

Tapestry representing the Massacre of St. Bartholomew.

Third Ante-room.

Tapestry representing the Death of Leonardi da Vinci.

Fourth Ante-room.

Hung with blue damask. Facing the window, a picture of The Martyrdom of the forty Jesuits at Japan.

Fifth Ante-room.

Hung with green damask. Facing the window, a picture of The Power of Love, by *Cav. di Vivo.*

Sixth Ante-room.

Hung with crimson damask. Facing the window, are pictures of Raphael and the Fornarina in his Studio, and of Pia de Tolomei, by *Carlo Saltelli.* The window of this room opens on the balcony from which the name of the newly elected Pope was announced to the multitude in the piazza below. Having received the permission of the Pontiff the eldest Cardinal Deacon, preceded by the cross, and accompanied by the Master of the Ceremonies, proceeded to this window, and having broken down the wall built to close it during the sitting of the Conclave, passed out upon the balcony and in a loud voice proclaimed the election in the following words :—

" *Annuncio vobis gaudium magnum : habemus. Papam eminentissimum et reverendissimum Dominum.* * * * * *qui sibi nomen imposuit* * * * *.*"

Seventh Ante-room,

Hung with blue damask Facing the window is a picture of St. John the Baptist by *Giulio Romano.*

The State Drawing Room.

The walls are hung and the gilt furniture entirely covered with gold coloured damask. From the ceiling hang two magnificent Venetian chandeliers of blown glass, with coloured flowers in the cinquecento style, from the *Salviati* manufactory at Venice. Around the walls are six Chinese vases.

The Throne Room.

The walls are hung with dark crimson damask and the canopy with crimson velvet. Around the room are eight magnificent Chinese vases, six surmounted with chandeliers, and two enormous lustres hang from the ceiling. Opposite the throne is a portrait of Charles Albert, King of Sardinia, the father of Victor Emanuel, by *Capisani.*

The Ambassadors' Waiting Room.

The walls are hung with blue damask. On the left, opposite the mirror, is a beautiful Sevres vase, and on the right two large Chinese vases, between which are portrait busts, of the King Victor Emanuel by *Albertoni,* and of the Princess Margherita, executed in 1869, by *Fantacchiotti.* From the ceiling hang two magnificent *Salviati* chandeliers. From this room we pass into

PRINCE HUMBERT'S PRIVATE APARTMENTS.

FIRST ROOM.

Small square room with vaulted ceiling. The walls hung, and the gilt furniture covered, with blue silk.

SECOND ROOM.

Gilt furniture covered with pearl-coloured damask. Opposite the windows is a portrait of Queen Maria Adelaide, wife of Victor Emanuel and mother of Prince Humbert, and opposite to it a portrait of Queen Maria Teresa, the wife of Charles Albert and grandmother of Prince Humbert. This used to be the Pope's bedroom.

A PASSAGE, hung and furnished with red striped material, leads to

PRINCE HUMBERT'S BEDROOM.

The walls are hung with blue damask with a yellow pattern, and the furniture and bed of carved walnut furnished with the same material. Over the head of the bed is a painting of the Madonna and Child, by *Domenichino*.

PRINCE HUMBERT'S RECEPTION ROOM.

Entirely furnished with green and gold coloured silk damask. On the large settee in the centre is a beautiful Chinese Vase, and on the walls two fine interiors of Spanish Cathedrals, by *Fayola*. From this room we enter the PRIVATE APARTMENTS OF THE PRINCESS MARGHERITA, commencing with

THE PRINCESS'S BEDROOM.

Most charmingly hung with tapestries of great beauty, illustrating the story of Don Quixote, formerly in the Palazzo Reale at Caserta. The bed is furnished with white figured damask.

The next room is THE BATH ROOM, from which, turning to the left, we pass through a double room, or rather two rooms thrown into one, to form THE PRINCESS'S LIBRARY—the walls of one portion of which are covered with stamped leather—and thence into

THE PRINCESS'S MUSIC ROOM,

One side of which is entirely lined with plate glass, held by most delicately carved frames, gilt, and on three sides windows opening to the ground, command a most magnificent panoramic view of Rome, a finer view even than that seen from the Janiculum. The walls are hung with tapestries from the Palazzo Reale of Caserta, *en suite* with those in the bedroom, the subjects being the continuation of the history of Don Quixote. The cradle, in the form of a silver shell, supported by a dolphin, with cherubs' heads around the bed, was presented to the Princess, for the birth of the Prince of Naples, by 40,000 children of the National Schools of the different cities of Italy. The ceiling has been recently painted in fresco by *Barilli*.

Repassing through the further side of the Library, we enter

The Princess's Workroom.

Hung and furnished with rich satin damask, white flowers on a crimson ground. The recesses of the windows are lined with looking glass, with seven charming little gilt baskets on each side for bouquets of flowers, and on the walls of the room, are a number of flower baskets. Between the windows, is a beautiful gilt and painted cabinet inlaid with crystal, and opposite, to the left of the fireplace, another cabinet ornamented with *ormolu* and porcelain panels, painted with baskets of flowers. At the right of the fireplace, and ends of the room, are etageres with the Princess's painting materials, and well-filled book cases, in which are many English works. By the side of the fire is a beautiful screen, and about the room are arranged little Japan work tables, luxurious arm chairs, and charming little settees, marvels of upholstery; and finally a sewing machine.

The Princess's Private Drawing Room.

Hung and furnished with beautiful blue flowered satin. By the fireplace are luxurious sofas, arm chairs, and a beautiful Japanese screen; and about the room, which like all those used by the Princess, has, notwithstanding its splendour, a thoroughly home-look, are a number of small tables and dwarf settees. On the right wall is a life-size portrait of Victor Emanuel, and below it in an oval frame a portrait of the Prince of Naples, of whom also there is another portrait on an easel.

The bas relief around the walls immediately below the ceiling is the Triumph of Alexander, by Thorwaldsen.

Passing through a kind of Ante-room, the walls of which are covered with stamped leather held by steel bosses, we enter the Princess's State Drawing Room; but first may turn into a large room to the right, where a number of very beautiful birds, of which the Princess is very fond, are generally kept.

The Princess's State Drawing Room.

Most sumptuously furnished throughout with satin of the Princess's favourite colour, a delicate pearl grey, with the exception of a few dwarf settees and light gilt chairs, covered with red silk damask shot with gold. In one corner is a large gold easel frame, containing a number of family miniatures, and towards the further end of the room a group in marble of Ino and Bacchus by *Benzoni*.

Cabinet,

Entirely hung with tapestries, the subjects from Don Quixote, *en suite* with those in the Bedroom and Music-room, and the gilt furniture covered with tapestry of birds and animals.

The Princess's Ladies' Waiting Room.

Hung and furnished with red damask. On one side is a marble statue of The Rebel Angel, by *Tabacchi*, 1870, and on the wall facing the window life-size portraits on horseback of Charles Emanuel II. of Savoy, and his wife Maria, by *Delfino*.

We then pass into the suite used for the state dinners.

LARGE ANTE-ROOM,

Used by the Prince and Princess as their private dining room. Hung with yellow damask, and having on one of the walls a very fine full length portrait of the Princess. This room is used for dancing during the Carnival balls.

From this room we turn to the left, into a small PRIVATE CHAPEL, in which there is a fine Annunciation, by *Guido.*

SECOND ANTE-ROOM,

Hung with tapestry. This is used as the supper room during the Carnival balls. From the windows there is a view of the Labyrinth.

STATE DINING ROOM.

This room has been newly decorated and the vault painted in fresco —the rising of the Star of Italy—by *Barilli.* Three magnificent lustres hang from the ceiling. From the windows there is a good view of the gardens of the Quirinal.

We then pass into a long

CORRIDOR,

by which we return to the Sala Regia. It contains a number of modern pieces of sculpture of no great merit, vases, tazze, carved cabinets, and some pretty pieces of tapestry, from the Pitti Palace at Florence.

MONTE CAVALLO.

The Piazza in front of the Quirinal Palace has received this name from the two magnificent groups of a man and a horse, called Castor and Pollux, which ornament the fountain. They were found among the ruins of the Baths of Constantine, which occupied this spot, and were first placed to ornament the Piazza by Sixtus V., 1585-90. According to tradition they stood in front of the Atrium of Nero's golden house, and are said to be the works of *Phidias* and *Praxiteles.* This may possibly have been derived from some inscription found at the time they were discovered, for there can be no doubt they are works of the Phidian epoch of art, in so far as being ancient copies in marble from bronze originals would constitute them. All persons with any knowledge of horses will at once perceive that the men and horses have been transposed; that the horse on the right pedestal belongs to the man on the left, and *vice versa*. In the time of Sixtus V. they stood in their proper positions, but were changed by *Antinori* in 1786, when he erected the Obelisk, and arranged them as we see, notwithstanding many petitions to the contrary presented to the Pope, Pius VI. On the morning after the change was made, a pasquinade bearing the words OPVS . PERFIDIAE . PII . SEXTI . was found pasted over the title OPVS PHIDIAE on the pedestal to the left.

The bason of the fountain is antique, of red granite, and measures 76 feet in circumference. It was found in the 16th century among the ruins of the Forum, near the arch of Septimius Severus, and was placed here to serve its present use by Pius VII., in 1818. The Obelisk, which measures 45 feet in height without the base, originally stood on one side of the entrance to the Mausoleum of Augustus; that now before the Tribune of S. Maria Maggiore standing on the other. They were brought to Rome by Claudius, A.D. 57.

On the left, as we look towards the Fountain, is the PALACE OF THE CONSULTA, now the MINISTRY OF FOREIGN AFFAIRS, numbered 63, built by *Ferdinano Fuga*, in the time of Clement XII., 1730-40.

A little further on the left, a long blank wall, with a gateway numbered 65, and a number of small square walled-up windows, encloses

THE ROSPIGLIOSI PALACE,

founded by *Flaminio Ponzi* for Cardinal Scipio Borghese, in 1603, on the ruins of the Baths of Constantine. It afterwards passed into the possession successively, of the Duke d' Altemps, of Cardinal Bentivoglio, and of Cardinal Mazzarin, and was increased in size by each from the de-
R

signs of *Carlo Maderno.*	The interior of the Palace is not shown to visitors, but the Casino, which contains the celebrated AURORA BY GUIDO, and a small collection of pictures, is open to the public on Wednesdays and Saturdays.

FIRST ROOM.

Frescoes on the ceiling.
THE AURORA: *Guido.*
The Triumph of Fame, *frieze on the left: Tempesta.*
The Triumph of Love, *frieze on the right: Tempesta.*
Four Landscapes: *Paul Brill.*

Paintings on the right wall.
The Virgin and Child: *School of Leonardo da Vinci.*
Portrait of a Man: *Vandyke.*

Pass to the right into

Sea Piece: *Salvator Rosa.*
At the right corner.
VANITY: *Titian.*

Facing the windows.
Some fragments of fresco paintings from the Baths of Constantine, on the remains of which the Palace stands.
The remainder of the paintings in this room are not worthy of mention.

THE SECOND ROOM.

The Paintings have no numbers affixed to them, but numbers, as given below, have lately been marked with white chalk on the wall against each. The principal works will be found in the following order:
Turn to the right.
1. Lot and his Daughters: *Annibale Caracci.*
2. SAMSON pulling down the pillars upon the Philistines: *Ludovico Caracci.*
6. Soldiers sacking a house: *unknown.*

Cross the first room to

7. *Idem: unknown.*
8. Venus and Cupid: *unknown.*
9. Martyrdom of St. Bartholomew: *Spagnoletto.*
13. THE TERRESTRIAL PARADISE, the fall of Adam and Eve: *Domenichino.*
19. Diana chasing Venus and Cupid: *Lorenzo Lotti.*
20. The death of Peter Martyr: *unknown.*
A horse in bronze, in the middle of the room.

THE THIRD ROOM.

Pass to the left.
44. PERSEUS DELIVERING ANDROMEDA: *Guido.*
43. Head of an old man.
42. The Genius of Abundance.
41. Portrait of *Nicholas Poussin* at the age of 56, by himself.
31. Our Saviour carrying his Cross: *Rubens.*

32. Our Saviour meeting his mother on the way to Calvary: *Daniele da Volterra.*
23. THE TRIUMPH OF DAVID: *Domenichino.*
12. Adam and Eve: *Palma.*
2. Head of an old man.
3. Poppea, second wife of Nero: *Florentine School.*
48. A Pietà: *Annibale Caracci.*

Opposite to the Rospigliosi Palace is the GARDEN GATE OF THE COLONNA PALACE, No. 12, *described, page* 108, into which admittance can generally be obtained by ringing the bell. On the upper terrace, to the left, are some COLOSSAL ARCHITECTURAL FRAGMENTS of white marble, of stupendous size; conjectured to have belonged to THE TEMPLE OF THE SUN, erected by Aurelian, on the Quirinal. The largest measures no less than 1490 cubic feet; giving an estimated weight of more than 100 tons. At the other extremity of the terrace are some extensive remains of THE BATHS OF CONSTANTINE, built A.D. 326, now converted into hay lofts. The lower terraces of the garden, as they slope down to the Palace, are exceedingly quaint and picturesque. Along the walks are some interesting antique Sarcophagi.

Returning past the Palace of the Consulta, and proceeding along the Via del Quirinale, we come, on the right, to the pretty little oval CHURCH OF S. ANDREA A MONTE CAVALLO, built by *Bernini*, at the expense of Prince Camillo Pamfili, nephew of Innocent X. The picture of the Martyrdom of St. Andrew, above the high altar, is by *Guglielmo Courtoys*, brother of the celebrated Borgognone. In the Chapel, to the left, is the monument, by *Festa*, of Charles Emanuel IV., King of Sardinia, who abdicated in 1802, entered the Jesuit order, and died in the adjoining convent in 1819.

Continuing onwards, we come to THE QUATTRO FONTANE, the four fountains, one at each corner where the streets cross, which lead from the Quirinal to the Porta Pia, in a direct line before us, and from the Pincean Hill, on the left, to the Basilica of Santa Maria Maggiore, on the right.

At the right hand corner is the Church of ST. CARLO ALLE QUATTRO FONTANE, built, together with the adjoining convent, by *Boromini*, in 1667; it was the first work which brought him into notice.

At the further corner is the ALBANI PALACE, built by *Domenico Fontana* for Cardinal Mattei, from whom it passed into the possession of the Albani family. It was purchased a few years ago by the ex-Queen Isabella of Spain. The Turkish Ambassador now occupies a portion of it.

Descending the hill to the left, we come, on the right, to

THE BARBERINI PALACE,

commenced for Urban VIII., 1623-44, by *Carlo Maderno*, and finished by *Bernini* in 1640. This palace, which is one of the largest in Rome, is almost entirely built of travertine taken from the Colosseum. Entering the door, on the right of the Portico, above which are the words AEDES BARBERINAE, we ascend the corkscrew staircase to the first door in the wall, which is that of

THE PICTURE GALLERY.

It contains a comparatively insignificant collection, arranged in three small rooms, but worth visiting on account of the celebrated portrait of *Beatrice Cenci*, by Guido, said to have been painted in the prison, the day before her execution.

FIRST ROOM.

4. The Annunciation: *School of Correggio.*
9. A Pietà: *Michael Angelo da Caravaggio.*
10. Sophonisba: *Guercino.*
11. The Apotheosis of St. Urban: *Simon Vouet.*
15. The Magdalen: *Pomarancio.*
16. Joseph and Potiphar's wife: *Bilivert.*
21. St. Cecilia: *Lanfranco.*
25. Jacob wrestling with the Angel: *Pomarancio.*

SECOND ROOM.

30. Holy Family: *School of Raphael.*
33. Portrait of Urban VIII.: *Andrea Sacchi.*
38. Our Saviour in the Garden; *Correggio.*
44. The building of the Temple; *Bonfonti.*
47. Diana and Actæon: *Locatelli.*
48. Madonna and Child, with John the Baptist and St. Jerome: *Francia.*
54. Madonna and Child: *Sodoma.*
57. Holy Family: *School of Raphael.*

58. Madonna & Child: *Giovanni Bellini.*
63. Portrait of his daughter: *Raphael Mengs.*
67. Portrait of *Massaccio*, by himself.
Three bas reliefs cast in iron at Berlin.
69. The Last Supper, *after Leonardo da Vinci.*
70. Our Saviour blessing the Cup, *after Domenichino.*
71. St. John the Evangelist, *after Domenichino.*

THIRD ROOM.

72. A SLAVE: *Titian.*
74. The Almighty reproving Adam and Eve: *Domenichino*
76. View of Castle Gandolfo, and the Lake of Albano: *Claude Lorrain.*
79. Our Saviour disputing with the Doctors: *Albert Durer.*
81. Portrait of the Mother of Beatrice Cenci: *Michael Angelo da Caravaggio.*
82. THE FORNARINA: *Raphael.*

83. Portrait of Lucretia Cenci, step-mother of Beatrice: *Scipio Gaetani.*
85. BEATRICE CENCI: *Guido.*
86. The death of Germanicus: *Nicholas Poussin.*
88. A Sea piece: *Claude Lorrain.*
90. Holy Family: *Andrea del Sarto.*
93. The Annunciation: *Botticelli.*
94. Attack on the Palazzo Vecchio at Florence: *Canaletti.*

Continuing up the corkscrew staircase we reach THE GRAND HALL, leading into the state apartments. It is worth going up to see on account of its great size and of the frescoes by *Pietro da Cortona*, with which the five compartments of the vault are decorated.

THE LIBRARY,

open on Thursdays, is one of the largest in Rome, and is particularly rich in manuscripts and rare editions. It was formed by Cardinal Francisco Barberini, nephew of Urban VIII., and contains about 10,000 manuscripts and 60,000 printed volumes.

At the bottom of the hill we enter THE PIAZZA BARBERINI, and crossing diagonally to the further side, where the smaller PIAZZI DEI CAPPUCCINI opens from it, we see at the summit of the ascent, on the left, THE CHURCH OF STA. MARIA DELLA CONCEZIONE, commonly called

THE CHURCH OF THE CAPPUCCINI,

from the Capuchin monks—*Franciscans*—who inhabit the adjoining convent. It is chiefly celebrated for the beautiful picture of ST. MICHAEL triumphing over Satan, by *Guido*, in the first chapel on the right ; and for THE CEMETERY connected with the Church, in which the monks, until **very** recently, were buried, and where the bones of some six thousands, accumulated during two hundred and fifty years, are piled up in all kinds of quaintly horrible designs against the walls. The earth, it is said, was brought from Jerusalem and has a peculiarly drying tendency. The graves are forty in number : the bodies were placed in the bare ground, and when the whole was filled and more room was required, the bodies longest buried were disinterred in rotation, and piled up with the others; or if, as often occurred, the fleshly portions had dried up, the mummy was dressed in the monkish attire it had worn through life, and placed in a niche composed of the bones of his dead companions.

The Church and Convent were built in 1624, by *Antonio Casoni*, and *Michele*, one of the monks, at the expense of the brother of Urban VIII., Cardinal Antonio Barberini, who belonged to this order, and whose sepulchral slab, bearing nothing but the words, HIC . JACET . PVLVIS . CINIS . ET . NIHIL., lies in front of the altar.

The entrance to the Cemetery is from the courtyard, to

the right of the Church; but, to obtain admittance, application must be made to one of the monks in the Church; or, if it is shut, at the Convent door, to the left.

From the Piazza Barberini, we proceed along the Via San Niccola da Tolentino, at the back of THE FOUNTAIN—*See page 35*—and pass, on the right, the CHURCH OF SAN NICCOLA DA TOLENTINO, built in 1614, at the expense of the Pamphili family. The façade was designed by *Battista Baratta;* and the high altar, by *Allessandro Algardi.*

At the end of the Via San Niccola da Tolentino, on the left, are the Gardens of THE MASSIMO, which occupy the site of THE CIRCUS AND GARDENS OF SALLUST.

Turning to the left, up the Via Sta. Susanna, we find at the left corner THE CHURCH OF STA. MARIA DELLA VITTORIA.

In 1605, a small Church, dedicated to St. Paul, was built here, by Paul V., for the barefooted Carmelites of the adjoining monastery; but, in 1621, it was thrown down to give place to the present edifice, of larger size, and more sumptuous decoration, erected in honour of a wooden image of the Virgin, carried before the Imperial army in the battle of the White Mountain, near Prague, and to the miraculous powers of which the victory over the Protestant troops of Frederick and Elizabeth of Bohemia was attributed.

At the request of the Duke of Bavaria, Paul V. sent Padre Domenico, a celebrated preacher of that day, to join the army. He found, among a quantity of lumber, in the Castle of Straconitz, a battered old image of the Virgin, without eyes. Carrying it among the troops he exhibited the injuries it had received, and attributing them to the Protestants, exhorted the soldiers in powerful language to revenge the sacrilege perpetrated upon "the Mother of God," and carried it in the battle as a rallying point. After the victory it was conveyed to Rome, and on the way, was exhibited processionally at all the places of importance through which it passed. Valuable presents and offerings were collected everywhere to a large amount; the Emperor presented it with an Imperial crown of solid gold, set with gems of great price; the Duke of Bavaria gave it a grand tabernacle, 7 feet 6in. in height, of ebony, ornamented with silver and silver bas reliefs;* the Archduke Leopold, a valuable silver lamp; the Infanta of Spain sent rich ornaments for an altar ; and the Elector of Cologne and Duke William of Bavaria gave reliquaries full of the relics of Saints, whose names form a long list, including six of the Apostles; presents of great value were given by the Grand Dukes of Florence and Mantua, the Duke of Bracciano, the Duchess Doria, and many others; and the humble little Church of St. Paul was rebuilt as we see it, to commemorate the triumphs of Rome over Protestantism, and dedicated to St. Mary of the Victory, as personified in this image. Until recently a number of the tattered flags taken in the battle were hanging from the cornice, together with many others afterwards captured in the religious wars in the Netherlands.

In digging the foundations, the beautiful statue of an Hermaphrodite, now in the Louvre, was discovered, and purchased by Cardinal Scipio Borghese at the expense of building the façade. The interior of the Church was built from the designs of *Carlo Maderno*, and the façade from those of *Gio. Battesta Soria*.

In the second chapel on the right, the picture of the

---

* The wooden image of the Virgin was placed in this tabernacle on the high altar, where both, together with all the other embellishments of the altar, were destroyed by fire on the night of the 29th March, 1833.

Virgin and St. Francis, over the altar, and the paintings on the walls, are by *Domenichino.*

In the third chapel, on the left, the Trinity over the altar is by *Guercino;* the portrait of Cardinal Cornaro, on the right, is by *Guido.* The Crucifixion, on the left, is a copy from a picture by *Guido,* now in the Duke of Northumberland's collection.

Above the altar of the Chapel of Sta. Teresa, in the left transept, is one of Bernini's most famous works, representing the ECSTASY OF STA. TERESA, a group characterised by all the worst exaggerations into which an exuberant and scenic style led that great genius, and, by an obvious "fault more serious than even a bad style." The heads in bas relief, curiously arranged in balconies on each side as if they were looking on, are portraits of Cardinals of the great Cornari family of Venice.

The group above the altar, in the opposite transept, represents St. Joseph sleeping, and the Angel telling him not to put Mary away, by *Domenico Guidi.* The bas reliefs, that on the left, of the Birth of Christ, and on the right, of the Flight into Egypt, were sculptured by *Monot.*

The high altar is undergoing restoration.

Opposite to this Church is the side of the FOUNTAIN OF THE AQUA FELICE (*see page* 34), and a few steps on the right is the CHURCH OF SANTA SUSANNA, the niece of Pope Caius, 283-96, and grand-niece of the Emperor Diocletian, by whose order she suffered martyrdom, for having refused, being a Christian, to marry his adopted son Maximianus Galerius. The Church was founded at an early period on the site of the house of her father Gabinus, who had built an oratory within it for Christian use. The first positive record of the Church dates from the year 499. It was restored at various periods, and was finally rebuilt, as we see it, by *Carlo Maderno* in 1603.　Around the walls are indifferent frescoes, by *Baldassare Croce*, illustrating the story of Susanna and the Elders.　Crossing the road we enter THE CHURCH OF SAN BERNARDO, and with it, commence our examination of what remains of

THE BATHS OF DIOCLETIAN,

the largest of the great Roman Thermæ.　The remains, in point of fact, are very extensive, but they have been so changed by conversion to modern uses, churches, prisons, hospitals, hay-lofts, barracks, and even railway offices, that it is not easy for the stranger to understand them as a whole; though as regards details, this transformation has had the result of preserving portions sufficiently entire, for us to appreciate the original construction much better than is possible among the ruins of the Baths of Caracalla, notwithstanding the alterations made to adapt these to the purpose they now serve.

These Baths, which covered an area measuring 1300 feet by 1200, remained entirely abandoned until after the commencement of the sixteenth century, when *Palladio* made an exact plan of the remains.　In 1535 they were bought by Bellay, the Ambassador of Francis I. of France, who had just been made a Cardinal, and a considerable portion of the ruins were converted by him into a Villa, and called the *Horti Belleani*.　Leaving, at his death, an enormous amount of debts, his property was divided among his creditors, and this, valued at 8,000 scudi, was allotted to St. Carlo Borromeo, who was one of the largest, and from whom it was redeemed at the expense of the Papal treasury, by his uncle Pius IV., 1559-66.

This circular building in which we are standing formed originally one corner of the outer range of edifices, enclosing the Baths and the open area around them, and was converted in 1600 into a Church dedicated to St. Bernard, without any change being made in the construction of the interior, beyond the formation of the recess for the high altar. We see the domed roof as it was originally built; the sunk panels with which it was ornamented; the single opening in the summit by which the room was lighted, and the niches in the wall once filled with statues of pagan gods or heroes, now replaced by Christian saints, the work of *Camillo Mariani*. The paintings over the lateral altars are works of very considerable merit by the little known painter *Giovanni Orlasi* (died 1731).

Turning, on leaving the Church, to the left along the Via Torino, and again to the left, on reaching the Via Nazionale, we enter a large semicircular area. It is bounded by a ruined wall, the outer wall of the great open air theatre in the outer range, from the seats of which, the spectators could witness the games given on the Stadium, that is to say in the enormous area intervening between where we are standing, and the great central edifice of the Baths directly before us. This central edifice has, on the right, where we recognise ruins, been converted into hay-lofts and a barrack; in the middle, into a Church dedicated to SANTA MARIA DEGLI ANGELI; and on the left into an Orphan Asylum. If, before crossing over to the Church, we turn back through the opening made for the Via Nazionale in the semicircular wall, and continuing to the left, along the remainder of the Via Torino, turn again to the left at the end, we shall come to another circular edifice, now converted into a Prison, which formed the corner at this side of the square of the outer range of the Thermæ, and corresponds exactly, in form and size, to the Church of St. Bernard. In fact these two circular buildings form the extremities of one line of the outer square, with the open air theatre in the middle.

From this point we can diagonally cross the Public Garden, with the FOUNTAIN OF THE AQUA MARCIA (*see page* 33) in the centre, to

THE CHURCH OF STA. MARIA DEGLI ANGELI.

This portion of the Baths of Diocletian was converted into a Church by *Michael Angelo* for Pius IV., 1555-59.

It was originally, as regards the main central portion of the Church, the great Tepidarium, the warm water bath, and in contemplating this magnificent hall, we can form some idea of the magnitude of these enormous establishments, when we take into consideration that it constituted rather less than one ninth part of the great central edifice of the Thermæ. In form a Greek cross, its limits are exactly marked by the sixteen columns, eight of which are monolyths of Egyptian granite, standing where they were originally placed,* while the others are brick columns, built to supply the place of those which had fallen, or more probably, been removed anterior to the sixteenth century. The length along the nave and across the transepts is 150 feet each way within the columns, and the height from the present floor to the ceiling is 96 feet.

At the end of the right transept—but beyond what was the great Tepidarium—which was limited to the Greek

---

* These columns, which are 16 feet in diameter, and measure 46 feet in height, including the capitals, and the bases as we see them, are in reality about eight feet longer than they appear. In altering the place into a church, it was found necessary to raise the floor, and the lower portion of the columns are buried to that depth, rings of marble—sham bases—having been fitted on to them at the floor. As there was a difficulty in painting the brick columns to imitate the red granite, a later architect *Vanvitelli*, daubed them all a dirty brown to make them match each other.

cross within the columns—is the Chapel of the Beato Niccolo Albergati, to which a beautiful pavement has been newly laid, by order of Pius IX., of marbles found at the ancient Marmorata, discovered on the left bank of the Tiber, in 1867.

The Church, as originally constructed by *Michael Angelo*, had its chief entrance here, and what are now the transepts, then formed the nave ; and, opening from it, were four large chapels, two on each side, constructed out of the warm water plunge baths on the sides of the Tepidarium, arranged in exactly the same manner we see at the Baths of Caracalla. In 1749, this arrangement was changed, in order to place the Chapel of the Beato Albergati here, which might easily have been situated in some other part of the Church. The handsome façade of travertine, built by Michael Angelo— one of his last works—was thrown down and destroyed; the side chapels were walled up; and the entrance, to which no façade has yet been built, changed to where it is now.

We enter through a circular chamber, converted into a kind of vestibule, which originally separated the great Calidarium—now destroyed—from the Tepidarium, and was, probably, also used for the hot-air bath. Immediately within the door, as we enter, are the monuments of the two celebrated painters, Salvator Rosa and Carlo Maratta, one on each side. On the right, as we pass from this vestibule into the body of the Church, is the celebrated Statue of St. Bruno, by *Houdon*. On the walls of the Church are a number of pictures of uniform size, originally in St. Peter's; but which, as they have gradually been replaced by mosaics, have been brought here. Four of these, on the walls within the altar, are especially worthy of observation. On the right, the presentation of the Virgin in the Temple, by *Romanelli,* and THE MARTYRDOM OF ST. SEBASTIAN, fresco, by *Domenichino;* and, on the left, The Death of Ananias, by *Pomarancio,* and The Baptism of Our Saviour, by *Carlo Maratta.* The meridian line traversing the floor, and on which a little spot of light shows the position of the sun each day at noon, was laid down by the learned Monsignore Bianchini, by order of Clement XI., in 1703.

The Villa, now called the Villa Negroni, at the further corner of the Piazza, to the left as we leave the Church, was built by *Domenia Fontana,* for Sixtus V., 1585-90, who occupied it anterior to his elevation to the Papal chair.

Passing this villa on the left, we continue along the VIA VIMINALE. THE VILLA STROZZI, on the right side, was the residence of the great poet ALFIERI, as recorded by a tablet recently placed upon the wall. At the end of the Via Viminale we turn to the left and see before us THE BASILICA OF SANTA MARIA MAGGIORE (*see page* 258), and at a short distance on the right side of the first turning to the right we shall find THE CHURCH OF SANTA PUDENTIANA (*see page* 255).

FROM SANTA MARIA MAGGIORE TO SAN PIETRO IN VINCULI.*

The nearest way from the Piazza de Spagna to the Basilica of Santa Maria Maggiore is to ascend THE SCALINATA (*see page* 37), and turning to the right at the summit, we shall find that the further street—the first portion of which

---

* This section is entitled as commencing at Sta. Maria Maggiore, for the convenience of those who desire to continue onwards from the Baths of Diocletian, after which, it is the chief point of interest; but for those who desire to commence at Sta. Maria Maggiore, we have, taking the Piazza de Spagna as a central starting point, indicated first, the objects of lesser interest passed on the way.

is called The Via Felice—leads in a direct line to the Basilica.

The Church at the top of the steps is The Trinita de' Monti (*see page* 37).

The house adjoining the Church was inhabited for forty years by the celebrated painter, Nicholas Poussin. In that, with a small semicircular portico, No. 9, at the angle where the Vias Felice and Gregoriana open into the Piazza, Claude Lorrain resided; and the first house of the Via Felice, on the right, No. 64, was built and occupied by the Zuccari. Some of the rooms on the ground floor have paintings in fresco by Federico Zuccari, and the walls of a small room on the second floor are covered with frescoes, illustrating the history of Joseph, by *Overbeck, Cornelius, Schadow,* and *Veit,* painted, when young men together, they were commencing their careers in Rome, and founding the modern school of German art.

Crossing the Piazza Barberini—in the little piazza from the left side of which is The Church of the Cappuchini, called *Sta. Maria della Concezione,* and their curious Cemetery (*see page* 246)—we ascend the Via delle Quattro Fontane, passing, on the left, the Barberini Palace (*see page* 244).

Descending in a direct line from the further side of the Quattro Fontane, we reach the foot of the rise of the Esquiline, on which the Basilica of Sta. Maria Maggiore stands, but before ascending to it, let us turn to the right, into the Via di Santa Pudentiana, which in ancient times was the *Vicus Patricius,* and a few steps will bring us to

THE CHURCH OF SANTA PUDENTIANA.

This Church stands on the site of one of those private

houses—celebrated in early Christian history, and rendered sacred through the memories attached to them—in which the first converts to the Faith assembled together in secret during the years of persecution, to offer up their united worship to God. Here stood THE HOUSE OF PUDENS, the wealthy senator, the friend of St. Paul, and whose name, together with that of his wife Claudia,* is mentioned by St. Paul in his second epistle to Timothy, iv. 21.

It was a palace of great extent, and within that portion, where NOVATUS, the son of Pudens, added baths to the other luxurious accommodation it afforded, Pius I., 142-57, at the request of PRASSEDE, the surviving daughter of Pudens, consecrated the first Christian Church, known as such, and dedicated it to her martyred sister PUDENTIANA.

This primitive Church gave place, between the years 772 and 795, to another, built on a higher level, by Adrian I., the apse of which was ornamented with the beautiful mosaic we see by Adrian III., 884-85.   The Church was restored by Gregory VII., 1073-86, and by Innocent II., 1130-43, who erected the campanile, and finally it was to a great extent modernised by Cardinal Enrico Gaetani in 1597.   The fourteen columns of grey marble, which divided the aisles from the nave, can still be seen in the wall into which they have been incorporated, but, from the segment of the apse, which has been reduced in size—and the mosaic correspondingly injured—it is evident that the nave, as originally built by Adrian I., was much wider than the position of these columns would indicate.

The fresco by *Ciampelli*, on the left as we enter the Church, represents Pudenziana and Prassede, collecting the

---

* Claudia was the daughter of the British King Caractacus.

blood of the martyrs; and, in the left aisle, is a low rectangular wall covered by an iron grating, in which the sisters are said to have deposited the relics and blood of more than 3000.

The handsome chapel close to this, originally called the Chapel of St. Pastor, was rebuilt by *Francesco da Volterra* in 1597, for the Cardinal titular, Enrico Gaetani, who converted it into his family chapel. Several of the " Hats" of late Cardinals titular are hanging from the roof. The bas relief over the altar represents the Adoration of the Magi, by *Paolo Olivieri;* and on the steps is a mark which, according to "a pious belief," was made by the Host falling bleeding from the hands of a priest who doubted the bodily presence.

Above the altar of the long Chapel, to the left of the tribune, is a group representing Our Saviour delivering the keys to Peter, by *Gio. Battista della Porta,* and on the left wall are some Christian inscriptions relating to members of the Pudentiani family, found in the catacombs of Santa Priscilla, and which have been recently removed here from the Lateran Museum.

The frescoes in the modern dome above the high altar were painted by *Pomarancio.*

Originally an ascent of ten steps led up to the Church : now we have to descend by two flights, recently constructed by the actual Titular, Cardinal Buonaparte, at whose expense also the façade has been decorated with painting in imitation of mosaic. The first " Titular" of St. Pudentiana was St. Pastor, brother of Pius I.; the last was Cardinal Wiseman.

Behind the Church, and beneath it, are remains of THE

s

HOUSE OF PUDENS,* in which, according to the historians of the Roman Church, St. Peter lived for seven years, during which he converted and baptised Pudens and his family, administered the affairs of the Church, and sent out many missionaries, who are mentioned by name, to preach the Gospel to the Gentiles. Among these he sent Aristobulus, one of the seventy-two disciples of Our Lord, to Britain. St. Paul, who especially names both Pudens and his wife in his second epistle to Timothy, is only incidentally mentioned.

Ascending the rise of the Esquiline—which has recently been lessened by partly filling up the valley, and raising the street in front of Sta. Pudentiana—we approach

THE BASILICA OF SANTA MARIA MAGGIORE,

passing on the way the small OBELISK, erected by Sixtus V. in 1587. It originally stood in front of the Mausoleum of Augustus, together with that, now above the fountain, on Monte Cavallo.

This Basilica, founded in the year 352, was the first Church dedicated to the Virgin Mary in Rome. It was first entitled *Sancta Maria ad Nives*, from the circumstance which led to its erection, and the *Basilica Liberiana*, a name it still retains, from its founder, Pope Liberius. It next received the name of *Sta. Maria del Presepio*, from what is said to be the Manger in which Our Lord was laid, preserved here. Next, it was called *The*

---

* A supposition has arisen that these remains were—like those of the house of Clement—entirely unknown until Cardinal Wiseman having, in "Fabiola," drawn particular attention to the Church, they were sought for and discovered by an English archæologist. This is entirely erroneous. The remains are mentioned by almost all the Italian archæologists from the fifteenth century to the present time, and some, in addition to written description, give plates of the portions, which until a comparatively recent period, were visible at the side of the Church. The claims to discovery asserted with so little foundation, aroused the indignation of the Ecclesiastical authorities, and prevented excavations which would doubtless have had most important results.

Basilica Sistina, from Pope Sixtus III., who rebuilt it; and lastly, *Santa Maria Maggiore*, from being the first Church dedicated to Mary.

The legends of the Church relate, that on the night of the 4th of August, 352, the Virgin miraculously appeared in a dream, simultaneously, to a certain Johannes Patti, a Roman patrician of great wealth—but who being childless was desirous of employing his money in good works—and to the Pope, Liberius, commanding them to found a Church, in her honour, where the highest point of the Esquiline would be found, the next morning, covered with snow. Imme_diately John arose he went to the Pope, and while communicating to him the dream, corresponding exactly to his own, word was brought that a remarkable event had happened on the Esquiline; part of it being thickly covered with snow. On this, Liberius, attended by his Court, and accompanied by John, repaired to the spot, and drawing the plan of the Basilica on the ground, the building was immediately commenced. This event is represented in a bronze bas relief above the altar in the Borghese Chapel where it is commemorated each year, on the 5th of August, by a solemn mass, during which a quantity of the leaves of a delicate white flower are scattered from the dome. Floating gently downwards they have all the appearance of snow flakes falling lightly on the vestments of the clergy, and at the conclusion of the service completely covering the floor of the Chapel.

The primitive Basilica, however, would seem to have been not very securely constructed, for seventy years later it was entirely rebuilt by Sixtus III., 432-40, as "a trophy against the Nestorian heresy," and dedicated by him to *Sta. Maria Mater Dei*, and to this period belong the mosaic in the arch of the tribune and the curious series of mosaic pictures, representing events taken from the Old and New Testaments, on the frieze above the columns. At the Council of Nicea these pictures were quoted as evidence in confutation of the Iconoclasts, and are spoken of at length in a letter written by Adrian I. to Charlemagne.

From the time of Sixtus III. to the present day, the form of the interior has undergone no material change, except in so far as through additional embellishments made from time to time, and by chapels being opened from the sides; the Sixtine and Borghese Chapels being especially designed to change the simple basilican plan to the cruciform. The Church was re-roofed by Adrian I., 772-95. Eugenius III., 1145-50, built a handsome portico, ornamented the façade with mosaic pictures, the work of *Filippus Rossutus,*—still visible in part, amid the barbarous additions made by Benedict XIV.,—and laid down the beautiful pavement of *opus Alexandrinum*, which has been entirely relaid, without any change in the design, during the present Pontificate.

Nicholas IV., 1278-92, thoroughly restored the interior, and in 1295 the beautiful mosaic, representing the Coronation of the Virgin, which ornaments the vault of the apse, was made by *Jacobus Torriti*, at the expense of the Cardinal titular Giacomo Colonna. It bears on the left side the inscription, JACOBVS . TORRITI . PICTOR . HOC . OPUS . MOSAICEN. FECIT., and on the right, A.D. MCCLXXXXV . DOMINUS. JACOBVS . DE . COLONNA . PRESBYTER . CARDINALIS.

The mosaics between the windows were, after the death of Jacobus Torriti, completed by *Gaddo Gaddi.*

The Campanile, which is the largest in Rome, was built by Gregory XI., 1370-78, after his return from Avignon. In 1450, Cardinal Rotomagense ornamented the ciborium above the high altar with the four porphyry columns which now support the more modern Baldachino. The ceiling of carved wood was designed and commenced by *Guiliano da San Gallo* for Calixtus III., 1455-58, and finished in the time of Alexander VI., 1492-1503, when it was gilt with the first gold sent from Peru. In 1485, Innocent VIII. restored the mosaic in the apse, and about the same time Cardinal d'Estoutville, Archpriest of the Basilica, opened the doors by the side of the tribune, and ornamented the High Altar with a new and richly sculptured Ciborium.

In 1575, Gregory XIII. restored the Portico, and Sixtus V., 1585-90, opened out the magnificent chapel on the right of the tribune, called after him the Sixtine, and Paul V., 1605-21, constructed that, corresponding to it on the opposite side, which, after his family name, is called the Borghese Chapel. In 1593 Cardinal Domenico Pinelli restored the mosaics of the frieze made by Sixtus III.

Up to the middle of the last century the exterior of the Basilica preserved all its original characteristics, when Benedict XIV., 1740-58 employed *Ferdinando Fuja* to modernise it. The portico, built by Eugenius III., was thrown down, and the beautiful mosaic on the front hidden by constructions, which, notwithstanding they possess a certain amount of palatial grandeur, are no compensation for what they conceal. Fortunately the construction of the upper portico permitted parts of the mosaic being left uncovered.

At the end of the portico, to the right as we enter, is a bronze statue of Philip IV. of Spain, by *Lucenti*.

The aisles are divided from the nave by 36 ancient columns of Greek marble with Ionic capitals—the spoil of some ancient edifice of importance—and four of granite, later additions placed when the line of columns, on the one side and the other, was broken, and the arches thrown across to form openings into the Sixtine and Borghese Chapels, to give the Basilica a cruciform plan.

The four bas reliefs on the wall of the tribune are fine examples of fifteenth century sculpture, and originally formed part of the ciborium erected by Cardinal d'Estoutville.   They represent—The Birth of Our Saviour, The Adoration of the Magi, The Assumption of the Virgin, and The Miracle of the Snow.   The beautiful confession, in front of the high altar, richly decorated with the rarest marbles, has recently been constructed by order of Pius IX.

To the right of the high altar is

THE SIXTINE CHAPEL,

built for Sixtus V., by *Domenico Fontana*, in 1586.   On the right is the monumental statue of Sixtus V., sculptured by *Gio. Antonio Valsoldo*, between four beautiful columns of *verde antique*, and above the statue, a bas relief by the same sculptor, representing his coronation.

On the opposite side is the monumental statue by *Leonardo da Sarzana* of St. Pius V., 1566-72, whose remains were placed here by Innocent XII., 1691-1700.   It was he who excommunicated Queen Elizabeth, gave thanksgivings for the Massacre of St. Bartholomew, and struck a medal to commemorate that event.   His body, uncorrupted, and dressed in the Pontifical robes, is preserved in the urn of precious *verde antique* below the statue, and is shown to the public each year on the 5th of May.

Above the altar in the middle of the Chapel, the whole of which has lately been restored by order of Pius IX., is a beautiful gilt bronze ciborium, supported by four angels, and richly inlaid with *pietra dura.* In the subterranean Chapel below is a *presepio*, commonly attributed to Bernini, but which was sculptured by *Cecchino da Pietrasanta*, and opposite to it is a statue of St. Gaetano.

On the opposite side of the Church, to the left of the high altar, is the magnificent

BORGHESE CHAPEL,

erected by *Flaminio Ponzio* for Paul V., in 1611, and dedicated to the " Mother of God." The plan is a Greek cross, like the Sixtine, and, in addition to a wealth of sculpture, in marble and bronze, fresco paintings, and gilding, expended on its embellishment, it is adorned throughout with a sumptuous profusion of the rarest marbles excavation among the remains of the ruined grandeur of ancient Rome could procure.

The architectural features and sculpture of the altar are entirely of bronze gilt, the flutings of the columns being inlaid with the richest oriental jasper. Above the pediment is a bas relief representing Pope Liberius marking out the plan of the Basilica on the snow. In a small chamber in the middle, entirely lined with *lapis lazuli*, and closed, except on grand festivals, behind small folding doors of a very rare marble, is the portrait of the Virgin "piously believed" to have been painted by St. Luke. It was this picture which, on the 25th April, 590, Saint Gregory carried in procession during the great pestilence, when, in crossing the Bridge of St. Angelo, he saw the Destroying Angel sheathing his sword on the summit of the Castle. (*See page* 46).

On the left side of the Chapel is the sepulchral monument which Paul V. erected to himself. Around the statue of the Pope, sculptured by *Tilla da Vigiù*, are bas reliefs representing, above, his Coronation, and on the sides, the reception of the Envoys of Congo and Japan; the fortification of Ferrara; the despatch of troops to the assistance of Rudolph II. of Hungary; and the Canonisation of Sta. Francesca Romano and St. Carlo Borromeo.

On the opposite side is the monument of Clement VIII., 1592-1605. His statue is by *Tilla da Vigiù*, and around it are bas reliefs representing The Taking of Ferrara, The Ratification of Peace between France and Spain, and other events during his reign.

The beautiful Corinthian Column in front of Sta. Maria Maggiore originally belonged to the Basilica of Constantine, from whence it was removed by Paul V., in 1613, and placed where it now stands, to support the bronze statue of the Virgin and Child, by *Augustus Bertelot* (*vide page* 142).

On the left side of the Via St. Antonio, which leads from Sta. Maria Maggiore by the left of the column, stands THE CHURCH OF ST. ANTONIO ABBATE, whose temptation by devils has formed the subject of so many paintings. It is chiefly remarkable for its beautiful 13th century Lombard Gothic doorway, one of the very few examples of this style in Rome. The Church was built between the years 1259-77 with money left for the purpose by Cardinal Pietro Capocci. In 1481 it was entirely rebuilt, with the exception of the doorway. It was in front of this Church, that, on the 17th of January of each year, the curious ceremony of blessing the animals used to be performed. It has not, in fact, been altogether discontinued, but is falling gradually into disuse.

The curious monument in the form of a cross, opposite to this Church, bearing the inscription "*In hoc signo vinces*," was erected in commemoration of the absolution given by

Clement VIII. to Henry IV. of France, when he seceded from the Protestant faith to Roman Catholicism in 1595. Taking our way along THE VIA MERULANA, which leads directly from Sta. Maria Maggiore, we see AN ANCIENT ARCH spanning the end of the first turning to the left, the Via di San Vito. It was erected about the year 260 A.D. by Marcus Aurelius Victor, Prefect of Rome, to the Emperor GALLIENUS and his wife Salonina.

The Church at the corner of the Via San Vito was built a few years ago by the English Redemptorists, and dedicated to St. Alphonso Liguori. It is a curious example of the full development of English Ritualism into the Roman Catholicism of the latter half of the nineteenth century, and, with its gaudily painted images and other decorations of the same character, forms an impressive contrast to the many churches of Rome herself, and particularly to the devotional simplicity of those of the earliest period.*

Proceeding a few yards along the Via San Martino—the first turning to the right from the Via Merulana—we find, on the right, the quaint old portico of

THE CHURCH OF SANTA PRASSEDE,

daughter of the Senator Pudens and sister of Santa Pudenziana. The earliest record we have of a church dedicated to this Saint is the mention of a certain Antonio Silvano, Titular of Sta. Prassede in the year 318. That church was restored by Adrian I., 772-95, and in 816

---

* It is commonly urged by Ritualists that in the decoration of their churches they seek to make them glorious to God through the highest efforts of art with which He has gifted man ; but the absolutely false art in this Church, contradictory to fact and untrue to nature, servilely imitated from a Monkish period without attainment to the sentiment which animated the artists of those days, may be instructively compared with that employed upon the walls of the Church of the Santa Sudari (*see page* 294), recently redecorated throughout with fresco paintings.

Stephen IV. built the adjoining monastery. Paschal I., 817-24, rebuilt the primitive church from the foundations, at the same time slightly altering its site, and is said to have deposited within it the relics of 2,300 martyrs taken from the Catacombs. He decorated it richly with mosaics, of which those on the vault of the apse, on the arch opening upon the tribune, and in the Chapel of St. Zeno, still remain. In 1564 St. Carlo Borromeo, then Cardinal Titular of the Church, restored it throughout and somewhat modernised it, without, however, entirely divesting it of its primitive Basilican characteristics. The restorations commenced by him were continued and completed by Cardinal Alessandro de Medici, who afterwards filled the Papal chair in 1605, as Leo XI. In 1730 the high altar was reconstructed in the form we see by Cardinal Pico della Mirandola. In 1830-31 the mosaics were repaired in some parts where they had become damaged, and during the present Pontificate the Church has been entirely repainted.

In the middle of the nave, towards the door, is a well, in which it is said that Sta. Prassede deposited the blood and remains of many martyrs.

The Third Chapel on the right, unfortunately only open to women during the Sundays of Lent, is part of the original edifice, as built by Paschal I., and from the great beauty of its mosaic decorations is called "The Garden of Paradise." It is dedicated to St. Zeno, and is sometimes also called the Chapel of the Column, from the column of blood jasper preserved within it, which was brought from Jerusalem in 1223, by Cardinal Giovanni Colonna, and is said to be that to which our Saviour was bound during the Flagellation. The Chapel is entered by a side door, opposite to which is the beautifully sculptured fifteenth century monument of Cardinal Alano Cetive (*obit* 1474).

The thirteenth century monument of Cardinal Anchero, *obit* 1286, in the chapel at the end of the right aisle, is well worthy of observation. It is in the form of a recumbent figure of the Cardinal lying on a couch covered with richly folded drapery, and below, coats of arms in mosaic. It is supposed to be the work of one of the *Cosmati.*

On the wall to the left on entering is a slab of black and white granite, placed between two columns, said to be that on which Sta. Prassede used to sleep, to mortify the flesh.

The Second Chapel to the left is dedicated to St. Carlo Borromeo, and contains, on the right, the wood of the table at which he used to feed and serve twelve poor men daily, in the contiguous palace built by him, for the use of the Cardinals titular of Sta. Prassede; and on the left, his episcopal chair. The paintings on the side walls are by *Louis Stern*, and represent St. Carlo in Ecstasy before the Sacrament; and St. Carlo Meditating on the Passion of the Redeemer.

In the Sacristy is a fine painting of The Flagellation, by *Giulio Romano.* On the pilasters on each side of the arch of the tribune are inscriptions recording a quantity of most marvellous relics preserved in this Church.

Turning to the right on leaving Sta. Prassede, we pass the house, No. 20A, in which the celebrated painter, Domenico Zampieri, commonly called *Domenichino*, lived.

Continuing onwards as far as No. 69 on the left side, we turn into a kind of long courtyard, and enter by a side door

THE CHURCH OF ST. MARTINO AI MONTI.

Pope Damasus, in his life of St. Sylvester, has left us the

record of that Pope having founded a Church on this site, and says that it was built in the field belonging to the priest Equitius, situated near the Baths of Domitian— then confused with the Baths of Trajan. In that Church St. Sylvester held a Council about the year 324, at which, according to some, 284, and to others, 230 Bishops were present. Constantine himself, and Calphurnius, Prefect of Rome, took part in its sittings. It is not known to whom the Church was dedicated, and in all probability it was destroyed and buried in its own ruins during one or other of the many disasters through which Rome suffered during the following 150 years, for we have no further record of it from the time of St. Sylvester till the seventeenth century.

About the year 500, however, Pope St. Symmachus built a new Church from the foundations, on or near the same spot, and dedicated it to St. Sylvester and to St. Martin, Bishop of Tours. It was restored successively by Adrian I. 772-95; Sergius II. 844-47; Innocent III., 1198-1216; by Cardinal Diomed Carafa, nephew of Paul IV., 1555-59; by Cardinal—afterwards Saint—Carlo Borromeo, who in the time of Pius IV., 1559-66, added the carved wood ceiling. In the year 1650 Padre Gio Antonio Filippini, General of the Carmelites, to whom the Church belongs, spent 70,000 scudi, about £24,000, in modernising it. His successor, Padre Francesco Scannapieco, built the façade in 1676, and finally, in 1780, the Cardinal Titular Francesco Saverio Zeladi, spent about £12,000 more in ornamenting the altar and tribune. The columns which divide the aisles from the nave were placed by Padre Filippini in 1650, and it is said that they were taken from the ruins of Hadrian's Villa. On the wall of the left aisle is a large fresco, by an unknown author, representing the Council held in the Primitive Church, about the year 324.

The Chapel at the end of the left aisle, dedicated to the Madonna of Mount Carmel, was built at the end of the last century. By the altar are two very beautiful antique columns of *giallo antico*. The paintings, representing the souls in purgatory, over the altar, Elias and the angel, on the left wall, and the Madonna giving the dress of the Carmelite order to St. Simon Stock, on the vault, are by *Antonio Cavallucci*, and by the same author are the paintings on the vault and wall of the apse. The landscapes on the walls of this Church are by *Gaspar Poussin*, with the exception of the two nearest to the first altar of the right aisle. At the commencement of the wall of the left aisle, is a view of the interior of St. John Lateran, before it was modernised by *Borromini;* and further on, upon the same side, a view of the interior of old St. Peter's, both by unknown authors.

The pavement of the Church is curiously formed of pieces of marble and tiles combined, and along the sides of the nave, against the columns, a number of curious sepulchral slabs are ranged, which formed the earlier pavement. They are engraven with effigies like those cut on monumental brasses, and are in a very fine state of preservation. On the floor of the left aisle, below the picture of the Council, are two very curious monumental slabs in relief.

During the works carried on in 1650, the Primitive Church, built by St. Sylvester, was discovered filled with accumulation. It was entirely cleared, and, in order to give access to it, a curious semi-subterranean Chapel was formed, partly by raising the floor of the tribune, and partly by lowering that of the confession.

Descending into this Chapel, an incline on the left leads us down into the primitive Church, where the Council, in the year 324, was held. It was evidently of great size, but it has been so much transformed by massive pilasters built within it—either to support the weight above, when it was abandoned and filled in, or the better to support the vault —on which modern buildings weigh—when it was discovered, about the year 1650—that it preserves little of an ecclesiastical character beyond the remains of fresco paintings, now almost entirely obliterated, on the walls, and an ancient mosaic of the Madonna. This ancient Church was evidently an earlier edifice, adapted to Christian worship, but there is no ground whatever for the popular belief that it originally formed part of the Thermæ, erroneously called those of Titus.

Leaving St. Martino by the principal entrance, we turn to the left along a narrow lane, which leads to

THE CHURCH OF ST. PIETRO IN VINCULI,

so called because of the chains preserved within it, with which it is said St. Peter was bound, when he was imprisoned in Jerusalem by order of Herod, or rather, one of the two chains which bound him there, miraculously joined to, that he is said to have borne in the Mamertine prison.

According to the legends of the Church, Eudoxia, wife of Theodosius the younger, made a pilgrimage to Jerusalem where Juvenal, the Bishop, presented her with the iron chains, ornamented with gold and jewels, which St. Peter had worn in prison. One of these she took with her to Constantinople, and the other she sent to Rome by her daughter—also called Eudoxia, and who became the wife of

Valentinianus III.—who presented it to Leo I., then occupying the Papal throne. On receiving it, Leo showed Eudoxia another chain which had bound St. Peter in Rome, and on the two being placed together they at once became miraculously united. As regards the Roman chain, it is said that Santa Balbina, the daughter of St. Quirinus, Tribune, and *custode* of the Mamertine Prison, being exhorted by St. Alexander I., 108-19, besought her father to search for the chain which St. Peter had worn, who complying with his daughter's request, found it. On her deathbed Santa Balbina confided it to the care of Santa Theodora, by whom, and by the Pontiffs between her time and that of St. Leo, it was preserved with the greatest veneration. In commemoration of the miraculous union of the chains, and for their preservation, Eudoxia founded this Church, about the year 442, entitling it *San Pietro in Vinculi.* It is also called the *Basilica Eudoxiana*, after its founder. It was restored by Pelagius I., 555-60. In the eighth century it was rebuilt by Adrian I., 772-95. Sixtus IV., 1471-84, reconstructed the vault of the Tribune, and Julius II., 1503-13, employed *Baccio Pintelli* to make considerable restorations. The ceiling of the nave was reconstructed by *Francesco Fontana*, in 1750, and painted by *Gio. Battista Parodi.* The aisles are divided from the nave by 20 antique fluted columns of white marble with Doric capitals, taken from some ancient edifice, and the arch of the Tribune is supported by two Corinthian columns of grey granite. The marble columns measure about seven feet in circumference, but have been shortened from their original length.

The tribune is adorned with frescoes of no very great merit by *Giacomo del Meglio*, illustrating events in the life of St. Peter. On the lower part of the tribune is the memorial and portrait of Guilio Clovio (died 1578), the celebrated miniature painter, many of whose works adorn manuscripts in the Vatican Library.

At the end of the right aisle is Michael Angelo's great masterpiece in sculpture, THE MOSES, which forms the central figure of the memorial monument of Julius II., whose body lies in a humble sepulchre in St. Peter's. There are few works against which so many critical objections can be made, and have been made, as upon this wonderful statue; but it is nevertheless one of the most marvellous creations ever hewn by the hand of man from a block of stone. It is replete throughout with the great genius of the sculptor; its majestic aspect almost inspires awe in the beholder; and it is so full of life, that one would scarcely be surprised to see it rise from its seat, or hear it speak in the commanding tone of the great ruler and lawgiver of Israel. Upon the brow is bound the symbol of the lawgiver—two small horns.

This statue was sculptured to form part of the magnificent cenotaph Julius II. had intended to erect to himself under the dome of St. Peter's, but the dissensions which arose between the Pope and the sculptor retarded its execution, and it was never completed. It was to have been of the colossal dimensions of eighteen cubits in length by twelve in width, and adorned with forty statues, many of which were to have been of bronze. Four of the principal statues, representing Active Life, Contemplative Life, St. Paul, and Moses, were to occupy the corners, of which only this before us was finished, or even commenced. In the middle, there was to have been a sepulchral chamber to contain the body of the Pope.*

* For a complete description of the design, see the life of Michael Angelo, written by his scholar Condivi.

The successors of Julius finding the completion of this colossal conception a work of too great magnitude, it was finally renounced, and instead of placing a monument to Julius in St. Peter's, this, in which the Moses was utilized. was erected here by Paul III., 1534-50. The statue of Leah, holding a mirror, symbolic of *Active Life*, on one side, and of Rachel, symbolic of *Contemplative Life*, on the other, are believed to be by *Raffaelle di Monte Lupo;* the recumbent figure of the Pope is by *Mazo del Bosco;* the Virgin and Child by *Scherano da Settignano,* and the Prophet and Sybil are by *Raffaelle di Monte Lupo.*

Over the altar of the chapel at the end of this aisle is a picture of St. Margaret, by *Guercino.*

To the left of the door, on entering, is the monument, with the portraits, of Antonio Pollajuolo, the famous sculptor and worker in bronze, and his brother Pietro, who worked with him. Above is a very curious fresco, illustrating a legend regarding the great plague in 680.

In the corner, to the left, is an interesting fifteenth-century monument, erected in 1465 to Cardinal Nicholas de Cusa, of whom the figure kneeling on the left of St. Peter is a portrait.

In the second Chapel to the left is a curious mosaic of the seventh century, representing St. Sebastian as an old man, placed—originally in the first Chapel—in commemoration of the great pestilence of 680, from which, it is said, Rome was liberated by the intercession of this saint.

In the Sacristy there is a very beautiful altar of fifteenth-century work; above which, in a kind of ciborium, delicately sculptured, the chains of Peter are preserved.

In this Church the Popes John II., 532-35, and Gregory VII., 1073-86, were elected.

T

The adjoining Convent and the Palace for the Titular Cardinal were built by *Guiliano da Sangallo.*

In the cloisters is a well-head, attributed to Michael Angelo; *Titi* says it was sculptured by *Simone Mosca.*

The Monastery opposite belongs to the Maronite Monks.

The house on the right is reputed to have been that of LUCRETIA BORGIA—and if we pass under the archway a very picturesque balcony belonging to it will be seen on the other side. The square tower beyond—now the belfry of the Church of St. Francesco di Paola—was originally the watch tower of the Frangipani fortress.

In the vineyard, to the left of the Church—the entrance to which is from the lane called the Via della Polvericra on the left—there are some magnificent pieces of ruin, the remains of THE BATHS OF TRAJAN, vulgarly called The Baths of Titus, standing above the remains of Nero's Golden House (see page 164); but it is not easy to obtain admittance to the vineyard.

The lane to the left of the Church leads—by keeping to the right—to the south-west side of the Colosseum; and, by keeping to the left, to the Via Labicana, where the entrance to the remains of the GOLDEN HOUSE OF NERO, commonly called the Baths of Titus, will be found immediately on the left after descending the incline; and on the right is THE COLOSSEUM.

AROUND THE PANTHEON.

From the Piazza di Spagna we pass down the Via Condotti, and crossing the Corso, a little to the right, to the Via Tomacelli, which opens between Nos. 421 and 422, continue along it to THE RIPETTA. This quay, or flight of steps leading down to the edge of the Tiber, was built by Clement XI., 1700-21, with stones taken from the Colosseum.

The river can be crossed at this point by means of the ferry boat, and from the other side there is a very pleasant walk—across what are believed to have been the fields of Cincinnatus—leading by the back of the Castle of St. Angelo to the Porta Angelica, and thence to St. Peter's.

On the wall of the house to the left of the Ripetta, as we look towards the river, is a brass guage, on which are marked the heights reached by the various inundations of the Tiber.

The Church opposite to this, dedicated to St. Rocco, was originally built in 1499. In 1657 it was amplified and moderuised by *Antonio de Rossi*, and in 1834 the façade was built by *Valadier*.

Immediately opposite the steps of the Ripetta is The Church of St. Girolamo degli Schiavoni, built for Sixtus V., in 1588, by *Martino Lunghi the elder*, and *Giovanni Fontana*.

Continuing, with the river on our right, along the Via Ripetta, which, after crossing the Via Fontanella Borghese, takes the name of Via della Scrofa, we reach, on the right, the short Via di S. Antonino dei Portoghesi, at the bottom of which is a short mediæval tower, called the *Torre della Scimia*. This is the " Hilda's Tower" of Hawthorne's novel of the Marble Faun.

The next street on the same side is the Via di S. Agostino, where, a few yards on the right, stands

THE CHURCH OF ST. AGOSTINO,

founded in 1484, by Cardinal Gilgliclmo d'Estoutville.

It was built by *Baccio Pintelli*, the famous architect of that period, with stone taken from the Colosseum. The interior was restored by *Vanvitelli* in 1750, and is now again undergoing complete restoration. The cupola of this church was the first erected in Rome.

The chief objects of interest here are a FRESCO OF ISAIAH and two angels, holding a tablet, by *Raphael;* on the third pilaster, to the left of the nave — much injured through having been retouched by *Daniele da Volterra*— and the group of THE VIRGIN AND CHILD, immediately to the left, on entering by the door to the right of the main entrance. It was sculptured by *Giacomo Tatti da Sansovino*, and is, for the time being, the favourite Madonna of Rome, having superseded in popular estimation that over the third altar to the left, in the Pantheon. This idol is believed to be endowed with supernatural power; prayers made to it are supposed to be especially efficacious in their results; it is literally covered with necklaces, brooches, rings, watches, bracelets, and other votive offerings of value; its foot— close to which is a little money box—is covered with metal, to protect it from being worn by the constant kissing it receives; the walls around are hung with votive pictures, representing the cures from illness and protection from the fatal results of accidents, which imme- diate prayer to it have obtained; before it hang many silver lamps, constantly burning; and on the floor, in front, a number of the devout may always be seen kneeling in prayer. There can be no question here that the prayers are made to the statue, and not to the personage it represents.

Returning to the left, on leaving the Church, and con- tinuing for a short distance along the Via della Scrofa—the first turning to the right—the street widens into the small Piazza San Luigi dei Francesi; on the right side of which is

THE CHURCH OF ST. LUIGI DEI FRANCESI,

the National Church of the French people, and especially placed under the protection of that nation. It was built by *Giacomo della Porta*, chiefly at the expense of Catherine de Medicis, and was dedicated on the 8th of October, 1589, to the Virgin Mary, St. Denis, and St. Louis, King of France. It contains a number of monuments to Frenchmen of distinction who died in Rome, and among others, to the celebrated archæologist, Seroux d'Agincourt, in the last chapel on the right, and to Claude Lorrain, on one of the pilasters of the left aisle.

The second chapel on the right, dedicated to St. Cecilia, is celebrated for the fine frescoes by *Domenichino* with which it is decorated. On the vault: Angels offering crowns to St. Cecilia and her husband Valerian; St. Cecilia borne to heaven by angels; and St. Cecilia refusing to worship idols. The large fresco on the left wall represents her martyrdom, and that on the right, her distributing her clothes among the poor. The painting over the altar is a copy by *Guido* from Raphael's picture of St. Cecilia, now ·in the Gallery at Bologna.

The fourth chapel on the right, dedicated to St. Denis, has a fresco by *Girolamo Siccciolunte* on the right wall. The fresco on the left wall and the battles on the vault were painted by *Pellegrino da Bologna.*

Over the high altar is a fine Assumption by *Bassano.*

In the chapel, to the left of the high altar, dedicated to St. Matthew, the altar piece, and the paintings on the side walls, representing the calling of St. Matthew, and his martyrdom, are by *Michael Angelo da Caravaggio.*

Returning along the left aisle, the last chapel contains a St. Sebastian bound to a tree, by *Girolamo Massei.*

The large building, to the right of the Church as we leave it, was built by *Paolo Marucelli*, in 1642, for Catherine do Medicis, and called the PALAZZO MADAMA. The interior has recently been altered to serve as the Chamber for THE ITALIAN SENATE.

Turning to the right, and passing between the Senato House and the side of the Church of St. Luigi dei Francese, we cross the small Piazza Madama into the short street called the Corsia Agonale on the opposite side, but a little to the left, and from it enter

THE PIAZZA NAVONA,

one of the largest Piazzas in Rome, measuring 10,924 square metres. It is in the form of a parallelogram, one end of which approaches a semicircle, and preserves the ground plan of THE CIRCUS ALEXANDRI, also called THE CIRCUS AGONE OR AGONALIS, on the foundations of the seats of which the houses are built. The name of the Piazza is a corruption from *Agone* to Nagone, Nagona, Navona.

In the centre is THE GRAND FOUNTAIN, erected by *Bernini* for Innocent X., 1644-55. From within a circular basin, measuring 73 feet in diameter, rises a mass of perforated rockwork, to which are chained four colossal emblematical figures, representing the four principal rivers of the world, THE DANUBE, THE GANGES, THE NILE, and THE RIO DELLA PLATA. The Mississippi was then unknown. On the summit stands an Egyptian obelisk; that which ornamented the *spina* of the Circus of Romulus. (*See page* 227.)

Crossing the Piazza, and continuing along the Via di S. Agnese immediately opposite, as far as the second turning to the right, we shall find

THE CHURCH OF STA. MARIA DELLA PACE,

built by *Baccio Pintelli* for Sixtus IV., 1471-84. In 1611 the tribune and high altar were constructed by *Carlo Maderno*, at the expense of Monsignore *Gaspare Rivaldi*. It was restored throughout by Alexander VII., 1655-67, and the actual façade and portico built by *Pietro da Cortona*. The chief object of interest in this Church is the fresco of THE SYBILS, BY RAPHAEL—the Cumœan, Persic, Phrygian, and Tibertine, on the wall above the arch of the first chapel to the right, belonging to the Chigi family. The prophets above the cornice were painted from Raphael's drawings, by *Rosso* the Florentine. The commission to paint these frescoes was given to Raphael by the celebrated banker, Agostino Chigi. The bronze bas relief within the chapel, the statue of Sta. Catherine of Siena, and two cherubs bearing the instruments of the Passion, on the right, are the work of *Cosimo Fancelli;* the statue of St. Bernardino and the two cherubs, on the left, are by *Ercole Ferrata.*

The second chapel on the right—of the Cesi family— was designed by *Michael Angelo.* The beautiful arabesques on the front were sculptured by *Simone Mosca.* The Adam and Eve on the upper portion was painted by *Filippo Lauri.* The picture above the altar is by *Carlo Cesi,* and the four paintings on the vault, by *Sicciolante.*

The four large paintings below the cupola are—The Visitation, by *Carlo Maratta;* The Presentation in the Temple, by *Baldassare Peruzzi;* The Nativity of the Virgin, by *Francesco Vanni;* and the Death of the Virgin, by *Morandi.*

The statues of Justice and Truth above the frontispiece of the high altar, were sculptured by *Stefano Maderno*. The Birth of the Virgin and the Annunciation, on the side walls, are by *Passignani*. The figures of St. Cecilia and St. Catherine of Siena, painted within the pilaster on one side, and of St. Augustine and Sta. Chiara, within that on the other, are by *Lavinia Fontana*.

In the chapel, to the left of the high altar, is a very beautifully sculptured altar-piece of the fifteenth century, from which the centre has been cut away to convert it into a kind of frame for the large crucifix of wood.

Over the altar of the last chapel, to the right on leaving the Church, is a fine fresco by *Baldassare Peruzzi*, which was discovered about forty years ago, beneath another subject painted over it at a later period. It represents the Madonna and St. Brigida, before whom Ferdinando Ponzetti —the founder of the chapel—is kneeling. The two delicately carved monuments to members of the Ponzetti family, on the external sides of this chapel, are well worthy of examination, as beautiful examples of fifteenth century work. That on the right was erected to two children, Beatrice and Lavinia, who died of the plague on the same day, in 1505. Their portraits are charmingly sculptured.

Returning to the Piazza Navona. On the side to the right, is the beautiful little

CHURCH OF ST. AGNES,

which stands on the site of the *fornices* in the Circus Agonalis, where it is believed the Virgin Saint and Martyr was exposed by order of Sempronius, Prefect of Rome, under Maxentius, in the year 310. In process of time these *fornices* were converted into an Oratory, of which there is record from as early as the eighth century. On the 28th January, 1123, it was reconsecrated to St. Agnes by Callixtus II., and in a Bull of Urban III., 1185-87, it is called *Ecclesia S. Agnetis de Cryptis Agonis.* Between that time and the year 1384, a Parish Church was built above it—but at what exact date is not known—for in that year Sta. Francesa Romana was baptized within it. In the year 1652, Innocent X. decided to rebuild the Church from the foundations, and employed *Girolamo Rainaldi* to make the plan and designs, but difficulties arising between the Pope and the architect, the execution of the work was confided to *Borromini*, who had completed the edifice as far as the vault of the church and the cupola, when he died; the remainder, including the lantern of the cupola, was finished by *Carlo Rainaldi*, the son of Girolamo.

The interior affords an example—very rare in Rome—of unity of design and decoration throughout, and an opportunity of examining good examples of the sculpture of the Bernini school, which, though theatrical and florid in style, is not without a certain merit of its own. The plan is a Greek cross.

Above the altar, at the right end, is a statue of St. Agnes, by *Ercole Ferrata*, and opposite to it, above the altar at the left end, a statue of St. Sebastian, said to be an antique statue altered to represent this saint, by *Paolo Campi.*

Above the high altar is a grand alto-relief, by *Domenico Guidi*, representing the Virgin and Child, with St. John, St. Joseph, St. Joachim, and angels.

At the angles of the cruciform plan, which are chamferred and formed into chapels, are the following four large alto-reliefs. Commencing from the right. The Death of St. Alexis, by *Francesco Rossi;* The Martyrdom of St. Emerentiana, by *Ercole Ferrata*; The Martyrdom of St. Cecilia, by *Antonio Raggi*; and St. Eustachius and his children among the wild beasts in the amphitheatre, by *Melchior Cafa* and *Ercole Ferrata*.

Above the door is the curiously arranged monument of Innocent X., by *Maini*.

The frescoes in the cupola were commenced by *Ciro Ferri* and completed by *Corbellini*.

Above the altar in the subterranean Chapel, said to mark the spot where St. Agnes was exposed, is an alto-relief representing the Saint, with her long hair covering her, commonly attributed to *Algardi*, but probably the work of his scholar, *Domenico Guidi*. The place said to have been her prison, and the spot where she was beheaded and burned, is shown in this subterranean Chapel.

Retracing our steps across the piazza and by the streets through which we entered it, and recrossing the Piazza Madama into the Via del Salvatore, between the Senate House and the Church of St. Luigi dei Francese, we continue in a direct line along the Via Giustiniani till we enter a square piazza with a fountain in the centre, and see before us

THE PANTHEON,

which carries us back to 27 years before the Christian era. With the exception of the external decoration of the inner and outer walls, it stands entire, as at the moment when completed; an example of how many other of the grand edifices of ancient Rome might have come down to us comparatively intact had they not been wantonly destroyed to afford building materials for the modern city. The Goths and Vandals who accomplished all this ruthless destruction were no other than the Romans themselves, a fact to which the history of this building alone bears eloquent evidence.

The Pantheon was built by Marcus Agrippa, the son-in-law of Augustus, to serve as the *Laconicum* or *Sudatorium* of his Thermæ—the first of these great bathing establishments erected in Rome—but, for some cause unknown to us, instead of applying it to the purpose for which it was intended, Agrippa converted it into a Temple dedicated to Jupiter the Avenger, and all the gods. We must either suppose that its founder, admiring the harmony of its proportions and the grandeur resulting from them, conceived the idea of devoting it to the service of the gods, or, what is more probable, that being the first edifice of the kind erected in Rome, there was some radical defect in its construction which unfitted it for a hot air bath; possibly the Romans were not sufficiently acquainted with the mechanism of these establishments to work it successfully on so large a scale. Be this as it may, there can be no doubt as to the original intention of the building, or that the magnificent portico of sixteen columns, monoliths, of Egyptian granite, which formed no part of the original construction, was added as part of the requisites for converting the edifice into a Temple.

The pediment was ornamented with a grand bas-relief in bronze, representing Jove hurling his thunderbolts against the Titans ; on the summit was a bronze statue of Jupiter Tonans in a quadriga — a four-horse chariot; and at the corners were bronze bulls, the whole executed by *Diogenes of Athens*, who, according to Pliny, was the sculptor who made all the bronze ornaments of the Pantheon. The dome was covered with plates of bronze gilt, and the casing of the ceiling and beams of the portico was of the same material.

Passing into the interior we see a large semi-circular niche, facing the door, in which stood the statue of the principal deity, Jupiter the Avenger, with, on each side, three rectangular niches, or recesses, for the statues of Mars; of Venus; of Romulus, or Quirinus, the founder of the city; of Juno, its protectress; of Pallas; and, according to the testimony of Dion Cassius, of the Deified Julius. The statue of Venus had ear-rings made from the fellow pearl to that which Cleopatra melted and drank.

The beautiful Corinthian columns of Phrygian and Numidian marble, each measuring 35 feet in height and 3¾ in diameter, which support the architraves of the recesses are antique, parts of the structure itself standing where they were originally placed. Occupying the spaces between these recesses are eight *Ædiculæ*, also believed to be integral parts of the building, but now converted into Christian altars. Above the cornice supported by these columns were caryatides of bronze, by *Diogenes of Athens*.

Consecrated by Agrippa to Jupiter the Avenger and all the gods, in the year 27, B.C., it was damaged by fire in the time of Titus, A.D. 80, and was repaired by Domitian in the year 93. In the time of Trajan it was again injured by fire through being struck by lightning in the year 110. This damage was repaired by Hadrian, and the building is also believed to have been restored by Antoninus Pius. In the year 202 it was again restored by Septimius Severus, as recorded by an inscription in small letters on the architrave of the portico. In the year 399 it was, together with all the other pagan temples in Rome, closed by the law of Honorius, and so remained till between the years 606 and 607, when Boniface IV., who was elected in 608 to fill the Papal chair, made a petition to the Emperor Phocas—whose column erected at that time still stands on the Forum—for this building, and consecrating it to the service of the Christian religion dedicated to the Virgin Mary and all the martyrs, on the 13th of May, in—it is believed—the year 610. Preparatory to this dedication, Boniface removed twenty-eight cart loads of bones from the Catacombs, and deposited them in the neighbourhood of the high altar.

With the exception that the statues of the Pagan deities were removed, and such other alterations made in the interior as were requisite for the conversion of the edifice into a Christian Church, it remained in all its original integrity until the year 645, when the Emperor, Constans II., stripped the bronze covering from the dome, and shipped it for Constantinople. He did not, however, profit much by his plunder. While on his way back to Constantinople he was murdered at Syracuse, and the vessels carrying the bronze were captured by the Saracens. The dome, thus despoiled of its bronze covering, remained exposed to the intemperature of the weather for upwards of seven centuries, until Martin V. commenced in 1425 to re-cover it with lead. The work was continued by his successor, Eugenius IV., and completed by Nicholas V. in 1452.

Eugenius IV. not only continued the work of covering the dome with lead, but also cleared the portico of a number of shops and taverns, which had been built up within and against it; and while doing this, and lowering the level in front, he discovered there, the magnificent Porphyry bath—popularly called the urn of Marcus Agrippa—which now serves as the sarcophagus to the monument of Clement XII.

in the Corsini Chapel at the Lateran (*see page* 179). A lion in basalt; a bronze head, supposed to be that of Agrippa; and the hoof of a bronze horse, with a fragment of a bronze wheel, which, in all probability, were fragments of the four-horse chariot that surmounted the pediment, were found at the same time.

Even as recently as the 17th century the Pantheon suffered at the hand of the spoiler. In the year 1632, Urban VIII. removed the bronze covering of the beams of the portico, that he might use the material for the construction of the bronze Baldachino under the dome of St. Peter's, and towards the casting of a hundred pieces of cannon for the Castle of St. Angelo.* It was then that the famous pasquinade appeared against Urban VIII., who belonged to the Barberini family, "*Quod non fecerunt Barbari fecerunt Barberini.*" An inscription to the left of the door records this act of Vandalism. At the same time, however, Urban replaced the column at the left angle of the portico, which had fallen or been removed. In 1662, Alexander VII· substituted for the other columns, wanting at this point, two of oriental granite, found in pieces near the Church of St. Luigi dei Francese.

In the year 1270, the clergy of this Church had built a rough bell tower upon it. This was removed by

---

* The weight of metal abstracted from the Pantheon by Urban VIII. was no less than 450,250 lbs., to which were added 87,508 lbs. taken from other ancient edifices; and of this, the cannon for the Castle of St. Angelo alone absorbed 448,286 lbs., the value of which was estimated at the time at a sum equal to about £13,500 of our money. The remainder of the metal was used for the Baldachino of St. Peter's. When the bronze taken by Urban from the beams of the portico alone weighed 450,000 lbs., what must have been the weight of that carried off by Constans II., which formed the entire covering of the dome. If, to this, we add the bronze bas relief in the pediment, the quadriga, and the bulls above the pediment, the bronze caryatides within, the bronze capitals of which Pliny speaks, and the bronze door still existing, we may be able to form some idea of the wealth of material lavished upon this edifice, and that at a time when a certain amount of republican simplicity was still observed by the Romans in the decoration of their buildings.

Urban VIII., who employed *Bernini* to re-disfigure the building by erecting the twin towers, one at each end of the pediment.

The last act of spoliation was committed in 1747, by Benedict XIV., who removed all the ancient marble and porphyry panelling from the attic, for which he substituted the wretched painted imitation we see.*

The portico measures 110 feet in length by 44 feet in depth. The sixteen columns—placed so that 8 show on the front and 3 on the sides—measure 47 feet in height, including the base and capital, and 5 feet in diameter.

The opening of the doorway measures 32 feet by 20, the upper 8 feet being closed by a bronze grating, which, like the bronze doors, is ancient and in its original place. The threshold is formed by one immense block of Chian marble, now called Africano. The flooring of the interior has been recently relaid with marble slabs, cut from the blocks found at the ancient Marmorata in 1867.

The interior measures $143\frac{3}{4}$ feet in diameter, or $2\frac{1}{2}$ feet more than that of the dome of St. Peter's. The diameter through the walls is 190 feet. The height from the floor to the apex through the opening is $157\frac{1}{2}$ feet. The opening in the dome is 28 feet in diameter, and within it is a ring of metal, all that remains of the bronze decorations. There are no works of art in this Church especially worthy of remark. The best are—the group of St. Anne and the Virgin, by *Lorenzo Ottoni*, in the fifth chapel on the right, and the

---

* When, in the history of the edifice, we have evidence of its having been despoiled of its materials and decoration three times after it was consecrated a Christian Church, viz.: first, of the bronze covering of the dome, by Constans II., in 653; secondly, of the bronze from the portico, by Urban VIII., in 1632; and thirdly, of the marble panelling of the attic, by Benedict XIV., in 1747, it is scarcely necessary to enquire by whom that ruthless destruction of the edifices of Pagan Rome was accomplished, which has been so conveniently shifted on to the shoulders of those much-wronged people, the Goths and Vandals.

monument of Cardinal Consalvi, Secretary of State under Pius VII., by *Thorwaldsen*—not one of his best works—in the Chapel of the Crucifix, on the left of the high altar.

In a chamber at the back of the third altar on the left, and under the statue of the once popular Madonna, which has been superseded by that at the Church of St. Agostino (*see page* 275), lie the remains of the Prince of Painters RAPHAEL D'URBINO.   Some controversy having arisen as to the correctness of Vasari's record regarding the resting-place of Raphael, search was made in the year 1833, and on the 14th September the remains were found intact.   When his will was opened, after his death, on the 6th of April, 1520, it was found that he had selected this spot as his place of sepulture, directing that the altar should be restored, and a statue of the Madonna—that now before us—by *Lorenzetto*, placed above it.   It was this same Lorenzetto who carved the statue of Jonah in the Chigi Chapel, in Sta. Maria del Popolo, from Raphael's model.

Turning to the right, on leaving the Pantheon, and ascending the incline by the side of the building, we enter the Piazza della Minerva, on the further side of which is the Church of

SANTA MARIA SOPRA MINERVA.

On the wall of the façade to the right of the entrances, are a number of small marble slabs marking the different heights to which the water of the Tiber reached in this Piazza during the great inundations, from that of 1422 to the last in December, 1870.

This Church is called Sta. Maria *Sopra Minerva* from its standing upon the ruins of a Temple to that deity, supposed, by some authorities, to be the same dedicated by

Pompey, after his victories in Asia. The Senate and people of Rome having given, in the year 1370, a smaller church which occupied this site—built during the Pontificate of S. Zaccharia, about 750—to the monks of the Dominican order, they determined to rebuild it on a larger scale, and collecting alms, and by the aid of different wealthy personages who undertook the expense of distinct portions, succeeded in raising this edifice. It is the only example in Rome of pointed Italian Gothic. It has recently been restored at the expense of about £23,000, and somewhat gaudily decorated. The seemingly beautiful clustered columns of Carystian marble which divide the double aisles on each side from the nave, are in reality artificial—they are made of scagliola, with the exception only of the lower four or five feet of each.

Passing up the right aisle.

Fourth Chapel. Frescoes on the vault by *Muziano.*

Fifth Chapel, dedicated to the Annunciation. Built by *Carlo Maderno.* Frescoes on the vault by *Cesare Nebbia.* Over the altar a very fine Annunciation, commonly attributed to Fra Angelico da Fiesole, but believed to be by *Benozzo Gozzoli.* It contains the portrait of Cardinal Torrecremata, who was living five years after Fra Angelico died, in 1455. On the left is the monument of Urban VII., 1590, with his statue, sculptured by *Ambrozio Buonvicino.*

Sixth Chapel, belonging to the Aldobrandini family, built by *Giacomo della Porta.* Over the altar is a Last Supper, by *Federico Barocci.* On the right side is the monument of Silvestro Aldobrandini—died 1558—the father of Clement VIII., by *Stefano Maderno.* The recumbent statue of the defunct, and these of Strength and Prudence on the sides, are by *Niccolo Cordieri.*

U

Opposite, on the left, is the monument of Luisa Deti—died 1557—the wife of Silvestro Aldobrandini, and mother of Clement VIII.; the recumbent statue of the defunct and the statue of Charity on the left are by *Cordieri*, the statue of Religion on the right is by *Camillo Mariani*.

Chapel of the Crucifix, on the right as we enter the right transept. Above the altar, is a Crucifixion painted in tempera, said to be by *Giotto*.

Chapel of St. Thomas Aquinas, at the end of the right transept, belonging to the Caraffa family, contains some fine FRESCOES BY FILIPPO LIPPI. The painting on the altar wall represents two scenes, the Annunciation, and St. Thomas Aquinas, presenting the donor, Cardinal Oliviero Caraffa, to the Virgin; and the Assumption, with the Apostles below. The painting on the right wall is The Disputation of St. Thomas. The Angels and Sybils on the walls were painted by *Raffaellino del Garbo*. Against the left wall is the monument of Paul IV., 1555-59, the founder of the Inquisition; the statue of the Pope is by *Giacomo Casignola*.

On the wall to the left, looking towards the chapel, is the interesting monument of Guglielmus Durandus, ob. 1290, ornamented with mosaic, by *Giovanni Cosmati*.

Chapel of the Altieri Family, the first on a line with the tribune, contains an altar piece by *Carlo Maratta*, representing St. Peter presenting to the Virgin the five saints canonized by Clement X., who was a member of the Altieri family. On the floor is a monumental slab in relief of one of the Altieri, who died in 1431, at the age of 110; and of another who died at the age of 90.

Chapel of the Rosary, adjoining. Frescoes on the vault representing the fifteen Mysteries of the Rosary, by *Marcello Venusti*. Frescoes on the side walls; incidents in the life of

St. Catherine of Siena, by *Giovanni de' Vecchi.* The Madonna and Child over the altar is attributed to *Fra Angelico.* Beneath this altar reposed the remains of St. Catherine of Siena, but within the last few years they have been removed to the high altar, where they lie in a marble sarcophagus, surmounted by a recumbent figure of the Saint, before which lamps are always burning.

On the right of the altar is a statue of John the Baptist, recently sculptured by *Obici,* and on the left a statue of CHRIST, by *Michael Angelo;* the brass drapery is an addition, and the foot has been covered with brass to prevent its being injured by kissing.

Within the choir—which has beautiful stained glass windows of modern manufacture—are the monuments of two of the Medici Popes, Leo X., 1530-22, and Clement VII., 1523-34, both sculptured by *Baccio Bandinelli,* with the exception of the statue of Leo, which is by *Raffaello di Monte Lupo,* and the statue of Clement, by *Giovanni di Baccio Bigio.*

Chapel of St. Domenic, at the end of the left transept, ornamented with black columns, contains the monument of Benedict XIII., 1724-30, who belonged to the Dominican order, designed by *Carlo Marchionni,* who also sculptured the bas relief and the angels holding the Pope's arms; the statue of the Pope and of the Virtue on the right are by *Pietro Bracci;* and the Virtue on the left is by *Pincellotti.*

Returning down the left aisle,

Second Chapel, dedicated to St. James. The picture of the Saint over the altar is by *Marcello Venusti.* Against the right wall is a grand statue of THE ANGEL OF THE RESURRECTION, forming part of the monument by *Tenerani,* erected to the Duchess Lanti, *ob.* 1840.

Fourth Chapel, dedicated to the Saviour and St. Filippo Neri, contains statues of John the Baptist and of St. Sebastian, by *Mino da Fiesoli*.

The Popes Eugenius IV., 1431-47, and Nicholas V., 1447-55, were elected in this Church.

Turning to the left, by the side of the Church, and then taking the first turning to the right, we reach the Convent, which, until recently, was the head-quarters of the Jesuits, and their principal Church,

THE GESU.

On the site where this Church and enormous Convent stand were two blocks of buildings divided by a street, and in each a Church, one dedicated to the Virgin, and the other to St. Andrew.

These were thrown down by Cardinal Alexander Farnese, in 1543, to make room for the General's house, founded that year, and in 1568 the Church was commenced by *Vignola*, who carried up the walls as far as the cornice. After his death, the work was continued by *Giacomo della Porta*, by whom the façade was designed.

Upon no Church of the same size in Rome has so much been expended on the decoration of the interior, with so little effect. The walls and vaultings are covered with sculpture, painting, gilding, and a profusion of the rarest marbles, to an extent which only escapes vulgarity through the superlative costliness of the materials. The eye becoming wearied by the excess of ornamentation thrown together without taste or style, is content to rest on details which, if skilfully put together, would have produced infinitely greater results.

The frescoes on the ceiling painted in illustration of the passage, In Nomine Jesu omne genu flectatur, are by Baciccio, as also those within the cupola and the vault of the tribune. The high altar was designed by *Giacomo della Porta;* the picture of the infant Saviour in the Temple is a recent work by *Capalti.* The front of the altar is panelled with veneers cut from a block of a very remarkable variety of spata fluore, supposed to be the celebrated *Murrhine* stone of antiquity, discovered some years ago at the Marmorata. The beautiful antique pale green marble, with white almond-shaped marks, of which the altar rail is made, is well worthy of examination.

The chief point of interest in the Church is the Chapel of St. Ignatius Loyola, the founder of " the Society of Jesus," which fills the end of the left transept. Notwithstanding a superabundance of ornamentation, the costly materials are here put together with a sumptuous magnificence approaching grandeur. The flutings of the bronze Corinthian columns are veneered with *lapis-lazuli.* In the pediment forming one of the accessories to the group of the Trinity, is a globe of lapis-lazuli of immense value. Within the niche above the altar—in front of which is an oil painting which serves as a kind of curtain—stands a silver statue of St. Ignatius, studded with jewels, nine feet in height, wrought by *Gio Federico Ludovisi* from the model by *Le Gros.* At the base of this statue are two angels with cornucopiae in their hands and holding between them a tablet on which are inscribed the words AD Majorem Dei Gloriam. On each side of the altar is a dramatic group of sculpture; one representing The Faith triumphing over Idolatry, by *Théodon;* the other, Religion beating down Heresy, by *Pierre Le Gros.*

(*Turning to the left from this Church, a few hundred yards, brings us to the Capitol.*)

Proceeding along the Via Cesarini, immediately opposite the Gesu, and continuing onwards in a direct course, we find in the line of the houses on the left, and near the end of the street, the small Church of the Stsimo. Sudario, the national Church of the Savoyards, recently redecorated with great taste.   The royal family regularly attend Mass here, the Church being the private property of the house of Savoy.   At the end of the street we find

ST. ANDREA DELLA VALLE.

a handsome Church, commenced in 1591, from the designs of *Olivieri*, and completed by *Carlo Maderno*, with the exception of the façade, which was built by *Carlo Rainaldi*.

It is chiefly celebrated for the frescoes, by *Domenichino*, on the vault of the tribune.   They are classed among his finest works, but notwithstanding their excellence, they were so severely criticised at the time, that he is reported to have gone to look at them in despair; and, after examining them for some time, to have turned away, saying, " they did not seem to him to be so very bad."

In the centre is the calling of Peter and Andrew; on the right the Flagellation of St. Andrew; on the left, St. Andrew being led to Martyrdom on the Cross; and above, his Glorification.   On the summit: St. John the Baptist, pointing out our Saviour to St. Andrew and John, the son of Zebedee, and saying, " Behold the Lamb of God," &c.

The Evangelists, in the angles above the four piers which support the cupola, are also by *Domenichino*.   The interior of the cupola, which measures 55 feet in diameter, and is the largest in Rome after St. Peter's, was entirely painted by *Lanfranco*.   The arrangement of the Glory is very fine, and particularly so when seen exactly from the centre of pavement, so that the windows of the lantern throw a complete circle of light.

The large frescoes on the wall of the tribune, representing three incidents in the Martyrdom of St. Andrew, are by *Mattia Preti*, Knight of Malta, commonly called *Il Calabrese*.

On the last piers of the nave, to the right and the left, are the curious fifteenth century monuments of the two Popes of the Piccolomini family, Pius II., 1458-64, and Pius III., 1503. These monuments were originally in old St. Peter's, and were brought here as being out of character with the edifice to which it gave place.

Buried under the accumulation on which this Church and the neighbouring houses stand, are the ruins of THE THEATRE OF POMPEY and of THE CURIA OF POMPEY, where Cæsar was assassinated.

Proceeding along the narrow Via di Massimi, at the further corner of the piazza to the left, we pass between Nos. 19 and 17, THE PALAZZO MASSIMO ALLE COLONNE, so called from its curious carved portico in a line with the houses. In the drawing-room of this palace is a remarkably fine antique copy of the celebrated Discobolus, by *Myron*—the finest of the several copies found—discovered near the Trophies of Marius on the Esquiline in 1761.

It was in the house adjoining that Conrad Sweynheim and Arnold Pannartz established the first printing press in Rome, in 1467.

Continuing onwards, we pass on the right THE CHURCH OF ST. PANTALEONE—rebuilt in 1621, and to which a new façade was added, by Valadier, in 1806—standing in a small piazza called after it. Then passing along the short Via di St. Pantaleo, we come to THE PALAZZO BRASCHI, now THE

MINISTRY OF THE INTERIOR, on the right; and find at the further angle of this building, and facing on a kind of triangular piazza, the celebrated fragment of an antique group of sculpture, called

PASQUIN.

In the days when Rome had no free press, it was on the pedestal of this fragment that the Romans used to affix those witty epigrams and biting satires on public persons and events, at making which they are so apt. Of course, they were speedily torn down, but the means of publication was sufficient. A written paper at once drew a crowd, and the few who had time to read, rapidly passed the pungent words along. These pasquinades were sometimes mere epigrammatic remarks, by Pasquin alone. At others, they were in the form of dialogues, carried on between PASQUIN and other statues, or fragments of statues, known to the people. His chief interlocutors were MARFORIO, the statue of Oceanus, in the Courtyard of the Capitoline Museum of Sculpture (*see page* 117); MADAMA LUCREZIA, the battered fragment of a colossal statue of Isis, in the Piazza San Marco (*see page* 116); THE BABUINO, the statue of an ape, in a niche next to the shop of No. 50, in the Via Babuino— in front of which there was a fountain, recently removed; and another old statue, to which the name ABATE LUIGI was given.

Retracing our steps towards the Palazzo Massimo, we find, on the right shortly before reaching it, the Via dei Baullari, along which we turn and proceed as far as the opening of the Piazza della Cancelleria, the further side of which is formed by

THE PALACE OF THE CANCELLERIA.

It was founded by Cardinal Ludovico Scarampo Mezzarota, and completed in 1517, from the designs of *Bramante*, by Cardinal Raffaello Riario, nephew of Sixtus IV., 1471-84. Directly it was finished the office of the Cardinal Vice-Chancellor was removed hither from the old Cancelleria, now the Sforza-Cesarini Palace. The architecture of the doorways was finished somewhat later. That facing upon the Piazza was designed by *Domenico Fontana*, and the other, towards the Church of S.S. Lorenzo and Damasus, by *Vignola*. This Palace was entirely constructed with materials obtained from ancient edifices; the travertine was taken from the Colosseum and from the Arch of Gordian, which spanned the Corso at the corner of the Via Lata (*see page* 103), and was thrown down for that purpose; the columns and great masses of red Egyptian granite employed in the portico, with a quantity of other material, belonged to the Theatre, Portico, and Curia, of Pompey, which occupied this neighbourhood.

The forty-four granite columns in all probability formed part of the *ecatostilo*, or portico of one hundred columns, attached to the Theatre of Pompey.

It was in this Palace that the short-lived Parliament, elected in virtue of the constitution given by Pius IX., and which made the commencement of his reign so glorious, held its sittings. It was here that the mob burst into the chamber, crying out for war against Austria, after the Pope, with the famous "*non devo, non posso, e non voglia,*" spoken to the people from the balcony of the Quirinal, withdrew his consent to the Roman Volunteers marching to join the forces of Carlo Alberto; and it was here in the

month of November, 1848, that the Prime Minister, Count
Rossi, was assassinated as he left his carriage, and was
entering the portico to ascend to the Chamber of Deputies.

Retracing our steps by the Piazza della Cancelleria to
the Via dei Baullari, we turn to the right—and crossing
the large Piazza called the CAMPO DE FIORI, the chief vegetable market of Rome, we see before us, at the end of the
street,

THE FARNESE PALACE,

without exception the grandest of the many grand Palaces
in Rome, not only in size but in architectural beauty. It
was built, as far as the cornice, by the celebrated architect,
Antonio Picconi, for Cardinal Farnese, afterwards Paul III.,
1534-50. The material employed was chiefly travertine,
the whole of which was taken from the Colosseum. When
Cardinal Farnese had ascended the Pontifical throne he
was desirous of surmounting his Palace with the most
magnificent cornice that could be designed. He confided
its execution to *Michael Angelo*, but was barely satisfied
with the result. Cardinal Alexander Farnese employed
Giacomo Barozzi da Vignola to construct the great hall
painted in fresco by *Annibale Caracci;* and finally *Giacomo della Porta* built the façade towards the Tiber.

The magnificent frescoes by *Annibale Caracci* and his
scholars, which adorn the grand hall of this palace, and
formed the chief attraction to strangers and to lovers of art,
are no longer shown to the public since the first floor was
let to the French Ambassador to the Pope. Strangers
must content themselves with looking at the courtyard,
which, however, is particularly fine. On the further side
is a sarcophagus, reputed to be that which contained the

body of Cecilia Metella. It was not however found within her monument, but near it; and the style of the carving indicates a much later period than that in which Cecilia Metella could have lived.

The great granite basins of the fountains in the Piazza, in front of the Palace, were originally enormous baths in the Tepidarium of the Baths of Caracalla, among the ruins of which they were found. They measure 17 feet in length by 4 in width.

Turning to the left, on leaving the Farnese Palace, and proceeding along the Vicoli de Venti, which is in a line with the front, we enter the small Piazza Capo di Ferro, the left side of which is formed by

THE SPADA PALACE,

built during the pontificate of Paul III., 1534-50, by *Giulio Mazzoni da Piacenza* for Cardinal Girolamo Capodiferro, from whom the Piazza takes its name. The Palace afterwards passed into the possession of the Mignanelli family, and in the time of Urban VIII., 1623-44, into that of Cardinal Bernardino Spada, by whose family name it is now called. He employed *Borromino* to modernise and enrich it with a quantity of ornament not in the very best style.

Ascending the staircase, we enter a large hall—now undergoing restoration — where stands the celebrated STATUE OF POMPEY, which there is fair reason for believing to be that at the base of which " great Cæsar fell." There has necessarily been a great deal of controversy on a subject concerning which there is no absolute proof; but, in brief, a statue, not that of an Emperor, but bearing in his hand the emblem of Sovereign Power, having a considerable resemblance to the portrait of Pompey on his coins, and found among the remains of the series of edifices—the theatre, temple, portico, and Curia—wherein Cæsar was assassinated—built by him on this spot, could scarcely be other than that erected to him, and especially mentioned by Suetonius. It would be absurd to suppose that there were two statues of Pompey erected in the same place, and that this is not the one at the base of which Cæsar fell.

As regards the edifices built by Pompey, considerable remains of them are still traceable among the lower stories of the houses, and many were visible in the sixteenth century.

The Pompey was found in the year 1553, under the wall dividing two houses in the Vicolo de Leutari, close by the Cancelleria, and its discovery gave rise to a dispute, which threatened to result in serious injury to the statue, if not its destruction. It was claimed by the owners of both houses; by one, on the plea that the head lay under his; by the other, because the greater portion of the body and legs lay beneath his. The matter was referred to the Judicial authorities, who gave the Solomonian judgment that it should be cut in two; each to take the portion which lay upon his property. At this juncture Julius III., 1550-55, interfered, and giving 500 scudi (about £100 sterling), to be divided between the litigants, made the statue a present to Cardinal Capodiferro, by whom this Palace was built.

From the hall we pass into the Picture Gallery, which is open to the public on Mondays, Wednesdays, and Saturdays from 10 to 3.*

* The attention of the Spada family especially is drawn to the porter, who, with his family, and particularly his son, a tall, thin youth, are notoriously uncivil and extortionate towards persons who visit this gallery.

FIRST ROOM.

5.—David with the Head of Goliath : *Guercino.*

7.—Urban Rocci, dressed as a Pilgrim : *French School.*

8.—The Triumph of David : *Pannini.*

9.—Fruit and Flowers : *Castiglioni.*

10.—Cardinal Naro Patrizzi : *Camuccini.*

13.—David dancing before the Ark : *Pannini.*

18.—Cain killing Abel : *Lanfranco.*

22.—A girl holding a pair of compasses, called Geometry : *Michael Angelo da Caravaggio.*

29.—The Death of Cleopatra : *Romanelli* (?)

30.—Youth carried off by Time : *Romanelli.*

39.—Fruit and Game : *Castiglione.*

40.—Portrait of Julius III., who rescued the Pompey : *Scipio Gaetani.*

48.—St. Christopher : *Antonio Razzi.*

53.—A Storm : *Tempesta.*

54.—The Roman Daughter : *Bolognese School.*

55.—Slaying the faithful Shepherd : *Luca Giordani.*

SECOND ROOM.

1.—Astronomy : *Sebastiano del Piombo.*

2.—Cardinal Bernardino Spada : *Guercino.*

3.—Madonna and Child ; *style of Murillo.*

4.—Jacob's Well : *Nicholas Poussin.*

9.—Attack on a Village : *Breughel.*

10.—Judith : *Guido.*

15.—St. John the Baptist preaching in the Desert : *Breughel.*

16.—The Visitation : *Andrea del Sarto.*

18.—The Revolution of Masaniello at Naples : *Cerquozzi.*

19.—The Woman taken in Adultery : *Il Calabrese.*

22.—Two Drinkers : *Michael Angelo da Caravaggio.*

26.—The Death of Lucretia : *Guido.*

32.— Time carrying off Beauty : *Solimène.*

36.—*Sic transit gloria Mundi :* Cupids playing with soap bubbles : *Unknown.*

43.—Our Saviour disputing with the Doctors, after that in the National Gallery, London : *Leonardo da Vinci.* (?)

THIRD ROOM.

2.—St. Anne and the Virgin : *M. A. da Caravaggio.*

3.—Dalila and Samson : *French School.*

4.—St. John the Baptist : *Giulio Romano.*

5.—Latona transforming the Shepherds into Frogs : *Chiari.*

6.—The Judgment of Paris : *Luca Cambiasi.*

7.—Adoration of the Shepherds : *Valentin.*

12.—Cleopatra and Mark Antony : *Trevisani.*

15.—The Mill : *Breughel.*

23.—David with the Head of Goliath: *Michael Angelo da Caravaggio.*

24.—The Death of Dido: *Guercino.*

26.—Sketch for the Fresco on the vault of the Gesu: *Baciccio.*

29.—Landscape: *Salvator Rosa.*

40.—A Portrait: *Moroni.*

41.—Madonna and Child: *Simone da Pesaro.*

42.—A Portrait: *Titian.*

48.—God the Father surrounded by angels: *Palmegiani.*

49.—Our Saviour meeting His Mother on the way to Calvary: *Palmegiani.*

58.—A Botanist: *Moroni.*

63.—The Rape of Helen: *Guido.*

66.—Horatio Spada: *Titian.*

71.—Portrait: *Moroni.*

73.—The Prodigal Son: *Guido.*

74.—Our Saviour driving out the Money Changers: *Il Calabrese.*

75.—The Massacre of the Innocents: *Pietro Testa.*

Fourth Room.

3—Winter: *Teniers.*

4—Cardinal Bernardino Spada: *Guido.*

15—Two Cherubs' heads: *M. A. da Caravaggio.*

16—The Vestals guarding the Sacred Fire: *Paolo da Cortona.*

17—The Woman taken in Adultery: *Venetian School.*

23—Deposition from the Cross: *Caracci.*

24—The Magdalen: *Guido Cagnacci.*

25—The Triumph of Bacchus: *Chiari.*

26—The Betrayal of our Saviour: *Gherardo della Notte.*

30—St. Cecilia: *Michael Angelo da Caravaggio.*

31—Cardinal Fabrizio Spada: *Carlo Maratta.*

34—A Head of a Saint in Fresco: *Unknown.*

38—The Magdalen: *Guercino.*

41—Portrait of a Girl: *Paolo Veronese.*

44—Madonna and Child: *Andrea del Sarto.*

49—The Sacrifice of Iphigenia: *Testa.*

50—The Birth of Bacchus: *Chiari.*

In some small rooms on the ground floor there is a collection of ancient sculpture for the most part worthless, with the exception of a small seated statue called Aristotle (?) (No. 5), and eight bas-reliefs of great beauty found in 1620, in the Church of St. Agnes, outside the walls, where they had been turned face downwards, and utilised as slabs for the pavement.

65—Pasiphæ and Dædalus.

66—Meleager.

67—Ulysses and Diomed robbing the Temple of Minerva.

68—Paris and Helen.

69—Adrastus and Hypsipyle finding the body of Archemorus.

70—Amphion and Zethus.

71—Bellerophon watering Pegasus.

72—Paris and Ænone.

Continuing onwards to the right, the street terminates in the Via dei Pelligrini, turning along which to the right we reach THE PONTE SISTO, and crossing it can pass on into the Trastevere, described in the following section. By keeping directly onwards—after crossing the bridge— along the Via S. Dorotea, we shall find the Via della Lungara on the right, and proceeding along it for a short distance we shall come to the Corsini Palace (*see page* 307) on the left. The Church of St. Onofrio (*see page* 304) is some distance further on in the same direction. Or if we keep straight on from the Via S. Dorotea, along the Via Garibaldi, we shall ascend the Janiculum to the Church of St. Pietro in Montorio, and from thence to the Villa Pamphili Doria, outside the Porta San Pancrazio.

THE TRASTEVERE.

Following the Section " *From the Piazza di Spagna to St. Peter's* " as far as the Castle of St. Angelo (*pages* 38 *to* 47), we turn to the left after crossing the bridge, and keeping to the left, pass along the Borgo Santo Spirito.

The long, low building on the left, with busts upon the parapet, is THE HOSPITAL OF SANTO SPIRITO, founded by Innocent III., 1198-1216. It was rebuilt in 1471, by *Buccio Pintelli*, for Sixtus IV., who added the great hall, which measures 376 feet in length, by 37 feet in width, and 44 feet in height. Afterwards *Palladio* added the cupola, and designed the altar below it, at the time when he was studying the ancient monuments, and it said this is the only work he executed in the city. Paul III., 1534-49, employed *Antonio San Gallo* to add a new wing. Gregory XIII. 1572-85, and Alexander VII., 1655-67, made further additions. Benedict XIV., 1740-58, directed *Ferdinando Fuga* to build another great hall, and finally, Pius VI., 1775-1800, made another great addition, on the opposite side of the street. This Hospital is capable of receiving upwards of 1600 patients.

At the further extremity of the Hospital, is THE CHURCH OF SANTO SPIRITO IN SASSIA, said to have been founded by Ina, King of the Saxons, in the year 717, together with a hospital for the use of the Saxon Pilgrims. Falling to ruin in the course of time, it was rebuilt by Innocent III., at the same time with the adjoining hospital, from the designs of *Marchionne*, a sculptor and architect of Arezzo. It was restored by Innocent IV., 1242-54, and was again rebuilt by Paul III., 1534-49, from the designs of *Antonio San Gallo*, with the exception of the façade, built by *Otavio Mascherino* in the time of Sixtus V., 1585-13.

Passing the Church, we turn immediately to the left, along the Via dei Penitenzieri, and after proceeding a short distance, pass through THE PORTA SANTO SPIRITO—commenced, but left unfinished, by *San Gallo*, in the wall of the Leonine city—and enter the Via della Lungara.

The long modern building on the left is the Lunatic Asylum, founded by Benedict XIII., 1724-30.

On the right a narrow street leads up the incline to

THE CHURCH OF ST. ONOFRIO,

built in 1419, by a certain Niccolo da Forca Paleno, a Hermit, of the order of St. Jerome, afterwards beatified. It is celebrated as containing the remains of the great poet TASSO, who is buried here, and who died in the adjoining Monastery on the 25th of April, 1595.

Against the wall, immediately to the left on entering, is the monument with a painted portrait, erected to his

memory by Cardinal Bevilacqua, above where his remains
rested beneath the pavement; the spot marked by a simple
slab. In 1857 they were removed and placed within the
grand memorial—erected by public subscription, headed by
Pius IX.—in the adjoining chapel, and the original slab in
the pavement was replaced by another. The new monument, executed by the sculptor *Fabris,* is not unworthy of
the subject, though the life-sized statue of the poet is
somewhat theatrical in character.

The room in the monastery, which Tasso occupied, and in
which he died, is shown to visitors. Until recently, women
were not permitted to see it, except on the 25th of April,
the anniversary of his death, but now they are admitted at
any time. It contains a number of relics connected with
the poet:—his chair; his inkstand; the cast taken from
his face after death, somewhat disfigured by having been
converted into a bust, and the eyelids separated; the crucifix which stood on his table; some of his writing; and
other objects.

In a glass case on one side, the leaden coffin is preserved,
which contained his remains up to the year 1857, and above
it, the original slab from the pavement.

Strangers will be struck with the extreme shortness of
the coffin, but in fact it is nothing more than a leaden box
made to contain his bones. He was first buried in a
common wooden coffin, close to the high altar. Six years
later, *i.e.,* in 1601, the grave was opened for the purpose of
removing the remains to the spot beneath the monument
erected by Cardinal Bevilacqua, when it was found that the
coffin had fallen to pieces, and nothing remained but fragments of wood and the bones of the poet, which were then
placed within this leaden box. The dates, of his death,

X

MDXCV., and of the removal of the remains, MDCI., are recorded on the original slab above.

On the wall is a full length portrait of Tasso, painted in fresco a few years ago, by *Filippo Balbi*, of Naples.

TASSO's OAK, the tree under which he used to sit in the garden of the monastery, is shown to visitors. It was much injured by the great storm in the autumn of 1842. From this spot there is a magnificent panoramic view of Rome.

The Church is very quaint in character. On the floor are a number of interesting monumental slabs, well preserved; some sculptured in low relief, others with figures incised upon them, after the manner of monumental brasses.

The frescoes on the vault of the apse are by *Pinturicchio;* those on the wall of the apse, below the little cornice, are by *Baldassare Peruzzi*—all much injured by restoration.

On the floor of the third chapel, on the left, is the monumental slab to the memory of the celebrated linguist, Cardinal Mezzofanti, ob. 1849, who is buried here.

The first chapel, on the left, with a vaulted ceiling supported by small columns, is dedicated to St. Onofrio.

The second, ornamented with stuccoes, is dedicated to the Madonna of Loreto; and against the wall beyond it is the monument of Archbishop Sacchi, ob. 1502, in the lunette, above which is a charming little fresco by *Pinturicchio.*

The monumental slab, placed upright against the wall to the right of the door before entering, is that of the founder of the Church, the Blessed Niccolo da Forca Paleno, ob. 1449. Three of the lunette frescoes on the right side of the little two-sided portico, and that over the door, covered with glass, are by *Domenichino*, much injured by exposure.

In the corridor leading to Tasso's room is a lunette, painted in fresco by *Leonardo da Vinci*.

After leaving the Church, the first turning on the right leads down a rapid incline, broken by steps,* to the Via della Lungara, along which we turn to the right.

On the right we pass the Botanical Gardens, and continue onwards till we reach

THE CORSINI PALACE,

on the same side. This splendid edifice was built by *Ferdinando Fuga*, in 1729, for Cardinal Nereus Corsini, nephew of Clement XII.—their monuments are in the Corsini Chapel, in the Lateran—on the site of the Riario Palace, built by the nephews of Sixtus IV., 1471-84. It contains a very fine collection of paintings, open to the public on Mondays, Thursdays, and Saturdays, from nine to three; and a fine library, open to students every day after one o'clock, excepting Wednesdays and festas.

FIRST ROOM.

9. The Plague at Milan: *Muratori.*
10. The Marriage of St. Catherine of Alexandria: *Carlo Maratta.*
15. St. Catherine of Alexandria holding the infant Jesus in her arms: *Zoboli.*
17. Men playing at cards in a village tavern: *Locatelli.*
18. A wine shop: *Locatelli.*
20. A *Bambochade: Locatelli.*
24. View of the port of Venice: *Canaletto.*
26. VIEW OF VENICE: *Canaletto.*
Portion of a Christian Sarcophagus, sculptured with a representation of the Vintage: *over the door.*
Pagan Sarcophagus: Tritons and Nereids, found at Syracuse.

* These steps are generally in such a filthy condition that ladies—unless they desire to witness a striking example of what Rome used to be until recently, when so much of the picturesque, loudly regretted by some, was removed—had better retrace their steps by the street up which they ascended, and, at its foot, turn to the right along the Via della Lungara.

Second Room.

26. Adam and Eve mourning the death of Abel: *Cerquozzi.*
29. The Prodigal Son: *Cerquozzi.*
31. Portrait of a woman: *Luini.*
32. Lucretia: *Carlo Maratta.*
40. Jacob's Dream: *Macon.*

Third Room.

1. ECCE HOMO: *Guercino.*
2. THE VIRGIN AND INFANT CHRIST: *Carlo Dolci.**
9. The Virgin and Infant Christ: *Andrea del Sarto.*
10. Birth of the Virgin: *Ludovico Caracci.*
15. The Virgin and Infant Christ: *Andrea del Sarto.*
17. The Virgin and Infant Christ: *Michael Angelo da Caravaggio.*
28. Interior of a Tavern: *Teniers.*
38. The Meet: *Wouvermans.*
44. POPE JULIUS II.: *Raphael.*
49. ST. APOLLONIA: *Carlo Dolci.*
50. PHILIP II., KING OF SPAIN: *Titian.*
51. The Infant Jesus and St. John the Baptist: *Carlo Cignani.*
52. Vanity: *Saraceni.*
53. Marriage of St. Catherine of Alexandria: *Paolo Veronese.*
81. The Annunciation: *Vasari.*
82. St. John the Baptist: *Carlo Maratta.*
88. ECCE HOMO: *Carlo Dolci.*
89. ECCE HOMO: *Guido.* †

Fourth Room.

11. Herodias with the head of St. John the Baptist: *Guido.*
18. St. Andrew kneeling before his Cross: *Andrea Sacchi.*
19. Martyrdom of St. Peter: *Guido.*
27. Two heads: *L. Caracci.*
28. St. Jerome praying in the Desert: *Titian.*
40. FAUSTINA MARATTA, daughter of *Carlo Maratta.*
41. The Fornarina: *Guilio Romano.*
44. A Hare: *Albert Durer.*
The Genius of fishing, statue: *Tenerani.*
The Genius of hunting, statue: *Tenerani.*

Fifth Room.

12. ST. AGNES: *Carlo Dolci.*
14. The Annunciation: *Carlo Maratta.*
16. The Holy Family: *Schidone.*
23. The Virgin and Infant Jesus: *Albani.*
24. Our Saviour and the Samaritan Woman: *Guercino.*
25. The Infant Christ: *Battoni.*
28. Our Saviour ordering St. Peter to pay the tribute with the money found in the fish's belly: *Luca Giordano.*
32. The Angel of the Annunciation: *Guercino.*
37. Our Lady of Sorrows: *Guido.*
38. ECCE HOMO: *Guido.*
39. St. John the Evangelist: *Guido.*
40. The Annunciation: *Guercino.*
45. The Crucifixion: *Guido.*

---

* This picture is generally on an easel, for the convenience of copyists, in the second room.
† Compare Nos. 88 and 89 with No. 1.

SIXTH ROOM.

15. Head of an old man: *Rubens*.
21. The two children of Charles V.: *Titian*.
31. The wife of Martin Luther: *Holbein*.
35. Portrait of Martin Luther: *Holbein*.
40. Cardinal Divitius de Bibiena: *Bronzino*.
43. Cardinal Albert of Brandenburgh: *Albert Durer*.

47. Portrait of Rubens: *Campiglia*.
50. Cardinal Alexander Farnese: *Titian*.
54. Lorenzo de Medicis: *Bronzino*.
67. Portrait of Mary Queen of Scots: *Oliver*.
68. Cardinal Nereus Corsini: *Bacciccio*.

SEVENTH ROOM.

11. WOMAN AND CHILD: *Murillo*.
13. Landscape: *Gasper Poussin*.
15. Angels removing the arrows from St. Sebastian: *Rubens*.
18. Our Saviour bearing His Cross: *Garofolo*.
22. The descent of the Holy Spirit upon the Apostles: *Fra Angelico*.

23. The Last Judgment: *Fra Angelico*.
24. The Ascension: *Fra Angelico*.
28. A Landscape: *Orrizonte*.
30. The woman taken in Adultery: *Titian*.
34. A Landscape: *Orrizonte*.

EIGHTH ROOM.

2. Holy Family: *Francia*.
6. A Cattle-field: *Claude*.
8. ECCE HOMO: *Vandyke*.
10. The history of Niobe: *P. da Caravaggio*.
11. Holy Family: *Nicholas Poussin*.
13. Contemplation: *Guido*.
15. Nymph surprised by a Satyr: *Gaspar Poussin*.
18. Susanna and the Elders: *Domenichino*.

21. Village by the sea side: *Gaspar Poussin*.
23. Sheep: *Gaspar Poussin*.
24. St. Jerome writing his Commentaries: *Guercino*.
25. St. Jerome meditating upon death: *Spagnoletto*.
26. Portrait of a Florentine Senator: *Bronzino*.
40. A Faun: *Gaspar Poussin*.
41. A Pastoral Scene: *Gaspar Poussin*.

CABINET.

10. ECCE HOMO: *Guido*.

22. A triptych: *Orcagna* (?).

NINTH ROOM.

2. An Interior: *Teniers*.
9. Pope Innocent X.: *Velasquez*.
26. Portrait of a woman: *Bronzino*.
28. A Battle Piece: *Salvator Rosa*.
29. *Idem: Salvator Rosa*.
30. The Virgin visiting St. Elizabeth: *Giorgione*.

33. Holy Family: *Barocci*.
35. A Battle Piece: *Salvator Rosa*.
36. Portrait of a young woman: *Titian*.
49. The Virgin and Infant Christ: *Gherardesca*.

Opposite the Corsini Palace is

THE FARNESINA,*

a kind of intermural villa, built by the wealthy banker
Agostino Chigi, from the designs of *Baldassare Peruzzi*, in
1506, as a place where to give those sumptuous entertain-
ments for which he was so celebrated.   It was at this villa
that he gave the grand banquet to which he invited Leo X.,
the Cardinals, Ambassadors, and other notabilities of the
day; and as the plate on which they had dined was removed from the table had it thrown into the Tiber, that it
might not be degraded by being put to inferior use.

It is more particularly celebrated, however, for the
beautiful FRESCOES BY THE HAND OF RAPHAEL, and from his
designs, illustrating the fable of CUPID AND PSYCHE, painted
on the ceiling of the first room—originally open towards
the garden—into which we enter.   The incidents of the
story are represented on the curved portion, in the following
order:—

1. Venus angrily pointing to Psyche on earth, of whom she was jealous, and commanding Cupid to punish her with the pains of love.
2. Cupid having become enamoured of Psyche, draws the attention of the Graces to her.
3. Juno and Ceres refusing to aid Venus to find Psyche.
4. Venus in her car, drawn by doves, hastening to claim the assistance of Jupiter.
5. Venus entreating Jupiter.
6. Mercury sent by Jupiter to find Psyche.
7. Psyche carrying the Vase from the Infernal regions to appease Venus.
8. Psyche presenting the Vase to Venus.
9. Cupid interceding with Jupiter against his mother's opposition and cruelty.
10. Psyche carried by Mercury into the presence of Jupiter and the gods of Olympus.

The two large frescoes on the flat of the ceiling represent
Psyche brought by Mercury before Jupiter and the Council

* Open to the public on the 1st and 15th of each month.

of the Gods on Mount Olympus; and the marriage of Cupid and Psyche. In the lunettes are " Loves" carrying the attributes of the gods. The continued garland of flowers, by which the subjects are bordered, was painted by *Giovanni da Udine.* The whole of these frescoes have been injured through being retouched by *Carlo Maratta.*

The beautiful fresco of GALATEA, BY RAPHAEL, on one of the compartments in the adjoining room, is believed to have been entirely painted by himself, with the exception of the group of Tritons on the right. The lunettes in this room were painted by *Sebastiano del Piombo* and *Daniele da Volterra.* The colossal head in chalk in the lunette near the left window is said to have been drawn by MICHAEL ANGELO, and left as a kind of visiting card for Daniele da Volterra. The frescoes on the ceiling are by *Baldassare Peruzzi.* The landscapes on the walls were painted, at a later period, by GASPAR POUSSIN.

In the upper rooms: the walls of the first are decorated with architectural paintings by *Baldassare Peruzzi,* and the frieze, with subjects from Ovid's Metamorphoses, is said to be by *Guilio Romano.* In the second, is the marriage of Alexander and Roxana; and Darius at the feet of Alexander, by *Sodoma.*

Turning to the left, from the Farnesina, we pass under THE PORTA SEPTIMIANA, a gateway rebuilt by Alexander VI., 1492-1503, on the site of that said to have been constructed by Septimius Severus, in the original wall of fortification.

The Via Garibaldi, on the right, leads up the side of THE JANICULUM to THE CHURCH OF ST. PIETRO IN MONTORIO, and to THE VILLA PAMPHILI-DORIA; *for these, see index.*

There is a little gothic window, with a painted arch, above the baker's shop, No. 20, in the Via di S. Dorotea, on the

left, which is said to be that at which Raphael first saw the
Fornarina; this street leads to the Ponte Sisto (*see page* 303).
Continuing in a direct line onwards along the Via della
Scala, passing on the right the little CHURCH OF STA. MARIA
DELLA SCALA, built in 1592, by *Francisco da Volterra*, with
a façade by *Ottavio Mascherino*, and through the little
Piazza of S. Egidio, we reach the side of the Basilica of

STA. MARIA IN TRASTEVERE,

and, turning to the left, along the Via della Paglia—which
also leads off to the right—we enter through the Portico,
which faces on the Piazza di S. Callisto.

This fine old Basilica, which surpasses in grandeur and
solemnity those of St. John Lateran and Sta. Maria Maggiore, has recently been repaired and redecorated throughout
with perfect regard to the restoration, where possible, of
its primitive simplicity, and particularly as regards the
tribune, with its ancient episcopal throne of marble.

Here stood the TABERNA MERITORIA, a kind of asylum for
disabled veterans, on the site of which the Church was
founded, in commemoration of an extraordinary occurrence
which happened here about the time of the birth of our
Saviour, and which was afterwards interpreted as being a
miraculous indication to the Romans of the grace of God
made manifest through the coming of the Redeemer. It is
narrated by Eusebius, of Cesarea, by Eutropins, and by
Orosius, that in the year 753 of Rome, shortly before the
birth of our Saviour, a spring of mineral oil burst forth,
and ran during an entire day in a rapid stream towards the
Tiber. The inscription **FONS . OLEI·** close to the high altar,
is said to mark the site of the well.

In consequence of the belief attached to this circumstance, a small Church was founded here by S. Callixtus, in the year 222, but during the subsequent persecutions it was abandoned, and fell to ruin. About the year 340, it was rebuilt by S. Julius II., and John IV., 702-4, decorated it with paintings. Gregory II., 715-31, restored it in part, and his successor, Gregory III., 731-41, strengthened the foundations and re-roofed it. Adrian I., 772-95, added aisles to what had been a single nave and enriched the Church with endowments; and his successor, Leo III., 795-816, adorned it with many precious objects. Gregory IV., in the year 828, built a monastery dedicated to Pope S. Cornelius, in connection with the Church, and, raising the pavement of the Tribune, formed the confessional in front of the high altar, beneath which he placed the bodies of Sts. Callixtus, Cornelius, and Calepodius. Leo IV., about the year 848, restored it throughout; but, notwithstanding this, his successor, Benedict III., 855-58, found it necessary to rebuild the tribune and other parts.

It is evident, from this continued series of repairs and restorations, that the primitive edifice was never in a very strong condition, and we find that Innocent II., 1130-43, rebuilt the Church from the foundations exactly as we see it—with the exception only of the richly carved ceiling, placed by Cardinal Pietro Aldobrandini, in 1617, from the designs of *Domenichino*; the portico, rebuilt by *Fontana*, for Clement XI., 1700-21; and such few later additions as monuments, &c., which are at once evident. Innocent II. laid the floor with the beautiful pavement of *Opus Alexandrinum*; * ornamented the vault of the tribune

---

* This pavement has been entirely relaid in the course of recent restorations, but the original design has been scrupulously preserved, and if it has now a very modern look, different from the antique appearance of the other pavements of the same kind elsewhere, it must be borne in mind that, like discoloured and damaged statues, they have that appearance through age, while this in reality gives us a more exact representation of the original character of the *Opus Alexandrinum*.

with the mosaic we see; erected a marble ciborium over the high altar, supported by four columns of porphyry, which still remain, though the rest of the ciborium, having disappeared, has been replaced with woodwork; and to the bodies of the saints beneath the high altar added that of St. Quirinus, taken from the Catacomb of S. Callixtus. What was left incomplete by Innocent was finished by his successor, Eugenius III., 1145-53, by whose order the mosaic on the façade was commenced, and finally completed, in the 14th century, by *Pietro Cavallini*, a pupil of Giotto's. This mosaic façade enables us to understand what those of Sta. Maria Maggiore and of the other great Basilicas were like. Nicholas V., 1447-55, Pius V., 1566-72, and other Popes, bestowed care upon this Church, and made alterations and additions as regards the chapels, but the architects employed in no way changed the general aspect of the edifice.

The aisles are divided from the nave by eleven columns on each side of red and grey granite, taken from ancient edifices, surmounted by antique capitals of great beauty. The majority of them are ornamented Doric, and are particularly interesting from the small busts of Isis, Serapis, and Harpocrates sculptured upon them. Some of the columns stand on richly ornamented antique bases.

The chapel at the end of the right aisle, designed by *Domenichino*, is dedicated to the Madonna of the Via Cupa, from a miraculous picture removed from that lane outside the Porta Pia, and placed over the altar. The iron railing which closes the chapel, and has the arms of England above the gate, was erected at the expense of Cardinal York, brother of the young Pretender.

The monument against the wall of the aisle before

entering this chapel was erected in 1524, to two members of the Armellini family; the figures in the central compartment represent St. Laurence and St. Francis.

Immediately opposite this, at the end of the left aisle, is a very picturesque gothic altarpiece : two spiral columns supporting a canopy ornamented with small statues of saints. The picture above the altar, representing the martyrdom of St. Philip, who, like St. Peter, was crucified with his head downwards, is said to have been painted about the year 1390, but having been entirely worked over, it has lost the characteristics of the period. It is, nevertheless, an interesting work. This altarpiece was erected at the expense of Cardinal d' Alençon, brother of Philippe le Bel of France, and nephew of Charles de Valois. It originally stood in the nave, and was removed to its present position by Cardinal d'Altemps in 1582, who, at the same time, had his portrait introduced at the right-hand corner of the picture above the altar.

The monument on the left is that of the Cardinal d' Alençon, ob. 1403, who erected the altarpiece. The bas-relief represents the transit of the Virgin.

The monument on the right of the altar is that of Cardinal Pietro Stefaneschi degli Annibaldi. It was sculptured at the commencement of the 15th century by a celebrated Roman sculptor of that period, named *Paolo*, whose name it bears, and who in all probability was the author of the monument of Cardinal d' Alençon.

The chapel, dedicated to the Sacrament, at the end of this aisle, was built by *Onorio Lunghi* the elder, for Cardinal d' Altemps, in the time of Pius IV., 1559-66. The vault is divided into compartments, ornamented with subjects from the life of the Virgin, painted in fresco by *Pasquale*

Cati da Jesi, by whom also are the frescoes on the side of the walls: one representing the Council of Trent, and the other the Consistory of Cardinals, held by Pius IV., when the acts of the Council were presented to him.

The beautiful mosaics on the vault and face of the apse were executed by order of Innocent II., 1130-43. The series on the wall below the vault—representing incidents from the life of the Virgin: *i.e.*, The Birth of the Virgin; The Annunciation; The Birth of Christ; The Adoration of the Magi; The Circumcision; and, The Death of the Virgin —were executed by *Cavallini*, about the year 1290; and by him also is the mosaic above the episcopal throne, representing the Madonna and infant Christ, with St. Paul on the right and St. Peter on the left, presenting to her Bertoldo Stefaneschi—ancestor of the Cardinal Stefaneschi, whose monument we have already noticed—majordomo to Nicholas IV., and at whose expense these mosaics by Cavallini were made.

About the middle of the left aisle is a monument to Innocent II., recently erected at the expense of Pius IX.

To the right of the main door on entering is a beautiful little ciborium for the holy oil, sculptured by *Mina da Fiesole*, and bearing the words **OPUS MINI**.

The stained glass windows in the front are modern, and were placed during the recent restorations.

Leaving Sta. Maria in Trastevere by the main entrance, we cross the piazza to the opposite left-hand corner, and continuing along the Via della Lungaretto, the sixth turning on the right brings us in front of the lateral entrance of the

BASILICA OF ST. CRYSOGONO.

This ancient Church—the date of its foundation is not

known, but there is record of its existence from the year 499—is connected with the history of England, through two of its cardinals titular. The first, Giovanni da Crema, was sent as Apostolic Legate to England by Honorius II., 1124-30, and presided at the synods held in London and Westminster. He was afterwards sent in the same capacity to David I., of Scotland. The second was Stephen Langton, Cardinal Archbishop of Canterbury in the time of John, when Innocent III., 1198-1216, laid England under an interdict, and finally succeeded, for the time, in making England and Ireland tributary to Rome.

The earliest record of this Church is the mention of three of its titulars as sitting successively in the Roman synod held in 499. Gregory III., 731-41, restored the roof, ornamented the walls and apse with paintings, and enriched the Church with many valuable gifts, among which was a ciborium of silver. Leo III., 795-816, Gregory IV., 827-44, and Benedict III., 855-58, presented it with sacred hangings. In 1623, Cardinal Scipio Borghese, nephew of Paul V., employed *Gio. Battista Soria* to restore it throughout, and from that period it has remained unchanged. No material alteration was made in the formation of the building; the twenty-two antique granite columns which divide the aisles from the nave, and the two magnificent porphyry columns which support the arch of the tribune, stand as they were originally placed. The vault of the apse was once covered with mosaic, but it has all disappeared, with the exception of a small portion above the episcopal throne, on which the Virgin and Child, with St. Chrysogonus and St. James, are represented. The picture of St. Chrysogonus, borne to heaven by angels, which forms the centre of the ceiling, is a copy from one by *Guercino*, which originally occupied the same position, but is now in the Duke of Sutherland's collection. This Basilica does not contain any works of art worthy of notice.

Leaving the Basilica by the main entrance, and crossing to the further right-hand corner of the piazza, we shall find another small piazza, called the Monte di Fiore. Excavations were made here in 1866, which resulted in the discovery of an *Excubitorium*, or

GUARD-HOUSE OF THE VIIth COHORT OF THE VIGILES,

whose barracks were situated in this region, but the exact locality is not known.*

The walls, to the height of about five feet from the pavement, are covered with wainscoating of stucco coloured red, which is entirely covered throughout with graphites, rude scratchings made by the soldiers. These are exceedingly interesting, inasmuch as the majority of them are made in imitation of inscriptions recording certain SEBACIARIA,† or illuminations with tallow lights made by the soldiers on different festive occasions. Many of these graphites give not only the names of the consuls for the year, but also the month and the day, so that there has been no difficulty in ascertaining what were the events in honour of which several of these *Sebaciaria* were made. One, for instance, dated the year 221, was made on the occasion of the adoption of Alexander Severus by Heliogabalus; and this graphite is very curious, from the circumstance that the

---

* The Vigiles, or firemen and police of ancient Rome, were instituted by Augustus, who divided them into seven cohorts—one for each two of the fourteen regions into which Rome was divided. The seventh cohort was quartered in the Tenth Region, the Trastevere.

+ This word is not found in any Latin Lexicon, but it is believed to have been derived from *Sebum*—tallow, and to signify an illumination with tallow lights; as Ceriolarium, derived from Cereum—wax, signifies an illumination with wax lights or candles.

Emperor's name was afterwards scratched out, evidently in obedience to the decree of the Senate, made after his death the following year, that his name should be erased from every public document. Another bears the name of Dion Cassius, the celebrated historian, who, together with the Emperor Alexander Severus, was consul A.D. 229, and states that the *Sebaciaria* was made in honour of the taking of the decennial votes, when, it also records, the Emperor gave each of the Vigiles ten gold pieces. A third records that the illumination was made in honour of the accession of Gordian III. to the Imperial throne.

On other parts of the walls are considerable traces of fresco painting, and on one side there is a kind of niche or recess, also delicately painted, in front of which is a doorway of great architectural beauty, and quite unique of its kind. It is entirely formed of brickwork. On each side are pilasters of the finest red brick, with bases and Corinthian capitals of yellow brick supporting a pediment. The capitals were carved after the doorway was built. The pavement is formed of black and white mosaic—Tritons and sea monsters. On the floor is a kind of octagonal basin, with concave sides, made of *opus signinum*, supposed to be a fountain. A passage cut through the accumulation leads to a bath chamber, on the walls of which are considerable remains of marble panelling, but it has not yet been ascertained if it formed any part of the guard-house.

Turning to the left, from the Monte di Fiore, along the Via San Crisogono, we take the first turning to the left, the Via de Genovesi. At some little distance along this street we find a small piazza on the right. Above the wall on the further side we see a square church tower, and crossing to the further right-hand corner we pass through a small doorway into a little court yard, and find the lateral entrance to

THE CHURCH OF SANTA CECILIA.

We have no record of the exact date at which this Church was built, but the name of the Titular of Sta. Cecilia is appended to the acts of the Roman Synod, held under Pope Symmachus, A.D. 499. There is every reason for believing that it marks the site, and was built among the remains of the house where this wealthy and charitable Roman lady and saint resided, and where she suffered martyrdom. She was married to a Pagan husband, Valerianus, with whom, according to the legends of the Church, she lived in a state of virginity, and was finally converted to the faith, together with her brother Tiburtius. Valerianus and Tiburtius were taken to the Temple of Jupiter on the Appian Way (*vide page* 230), where they suffered martyrdom, by decapitation, by order of Almachius, Prefect of Rome. Later, Almachius, desiring, it is said, to obtain possession of Cecilia's wealth—which, however, she had almost entirely distributed among the poor—ordered her to be executed within the precincts of her palace. An attempt was first made to stifle her in the vapour bath, but that failing, an executioner was sent to behead her. Three blows having been made ineffectually, the execution, in accordance with the Roman law under such circumstances, was stayed. For three days she continued to teach and exhort those around her to live for Christ's sake only, and then, beseeching Pope Urban to take care of her poor people, and to dedicate her house to Christian uses, she died from loss of blood on the 22nd of November, in the year 280; and her body was placed in the catacomb of St. Callixtus, near those of her husband and brother.

By the beginning of the ninth century, the Church, having fallen into a very ruinous condition, Paschal I., 817-24, determined to rebuild it. He had removed the bodies of many saints and martyrs from the catacombs to places of greater security in the churches within the walls, and was desirous of finding the remains of Sta. Cecilia to place them in this. Having searched for some time ineffectually, he supposed they had been stolen by Astolphus, King of the Longobards; when one Sunday, having fallen asleep near the high altar of St. Peter's, Sta. Cecilia appeared to him in a dream, and told him "that he had approached so near to her resting place that if he had liked he might have spoken to her." On this, Paschal recommenced the search, and found her body, together with those of her husband, Valerianus, and Tiburtius, her brother, and that of Maximus, the chamberlain of Almachius, who having been converted through their martyrdom, at which he was one of the presiding officers, also suffered for the faith. He discovered, at the same time, the remains of the Popes Urban and Lucius, and removing them, together with those of Sta. Cecilia, Valerianus, Tiburtius, and Maximus, from the catacomb of St. Callixtus, placed them beneath the high altar. The beautiful mosaic on the vault of the apse is part of the enrichment with which Paschal I. embellished the Church. In 1283, during the Pontificate of Honorius IV., the Church was restored throughout, and at that time the ciborium, still standing over the high altar, was made by a certain Arnulphus, whose name it bears, HOC OPUS FECIT ARNVLPHVS ANNO DOMINI MCCLXXXIII. On the corners are statuettes of

Y

Cecilia, Valerianus, Tiburtius, and Pope Urban. The Church was again restored throughout in the year 1599, by Cardinal Paolo Sfrondati, nephew of Gregory XIV., and in the course of the works necessary to this purpose the remains of the martyred saints were disclosed beneath the high altar. *Bosio*, the celebrated writer on the Catacombs, who was present at the time, has left a description of the condition in which they were found. On removing the altar, three arches were revealed beneath. In the first a coffin of cypress wood was found, lined with a kind of serge woven with green and red threads, and in it the body of Sta. Cecilia, enveloped in a veil of dark coloured silk, beneath which was her robe of cloth of gold, stained with blood; the robe she had worn during life, and which was upon the body when originally discovered by Paschal I. The saint was lying on her right side, with her knees somewhat drawn up, her arms extended, and her face turned towards the ground; in the attitude, in fact, in which we see her represented in the beautiful statue which occupies the niche below the altar. During the days while her embalmed body lay exposed to public view, and while all Rome flocked to see it, the sculptor, *Stefano Maderno*, made an exact copy from it, and produced in marble not only a perfect record of the condition and pose in which the body was found, but also one of the purest and most touching statues ever carved by the hand of man.

At the same time, also, one of the bath chambers belonging to Cecilia's house was found, and as the *calorifories*, or earthenware pipes, for conveying the heat, which surrounded the room, prove that it was a vapour bath, it is supposed to be that in which the attempt to smother St. Cecilia was first made. A door from the right aisle leads into this bath

room, but it has been so much changed by the introduction
of modern altars, fresco paintings, and the like, that it conveys but little idea of what its original formation was,
except indeed to those who are acquainted with the construction of the Roman baths.

In 1725, other restorations were made to the Church by
Cardinal Acquaviva, and in 1823, Cardinal Giorgio Doria
enclosed the twenty-four columns of grey granite in the
common looking pilasters which now divide the aisles from
the nave.

On the right of the door after entering, is an interesting
monument erected to Adam of Hertford, ob. 1397, who
was Cardinal Titular of this Church, and administrator of
the diocese of London. The body of the tomb is ornamented
with the arms of England of the time. On the left side is
the monument of Cardinal Niccolo Fortiguerra, ob. 1473,
who was papal legate under Pius II., 1458-64, and Paul II.,
1464-71.

The painting of the martyrdom of the Saint, on the wall
of the tribune, is attributed to *Guido.*

On the cornice of the portico, which is supported by two
granite columns, and two of Chian marble, commonly
called *Africano,* is a curious mosaic frieze, with medallion
portraits of Cecilia, Valerianus, Tiburtius, and Urban I.,
supposed to be of the ninth century. In the courtyard
before the Church is an ancient marble vase, called a *Can-
tharus,* of large size.

Leaving the Church by the main entrance, and crossing
the court, we turn to the left, and then taking the first turning to the left, the Via de Genovesi, proceed along it as far
as the second street on the right, the Via Anicia, at the end
of which we shall find an archway, called the Arco di

Tolomei.   We pass under this, and continue onwards in as
direct a line as possible, till the street ends in one which
traverses it at right angles ; then turning to the right, the
first turning on the left, the Via Piscinula, leads across the
Ponte di S. Bartolommeo, to the ISOLA TIBERINA, commonly
called

THE ISLAND OF ST. BARTHOLOMEW.

After the expulsion of the Tarquins, the crops of corn
which they had sown on the Campus Martius, and which
were just ripe for the sickle, were cut down and flung into
the Tiber.   The river being shallow, after the heat of the
summer, the sheaves stranded on a mud bank in the middle
of the stream at this point, and created a nucleus, which,
being afterwards purposely increased, formed this island.
It was dedicated to Esculapius, and on the site of the Temple
to that deity,

THE CHURCH OF ST. BARTOLOMMEO

was built, by—it is believed—the Emperor Otho III., at the
commencement of the eleventh century.   It is situated at
the further side of a small piazza, a short distance on the
right, after crossing the bridge.   From an inscription upon
the architrave of the central door, it is believed that
Paschal II. either restored or embellished the Church, in
1113.   In the year 1180, Alexander III. erected a new confession, the work of the sculptor *Niccolò di Angelo*, the
same who carved the great marble candelabrum for the
Pascal candle, in the Basilica of St. Paul, outside the walls ;
and, in 1284, Ognissanti Callarario de Tederini erected a
handsome marble ciborium.   During the great inundation
of 1557, this Church was almost entirely ruined. The confession and ciborium were broken to pieces, and the mosaic

with which the front was decorated, was destroyed, with the exception of half the figure of the Saviour holding an open book, on which are the words EGO . $\overline{\text{SV}}$. VIA . VERITAS . ET . VITA. This fragment is now preserved in the choir above the portico.   The Church remained closed till the time of Gregory XIII., 1572-85, when the Titular Cardinal, Santorio, employed *Martino Lunghi*, the elder, to commence its restoration, which was completed by Cardinal di Trejo, in 1625. It was again devastated in 1798, and restored in 1806, and has recently been redecorated and painted by the Padre Bonaventura Gofredo, one of the monks of the Franciscan order, whose convent is attached to this Church.

We enter through a portico sustained by four granite columns.   The aisles are divided from the nave by seven columns on each side.   Some of the chapels are decorated with paintings by *Antonio Caracci*, a descendant of the great painters of that name, but beyond these, the Church does not contain any works worthy of special observation. Under the high altar is a porphyry urn, containing the relics of St. Bartholomew, and in front of the tribune is a curious well-head of the 12th century, supposed to be the work of the *Niccolò di Angelo*, above mentioned. The figures upon it represent the Saviour, St. Adalbert, St. Bartholomew, and the Emperor Otho III.

In the piazza in front of the Church is a handsome cross with four statues of saints, erected in 1870, by order of His Holiness Pius IX.

Continuing onwards to the right, we reach the PONTE QUATTRO CAPI—the ancient PONS FABRICIUS—which takes its modern name from the four-faced terminal figures which stand at the opening.

The Via Fiumara, on the left, after crossing the bridge,

forms the lower part of The Ghetto; but we continue
directly onwards, and passing a Church, said to have been
built by a converted Jew, on the front of which the Crucifixion is painted, with, below it, in Hebrew and in Latin,
the words from the 65th chapter of Isaiah, " I have spread
out my hands all the day to a rebellious people," we turn
to the right into the Via del Monte Savello. The architectural fragment, in travertine, slightly projecting from the
house, No. 70, is a portion of the Theatre of Marcellus;
and the gateway to the left, as we stand looking at this,
with Bears on the imposts, is the entrance to the Orsini
Palace, built upon the *Cavea, Orchestrum,* and *Pulpitum*
of the theatre.

Passing onwards, and taking the first turning to the left,
we find ourselves in front of that portion of the exterior of
the Theatre of Marcellus, which is still visible, and can
from this point continue the route laid down in the following section.

FROM THE THEATRE OF MARCELLUS TO ST. PAUL'S, OUTSIDE THE WALLS.

Passing from the Piazza di Spagna along the Via Condotti, we turn to the left into the Corso, and continuing on
as far as the Piazza de Venezia, and turning immediately to
the right, take the streets as follows:—The second turning to
the left past the front of the Church of the Gesu (*see page*
292), along the Via Ara Cœli, and taking the third turning to the right, the Via Tor de Specchio, immediately at
the foot of the ascent to the Capitol, we pass directly
into the Via Montanara, a short distance along which we
shall find the grand remains of

on the right side. This magnificent ruin stands more than half buried among the modern houses built around it,—under the Orsini Palace, erected upon its stage and ranges of seats, —and in some twelve feet of accumulation, which fills up two thirds of its lower arcade to the height of the modern pavement. The upper part of the range of arches which opened from the ancient level, and formed the grand arcade, once crowded with the patrician ladies and togad senators of Imperial Rome, is now converted into a series of squalid shops, and against the piers sit vendors of cigar ends to the plebs of modern Rome.

It was founded by Julius Cæsar, who, according to Dion Cassius, desired to build a theatre like that of Pompey, but, being unfinished at the time of his death, it was continued and completed by Augustus, who dedicated it B.C. 13, to his nephew Marcellus, then recently deceased; the same Marcellus whose death is lamented by Virgil, in the lines ending " *tu Marcellus erit.*" We read that it was capable of giving accommodation to 30,000 spectators. The exterior was divided into separate stories, as we have seen in the Colosseum, and, in fact, the architect of that edifice would seem to have designed its exterior in close accordance with the architectural lines of this theatre. The two lower arcades were open porticoes, the piers ornamented with engaged columns, the lower of the Doric, the upper of the Ionic order. The arches of the lower portico have been converted into shops, and those of the upper, walled in, are now used as the servants' offices of the Orsini Palace. Above the porticoes was an attic pierced with rectangular windows, and ornamented with pilasters, possibly, of the Corinthian order. The material is travertine.

It was injured during the Neronian conflagration, A.D. 65, and was restored by Vespasian. It was again damaged by fire in the time of Titus, and restored by Septimius Severus. After the death of Gregory VII., in 1086, it was turned into a fortress by the Pierleone, and during the two following centuries, was subject to that series of vicissitudes through which the Colosseum and other noble edifices suffered in the contentions between the turbulent Barons of that period. The Pierleone sheltered Urban II. within it, in the year 1099, and in it that Pope died in 1118. About—it is conjectured—the year 1220, it passed into the hands of the Savelli, in whose possession it remained until that family became extinct in the year 1712, when it was purchased by the Orsini, who still retain it.

Turning to the right, and passing the remains of the theatre on the left, we enter a narrow squalid street, the Via del Teatro di Marcello, which occupies one side of

THE PORTICO OF OCTAVIA.

The fronts of the houses on the one side and the other mark the double row of the columns, many of which, though hidden, are incorporated into the walls, as we see two in the house No. 11, on the left side, where the wall has been recessed back. At the end of this street we find the grand vestibule, formed by magnificent Corinthian columns of white marble, sustaining a double pediment, one facing outwards, and the other inwards upon the area enclosed by the portico. This portico was in the form of a rectangular double line of columns, and measured 750 feet in length upon the sides, and 500 across the front and end. The pediments of the vestibule were each supported by four columns and two pilasters, of which, towards the inside, one column is wanting, and upon the outside, two, to supply the place of which a brick acrh was built at some comparatively early, but unknown, period. Passing to the further end of the vestibule, and along the filthy fish market in a line with the street, by which we approached the Vestibule, we shall find, just visible through fractures in the wall on the left, four other columns of the portico, in a direct line with those in the Via del Teatro di Marcello.

The portico was originally built by Quintus Cecilius Metellus, about 147 B.C., to enclose the Temples of Jupiter,* built by him, and of Juno Regina, erected by Marcus Æmelius Lepidus, in the year 178 B.C. In the year 32 B.C., both the Temples and the portico were rebuilt on a scale of greater magnificence by Augustus, who dedicated the portico to his sister Octavia. The architects employed were *Sauros* and *Batracos ;* and Pliny relates, that, as they were not permitted to place their names upon the work, they hit upon the device of carving among the foliage of the capitals, a frog and a lizard. A curious circumstance is related by Pliny regarding the statues of the Divinities. When the Temples were completed, and the pedestals ready to receive the statues, the slaves who carried them placed, by mistake, the statue of Jove in the Temple of Juno, and that of Juno in the Temple of Jove. Directly the mistake was discovered, the Augurs were consulted, and they decided that the statues should remain as they were, because, for some inscrutable reason, the gods had so willed it. This grand portico, containing within its area two magnificent temples, was peopled along its four sides with masterpieces

* This was the first marble Temple erected in Rome:

of Greek sculpture; and in the area in front of the Temples
were ranged the 75 bronze equestrian statues of the generals
and friends of Alexander the Great, who perished at the
passage of the Granicus.   They were the work of Lysippus,
and were brought away from Macedon to Rome by Metellus.

These magnificent edifices, and the many works of art
which adorned them, were destroyed during the great conflagration, in the time of Titus, A.D. 80, and continued in ruins
for 123 years, when they were rebuilt by Septimius Severus,
as recorded by the inscription upon the outer pediment.
The inside of the inner pediment, where the marble facing
has been destroyed, shows the old material, parts of
columns and cornices, with which it was, in part at least,
reconstructed.

The Church built within the portico, and which has its
entrance from the vestibule, is called St. Angelo in Pes-
cheria.   It dates from the eighth century; was rebuilt in
1610, and has been recently restored.   It contains nothing
of particular interest.

Returning by the Via del Teatro di Marcello, and repassing the Theatre of Marcellus on the right, we continue
along the Via Montanara, as far as No. 72, where a little
piazza opens on the right in front of

THE CHURCH OF SAN NICCOLA IN CARCERE.

It takes its name from a tradition which connects it with
the prison built by Appius the Decemvir, the same in which
that celebrated event occurred, of the life of a man condemned to death by starvation being saved by his daughter,
who visited him daily, giving him milk from her breast.*

---

* This story is differently told.   Pliny and Valerius Maximus say it was a mother
condemned to death, and Festus that it was a father.

The scene, however, of this touching event, which occurred in the year 149, B.C., was obliterated by Julius Cæsar; for Pliny, after narrating the story, and stating that the spot in the prison where it occurred was dedicated to the daughter's piety, says that it was situated "where the Theatre of Marcellus now is."

This Church is exceedingly interesting from the circumstance that it is built among the remains of three temples—THE TEMPLE OF HOPE, built about 253 B.C., by Aulus Attilius Calatinus, in fulfilment of a vow made during his Carthagenian campaign; THE TEMPLE OF JUNO MATUTA, built by Cneius Cornelius Cethegus, in the year 195 B.C., in fulfilment of a vow made at the commencement of the victory he gained three years before over the Cisalpine Gauls ; and THE TEMPLE OF PIETY, vowed by the Glabrio, who gained the great victory over King Antiochus at Thermopylæ, but which was built and dedicated by his son, M. Acilius Glabrio, in the year 181 B.C.   No doubt the story of the piety of the daughter who saved her parent's life became, in process of time, confused with that of the piety of the son who fulfilled his father's vow, and thus the event which occurred in the neighbouring prison became connected with this Church.

Of these three Temples considerable remains can still be traced, but it will be necessary for the visitor to have recourse to the Sacristan to point them out.

The platforms on which the Temples were built, and the crypt* of that of Piety, can be examined by descending into the subterraneans of the Church.

* When Byron was in Rome, this crypt was shown as the actual spot in the prison where the daughter saved her parent's life, and to it he has dedicated the stanza in Childe Harold commencing, " There is a dungeon, in whose dim drear light."

Beyond the remains of these temples there is nothing worthy of notice in the Church. It is supposed to have been built in the time of St. Gregory I., 590-604, but there is no positive mention of it till the year 1100. In 1599 the Cardinal Pietro Aldobrandini employed *Giacomo della Porta* to restore it, and it has recently been redecorated throughout.

Continuing down the Via Montanara, as far as No. 96 on the right, we find, at a short distance on the right hand side of the Via di Ponte Rotto, the picturesque remains of a baronial mansion of the middle ages, which is called

THE HOUSE OF RIENZI.

Whether it ever belonged to "The Last of the Tribunes," or was inhabited by him, it is impossible to ascertain. The inscription, however, shows that it was built by Nicholas, the son of Crescentius and Theodora, and was given by him to his son David, and there can be little doubt but that the Crescentius and Theodora named, are the same persons who figured so prominently during the disturbances in the time of the Emperor Otho III.

The house is a remarkable example of the manner in which, during the 10th and 11th centuries, corbels, cornices, and other architectural features of ancient edifices were utilised as ordinary building materials, and made to serve the purpose of decoration in a very rude quaint manner. On the side towards the Via Montanara, a massive and evidently richly sculptured architrave has been incorporated into the wall with the bottom outwards, that it might serve for the inscription mentioned. Connected with the inscription are a number of initial letters, which, with much ingenuity, have been explained as referring to Cola di Rienzi, but it is, at best, a mere matter of conjecture that they do so. A few steps further leads us on to

THE PONTE ROTTO,

which can now be crossed by means of the suspension bridge, erected a few years ago. Here was the Pons Æmilius of ancient Rome. The actual construction was built by Gregory VIII., in 1575, and during the inundation of 1598, the arches on this side of the river were carried away. From that time it has been known by the name of the Ponte Rotto, or broken bridge.

From the suspension bridge we have a fine view, on the one side of the ISLAND OF ST. BARTHOLOMEW (see page 324), and on the other of THE AVENTINE. The piers of a ruined bridge which appear just above the surface of the water, as we look towards the Aventine, are the remains of the celebrated PONS SUBLICIUS, which Horatius kept. On the left we see the little TEMPLE OF VESTA (so called), and below it, if the water is not too high, the mouth of THE CLOACA MAXIMA, with its three arches of masonry, one within the other.

Returning from the bridge we see, immediately opposite to the house of Rienzi,

THE TEMPLE OF FORTUNA VIRILIS,

the most ancient of the Roman temples remaining, and which has been preserved almost intact, through its having been converted into a Church dedicated to the Virgin, in the year 872, by a certain Stephen, who walled up the spaces between the columns of the portico to increase its size. In the time of Pius V., 1566-72, it was given to the Armenians, and from that time has been called SANTA MARIA EGIZIACA.

This Temple dates from about the year 214 B.C. The original Temple of Fortuna Virilis, built by Servius Tullius, 557 B.C., was burnt down in that year, and immediately afterwards rebuilt as we see. (Pliny XXIV., 47.) It is exceedingly interesting, not only as showing the manner in which the Temples were constructed of the native stone of the country, before marble was introduced, but as the purest example of the Ionic order existing among the remains of ancient Rome. Not only, therefore, have we evidence of the date given by the material, but the style proves the edifice to have been built at a time when the Romans had become well acquainted with the Grecian orders, but before they commenced to debase their proportions by attempting to improve and embellish them.

A few steps further bring us to the beautiful little circular edifice called

THE TEMPLE OF VESTA.*

Nothing whatever is known concerning this edifice, either as regards the period when it was built, or the deity to which it was dedicated. It is attributed to Vesta, on account of its circular form, but the Temples of Hercules were also round, and some are disposed to think it may have been dedicated to him. All that can be said is, that the arguments for and against each theory are equally strong.

It is a *perypteros*, formed by twenty Corinthian columns, of which one only is wanting; and, judging from the workmanship, was probably built about the end of the first century. We owe the preservation of this Temple, also, to its having been dedicated to Christian uses. The spaces

---

* This must not be mistaken for the celebrated Temple of Vesta. It stood at the corner of the Forum. (See page 138.)

between the columns were walled up by the Savelli family, who had the building consecrated, under the title of St. Stefano delle Carrozze. In 1560, the dedication was changed to that of STA. MARIA DEL SOLE. At the commencement of this century, the spaces between the columns were re-opened, and the building restored, as far as possible, to its original condition. At the same time some of the accumulation, which covers the ancient level around it, was removed on the right side, to show the foundations of the steps which surrounded it.

Almost immediately opposite is

THE CHURCH OF STA. MARIA IN COSMEDIN.

This Church is said to have been built by Pope Dionysius, 259-69—or about fifty years before St. John Lateran was constructed,—within the remains of an ancient edifice, of which nine Corinthian columns are visible, incorporated into the walls of the original building. These columns are supposed by some to be part of a Temple of Ceres and Proserpine, by others of a Temple dedicated to Pudicizia Patrizia, and by others again to be the remains of a portico called the Schola Græca. In 772 St. Adrian I. embellished the Church sumptuously, and from the splendour of the ornamentation it received the name of Sta. Maria "*in Cosmedin*," from the Greek κοσμος. In 1118, Pope Gelasius II. was elected within it, and in 1191, Celestine III. Here also the Antipope Benedict XII. was proclaimed. By the commencement of the 18th century it had become surrounded by accumulation to the depth of six feet, so that it was necessary to descend into the Church by a flight of steps.

In 1715, Clement XI. removed this accumulation by

lowering the Piazza to its present level. In 1718, the Titular Cardinal Annibale Albani employed *Giuseppe Sardi* to build the present façade.

The popular name of this Church is THE BOCCA DELLA VERITA, from a curious circular marble mask of large size, at the end of the portico on the left. It originally formed the opening to a small drain, or an outlet for the water of a fountain; but the people believe that it once stood upon the altar of Jupiter Ammon, as an instrument of ordeal for those accused of perjury, on whose hands, when placed within it, the mouth closed if they were guilty.

The pavement of the nave is constructed of beautiful *Opus Alexandrinum*. The raised portion towards the altar formed the platform for the choir, of Phrygian marble, like that in the Basilica of St. Clemente, but only the ambones now remain. The little tabernacle, richly ornamented with mosaic, against the left pier of the apse, is the work of *Diodati Cosmati*, by whom it may be presumed is the mosaic work in the marble baldachino, supported by four columns of red Egyptian granite, above the high altar.

A small portion of the fresco painting, with which Adrian I. adorned the walls, may be seen close to the mosaic tabernacle, but it will be requisite to get the Sacristan to move back the woodwork which conceals it. The ancient episcopal chair, with lions on each side, at the end of the apse, is believed to date from the twelfth century. Above, is an ancient painting of the Madonna, attributed to the same period. In the left wall, looking towards the altar, we recognise three of the Corinthian columns of the Temple of Pudicizia Patrizia (?), and six in the front wall of the Church. In the Sacristy there is an exceedingly interesting mosaic, representing the Virgin and St. Joseph, of the time of John VII., 705-8.   It is a fragment of that which adorned the Chapel of the Madonna in old St. Peter's, from whence it was removed here.

On leaving this Church, we turn to the right, and keeping along the wall opposite to the Temple of Vesta, leave the piazza at the corner, and continuing directly on across the Via dei Cerchi, find the short Via di San Georgio in Vela-bro, on the right, at the end of, and below which, we see a massive ruin,

THE JANUS QUADRIFRONS,

built entirely of great solid blocks of white marble.   It is a magnificent example, and the' only one left to us, of the grand four-fronted arches, of which many existed in ancient Rome, built at the spots where two roads crossed.

Here, in the middle of THE FORUM BOARIUM—the cattle market—the Via Nova and Vicus Jugarius intersected each other, and the arch, while forming a grand piece of street architecture, afforded shelter to the cattle dealers, in the transaction of their business, both from the rain in winter and from the sun's rays during the heat of summer. These arches, in fact, served the purpose of second class basilicas for the use of the frequenters of the lesser *Fora*. The many holes at the junction of the blocks were made to abstract the metal pins.

Close by stands a small square arch, richly ornamented, which affords an example of honorary monuments of this description; it is called

THE GOLDSMITH'S ARCH,

from the circumstance of its having been erected by the money-changers and merchants who had their shops in this market-place, in honour of Septimius Severus, for some

z

privileges he had granted them. The inscription, like that upon the triumphal arch of Septimius Severus, on the Forum, bears evidence to the record that Caracalla, after the murder of his brother at Geta, obliterated his name from every public monument. It will easily be perceived that the original words at the end of the third line were obliterated by lowering the surface of the ground, and replaced by those we now read. One end of this arch is embedded into

THE CHURCH OF ST. GIORGIO IN VELABRO,

built up against it. This ancient Church, dedicated to St. George of Cappadocia, the patron saint of England, is believed to have been built in the fourth century. In the seventh it was restored by Leo II., 682-84; and in the eighth it was rebuilt by Pope Zaccaria, 741-52. Gregory IV., 827-44, ornamented the tribune, and added two porticoes, and about the year 1295 the Titular Cardinal, Giacomo Gaetano Stefaneschi, restored the portico on the front, as we read in the metrical inscription in Gothic letters upon the cornice, and employed the celebrated painter *Giotto* to paint the wall of the tribune. Unfortunately these frescoes have been so entirely repainted over by inferior hands that not a trace of the master's touches can be recognised. The Church was again restored by Cardinal Giacomo Serra, and in 1703 Cardinal Giuseppe Imperiali restored the ceiling, and had it painted by *Francesco Civalli*, and at the same time erected the iron railings between the columns of the portico. Finally, it was again restored in 1819, by the confraternity of Sta. Maria del Pianto, to whom it had been conceded by Pius VII., but without any alteration being made in its original form.

The aisles are divided from the nave by fifteen columns of different marbles and orders, spoils from ancient edifices. The ciborium, ornamented with *cosmati* mosaics, is supported by four columns of black granite, closely resembling porphyry.

Unfortunately, this interesting Church is seldom to be found open.

Returning to the Church of Sta. Maria in Cosmedin, and continuing onwards along the Via della Salara, the first lane upon the left, called the Via di S. Sabina, leads up to the Aventine (*see page* 350).*

A little further on, we pass under a modern arch, which spans the road, and which marks the site of THE PORTA TRIGEMINA, in the Servian circuit. A few yards further on, the road runs along the bank of the river, and turns to the left by the modern marble yard.

The extensive building, on the opposite side of the river, is the great HOSPITAL OF SAN MICHELE.

If, instead of continuing along the road, we pass through the marble yard and proceed a few hundred yards along the river bank, we shall come to the spot where THE ANCIENT MARMORATA, AND THE QUAYS for landing the merchandise brought up the Tiber, was discovered in the year 1869, together with several hundred blocks of rare marble, of different qualities, many of large size, lying just where they had been disembarked. Unfortunately, the mud and sand from the river has been allowed to gather again over these quays, until they are once more almost entirely hidden.

In the vineyard which borders the river, and back about a hundred yards from the bank, stand some magnificent re-

---

* The hurried traveller might do well to turn aside here and visit the objects of interest on the Aventine, and then, returning to this spot, continue this section.

mains of THE EMPORIUM of ancient Rome, for the reception of the merchandise landed here. They are very interesting, not only from their great extent, but as affording one of the very few existing examples of *Opus incertum*, that mode of construction which preceded the *Opus reticulatum*, and passed out of use about two hundred years before Christ. The vineyard, in which the ruins of the Emporium stand, is private property, but, on proper application, admittance can be obtained. The entrance is on the right, directly after passing the modern marble yard.

A few yards along the road, after passing the modern marble yard, we come to a brick arch, in a somewhat ruinous condition. This, and other immense buttress-like masses of brick wall, we have just passed upon the left, jutting out from the side of the Aventine, are remains of THE GREAT GRANARIES, in which corn brought up the Tiber was stored.

A little further, on the right, we find a gateway in the wall which borders the road. Passing through this, and turning immediately to the left, we come to

THE PROTESTANT CEMETERY,

dedicated for the interment of persons of all nations not Roman Catholics, but especially dear to Englishmen, for the sake of the many buried here, whose names are household words. A little to the right on entering is the monument to the sculptor, Richard Wyatt, with his medallion portrait sculptured by John Gibson, at whose expense the monument was erected. A little further to the right, and on the higher ground, is the spot where Gibson himself lies buried. Next to his monument is that, richly inlaid with *cosmati* mosaic, to the memory of the Rev. Francis Woodward, chaplain to the English Congregation in Rome for fifteen years. Further again, on the right, lies Henry S. P. Winterbotham, H.M.'s Under-Secretary of State for the Home Department, who died so prematurely, in 1874. On the higher ground, behind his grave, lie the remains of the sculptor, Alfred Gatley. The heart of the poet Shelley lies under a plain slab at the foot of one of the towers in the Aurelian wall, which rises at the back. To reach the spot we must ascend the path which leads directly upwards from the gate, and, turning to the left, shall find it on the right, after proceeding a few yards along the wall. Keats, on whose simple headstone are inscribed the words, "Here lies one whose name was writ in water," lies in what is called the old cemetery, to the left of that now in use, and which was surrounded by a low wall and ditch, and closed in the year 1825. Near his grave are those of John Bell, the eminent surgeon, and author of the "Anatomy of Expression;" and of Augustus William Hare, "the elder of the two brothers who wrote the 'Guesses at Truth.'" There is an atmosphere of quiet solemn repose about the place which is eminently impressive, but it is a pity that many of the monuments are not as well cared for as others, upon which the friends and relations of the departed are still mindful enough to spend money. It is a pity there is not a fund which would insure the whole being kept in proper order, without reference to whether those left behind have become forgetful, or have also passed away.*

---

* Should any of the readers of this book be unfortunate enough to lose any relation in Rome, they are especially cautioned against the solicitations of the custode of this cemetery for the execution of any monument they may desire to erect, or his recommendations of any one to undertake the task. It is scarcely necessary to say, that he puts himself forward through interested motives, not advantageous either to those who require such works, or those who execute them. The best course persons can follow is to ask some sculptor of their own nation to recommend to them a good reliable mason, and to superintend the execution of the work for them. Some of the best executed monuments in the cemetery have been made by the Guiseppe Sassi—whose address is given among others at the end of the introduction. He is a simple mason, with very little, or nothing, to show in his workshop, but is an excellent workman, and thoroughly understands his business.

At the lower level of the cemetery is a kind of chapel, erected at the expense of Mrs. King, the mother of the Mr. King who was formerly United States Ambassador to Rome, for the temporary reception of those whose remains are to be carried back to their native lands.

At the back, and partly upon the ground of the old cemetery, stands

THE PYRAMID OF CAIUS CESTIUS,

one of the sepulchral monuments upon the old Ostian road, enclosed by Aurelian in the line of his wall of fortification. It is formed of concrete, faced with blocks of pure white marble, now black with age and exposure to the weather. The Caius Cestius, whose name it records, lived in the time of Augustus, and the inscription, seen on the other side from the road leading to St. Paul's, narrates that it was erected by his executors, among whom were M. Valerius, Messalla Corvinus, and L. Junius Silanus, within the period of 330 days. In the year 1663, it was cleared of the accumulation which had risen around it to the height of about 16 feet, and the sepulchral chamber, decorated with paintings, discovered. The pyramid measures 114 feet in height, and at the base 90 feet on each side.

The great mound we see on the left, as we leave the Cemetery, is

MONTE TESTACCIO,

an artificial hill of about 160 feet in height, formed entirely of broken pottery. As there is no rubbish among these fragments, and as they are all portions of vessels which had never been used, it is evident that there must have been a manufactory of terra cotta vessels, *ollæ, dolia, amphoræ,* and the like, at this spot, so extensive that the mere accumulation of the vessels broken in the firing,. or otherwise, was sufficient to form this enormous mound. Chambers have been hollowed out in the sides, and converted into wine cellars. The air passing through the interstices between the fragments, makes these chambers intensely cold, even during the hottest days of summer, and especially fitted for the purpose to which they are applied. The place is a great resort for the Roman people during the summer afternoons, on account of the coolness and excellent quality of the wine sold here.

Returning to the road, and continuing onwards to the right, we pass on to the Ostian way, through THE PORTA SAN PAOLO, rebuilt by Belisarius, on the site of the Porta Ostiensis, of the earlier empire. Immediately on the right, is the Pyramid of Caius Cestius (*see page* 342), and, after passing under the railway bridge, we come to A HUMBLE LITTLE CHAPEL, upon the left, above the door of which is a rude bas-relief, representing St. Paul and St. Peter embracing. This is said to be the spot where they bade farewell to each other when on their way to martyrdom.

Another three quarters of a mile brings us to an immense building, like a great factory, with a bell tower at one end, surmounted by what, in the distance, looks like a gigantic birdcage. This is

THE BASILICA OF ST. PAUL,

outside the walls, but, however unprepossessing the exterior may appear, or however open to criticism the tower may be, the interior is grand and magnificent beyond description.

This ancient Church—the Basilica which, in olden times, was under the special protection of England—was burnt to the ground on the night of the 15th of July, 1823—that which preceded the death of Pius VII., and has since been rebuilt, or rather is still in course of rebuilding, for the façade, which faces towards the river, is not yet finished.

On this spot, where the body of St. Paul was buried, immediately after his martyrdom, Anacletus, the third Bishop of Rome, 78-91, built an oratory, in place of which Constantine the Great founded a Church, in the year 324, at the prayer of St. Sylvester, at the same time when the church in honour of St. Peter was founded upon the Vatican. In the year 386, the Emperor Valentinianus II. commenced to rebuild the Church, which was completed by Theodosius and Honorius, as is recorded on the arch which separates the tribune from the nave, as follows :—

THEODOSIVS . COEPIT PERFECIT HONORIUS AULAM DOCTORIS MUNDI SACRATAM CORPORE PAULI.

The Basilica was afterwards restored and embellished successively by the Popes St. Leo I., 440-61, St. Symmachus, 498-514, Hormisdas, 514-23, John I., 523-26, St· Gregory I., 590-604, Sergius I., 687-701, John VI., 701-5, Gregory II., 715-31. In the time of Leo III., 795-816, it was in great part destroyed by a terrible earthquake, and was restored by him ; but during all these restorations and embellishments the original formation of the edifice, as built by Theodosius and Honorius, was preserved.

The ancient quadri-portico, through which the Basilica was entered, having fallen to ruin, Benedict XIII. built a new portico, in the year 1725, composed of seven archways supported by fourteen marble columns, and at the same time repaired the mosaic with which the front was covered, the work of *Pietro Cavallini*, the celebrated pupil of Giotto.

The Church was entered through three doorways, with

bronze doors, the central of which was remarkable for its beauty, and was made in Constantinople in the year 1070, during the pontificate of Alexander II., and at the expense of a certain Pantaleone Castelli, Roman Consul. The two aisles on each side were divided from the nave by eighty antique marble columns, twenty-four of which were of the richest Phrygian marble of the Corinthian order, and measured 38 ft. 6 in. in height and 12 ft. in circumference. It is supposed that they originally formed part of the Basilica Æmelia on the Forum. The Church measured 423 feet in length and 153 in width. The upper walls of the nave were decorated with frescoes representing subjects from the Old and New Testaments, painted by order of the Pontiffs, St. Leo I., 440-61, and St. Symmachus, 498-514. Beneath these were portraits of the Popes in chronological series, commenced by order of St. Leo I., and including all from St. Peter's to his own. Next, Pope St. Symmachus completed the series down to his time, after which the portrait of each succeeding Pope was regularly added, down to that of Pius VII., 1800-23.

The end of the nave, where it opens upon the transepts, was spanned by an immense arch, supported by two colossal columns of Greek marble, called *salino*, measuring 17 feet in circumference, and richly ornamented with mosaic, representing our Saviour with the twenty-four elders of the Revelations, twelve on each side. This arch was erected and ornamented in the year 440, at the expense of Galla Placidia, sister of the Emperors Arcadius and Honorius. The vault of the tribune was enriched with mosaic, commenced in the year 1226, under Honorius III., by *Pietro Cavallini*, and completed by the order of a certain Arnolfo Sacristi, and of Gaetano Orsini, who afterwards became

Pope, under the title of Nicholas III., 1277-81. Beneath the arch of Galla Placidia stood the high altar, covered by a marble ciborium, ornamented with mosaic, the joint work of *Arnolfo di Lapo* and *Paolo Cosmati.* The body of the altar was formed by an ancient Christian sarcophagus of white marble, covered with bas-reliefs, which was removed by Sixtus V., 1585-90, to the new chapel he had built at Sta. Maria Maggiore, and has since been transferred to the Lateran Museum. Beneath the altar was the *Confession,* where repose the remains of the Apostle of the Gentiles.

With the exception of a few, though important details, all these things were destroyed by the fire in 1823, but the above description, when compared with the Basilica as it now is, will be sufficient to show that it has been rebuilt with the most scrupulous regard to its original form, and, as its plan and internal arrangement were never altered during the many restorations it underwent, we, as a matter of course, have in the new Church an exact representation of one of the larger Basilicas of the Constantinian period. At the very commencement of his reign, Leo XII., 1823-28, decreed that the Basilica should rise from its ruins with all the splendour and magnificence possible. Letters apostolic were sent to all the Bishops of the Catholic world, and to the faithful of all nations. The appeal was generously responded to, a large amount was set apart from the revenues of the State, and the result we now see before us. The walls have been rebuilt upon the original foundations; the 80 columns have been replaced by so many monoliths of granite of the Semplon, and two of colossal dimensions supply the place of those of Greek marble, which sustained the arch of Galla Placidia. The ancient mosaics upon the face of the arch, and upon the vault of the apse, have been carefully restored to almost their primitive condition, though that of the apse still shows considerable trace of the fire. Other paintings on the wall of the nave, by *Gagliardi*, *Podesti*, and other modern Roman artists, supply the place of those executed during the pontificate of St. Leo I., and the chronological series of Papal portraits has been replaced by another, executed in mosaic. The ancient ciborium, fortunately, remained almost uninjured, and still occupies its original position, covered by a more magnificent baldachino, supported by four splendid columns of oriental alabaster, the offering of Mahomet Ali, Viceroy of Egypt, standing on pedestals inlaid with a portion of a large quantity of lapis lazuli and malachite, sent by the Emperor of Russia for the adornment of the Church. The Viceroy of Egypt also sent the columns of oriental alabaster, which stand on the inner side of the main entrance, not yet finished, and all the panelling, of the same material, which adorns the end walls of the transepts and other parts of the basilica. The Confession has been reconstructed with greater magnificence, and the floor of the apse, to which we ascend by two steps of red oriental granite, is paved with ancient marble of the rarest quality. The sides of the apse, and the altars at the ends of the transepts, have been ornamented with beautiful Corinthian columns of Phrygian marble, most skilfully made from the fragments which remained uncalcined of those which originally ornamented the nave, fitted upon cores of peperino.

Above the altar, dedicated to St. Paul, at the end of the left transept, is a picture of his conversion, by *Camuccini*, and in the niches, on the sides, are statues of St. Gregory, by *Laboureur*, and St. Romualdo, by *Stocchi*.

On the left of this altar, as we turn from it towards the

tribune, is the chapel of St. Stephen, ornamented with pictures illustrating his martyrdom, and, above the altar, a statue of the Saint, by *Rainaldi.*

Next to this is the chapel dedicated to the Ancient Crucifix, which stands over the altar, said to have been carved by *Cavallini*, the pupil of Giotto. It was this crucified figure of our Saviour which is said to have spoken to St. Bridget, of whom there is a statue in the chapel. In one corner is a very ancient wooden statue of St. Paul, in the condition in which it was rescued from the fire.

Passing the apse we come to the Chapel of the Sacrament, built by *Carlo Maderno*, in 1629, and which was left almost uninjured by the fire; and next to it the chapel of St. Benedict, with a seated statue of the Saint, by *Tenerani.*

Above the altar at the end of the right transept, is an exceedingly beautiful mosaic copy—recently placed—of the Madonna di Monte Luco, by *Giulio Romano* and *Francesco Penna*, now in the third room of the Picture Gallery at the Vatican. (*See page 75.*)

At each side of the nave, as we ascend to the higher level of the transepts, are colossal statues of St. Peter and St. Paul, by *Obici* and *Girometti.* The windows in the lateral walls are filled with richly stained glass, each window giving a full length representation of an apostle or saint.

The cloisters of the Benedictine Monastery, attached to this Church, are well worth visiting Ladies can only see them through the railing which closes the entrance. They are in the form of a quadriportico, sustained by twisted columns, in pairs, enriched with *Cosmati* mosaic of the 13th century, above which is a cornice richly ornamented in the same manner. On the walls are a number of Christian inscriptions and monuments, which originally stood in the old Basilica.

A little beyond the Basilica of St. Paul, the road bifurcates, and upon that on the left, at the distance of about two miles, we find

THE CHURCH OF ST. PAOLO ALLE TRE FONTANE,

built upon the spot where St. Paul suffered martyrdom by decapitation. It is said that when his head was severed from his body it bounded, touching the ground three times, and at each spot a fountain gushed forth. The present Church, enclosing the fountains, was built in 1599, by *Giacomo della Porta*, for Cardinal Pietro Aldobrandini. The pavement has been recently ornamented with a very valuable mosaic, representing the Four Seasons, discovered in the excavations now being carried on at Ostia.

There are also two other Churches here; one dedicated to Sta. Maria Scala Coeli, so called because St. Bernard, praying here one day for the dead, and passing into a state of ecstasy, saw ladders reaching from earth to heaven, by which a great number of souls were ascending from purgatory. The Church stands above the ancient cemetery of St. Zeno, where, it is said, more than ten thousand martyrs, who suffered during the reign of Diocletian, were buried. It was rebuilt by *Gia. Battista della Porta*, in 1582, for Cardinal Alessandro Farnese. The mosaics in the vault of the tribune were executed, shortly afterwards, by *Francesco Zucca*, a Florentine, from the designs of *Giovanni de Vecchi*. The other is The Ancient Basilica of S.S. Vincenzo and Anastasio, built by Honorius I., in 625. It was restored by Adrian I., about the year 772, and, in 796, Leo III. rebuilt it from the foundations. Charlemagne endowed it with a large extent of land in the territory of Siena.　Innocent II., in 1128, rebuilt, from the foundations, the monastery attached to it, and invited St. Bernard to send monks from Chiaravalle to inhabit it.　He appointed as its first Abbot Pietro Bernardo Pisano, who afterwards became Pope, under the title of Eugenius III., 1145-50.　The Basilica was again rebuilt by Honorius III., in 1221, since when, stripped to the walls, it has fallen into entire neglect.

It is entered through an atrium, once richly decorated with fresco paintings, now almost entirely obliterated.　A figure is pointed out as that of Pope Honorius.　In the interior are rude frescoes of the Apostles, said to have been designed by Raphael.

THE AVENTINE.

Starting from the Piazza de Spagna, we follow the route laid down at the commencement of the last section (*see page* 326), to the Church of Sta. Maria in Cosmedin, and passing it, along the Via della Salara, take the second turning on the left, the Via di Sta. Sabina (counting the street by the side of the Church as one).　It is a lane leading up the side of the hill, and on reaching the summit we turn to the right, and immediately upon the right find

THE CHURCH OF STA. SABINA.*

We ring the bell of the door upon the left, and gain access to the Church through the ancient portico and main entrance.　The appearance of the portico is very much· changed from what it was originally; the spaces between

* The little portico before the door—which is a lateral entrance, now closed—was once supported by columns of very rare green granite, but they were removed by Pius VII. to ornament the Nuovo Braccio in the Vatican Museum.

the columns have been walled up, and the half, on the further side of the handsome carved wood door, has been encroached upon by the buildings of the Monastery, so that we can only recognise four of the fluted columns of Phrygian marble, and four of the granite columns of which it was formed. The door of cypress wood, with subjects from the Scriptures carved upon the panels, dates from the 13th century. It has since been restored and strengthened; the scroll-work which divides the panels is a later addition or restoration.

According to some authorities this Church was erected on the site of the house belonging to the Saint, and in which she suffered martyrdom, during the reign of Hadrian; and according to others, on the site of a temple of Diana, or of Juno Regina, the twenty-four beautiful Corinthian columns of Parian marble belonging to which were utilized to divide the aisles of the Church from the nave. In fact, it would almost appear as if they had been left standing in their original positions, and the wall of the Church built round them. The beautiful carved imposts and architrave of the chief entrance also have all the appearance of having belonged to the veritable doorway of the temple, whether in its original position or not.

The Church was built, or the temple converted into a Church, by a certain Illyrian priest, named Peter, in the year 425, during the reign of Celestine I., as recorded by an immense inscription, commencing *Culmen Apostolicum cum Caelestinus haberet*, in mosaic, in the interior of the Church, over the main entrance. At each side of the inscription is a female figure, with a book in her hand, and below the one are the words, *Ecclesia ex circumcisione*, and below the other, *Ecclesia ex gentibus*. This mosaic originally covered the whole inside of the front wall, but was reduced to its present form by Sixtus V., 1585-90. In the spandrils of the arches which spring from the columns there are also curious mosaics of *pietra dura*, porphyry, serpentine, &c., part of the original decoration. Between the years 590 and 604 St. Gregory the Great preached several of his Homilies within its walls. In 824 it was restored by Eugenius III. Honorius III., 1216-27, having confirmed the Dominican order, gave this Church to St. Dominick, together with a considerable portion of the adjoining Pontifical Palace, which he converted into a monastery, and here he lived with his monks. In 1238 the Church was newly consecrated by Gregory IX. In 1441 it was again restored, by Cardinal Julius Cesarini, and finally Sixtus V., 1585-90, restored it as we see, of which the inscription in the middle of the tribune is a record.

On the pavement are several interesting sepulchral slabs, on which portraits of the defunct are incised, after the fashion of monumental brasses; and one particularly, to the memory of Munio da Zamora, the seventh general of the order, who died in the year 1300, during the pontificate of Boniface VIII., and whose figure is represented in mosaic.

Above the altar of the Chapel of the Rosary, at the end of the right aisle, is a very beautiful picture by *Sassoferrato*, representing the Madonna of the Rosary with St. Dominick on one side and St. Katherine on the other, and on the wall near it is the very fine 15th century monument of Cardinal D'Ausia, who erected the chapel.

About midway along the right aisle is the Chapel of St. Hyacinth, of which the walls are painted in fresco by the *Zuccheri*. That on the right, representing the canonisation of the saint, by *Federico Zucchero*, and that on the left, representing St. Dominick giving the habit to St. Hyacinth and to the blessed Geslas, by *Taddeo Zuccheri.* The painting above the altar is by *Lavinia Fontana.*

Immediately opposite, in the left aisle, is the handsome chapel of the D'Elci family, dedicated to St. Katherine. The frescoes on·the vault of the cupola are by *Giovanni Odazi.*

Through the immense quadriporticus of the cloister, supported by small columns, from which rise narrow Lombard arches, we pass into the garden, where still flourishes a fine bitter orange tree, planted by St. Dominick. Women can only see this through a window which opens from the portico.

Some interesting excavations were made in the year 1856 upon the side of the Aventine to which this garden leads, but they are now filled in again.

Turning to the right on leaving Sta. Sabina, a few steps brings us to a doorway, above which are the words *Istituto dei Ciechi.* Through it we enter a rectangular courtyard, on the further side of which is

THE CHURCH OF ST. ALESSIO,[*]

dedicated to the pilgrim saint, Alexius, whose story is represented on the ancient fresco painting upon one of the piers of the subterranean Basilica of St. Clemente.

According to tradition this Church was founded in the fifth century, upon the site of the house of Euphemianus, the father of Alexius, and was originally dedicated to St. Boniface, but there is no positive record regarding it earlier than the 10th century, in which the best authorities believe it to have been built.

Originally the aisles were divided from the nave by six-

---

[*] To obtain entrance to the Church, ring the bell of the door on the left.

A A

teen columns, but in the year 1750 the Church was entirely modernized, and reduced to its present uninteresting condition by Cardinal Angelo Maria Quirini, who employed *Tommasso di Marchis* for the purpose. It has recently been re-decorated without receiving further alteration.

At the entrance end of the left aisle there is preserved, in a glass case, what is believed to be a portion of the wooden staircase under which the poor pilgrim Alexius was in charity permitted to sleep while he abode for seventeen years, in his father's house, unrecognised by his relations and his deserted bride. In front of this relic is a mediocre statue of the saint.

On each side of the episcopal chair, at the end of the tribune, is a small column very beautifully inlaid with Cosmati mosaic, vestiges no doubt of the decoration of the original Church, of which also the beautiful *opus Alexandrinum* of the pavement—restored though it is—formed part. In a large recess in the passage leading to the Sacristy is a fine (for the period) monumental statue of Cardinal Guidi de' Bagni, who lived in the time of Urban VIII., 1623-44, by *Domenico Guidi*.

Below the tribune is an interesting crypt well worth visiting. It is probable that this is the level of the primitive Church, and that the small columns which now support the pavement above, formed part of the construction of the original tribune. At the back of the apse are the remains of an ancient episcopal chair.

Upon the wall of the quadriportico which surrounds the garden of the monastery, filled with orange trees, and through which we enter the Church, are some interesting inscriptions, which were removed from the interior of the Church when it was modernized in 1750.

Continuing on to the right, after leaving this Church, we come to a kind of piazza, formed on the left side by a series of broad pilasters, ornamented with trophies. Opposite to these, there is a gateway, through which, by ringing at the bell, we can gain admittance into the garden of THE PRIORATO OF THE KNIGHTS OF MALTA; but, before doing so, let us peep through the key-hole, and obtain one of the prettiest views of St. Peter's to be seen in Rome.

Passing along an avenue of laurels, we reach the declivity of the Aventine, and from the garden terrace can enjoy a magnificent view of the river, with THE JANICULUM and St. Peter's beyond, and the city lying spread out upon the right.

To the left of the terrace is

THE CHURCH OF STA. MARIA AVENTINA,

sometimes also called St. Basilio, attached to the Priory. Nothing is known regarding the early history of this Church beyond the fact that it was one of the twenty Abbacies of Rome. It was restored by St. Pius V., 1566-72, who built the contiguous habitation. In 1765 it was completely modernized by *Gio Battista Piranesi* for Cardinal Rezzonico, but possesses no features of the least interest beyond a few quaint monuments of Grand Masters of the Order of St. John of Jerusalem, looking singularly out of character with the modern niches in which they are now arranged.

On the right is the statue of the architect, Piranesi, also looking very much out of place.

Returning past the Churches of St. Alessio and Sta. Sabina, we continue onwards until we find a turning to the right, and proceeding a short distance along this we find, on the left,

THE CHURCH OF ST. PRISCA,

said to have been built by Pope Eutichianus, 275-83, on the site of the house in which St. Peter lived, and where he baptised Sta. Prisca and many others to the faith of Christ. It was first dedicated to St. Aquila, and is mentioned in the acts of the Second Roman Council, held by Pope St. Symmachus in 449, by the title of S.S. Aquila and Prisca. It was restored by Adrian I., in 772, and afterwards by Callixtus III., 1455-58. In 1600 Cardinal Benedetto Guistiniani altered it considerably, and rebuilt the façade from the designs of *Carlo Lombardo di Arezzo.* Finally, it was reduced to its present condition by Clement XII., 1730-40. It is very seldom open, except on the *Festa* of St. Prisca, which falls on the 18th of January.

In the vineyard belonging to Prince Torlonia, the entrance to which is immediately opposite to this Church, a considerable portion of THE WALL OF FORTIFICATION, BUILT BY ANCUS MARTIUS around the Aventine, when he enclosed it within the limits of the city, was discovered a few years ago. It is some fifty feet in height, and is the most remarkable among the remains of the Regal period yet discovered. A polite request to enter the vineyard is always granted.

In another part of the vineyard some very interesting remains of a Roman house have been discovered, beneath a modern building belonging to the Jesuit Fathers.

If on leaving the vineyard we continue along the lane to the right, it will be found to terminate in another crossing it at right angles. Following this to the right, will take us to the Porta San Paolo (*see page* 349), and to the left, direct to the Colosseum, past the Church of St. Gregory (*see page* 208).

Turning to the left, on leaving the vineyard, and keeping to the left, we make our way back to the lane by which we ascended the Aventine, and from thence can take the latter half of the last section, on to St. Paul's outside the walls, commencing at page 343.

CHURCHES, VILLAS, &c., NOT SITUATED WITHIN THE DIFFERENT SECTIONS.

Ascending the side of the Janiculum by the Via Garibaldi (*see page* 311), we come to

THE CHURCH OF ST. PIETRO IN MONTORIO,

from the terrace in front of which there is a magnificent view of the city.

This Church is called *in Montorio* from the golden coloured sand with which the hill abounds. It is said to mark the site of St. Peter's martyrdom, though according to some authorities, he was crucified upon the Vatican. There is no record of the date when a Church was first founded here, but tradition ascribes it to the time of Constantine. It is only known that in ancient times the Church went by the name of Sta. Maria, and also St. Angelo, and that it was one of the twenty Abbacies of Rome. In progress of time it became abandoned, and remained so until the year 1472, when it was conceded to the Franciscans, for whom Ferdinand IV. and Elizabeth of Spain rebuilt the Church, from the designs of *Bacio Pintelli.*

The first chapel on the right is celebrated for its paintings, executed in oil, upon the walls by *Sebastiano del Piombo,* from drawings by *Michael Angelo;* but, unfortunately, they have become so black as to be scarcely recognisable. The principal subject is the Flagellation, on the end wall.

The fourth chapel on the right has an altarpiece, representing the Conversion of St. Paul, by *Vasari.* The statues of Religion and Justice, the monument of Cardinal del Monte, and other sculptures in the chapel, are by *Ammannati.* The cherubs which support the balustrade are particularly fine.

Raphael's celebrated Transfiguration was painted for this Church, and occupied the place on the wall of the choir behind the high altar, where there is now a copy of Guido's Crucifixion of St. Peter. It was removed from the Church and taken to Paris by Napoleon I., and when, in 1815, it was returned, with the other works of art carried off by the French, it was placed by Pius VII., for better preservation, in the Picture Gallery of the Vatican.

The first chapel after passing the high altar was painted by *Leonardo Milanese,* and the picture over the altar, of St. John baptising in the Jordan, is by his master, *Daniele da Volterra,* though by some it has been attributed to *Cecchino Salviati.*

The second chapel contains a Dead Christ and other subjects from the Passion, attributed to *Vandyke,* but nothing positive is known regarding them.

The fourth chapel was restored by Bernini, and contains some exceedingly interesting sculptures of the seventeenth century by *Andrea Bolgi.*

The fifth chapel contains a fresco of St. Francis receiving the Stigmate, painted by *Giovanni de' Vecchi,* from, it is said, a design by *Michael Angelo.*

Between the third and fourth chapels on the right there

is a door which leads into the cloister of the convent, where there is a beautiful little circular temple, built by *Bramante* at the expense of Ferdinand of Spain, upon the spot where it is said that St. Peter was crucified.

Continuing our ascent up the Janiculum—and from each higher point we obtain a still more extended view over the city—we come to the grand FOUNTAIN OF THE AQUA PAOLO, built by *Fontana*, in 1612, for Paul V., whose name it bears. It is supplied by the waters of the Lake of Bracciano, conveyed by the old aqueduct of Trajan. The six Ionic columns of red granite which ornament the fountain were taken from the remains of the Temple of Minerva, which stood in the Forum Transitorium, and of which considerable remains were in existence in the 16th century.

Ascending still further, we reach the PORTA SAN PANCRAZIO, which marks the site of THE PORTA AURELIA, in the Aurelian Circuit. The modern gate was entirely destroyed by the French when they besieged Rome in 1849, and entered at this point. It has since been rebuilt by Pius IX.

Immediately beyond the gate is the entrance to

THE VILLA PAMPHILI DORIA,

built from the designs of *Antinori* and *Algardi*, for Innocent X., who presented it, in 1650, to Olympia Maidalchini, the wife of his brother. The villa is not opened to the public, nor does it contain anything to interest, but the grounds, which are open to pedestrians and to *two-horse* carriages on Mondays and Fridays, after twelve o'clock, are well worth visiting, and form one of the pleasantest drives in the neighbourhood of Rome. They contain some very fine stone pines, and during the spring the grass is completely carpeted with violets and wild anemonies. From the terrace, in front of the villa, there is a very fine view of St. Peter's, and the country in that direction. Some interesting COLOMBARIA were discovered in the grounds of this villa a few years ago.

Proceeding along THE VIA VENTE SETTEMBRE from the Church of Sta. Maria della Vittoria (*page* 247), which we pass on the left, we reach THE PORTA PIA, which marks the site of the ancient PORTA NOMENTANA. It was in great part rebuilt by Michael Angelo in 1564, for Pius IV., but was not completed till the commencement of the reign of H.H. Pius IX. It is decorated externally with statues of St. Agnes and St. Alexander, to whose Basilicas it leads.

It was at this point that the Italian army entered Rome on the 20th of September, 1870. The gate received considerable damage during the attack, but the place where the breach was made is situated a few yards along the wall, turning to the left after passing through the gate. The spot is marked by a commemorative tablet, and close to the gate is another tablet, erected on the 20th of September, 1874, bearing the names of the Italians who fell during the attack.

A little distance along the road outside the gate, we pass, on the right side, the modern VILLA TORLONIA. It can be visited by order obtainable at the Palazzo Torlonia, in the Piazza Venezia, but, beyond being handsomely furnished, possesses no particular attractions. The grounds are chiefly remarkable for the number of imitation ruins with which they have been ornamented.

The handsome building we see in the grounds on the left is the Villa Albani. (*See page* 369).

At the distance of about a mile and a half from the gate, we find

THE BASILICA OF ST. AGNESE.

This ancient Basilica was founded by Constantine the Great, at the request of his daughter Constantia, on the spot where the remains of St. Agnes were laid in the Catacombs situated here. It was built down within them, and, judging from the depth, upon the floor of the second tier, like that of Santa Petronilla, recently discovered (*see page* 225), and from the position of this Basilica with regard to the Catacombs, which branch off on the same level with the floor of the Church, the stranger can understand the manner in which the Basilica of Sta. Petronilla was constructed.

At the beginning of the sixth century it was restored by Symmachus I., 498-514, but notwithstanding this, it had fallen into so insecure a condition by the commencement of the next century, that Honorius I., 625-40, rebuilt it from the foundations, and among other sumptuous decorations he lavished upon it, ornamented the vault of the tribune with the mosaic still existing. During the siege of Rome by Astolphus, in the year 755, the Basilica, together with all the other edifices in this district, suffered great damage, which was repaired by Adrian I., 772-95, after Charlemagne had overthrown the Longobard rule in Italy. It was again devastated in 1241, when, in the time of Gregory IX., Frederick II. advanced against Rome, and levelled with the ground castles, towers, palaces, and churches. It was restored immediately afterwards, and Alexander IV., in 1256, consecrated with great solemnity the three altars, dedicated to St. John the Baptist, St. John the Evangelist,

and St. Emerenziana.   In the fifteenth century it was again
restored by Cardinal Guiliano della Revere, and again
shortly afterwards by Julius II., 1503-13.

During the fearful sack of Rome in 1527 it a third time
suffered damage, and ultimate ruin, at the hand of the
enemy, and was rebuilt by the celebrated Cardinal Giromalo
Verallo.   During the works necessary for the reconstruction
of the steps which lead down into the Basilica, a number of
antique statues were discovered, and the eight splendid
bas-reliefs now in the Spada Collection.   (*See page* 302).

At the instance of Cardinal Paolo Emilio Sfrondato,
nephew of Gregory XIV., and who was called the Cardinal
of St. Cecilia, Paul V., 1605-25, reconstructed the high
altar as we see it, and on the *festa* of the saint, the 21st of
January, 1621, placed her remains with great pomp in an
urn of silver.   Finally, the Basilica has been redecorated
throughout by H.H. Pius IX., as a thank-offering for his
escape, when, in 1854, the floor of the refectory in the
adjoining convent, where he was dining, gave way, and he
was precipitated, with all in the room, into the chamber
beneath.   This occurrence is represented by a large fresco,
a very mediocre work, painted on the wall of a room facing
on the courtyard, through which we pass into the Church.
It can be seen through a large window placed in front of it.

Notwithstanding the many vicissitudes which have be-
fallen this Church, and the repeated restorations and
rebuildings it has undergone, it still—with the exception of
the choir and ambones, which have disappeared—preserves
the complete basilican model in a purer form than any other
church, and in fact it is the only one which retains the
upper portico, or gallery—answering to some extent to the
clerestory in Gothic churches—described by Vitruvius as

that portion in the civil basilicas set apart for women. The aisles are divided from the nave by fourteen columns of considerable beauty. Eight of these are of *Breccia di Serravezzo,* four of *Lucullan,* or *Porta Santa,* very handsomely marked, and two of Phrygian marble, beautifully fluted, which resemble so closely the fragments of fluted columns of Phrygian marble found in the ruins of the *Pulvinar* of the Stadium of Domitian, on the Palatine, that we may conjecture they were taken from that place. Clement VIII., 1592-1605, would have removed the four columns of Lucullan marble, to ornament the Aldobrandini chapel, in the Church of Sta. Maria Sopra Minerva, had he not been dissuaded by Cardinal de Medici, who became his successor under the title of Leo XI.

The small statue of St. Agnes, on the high altar, is an antique draped torso of very rare oriental alabaster, to which *Niccolo Cordieri* adapted the head, hands, and feet, in gilt bronze.

In one of the chapels on the right is a beautiful bust of the Saviour, said to be by *Michael Angelo.*

On the walls of the staircase are a number of Christian inscriptions, found in the neighbourhood of the Church. THE CATACOMBS connected with this Church are among the most interesting in Rome, and more particularly so from the circumstance that the remains of the occupants are in many parts still lying untouched in their places.

Close to the Basilica of St. Agnes, and within the same enclosure, is the curious and interesting

CHURCH OF STA. CONSTANTIA.

It was a mausoleum built to receive the bodies of members of the family of Constantine the Great. In it were placed the remains of Constantina, the wife of Gallus Cæsar; of Helena, the wife of Julianus, who became Emperor in the year 360; and of Constantia, daughters of Constantine. Constantia is said to have consecrated her life to God, and to have died a virgin in the monastery attached to the Church of St. Agnes, and her remains were placed within this mausoleum in a magnificent porphyry sarcophagus, now in the hall of the Greek Cross in the Vatican Museum (*see page* 77).

In honour of Constantia, Alexander IV., 1254-61, dedicated the Mausoleum as a Christian Church, and thus it has come down to us in its original form entirely unaltered, except in so far that the portion supported by the twenty-four columns was rebuilt by Alexander, when he adapted it to Christian purposes. The beautiful mosaic upon the vault remains almost intact as it was originally composed, when the Mausoleum was erected in the time of Constantine.

THE BASILICA OF SAN LORENZO FUORI LE MURA

is situated on the road to Tivoli, about three-quarters-of-a-mile outside the Porta San Giovanni.

Here was the *Campus Veranus,* in which was situated the Catacomb of Sta. Cyriaca, where, among many other saints and martyrs, the body of St. Lorenzo, the first deacon of the Roman Church, was laid. It is said that Constantine founded this Basilica, at the prayer of St. Sylvester, in the year 330, and, according to Anastasius, the librarian, it enclosed the spot where the saint was buried, and had a tribune ornamented with porphyry and much silver. Sixtus III., 432-40, with the consent of the Emperor Valentinianus, ornamented the Confession with columns of porphyry, and enriched the Basilica in many parts with friezes of silver.

St. Leo I., 440-61, influenced Galla Placidia to restore and enlarge it, and to level the rising ground against which it was built, and which threatened to give way upon it. St. Hilary, 461-68, added a monastery and other buildings, and increased the endowments. St. Pelagius II., 578-90, rebuilt the tribune, of which the great arch of mosaic, immediately over the steps we now ascend to the presbytery, still remains. Gregory II., 715-31, restored it in part; Adrian I., 772-95, re-roofed it; and Leo III., 795-816, adorned it with hangings. About the year 1216, Honorius III. made very important alterations and additions. He closed the entrance, which faced in exactly the contrary direction from the present; threw down the tribune, with the exception of the arch of Pelagius II., and filling the floor to the height of the actual presbytery, converted the primitive basilica into, as one might say, the tribune of another he built out from it, opening from the portico through which we now enter. Nicholas V., 1447-55, restored it without making material alterations. It was again restored in 1647, and it has recently been re-decorated throughout, and adorned with a number of fresco paintings of a high class of merit by *Fracassini.*

The low portico through which we enter is supported by six antique columns of the Ionic order. The cornice above them is ornamented with a mosaic frieze of the thirteenth century, of which a considerable portion has been recently restored. The decoration of the front wall above the portico is imitation mosaic, in the same style in which it was originally ornamented. Within the portico are some exceedingly interesting sarcophagi, and the walls are painted in fresco with subjects very quaintly illustrating the lives of St. Stephen, St. Lawrence, and Honorius III.,

1216-27, to whose time they are attributed. Unfortunately, they were entirely repainted over in the course of the recent restorations.

We pass from the portico into that portion of the Basilica built by Honorius III. The aisles are divided from the nave by twenty-two antique columns of granite and *cipollino*. Their capitals, and the cornice above them, are miscellaneous materials from Pagan temples. In the volutes of some of the capitals we can recognise the frog and the lizard—the emblems of the architects, *Sauros* and *Batracos*, the great architects who built the Portico of Octavia * (*see page* 328).

On each side of the nave are the ambones, ornamented with *Cosmati* mosaic, but the enclosure of the choir has disappeared.

At the end of the nave we find the great arch of mosaic, and leaving the portion added by Honorius III., enter what remains of the primitive Basilica of Pelagius. From the aisles, on the one side and the other, we descend to its ancient level, lower than that of the Church of Honorius, and from the nave we ascend by several steps to the raised level formed by Honorius, above that of the Church of Pelagius, when he converted it into the presbytery or tribune of the Basilica, as altered by him. At the time when he made these alterations, he buried the columns of the Church of Pelagius to the height of the level of the portion he added.

This filling in has been recently removed, disclosing once more the primitive level.

* It is erroneously supposed by some that these capitals may have belonged to the Portico of Octavia, or to one of the two temples within it; but those temples and the portico which surrounded them were of the Corinthian order, as may be seen from the remains still existing.

It may not be easy for strangers to make out the different portions at a glance, but a little study will enable them to understand the features of the primitive Basilica, and the alterations and additions made by Honorius.

The Basilica of Pelagius consisted of a nave and two aisles, divided by fine Corinthian columns, taken from some ancient edifices of importance, of which twelve still remain, ten of Phrygian, and two of white Carara marble. The cornice above the capitals is formed of miscellaneous materials, portions of antique cornices put together without regard to uniformity, and above the cornice is the gallery, on the one side, and on the other, supported by twelve small columns, in accordance with what Vitruvius describes in the civil Basilicas as the portions set apart for women.*

The screen and episcopal chair, at the back of the raised presbytery of Honorius, are ornamented with very beautiful *Cosmati* mosaic of the thirteenth century. They were very carefully and exactly restored during the recent restorations. Turning towards the entrance and looking upwards, we can, from this point, see the inside of the arch of Pelagius, richly ornamented with mosaic. In the centre is the figure of our Saviour, seated on the globe, in the act of blessing. On his left are St. Peter, St. Lawrence, and Pelagius II., with the words PELAGIUS SECUNDUS; and on his left St. Paul, St. Stephen, and St. Hippolytus.

Beneath the ciborium, which is supported by four ancient porphyry columns, repose the remains of Saint Lawrence and Saint Stephen.

To the left of the door, as we leave the Church, is a very

---

* Compare the construction of this portion of the primitive Basilica with the Basilica of St. Agnes outside the walls. (*See page* 361).

beautiful antique sarcophagus, ornamented with a bas-relief representing a nuptial scene, and surmounted by a mediæval canopy.   According to Mabillon, the remains of Cardinal Guglielmo Fieschi, nephew of Innocent IV., 1243-54, repose within this sarcophagus.

The frescoes upon the attic of the nave, painted by *Fracassini,** in illustration of the lives of Saint Stephen and Saint Lawrence, are works of very great merit, and well worthy of observation and study.

The granite column in front of the Basilica, surmounted by a bronze statue of St. Lawrence, by *Galetti*, was erected by H.H. Pius IX., in 1865.

Adjoining this Basilica is THE CEMETERY OF ST. LORENZO, the great cemetery of Rome, originally opened by Napoleon I., but not brought into general use until after the great cholera of 1837.

Ascending the Via San Basilio from the Piazza Barberini (*pages* 246 and 255) until it turns to the left, we shall see before us the entrance to

THE VILLA LUDOVISI,

built by Cardinal Ludovisi, nephew of Gregory XV., 1621-23.   The grounds, which were laid out by *Le Notre* in the quaint style of the period, are very extensive, and command some fine views.   The only portions of the villa itself opened to the public are the casinos.   That on the right, as we enter the grounds, contains some fine pieces of antique sculpture; and that at the end of the garden is celebrated

* This highly talented painter was prematurely cut off a few years ago, at the early age of 37.

for THE FRESCO OF AURORA, painted by *Guercino*, on the vault of the large room on the ground floor, and " Fame attended by Force and Virtue," also by him, on the first floor. The landscapes in the smaller rooms are by *Guercino* and *Domenichino*, and the groups of cupids by *Taddeo Zuccheri*.

THE SCULPTURE GALLERY.

We pass on into the second room, for the first does not contain any works worthy of notice.

SECOND ROOM.

1. MARS reposing, found in the neighbourhood of the Portico of Octavia, and restored by *Bernini*.
7. ORESTES DISCOVERED BY ELECTRA.
9. Colossal bronze bust of Marcus Aurelius.
26. Bacchus.
28. ARRIA AND PÆTUS (?). *See Dying Gladiator, page* 118.
29. Bacchus.
30. Mercury.
34. Venus.
41. THE LUDOVISI JUNO, a wonderfully beautiful colossal head.
43. PLUTO CARRYING OFF PROSERPINE, by *Bernini*.
46. Bust of Augustus.
47. Bust of Antinous.
52. Bust of Clodius Albinus.

Turning to the left, on leaving the Villa Ludovisi, we proceed onwards, and passing out of the city by THE PORTA SALARIA,* find on the right,

THE VILLA ALBANI,

designed and built in 1760, by Cardinal Allesandro Albani, who employed the architect *Carlo Marchionni* to carry out the work.

It was in this villa that Cardinal Albani formed that magnificent collection of antique sculpture—in great part the result of excavations made at the time—which was the

* This gate, which suffered severely during the three hours' siege of 1870, has been recently rebuilt. When the remains of the gate were taken down, the ruins of several sepulchral monuments, now visible outside the gate, were discovered

B B

chief object of Winckelmann's studies, and the basis of his works on the history of art. Together with other spoils carried away from Rome, Napoleon I. took no fewer than 294 pieces of sculpture from this celebrated collection ; and when the works of art taken to Paris were, at the Peace of 1815, restored to their owners, the Albani family, unable to bear the expense of transport, sold them to the King of Bavaria. The Antinous, No. 994, only was brought back. The fame of this collection, therefore, is due to works no longer forming part of it. Those remaining are many, but, with a few exceptions, not of any very great interest.*

51. Seated statue of Augustus, with the attributes of Jupiter.
54. Tiberius in military costume
59. Lucius Verus.
61. Seated statue of Faustina(?)
64. Trajan.
72. Marcus Aurelius.
59. Lucius Verus
79. Seated statue of Agrippina the elder.
82. Hadrian.
87. Augustus.
19. A Caryatid. On the back of the basket are the names of the sculptors, *Creton* and *Nicolaos*.
16. A Canephora, found near Frascati, in 1761, together with Nos. 24 and 91.
24. A Canephora, see No. 16.
46. Brutus.
90. Pertinax, in high relief.
91. A Canephora, see No. 16.
93. Juno.
103. Bacchante.
106. Faun, with the infant Bacchus on his shoulder.
110. Faun, copy from the celebrated statue by *Praxiteles*.

120. Caius Cæsar, grandson of Augustus.
131. Sarcophagus, with relief, representing the marriage of Peleus and Thetis, placed between two very fine antique fluted columns —one of *Cottanello*, and the other of *Alabastro fiorito*, found at the Emporium (*see page* 340) during the Pontificate of Clement XI.
132. Lucius Verus.
143. Livia performing sacrifice.
152. Female bust.
162. Bas relief of Diogenes receiving Alexander.
163. Dædalus and Icarus
165. An ancient fresco painting, found during an excavation on the Esquiline.
185. Leda and the swan.
186. Plinth, bearing the name of *Athenodorus, of Rhodes*, one of the sculptors of the Laocoon.
205. Iphigenia in Tauris recognising Orestes and Pylades.
219. Faun.

* In this collection the works are consecutively numbered, without reference to the rooms in which they are placed.

223. Achilles and Memnon.
484. Statue of Hylas.
600. Bust of Domitian.
617. Bust of Hadrian.
624. Bust of Balbinus.
632. Bust of Philip the elder.
641. Marsyas.
656. Bust of Pertinax.
671. Lucilla.
676. Jupiter Serapis.
711. Juno descending from Olympus.
729. Bust of Otho.
741. Statue of Hercules.
757. Statue of Bacchus.
885. The Slaughter of the Children of Niobe.
893. *Alimentariæ Faustinianæ*, fragments of a frieze with what is supposed to be a representation of a distribution of corn to the people by Antoninus Pius, in honour of his wife Faustina, after her death.
905. Apollo, seated.
906. An Athlete, supposed, from the inscription on the trunk, to be a copy from a work by *Stephanos*, a pupil of Praxiteles.
193. Faun.
915. Cupid bending his bow.
922. Mercury.
928. Faun.
931. Diana, alabaster statue, with head, arms, and feet of bronze.
933. Ancient bronze copy of the Farnese Hercules.

942. Diogenes and his dog.
952. THE APOLLO SAUROCTONOS, a bronze copy from the celebrated statue by Praxiteles, erroneously supposed by Winckelmann to be the original.
960. Bas-relief of the poet Perseus (?)
964. Æsop.
977. Hercules and Apollo contesting for the Delphic Tripod.
980. Leucothea with the infant Bacchus.
985. Lynceus and Pollux.
994. ANTINOUS CROWNED WITH THE LOTUS FLOWER, found at Hadrian's Villa; a highly finished work of its period, but by no means entitled to the high rank given to it among works of art.
997. Statuette of a Satyresse.
1008. Hercules in the gardens of the Hesperides.
1009. Dædalus and Icarus.
1013. Antinous with the attributes of one of the Dioscuri.
1023. Gordian III.
1026. Messalina.
1031. ZETHUS, ANTIOPE, AND AMPHION, a bas-relief of great beauty.
1034. Hermes of Theophrastus.
1036. Hermes of Hippocrates.
1037. Osiris.
1040. Hermes of Socrates.

THE VILLA BORGHESE

is situated immediately outside the Porta del Popolo, on the right hand (*see page* 88). It stands in the midst of very extensive grounds and gardens, which are open to the public every day during the week, with the exception of Monday, and form one of the pleasantest drives in the neighbourhood of Rome.

The Casino, which contains a fine collection of ancient sculpture, is only open on Saturdays, in the afternoon. It was built by *Vansanzio*, for Cardinal Scipio Borghese, nephew of Paul V., 1605-21.

The Grand Hall.

The vaulted ceiling was painted by *Mario Rossi*, the chief subject representing the arrival of Camillus at the Capitol. The floor is laid with exceedingly interesting mosaics, representing gladiators and scenes in the Amphitheatre, found in 1834 among the remains of an ancient Villa at La Giostra, near the Torre Nuova on the Via Labicana, above Tusculum.

1. Statue of Diana.	15. Bacchus.
3. Isis; colossal bust.	16. Antoninus Pius; colossal bust.
5. Juno; colossal bust.	Curtius leaping into the gulf; large alto-relief on the wall facing the entrance.
7. Tiberius.	
9. Caligula.	
11. Bacchus.	
14. Hadrian; colossal bust.	

First Room.

1. Juno, with the sceptre and patera, in the middle of the room.	9. Leda and the swan.
3. Urania.	16. Flora
4. Ceres.	20. Bas relief: the Birth of Telephus.
5. Venus Genetrix.	21. Venus leaving the bath.

Second Room.

1. Fighting Amazon, on horseback: in the middle of the room.	6. Bust of Hercules.
3. Bas relief of the labours of Hercules; part of a sarcophagus.	10. Bas relief of Tritons and Sea Nymphs, with a head of Oceanus in the centre.
4. Bas relief; part of a sarcophagus.	15. Hercules holding the distaff.
	21. Venus, resembling that of the Capitol.

Third Room.

1. Apollo, with the Lyre: in the middle of the room.	8. Melpomene, the Muse of Tragedy.
2. Child playing with a goose.	10. Clio, the Muse of History.
3. Scipio Africanus.	13. A seated statue of Anacreon.
4. The Metamorphosis of Daphne.	14. Lucilla.
6. Venus and Cupid.	16. Erato, the Muse of Comedy.
7. Bust of a Bacchante.	18. Polyhymnia, the Muse of Music.

In the corridor leading to the great gallery, there is a very fine bust of Cardinal Scipio Borghese, by *Bernini*.

THE GREAT GALLERY.

The subjects on the vault, painted by *Domenico de Angelis*, illustrate the story of Acis and Galatea. Around the gallery is a series of modern busts of the first eleven Cæsars, the heads sculptured in porphyry, and set into cuirasses of veined alabaster.

FOURTH ROOM.

3. Faun; an ancient copy from the celebrated statue by *Praxiteles*.

6. Titus.

7. The Hermaphrodite.

10. Tiberius.

11. Marble copy of the bronze statue of the shepherd Martius, plucking the thorn from his foot, in the Capitoline Museum.

15. Fragment of a statue of Hylas, found in 1830, near Mentana, the ancient Nomentum.

FIFTH ROOM.

1. Statue of Tyrtæus, in the middle of the room.
2. Minerva.
4. Apollo.

5. Lucilla (?) colossal bust.
10. Leda and the swan, found in 1823, near Frascati.
15. Æsculapius and Telesphorus.

SIXTH ROOM.

1. Group of a Boy on a Dolphin, in the middle of the room.
3. Isis.
4. Paris.
8. Ceres, with drapery, in black marble.

10. A Gypsy, in bronze and marble : a work of the seventeenth century.

19. Hadrian, colossal bust.

22. Venus.

SEVENTH ROOM.

1. A Dancing Faun, in the middle of the room, discovered in 1832, in the remains of an ancient villa, at the 32nd mile on the Via Salara.
2. Ceres.
3. Mercury Liricinus.
4. Satyr.

6. Bust of Seneca.
7. Bust of Minerva.
8. Faun (*see No. 3, in fourth room*).
9. Pluto.
14. Seated statue of Periander.
19. Group of Bacchus and Libera.

Returning to the Great Gallery, we find, at the further end, a spiral staircase leading to the rooms on the first floor.

THE GALLERY.

In the middle of the room are three very fine works by *Bernini*. No. 2, the group of ÆNEAS AND ANCHISES, said to have been executed by him when he was only fifteen years of age. No. 1, the group of APOLLO AND DAPHNE, his finest work, executed when in his eighteenth year; and the statue of DAVID slinging the stone at Goliath. The four marble vases, with subjects representing the Seasons, are by *Laboureur*.

FIRST ROOM.

Statue of Innocence holding the Dove, by *Aurelij*.
1. Bust of Paul V. : *Bernini.*
2. Bust of Cardinal Scipio Borghese: *Bernini.*

27. Portrait of Marc Antonio Borghese, the father of Paul V. : *Guido.*
7. Portrait of Paul V. : *M. A. da Caravaggio.*
8. Portraits: *Scipione Gaetani.*

SECOND ROOM,

contains a number of pictures by *Marchetti*, representing pageants of the seventeenth century, ruins, and architectural views.

THIRD ROOM,

has a very beautiful painting by *Gagnereau*, upon the ceiling, representing a nymph surprised by a satyr.

FOURTH ROOM.

In the middle of this room is the celebrated statue of VENUS VICTRIX, by *Canova*, for which Pauline Buonaparte, the sister of Napoleon the First, sat, and of whom it is a portrait.

FIFTH ROOM.

In the middle of the room is a statue of a Bacchante, by *Tadolini*, 1842. The vaulted ceiling was painted by *Novelli*, with subjects illustrating the fable of Cupid and Psyche. The landscape paintings on the walls are by Jean Francois Bloemer, of Antwerp, called in Italy *Orrizonte*.

The SIXTH and SEVENTH ROOMS contain a number of paintings of no particular merit. The name of the artist is attached to each.

APPENDIX.

THE COLOSSEUM.

The works of excavation have now been carried suf-
ficently far to enable the visitor to form some conception
of their great importance. At the depth of twenty-one
feet below the modern level, which some were pleased to
think was that made sacred by the blood of many martyrs,
the veritable Arena has been discovered paved with *opus
spicatum*, or herring-bone work. Upon it are a number of
constructions, the exact nature of which has not yet been
ascertained, nor will it be possible to arrive at any positive
conclusion regarding them until the entire area has been
cleared of the accumulation which covers it. The rude
manner, however, in which they are built indicates a period
long posterior to that of the Flavian Emperors, and although it is possible that some portions may have been
erected to raise the level of the arena, or to support a
pensile flooring, there can be little doubt the majority of
them are the remains of constructions of the Frangipani
family, who, in the eleventh century, converted the Colosseum into a fortress.

At the end furthest from the Forum three enormous
corridors have been found, opening into and from the
arena. That in the centre is somewhat above its level,
and continues in a direct line for a considerable distance,
but its termination has not been reached. It is conjectured that it leads to the great *Vivarium*—the menagerie
where the wild beasts were kept—which is known to have

been situated near the Porta Maggiore. From its sides a series of large chambers open off, possibly rooms for the Gladiators and *Bestiarii* to wait in until their time came for appearing on the arena ; and about half-way along the distance which has been cleared of the Tiber mud with which it was filled, another passage branches from it at right angles in the direction of the Cœlian, that is, to the right as we go from the building. This branch, from the indication of steps in it, was possibly an entrance into the long passage from the upper level at this point.

Below this long passage, and opening from and below the level of the arena, there is a great drain, at the mouth of which are some of the iron bars, the remains of the grating to prevent solid bodies washing down it. It is conjectured that this drain was for the purpose of carrying off the water at times when the arena was flooded for naval shows, though there is much controversy as to whether exhibitions of this nature were ever given in the Colosseum.

The side corridors branch off on the one side and the other from that in the centre, and at the distance of 78 feet turn at right angles, the one to the right, the other to the left, and connect with that between them. In each of these corridors there is a series of great bronze sockets, into which it is supposed that the pivots of swing gates, forming so many dens or cages for the wild beasts, were inserted. The animals were, in all probability, brought from the menagerie along the central passage, and turned to the right and to the left into these lateral corridors, where they were kept divided into groups between the different gates, to be turned loose upon the arena as required.

At the north side of the Colosseum, towards the Esqui-line, the mouth of another great corridor has been found opening upon the arena. It is expected that a corresponding corridor will be found opposite to this, on the south side, towards the Cœlian; as also, that at the end towards the Forum, three others, corresponding to those at the east end, will be discovered.

On the side towards the Cœlian, but rather to the east of the south end of the lesser axis, a long passage has been discovered, which, from the indications remaining, was originally paved with mosaic, and had a vaulting adorned with stucco ornaments. This is believed to be the passage made for the convenience of the Emperor Commodus, and in which the attempt was made to assassinate him.

In the course of the excavations several marble slabs, parts of the seats, have been found, on which are *graphites* deeply scored into the marble: rude representations of scenes in the amphitheatre, made, no doubt, by spectators while waiting for the games to commence. These have been placed on pedestals, at the opening of the great central corridor, at the east end. A number of fragments of the marble elbows of the *Cunei* have also been found, ornamented with sphingi, dolphins, greyhounds, and the like. These are now in one of the chambers off the side of the long passage.

The latest discovery made is the remains of a kind of stage or flooring, formed of great beams and cross-bars of timber, in a wonderful state of preservation, though black with either the effect of fire or through having lain buried in the wet clay for centuries. Where this flooring was placed has yet to be determined.

THE HOUSE OF MÆCENAS.

To the left of the road leading from the Church of Sta.

Maria Maggiore towards St. John Lateran, and at a short distance after passing the Church of the Redemptorists (*see page* 265), a portion of an ancient house of a very interesting character has been discovered. It is a kind of lecture-room or hall for holding philosophical discussions, and is in the form of a parallelogram, with at one end a semicircular range of seats rising one above the other.

The walls were beautifully painted in fresco, of which considerable remains, in a very fine state of preservation, are still existing. As the house of Mæcenas is known to have been in this vicinity, it is pleasant, at least, to suppose that this room may have formed part of it.

Near to this a very fine fragment of the

AGGER OF SERVIUS TULLIUS

has been found, and the arrangement of the new streets in this quarter are being laid out in such a way as to permit of its preservation.

THE VENUS OF THE ESQUILINE.

At the distance of some fifty or sixty yards beyond the house of Mæcenas, in the direction of Sta. Croce in Gerusalemme, a treasure trove of antique sculpture was made during the Christmas week of last year. It consisted of a very lovely STATUE OF VENUS; a remarkable BUST OF COMMODUS, with arms, and draped in the skin of the Nemean Lion; TWO TRITONS; a STATUE OF BACCHUS; and two FEMALE PORTRAIT STATUES, together with some other pieces of sculpture, all found together.

INDEX.

Care has been taken to Index the names of the different streets and piazzas traversed in this Itinerary, so that the Visitor, wherever he may find himself, has only to refer to the name of the street in order to open this book at once at the description of the locality. As a matter of course, only the principal streets are mentioned, but the pedestrian can scarcely walk far without passing one or other of these.

www.ingramcontent.com/pod-product-compliance
Lightning Source LLC
Chambersburg PA
CBHW021532110726
47902CB00004B/842